P9-DDI-450

Close
to
You

Center Point
Large Print

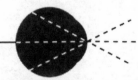

**This Large Print Book carries the
Seal of Approval of N.A.V.H.**

Close
to
You

KARA ISAAC

CENTER POINT LARGE PRINT
THORNDIKE, MAINE

LP
F
ISA

This Center Point Large Print edition is published
in the year 2016 by arrangement with Howard Books,
a division of Simon & Schuster, Inc.

The text of this Large Print edition is unabridged.
In other aspects, this book may vary
from the original edition.
Printed in the United States of America
on permanent paper.
Set in 16-point Times New Roman type.

ISBN: 978-1-68324-104-1

Library of Congress Cataloging-in-Publication Data

Names: Isaac, Kara, author.
Title: Close to you / Kara Isaac.
Description: Center Point Large Print edition. | Thorndike, Maine :
Center Point Large Print, 2016.
Identifiers: LCCN 2016024197 | ISBN 9781683241041
    (hardcover : alk. paper)
Subjects: LCSH: New Zealand—Fiction. | Large type books. | GSAFD:
Love stories. | Humorous fiction.
Classification: LCC PR9639.4.I83 C58 2016b | DDC 823/.92—dc23
LC record available at https://lccn.loc.gov/2016024197

For Josh

Thank you for supporting (and co-funding!) me chasing the crazy almost-impossible dream, even though my stories are woefully lacking in weapons/explosions/car chases/terrorists/epic gun battles, and contain way too much talking.
I love you.

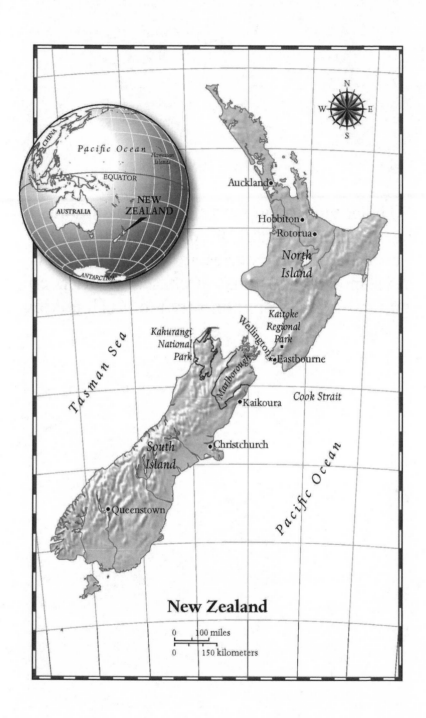

New Zealand

One

The pathetic state of Allison Shire's existence was perfectly summed up by the size-twelve prosthetic feet mocking her from the floor of the Mercedes minibus. Their hairy tops taunted her in ways she didn't even have words to express. Nasty wretched fake hobbit feet.

Leaning back in her leather seat, she stretched out her real size-seven feet and wiggled the toes that poked out from the bottom of her dumpy dress. The green floral material bore a startling resemblance to the curtain clothes from *The Sound of Music*. If only. Give her hanging off trees and crooning "My Favorite Things" any millennium.

Instead, here she was, trapped in her own personal version of Sisyphus's eternal struggle. Or maybe Dante's first circle of hell—Limbo.

Allie attempted to steer her thoughts into a more neutral direction. No one ever mentioned that one of the downsides to an English-lit degree was an endless litany of depressing comparisons for a train-wrecked life.

She stared out the window to her left, where she saw yet another poster advertising the super-extended-version DVD release of the final *Hobbit* movie. No matter where she went, there it was. No escape.

Closing her eyes, Allie attempted to block it all out and luxuriate in her last few minutes of freedom, but even in her mind she couldn't escape the irony of it all.

If life had gone according to plan, she'd be delirious about Peter Jackson's success in turning New Zealand into Middle-earth for two epic trilogies. Plan. *Ha.* Her life could not have gone less to plan if she'd set out to do the direct opposite. If only getting her life back on track were as easy as returning a magical ring to the fires of Mount Doom.

Cracking open both eyes, Allie sighed. She couldn't delay any longer: the time had come. Leaning over as much as the extra padding around her waist allowed her to, she grabbed the top of the left prosthesis and shoved her foot in. The rubber suctioned around her lower calf tighter than a swimsuit on a *Baywatch* babe; her foot was now encased in its second home for the next three weeks. She jammed her right foot into the other prosthesis, repeating the process.

The last moments of blissful silence were broken by her phone belting out its most obnoxious ring. Her whole body tensing at the sound of the opening notes rising up from the seat beside her, she eyed the flashing screen. It was always a fifty-fifty call as to which would cause less pain—answering or paying the price later for allowing it to go to voice mail.

Sighing, she picked it up. "Hello, Mother."

"Allison." Her mother's clipped tone came across as clear as if she were sitting right next to her. Allie's shoulders loosened a little. The calls that heralded untold torment always opened with "Allison Marie."

"Did you borrow your grandmother's heirloom silver salad servers last time you were home?"

"No." She resisted asking her mother what on earth someone who lived out of a suitcase would want with the family silver. Instead she waited, resigned to what was coming.

"I knew it! Your father is determined to drive me crazy."

She loved how her mother wielded the designation *your father* like she had no connection with the man.

Allie bit back the urge to say that her father wouldn't know a pair of salad servers if he sat on them. An overwhelming amount of evidence showed that even the most inane of comments could be misconstrued as a defense of him and would cause fire and brimstone to rain down on her head. Welcome to a front-row seat to the most dysfunctional marriage in the Southern Hemisphere.

"Have you asked Susannah?" Her socialite Martha Stewart protégée of an older sister had probably taken them for some dinner party or other and forgotten to return them.

9

"What would Susannah want with them? She has that lovely set of Chippendale ones."

Allie fought the urge to bang her head against the window. "Mother, I hope you find them, but I have to go. I'm at the airport to collect some guests."

Her mother sniffed. Only Veronica James-Shire could imbue even a nasal sound with disdain. "Really, Allison, when is this nonsense going to end? This living like a gypsy, hobnobbing with who knows what kind of riffraff—it's almost more of an embarrassment than your original little stunt. Especially now that Grant's political star is rising."

She highly doubted her brother-in-law cared about her job, since that would require him giving more than a millisecond's brain space to someone who served no purpose in boosting him higher up the political totem pole.

Allie dug deep and forced some gaiety into her tone. "I'm sure Grant has far more pressing issues to worry about than me. Lovely chatting, Mother. Good luck with the salad servers." Stabbing the END button, she stood, shoving her phone into the pocket of her dress.

Clomping to the front of the minibus, she lifted a wig of frizzy red hair off her usual seat beside the driver. She tucked her own auburn bob under the cap, tugged at the curls until they sat straight on her head, and then pulled a face at her freckly hobbit self in the mirror. Why couldn't she have been born tall and slender? At least then she would have gotten to be an elegant, regal-looking Elf.

If she'd known she was going to spend three years in PhD torment for it all to end in this, she never would have bothered. In fact, pretty much everything that had gone wrong with her life could be traced back to that fateful decision. She'd give everything she had, which wasn't a lot, to go back and have a do-over.

The clock on the dashboard flashed up the digits that marked the commencement of another three weeks of stuffing her true self down where no one could find her. Time for Allison Shire, Hobbit Hater, to be banished and Dr. Allison Shire, Tolkien Lover, to appear. She'd play the part like her life depended on it. Because it did.

The last time Jackson Gregory had flown economy long-haul, George Bush Jr. had been president. The last time he'd taken a bus, Junior's predecessor had been in a bit of trouble over an intern. So he had no idea how he'd ended up spending seventeen hours with his knees up to his eyeballs, on the verge of subjecting himself to almost three weeks crammed in a decrepit road behemoth roaming a country he knew nothing about. On top of all that, he had to pretend to be obsessed with some movies he hadn't even seen until yesterday.

Okay, if he was honest, he was excruciatingly aware of how he'd gotten here. He just preferred to forget along with the rest of the last six months of his life, which had ended with financial vultures picking over the remains of his corporate carcass like it was an all-you-can-eat buffet.

He picked up his pristine guidebook and thumbed through it as the plane commenced its descent to his final destination. Wellington, New Zealand. Home to not even half a million people. It was barely the microbe of a sneeze in terms of world geography. The entire nation couldn't even corral five million within its dual-island borders. Countries shouldn't be allowed to exist if they weren't at least the size of Texas. No, forget Texas. At least the size of Montana.

He kept his expression neutral as he closed the guidebook. New Zealand better have real coffee. Next to him, his great-uncle emitted a rumbling snore from his open mouth. Not that he even needed the sleep, since he'd spent the L.A.-to-Auckland leg ensconced in lie-flat luxury at the front of the plane.

The intercom crackled, and the pilot informed them they were making their final approach. Leaning his head against the cool Plexiglas, Jackson peered down at the choppy waves below. Hills rose around all sides of the harbor, houses haphazardly teetering along the steep sides like something out of a children's book. A city built in hills right on top of a fault line. Crazy people. All of them.

His eyes scanned the vista as the plane lurched from side to side, bouncing from air pocket to air pocket as it descended closer to the roiling water. He had yet to see any evidence of anything they could land on, not even so much as a large grassy field with a strip cut through it.

At least the one thing he did have left to his name was a decent life insurance policy, the beneficiaries of which he'd had the foresight to change from she-whose-name-shall-not-be-mentioned to his parents before he left. Wouldn't that have been the ultimate irony? The woman who had stripped him of everything he'd worked for also getting a few million dollars because of his exit from the planet.

Over his dead body. Which, actually, was beginning to look like a distinct possibility.

At the last possible moment, a strip of tarmac appeared out of nowhere; the only thing between it and the ocean was a flimsy fence and a sea wall constructed of large boulders. The plane dropped onto the concrete like it had discovered gravity and bounced a couple of times, the engine whining as the pilot hit the brakes. Peering out the window, Jackson caught a glimpse of a set of squat buildings as they taxied off the runway and the flight attendant droned on about staying seated, moving overhead luggage, and using cell phones.

The eyes of the elderly man sitting next to him fluttered open, gray orbs appearing underneath sparse eyelashes.

Stretching his spindly arms out in front of him, Louis—Jackson couldn't bring himself to call him Uncle Louis when he had only met the guy a couple of weeks ago—rubbed his hands together and grinned with the glee of someone seventy years younger. "Here we are. You ready for the trip of a lifetime, Jack?"

Jackson. He bit back the correction on the tip of his tongue. He'd left Jack behind in the cornfields of Iowa well over a decade ago and had no desire to find him ever again.

Something twinged in him at the unbridled excitement on his great-uncle's face. The old man honestly thought he was being accompanied by a fellow Tolkien fan. Jackson stuffed the feeling of unease back down. The old guy would never know the truth. And Jackson would be whatever he had to be for the next three weeks, do whatever it took, to get Louis to write the check he so desperately needed.

Allie stood at gate 17 waiting for her remaining tourists to disembark. Taking a final glance at her client clipboard, she pondered the list of names, nationalities, and ages that would soon become faces. Hans and Sofia, a German couple on their honeymoon. Elroy and Esther, an American father with his tween daughter, and Louis and Jackson, an American man in his late eighties and his aide.

The remaining two, elderly twin sisters from England, had already arrived and were getting settled in at the Museum Art Hotel.

The Germans and father/daughter duo were clearly true believers, as they'd been peppering the office with obscure questions that only true Tolkien obsessives would ask. The English sisters had forwarded a list of requirements as long as Allie's arm already, marking them out as high-maintenance. Only the American and his much younger attaché were an unknown quantity, all details having come through one of their travel partners in the States.

She steeled herself, shoved her clipboard under her arm, and held up her sign with the Southern Luxury Tours logo and six names listed. The obsessives came first, virtually tumbling down the gangway in their eagerness and duly exhilarated by her ridiculous costume. It even earned her a rib-crushing bear hug from Hans, who turned out to be built like a tank. Handing the guests off to Marge, their driver, to go and collect their baggage, she waited for the final pair.

A few minutes later she spotted them. The

elderly man had a cane but a surprisingly sprightly gait. His face was lined, but the slate eyes that peered out from under bushy eyebrows still held a lot of life. His aide was made for television. Dark hair, blue eyes, chiseled jaw, the whole cliché. Though rumpled, he screamed money from the soles of his Armani shoes to the tip of his trendy haircut. The whole ensemble would have been attractive if his expression hadn't been that of someone who had just sucked a very sour lemon.

She struggled to keep her face in friendly neutral. *Excellent.* Just what she needed for the next three weeks.

The older gentleman walked straight up to her and held out his hand. "You must be our guide. I'm Louis Duff and this is my aide, Jack Gregory."

The flicker of a wince crossed the aide's face when his boss called him "Jack." So he preferred "Jackson." *Interesting.* She filed the tidbit away for future reference.

"Please tell me you at least have real coffee in this country." The guy spat out the words in a voice that sounded like he'd eaten gravel for breakfast. What a charmer. Clearly he'd missed a few crucial pages in the *Lonely Planet* guide-book she could see poking out the top of his leather man-bag. In particular, the ones where they'd christened Wellington the coolest little capital in the world and raved about the amazing coffee and food scene.

She ignored him and smiled at the older man as she shook his hand. "Lovely to meet you, Mr. Duff, and welcome to New Zealand. I'm your primary guide, Dr. Allison Shire." Her academic title was out of her mouth before she realized. Usually she introduced herself as Allie. Let people work it out as they went along that she was probably the best-qualified tour guide on the planet. She didn't even know why this time was different, except there was something about the assistant that grated on her—and they hadn't even really met beyond his upturned nose. Like she needed to prove herself in spite of her ridiculous garb.

Mr. Snobby didn't even bother to hide his surprise. "Doctor?"

She stared him down—or up, considering the top of her head only just passed his shoulder. "Would you like a copy of my PhD?" She held back where it was from. She'd keep that in reserve. Let him think it was from some third-rate place. She could see from the way he'd looked around the terminal that he'd already written her beloved country off as something barely higher on the international food chain than some war-ravaged African nation.

His mouth opened, then closed. Good.

Mr. Duff chuckled. "Please excuse Jack, Dr.

Shire, he's still a little grumpy from his time in coach."

He wasn't just grumpy, he was an arrogant sod. But she'd dealt with far worse. She pasted on a smile. "Right, let's get that coffee then."

Six more tours, Allie. Just six more tours. Then you'll never have to be seen as inferior by people like him ever again.

"Can we have two flat whites and a hot chocolate please, Matt?" Dr. Shire gave the order to the guy working the coffee machine. *Doctor.* Whatever.

"Actually, I'd prefer a latte." Jackson hadn't gotten where he had by letting anyone force their preferences on him.

She raised an eyebrow. "You asked for real coffee. I'm ordering you a *real* coffee."

It was worse than his worst nightmares. Not even his wildest imagination could have conjured up some frumpy girl who barely came up to his chest, dressed as a *hobbit,* denigrating his beverage choice. And don't get him started on the so-called *Doctor.* Yeah right, if buying it off the Internet counted.

Three takeout cups appeared on the counter. She picked up the larger one and handed it to is uncle, then handed one of the smaller ones to him. He took a tentative sip, preparing himself for something horrid.

The smooth combination of coffee and milk hit his tongue. It was good. Really good. He struggled to stop himself from closing his eyes in bliss. Couldn't give little Miss Hoity Toity the satisfaction of seeing that he liked it.

"We should go and collect your bags." She directed her comment to his uncle, who nodded and started walking faster than his age and cane should have allowed.

Fifty feet later the space opened up to a large atrium encircling a food court and retail shops. Large glass windows overlooked the runway. Hanging from the high ceiling, supervising it all, were two huge eagle sculptures, one with the wizard Gandalf perched on top of its back. Twenty feet farther on, surrounded by fish, hung the little goblin-like creature who had a thing for the ring. "It's—" Jackson's mind blanked.

She stopped, looked at him, waiting. Fortunately, his uncle had paused a few steps ahead of them and was also staring above their heads, so he hadn't seen his nephew, who was supposedly as ardent a Tolkien fan as he was, flailing over the most basic of character names.

Think, Jackson, think. He'd crammed two of the movies on the plane. If he failed this most basic of tests he had might as well kiss the money good-bye right now and go home. There was no way he was going to survive three weeks.

It sounded like goblin but wasn't. Gobbin? Grobbin? Gollin? "Gollum!" He announced the name triumphantly, like he was wielding some kind of trophy.

"Oh boy." The hobbit—or should it be hobbitess? —stared at him with an incredulous look on her face as she muttered under her breath.

"I was just surprised." His pathetic excuse sounded lame, even to him. He was going to have to make up a lot of ground to convince her he was a legit fan. Not that he cared what she thought, but if she didn't believe it, it would only be a matter of time before she blew his cover with his uncle. That couldn't happen.

The man himself appeared beside him. "Isn't he brilliant? I've always felt sorry for poor Sméagol."

Sméagol? Who on earth was Sméagol? This was Gollum. Wasn't it? He looked down at Hobbit Girl, the confusion obviously clear on his face because she was struggling to cover a smirk.

"Yeah, me too." Time to change the topic, fast. "We should go and get our bags, right?"

He tried to catch the girl's eye. His uncle had paid top dollar for this trip, and Southern Luxury Tours marketed themselves as the most luxurious in New Zealand. Presumably that included doing their jobs with some sort of discretion.

She smiled sweetly. "We never rush anything on our tours. They're all about the experience. I'm sure your bags have already been collected, so we can stay here and admire Sméagol as long as Mr. Duff likes."

He closed his eyes for a second. What a pain. He was going to have to find a way to get the girl on his side before she became a liability. There was no way he was going to allow his family's future to be compromised by some snarky tour guide with a fake degree.

Fortunately, the one thing Jackson Gregory had never struggled with was charming the ladies. She'd be looking at him like he'd hung the moon in no time.

Allie eyed Jackson across the aisle of the company's luxury Mercedes touring bus. There was something about him, deeper than the patronizing arrogance, that jarred her. She didn't know what, but she didn't like it.

She couldn't give two hoots that he wasn't a Tolkien fan. Frankly, they were great to have on a tour. The more the better. It was the obsessives who drove her nuts, wanting to dissect every last nuance of the books, convene a debate club every other second on the shortcomings of the movies, and practice their Elvish. She'd had plenty of rich people bring their assistants who couldn't give two figs about *The Hobbit* or

The Lord of the Rings. They usually spent their days managing things back on home turf and making sure their boss's every whim was catered to.

People who had sheep phobias, people who freaked out at the sight of green food, people who had to have their hotel room at exactly 19°C, people who always had to have the bathroom on the right side of the room, people who ordered special food flown in from all over the country—she'd seen it all. Jackson Gregory was not a Tolkien fan, but he desperately didn't want his boss to know. Maybe it was for the dullest of reasons, but she was going to find out what they were. She liked Mr. Duff. There was no way he was getting taken advantage of under her watch by some guy who looked like a C-grade soap opera star. Especially not when he clearly had some serious money if he had paid for Jackson to come on the tour. In her experience, serious money tended to attract some serious lowlifes.

She pushed down the swirling emotions that threatened to come up at the thought. Only six more months and she'd be finished dealing with all the carnage that Derek had left in his wake. Then she could return home having salvaged some pride. Think about starting to rebuild her career.

She'd learned her lesson. Love had no place for Allison Shire, and she was fine with that.

Two

Jackson dropped his bag on the floor of the hotel room that was to be his home for the next week and looked around with a critical eye. His uncle was safely ensconced upstairs in an executive suite with harbor views, while Jackson found himself buried in the bowels of the hotel in what was euphemistically called a "classic deluxe" room.

To be fair, it was perfectly adequate. Queen-size bed with comforter, walls featuring large, bright floral prints, generic bedside tables, and a large armchair all positioned for a view of the plasma television hanging on a mirrored wall. He had just gotten used to living the high life—much like his uncle was currently enjoying, in his double-size room with marble bathroom and sweeping views.

He blew out a breath. Sometimes it still surprised him how much life had changed since the day he walked into his condo and discovered it stripped of every sign that his ex-girlfriend had ever existed.

Jackson shoved her out of his mind. So he was going to have to make a few sacrifices to get things back on track. So what? This was still a life of comparative luxury compared to how he'd lived during the years he'd spent pouring every cent he made into trying to build his company and gain the interest of serious investors.

Besides, this was a business trip. One he'd managed to get on by the sheer chance of his uncle's real assistant quitting a few weeks before. Nothing mattered except accomplishing his goal. He would sleep at the cheapest, nastiest hostel in town and risk getting some horrid foot fungus from the shared bathrooms if that was what it took.

The soft bed called to him, inviting him to sink his weary body down and close his eyes. Just for a few minutes. He hadn't slept properly in two days. He shook his head. No! Sleep was for the weak. He had three hours before the tour officially started, and he needed to use every second of that time to prep.

Dropping his carry-on onto the desk, he unzipped it and pulled out the material he'd have to ensure no one on the tour ever saw. Copies of *A Cheat's Guide to "The Lord of the Rings"* and *A Cheat's Guide to "The Hobbit."* DVDs of all six movies. Two large folders packed with hundreds of pages of information he'd printed off the Internet about Tolkien's books and the movies.

Picking up the two guides, he kicked his shoes off, grabbed a soda out of the minibar, and dropped into the armchair.

Though he had no doubt of his abilities to charm the tour guide, there were seven other people on this tour he also had to convince of his Tolkien credentials. And he had three hours to start covering some huge holes in his most elementary knowledge. For starters: who the heck was Sméagol?

Allie allowed her body to sag into one of the plush seats that made up the informal area of the hotel's bar. Tilting her head back, she closed her eyes and gave herself a few seconds to relax. She was a little early. Hopefully John, the hotel's manager, would be a few minutes late.

She absorbed the silence like a sponge. At eleven in the morning, both the bar and the restaurant were still half an hour from opening for lunch. Thank goodness. The last thing she wanted was to be seen by the ladies-who-lunch set who frequented the restaurant.

At least she'd had time to shed the hobbit feet and wig in her room, though she was still in the horrid dress because it was too much effort to get out of all the obnoxious padding only to have to wrestle it all back on in a couple of hours.

"An ice-cold Diet Coke with a slice of lemon for the lady."

She opened her eyes as John placed a tall glass on the table in front of her. "You're a lifesaver. Thanks."

The manager settled his lean frame into the seat opposite her, all business in his perfectly pressed navy suit and carrying a hotel-branded folder. Flicking it open, he eyed Allie's clipboard, which sat on the table between them. "So how bad is it?"

Allie picked up her glass and took a long sip. "Not too bad in the grand scheme of things."

She'd lost count of how many of these meetings the two of them had had. When people paid what SLT charged for a tour, they had high expectations. And on every tour, there was at least one person who would find fault wherever they went. Fortunately, after his years in high-class hospitality, there was almost nothing John hadn't dealt with. Though, admittedly, a few of her tourists had added to his repertoire.

Allie picked up her clipboard and consulted her notes. "The Barrett sisters would like their minibar emptied and filled only with glass bottles of sparkling Evian. The small ones. They would like the potted plant removed, their beds remade with the Frette sheets they brought themselves, their bathrobes replaced with brand-new ones, and an organic fruit basket."

John scribbled away. "No problem. That all for them?"

Allie paused, unsure how to frame the final directive. "And they, um, would like all their room service attendees to only be attractive gentlemen under fifty."

John threw back his head and let out a laugh, his perfectly coiffed dark hair not moving so much as a millimeter. "What are they? Like seventy?"

They were seventy-seven. "Over."

He shook his head and scribbled a note. "Oh well. Guess at that age you're entitled to get your fun wherever you can find it."

She consulted her notes again. "Mr. Johnson wants to confirm that the only thing accessible on his daughter's TV are the *Lord of the Rings* and *Hobbit* movies, and the German couple would like this added to the minibar." She handed over the name of a German spirit she couldn't even pronounce.

He took the piece of paper and raised an eyebrow. "I'll see what I can do."

She closed the cover of her clipboard. As far as tours went, so far the participants in this one were surprisingly undemanding. Though she was sure the Barrett sisters would up their game if they found that out. "And that is it."

"Nothing for Mr. Duff or Mr. Gregory?"

She shook her head. "Not yet, anyway."

"Excellent." John pulled a few envelopes out of his compendium and handed them to her. "These came for you."

"Thanks." Allie took the mail and gave it a quick shuffle, pausing at one marked as being from the University of Virginia. Its paper-thin width told her all she needed to know. The only question was which template their HR department had used to say, *Thanks, but no thanks*. She flipped past it, then did a double take at the familiar logo on the top left-hand corner of the next. Her heart sped up. Could this be it? The news she'd been waiting two years for?

Placing the envelopes on the table, she tried to keep her face neutral, as if they contained nothing of particular interest, even as the pounding of her heart filled her ears. She clasped her hands in her lap to prevent herself from grabbing up the innocuous-looking rectangle and tearing it open.

John tapped his notes with the tip of his pen. "I'll get onto these straightaway. We'll make the changes to the rooms while you're at the Weta Cave."

Allie conjured up a smile. "Thanks. I appreciate it."

Standing, he looked down at her almost empty glass. "Need another before I go?"

Was the man ever going to leave? The cream envelope on the table enticed her like the famous ring called to Gollum. "No, thanks."

"Okay. Well, you know where to find me."

He started walking away, then paused and turned back. She battled the urge to scream. "Oh, I almost forgot. We have some rooms opening up tomorrow. I could upgrade Mr. Gregory to a deluxe room."

She suppressed a smile. "Don't worry about it. Mr. Gregory is fine right where he is." The snooty aide would never know that she'd banished his supersize ego to a hobbit-size room, but it would give her something to smile about if he gave her as much grief as she was anticipating on this tour.

John nodded and finally, finally, disappeared from sight.

Allie waited a few seconds for the sound of the elevator's familiar *ding* before allowing herself to lean forward and flick the top envelope from the pile, revealing the letter from her lawyer.

Picking it up, she sucked in a deep breath. Stared at the creamy embossed paper in her hands. The envelope was thicker than usual, which meant it had to contain something more than the ordinary single-sheet quarterly invoice.

She tried to temper her expectations. She'd been mistaken before, thought they had finally reached the end of the road, only for Derek's lawyers to manage to cause another delay. But surely this had to be it.

The glue released as she slid her finger under the flap, and she reached inside to extract the folded document.

God, please let this be it. The desperate prayer surprised her. It had been a long time since she'd asked Him for any kind of intervention. As her mother liked to remind her, she'd made her bed and now she had to lie in it. There were other people out there far more deserving of the Almighty's help than she was.

She flipped open the pages, caught her bottom lip between her teeth.

Dear Ms. Shire,

We regret to inform you that Judge Finlayson has granted opposing counsel's request for a further continuance . . .

Her vision blurred and she couldn't read what followed. Didn't need to.

Bad enough that she'd married a guy who—it turned out—had already gotten himself hitched during a drunken weekend in Vegas to some girl he'd known for five minutes. But how could getting an annulment be this hard? She'd read the Family Proceedings Act so many times she could recite it. In particular, the section declaring any marriage to be void where either party was *already married*. And yet, almost two years later, she was still shackled to him while lawyers argued.

Allie flipped to the next page, a mirthless laugh escaping her lips at the sight of the jump in the quarter's bill. She added it to her mental tally of legal fees. At the current rate, it would probably be cheaper to strike a deal to pay Derek off to drop his opposition.

It might have even been a viable option if the

court hadn't frozen most of her assets at the beginning of this wretched saga. And there was no way she could cobble together enough now to satisfy her so-called husband.

She threw the papers on the table and knocked back the last of her drink. Wished for something stronger.

All those people who waxed lyrical about following your heart were idiots.

Jackson slapped his cheat's guide shut and stretched his legs. After all that, Gollum and Sméagol were the same creature. No wonder the guide had seen right through him. How could he have forgotten such a basic piece of information?

Opening his suitcase, he pulled out a fresh polo shirt and a pair of Calvin Klein jeans. Decent attire was one of the few luxuries he had left. At least the vultures hadn't literally stripped the clothes from his back.

His eyes lingered for a second on the family photo he'd thrown into his suitcase at the last moment. His parents and sister and her family grinned back at him. He wasn't normally the sentimental type. Business dealt harshly with those who were, but given that the woman he'd been considering spending the rest of his life with had turned out to be a traitor and that his so-called friends had disappeared as fast as his money, there was something oddly comforting about it.

Picking the silver frame up, he placed it on the bedside table. He might never understand their contentment with their lot, but they were all he had left that mattered. Them, and raising his reputation from the ashes.

Getting changed quickly, he tucked his wallet and phone into his pocket and stepped out the door. His skin felt gritty from hours of travel, but a shower would have to wait until tonight.

Taking the elevator down to the lobby, he stepped out and scanned the room for his uncle. At least so far he was proving to be reasonably low-maintenance on the assistant side of things.

A flash of frizzy red hair caught his eye. Did she have no shame? He would take a jump off a high building before he'd ever wear anything so hideous. Though with that unfortunate figure, there was only so much she could do.

He heard the thought resonate through his head, as if someone else had spoken it aloud, and flinched. When had he gotten so mean?

Striding across the room, Dr. Shire turned as he approached. "Ah, Mr. Gregory. Mr. Duff hasn't joined us yet, but let me introduce you to your companions on this tour for the next few weeks."

He hadn't even so much as glanced at whom she'd been talking to. He looked left, pasting an expression of polite interest on his face as he did.

As he registered what was standing there, he barely managed to keep his jaw from becoming unhinged. A man who looked to be in his forties stood in front of him in a full Legolas costume, from the long blond wig to the black boots to the bow-and-arrow set he clutched in his left hand. The guy beamed like he had swallowed a lightbulb.

He stuck out his hand and gave Jackson's a vigorous shake. "Elroy. Elroy Johnson from Minnesota. And this is my daughter, Esther." He gestured to a slender girl beside him who looked to be in her early teens in a light-green flowing dress, Elf ears, and tiara.

She cut an annoyed glance at her father. "Arwen."

Oh, brother. Seriously? He gave her a nod. "Nice to meet you, Arwen."

Now the scathing glance was turned on him. "You forget to whom you are speaking. I am Arwen, queen of the reunited kingdom of Arnor and Gondor." Her next words were complete gibberish. Followed by a string of even more. The tween looked at him like he was not only supposed to have a clue as to what she was saying, but be doing something in response.

He felt a poke in his ribs. "You need to kneel."

He gaped down at Allison. "You have got to be joking."

She shook her head, no hint of a joke on her face.

Kneel? In a hotel lobby in New Zealand to a deluded teenager? He looked back at the girl, whose face now held an expectant, imperious expression.

Suddenly he felt a tap at the back of one of his knees. Turning, he saw his uncle, in full Gandalf regalia. Of course he was.

He held out his cane and rapped the back of Jackson's leg again. "I'd suggest you do as Her Highness has commanded."

He turned back from Louis's piercing, unblinking gaze, dropped to one knee, and bowed his head. "I apologize, Your Highness."

Silence. After a few seconds his old Achilles injury started suggesting he might not want to stay kneeling for too long.

Finally, the girl deigned to speak. "You may rise."

Standing up, he saw that four more people had joined their congregation: two old ladies dressed in floral dresses similar to Allison's, and a stocky guy and a slim blond girl. He wore a *Lord of the Rings* T-shirt and she wore one with TEAM ÉOWYN emblazoned across the front. Swords—replicas, he hoped—hung from their waists. He was the only person in the entire group dressed normally.

The tour hadn't even started yet and he'd

already messed up. He addressed his uncle. "I'm sorry, sir. I didn't realize this was a dress-up event."

Allison spoke. "It's not. Nothing is, apart from the Hobbiton day, but we encourage our guests to assume personas if that will help them get the most out of the tour." She raked her gaze up and down his body. "We have some costumes available. I could go and get something if you would like." Her eyes twinkled with amusement.

There was nothing he wanted less than to look like he belonged with this bunch of losers and misfits. He opened his mouth to decline her offer, but his uncle got there first. "I think that would be a most excellent idea. We would hate for Jack to feel left out."

He barely managed to bite back the expletive that flew through his head. For the first time, it crossed his mind that it was possible the next three weeks were not going to be worth the prize at the end of the tunnel.

Three

Allie almost wished she'd accepted the offer of the room upgrade for Jackson. Almost. But not quite. And she had been kind to him, in a sense. At least she'd provided him with an Aragorn costume to wear, which was the least ostentatious of the options she had on hand.

Though even that had backfired on her, since Esther took her role of Arwen more seriously than most teenagers took Justin Bieber. The unfortunate result? In Middle-earth, where the twelve-year-old was adamant they now resided, this made Jackson her husband.

Allie tried to ignore the fact that Aragorn was one of her favorite characters—the book version, not the movie one—and that Jackson made a particularly good-looking one. At least he didn't need any help to perfect Aragorn's brooding nature. He had that one nailed. Staring straight ahead, only acknowledging his queen when he absolutely had to.

The rest of the group were all entranced with the Weta Cave, the tiny museum the now-world-famous Weta Workshop had set up to showcase their visual-arts achievements, not to mention flog large amounts of expensive merchandise to aficionados of all the movies they'd been involved in.

Allie glanced at her phone. A text from Kat flashed up, double-checking on their arrangements for Friday. Finally, something to look forward to. Allie couldn't wait to see what her best friend made of the group. At least they'd all been remarkably well behaved on the tour of the workshop, seemingly awed to be in the presence of someone who had actually worked on their beloved movies. And no one had tried to steal anything. As far as she knew. Which was more than she could say for a few people on some of her other tours.

Hans swung around in front of her, almost taking out part of the *Lord of the Rings* figurine exhibit with his replica sword. "How wonderful would it be to work here?" He swung his large arms around, one hand just missing a glass case.

Hans reminded her of the three large trolls that resided outside the entrance to the cave. Big and bumbling and not exactly the sharpest weapon in the armory. But he was good-natured and easygoing. Give her that over someone brilliant but nasty any day.

Allie pasted on a smile. "They are truly talented. Five Oscars and counting." Which was true. Their work was spectacular—even she could admit that, as jaded as she'd become.

"Do you know people who have actually worked on the movies?" He swung in the other direction, and this time his sword clanged against Sofia's.

"More than I can count." Actors, extras, costumers, set designers, visual designers, IT people, caterers. You name it, she had friends who had done it. You pretty much couldn't throw a stone in Wellington without hitting someone who had been involved in the movies at some point.

"They are the luckiest people in the world! To be involved in such . . . such . . . genius!" This time both arms flew up, and the left one smacked into the glass protecting the *District 9* display.

She couldn't help but smile at his childlike enthusiasm. Though her cynicism now ran deep, she would never disillusion her starstruck tourists with the reality behind the glamour. She wouldn't let them know, for example, that in Wellington, partners of people who worked at Weta were known as "Weta Widows," since the hours their loved ones worked sometimes rivaled those of people working in an Asian sweatshop. Nor would she tell them the tales of how, when deadlines were looming, people had been known to not leave the premises for days on end, snatching a few hours of sleep under their desks when they could.

However, he was right. At least they got to

be involved in the creation of artistic greatness.

Allie turned to Sofia. They hadn't really spoken, but she liked the girl already, if only for taking the fan road less traveled. "Great T-shirt."

Sofia blew a breath that puffed up her fringe. "Thanks. I get so mad at people who act like Arwen is the only female in the *Rings*." She put her hand on the hilt of her sword as if prepared to prove it. "Éowyn is so much stronger and more complex than some Elf princess. And Tolkien made her that way. Not screenwriters."

Allie was about to reply when a thump echoed from behind them. "Excuse me." Ducking past them, she peered into the main room to see if any of her people had been the cause. The Barrett sisters were making one of the poor staff open up almost every merchandise display case, their voices carrying through the small space as they bickered over what to buy.

Off to the side, she caught a glimpse of Jackson, trapped in a pincer movement by Elroy and Esther, up against the case that housed the armor of Théodred. A life-size Gandalf sculpture watched from off to the side, as if amused. Elroy stepped back, attempting to demonstrate some sort of Elvish combat move, while Esther hung on Jackson's arm like an adoring fan.

Allie felt a spark of irritation. The girl was only twelve, for crying out loud. Her father shouldn't be letting her drape herself all over some guy she didn't even know. A flash of panic passed across Jackson's face as he tried to extract himself from Esther's hold and got nowhere.

Across the room, their eyes caught, and he shot her a look she couldn't decipher. She suppressed the urge to wade in there and pry the limpet off his arm. Purely for professional reasons.

That was it. The Aragorn costume was going to have to be retired for this tour. The last headache she wanted—or needed—was a socially awkward girl with an inappropriate crush for the next three weeks. It was bad enough handling the occasional drama between people who were over the legal age of consent.

"You think I was mean." Mr. Duff made the observation from beside her, eyebrows tenting beneath his wizard's hat.

She looked into his sparkling eyes. "I wouldn't say that, sir. He just doesn't seem the dressing up type."

The elderly man observed his assistant, who was now trying to save himself by pretending to be avidly interested in a replica of some armor from one of the movies. "Please, call me Louis. And it will be good for him. Jack needs to loosen up a bit, not take himself so seriously. Discover there's more to life than living in the fast lane."

"And you think making him dress up will achieve that?" She doubted it. If anything, the guy had only gotten himself wound up tighter as the afternoon had progressed, and she was pretty sure Esther's unswerving attentions weren't the only reason.

Louis donned a mischievous grin. "I have something he wants very badly. I suspect there's not much he wouldn't be prepared to do in order to get it. Little does he know that a couple of hours in costume is the tip of the iceberg of what I've got planned for him."

Interesting. The old man was clearly much more clued in than she'd thought. "Most of my clients couldn't care less about their assistants as long as they do their jobs."

The old man shot her an appraising look. "Most tour guides have barely managed to graduate high school, and yet here I am with one who has a PhD from Cambridge."

Touché. Her mouth went dry. She wasn't sure why. Anyone who Googled her name would be able to find that information within a few pages. At one point it had even been on Southern Luxury Tours' website as part of their marketing pitch when they'd repositioned themselves to attract the highest caliber of clients.

But there was something in the old man's look that gave the impression he was only scratching the surface of what he knew about her. Information she had worked very hard to ensure remained hidden.

• • •

The door to Jackson's hotel room swung closed with a quiet click behind him, his attempt at slamming it thwarted by the annoying device installed in the top corner.

Storming into the small space, he stripped off pieces of his ridiculous costume as fast as his fingers could free him from the various buckles and buttons that constrained him.

Walking into the bathroom, he yanked on the tap, turning on the shower, and threw the bath mat onto the floor as water pounded into the tub. At least the country had decent water pressure. Steam filled the hotel bathroom, obscuring his vision and offering a brief respite from reality.

He looked at his watch, groaned, and shut the water off. Not enough time for a shower before he had to meet his uncle for a drink. Louis had sidled up to him as they were leaving Weta and informed him they needed to meet in the bar before dinner for a chat.

Turning on the cold water, he splashed it over his face and ran his fingers through his hair. Everything hurt, and he had a cracking headache because of the socially awkward Esther/Arwen, who had leeched onto him for the entire afternoon. One second, she'd been looking at him with disdain for pronouncing a character's name wrong or not knowing some tiny pedantic detail from one of the books. Then the next, she'd been wrapped around his arm tighter than cling wrap and reminding him that in Middle-earth they were married.

It was creepy. In spite of his best efforts to disentangle himself, she'd stayed glued to his side for the entire three hours. Worse, his attention was torn between trying to eyeball the girl's father and get him to take some responsibility for his daughter and his growing alarm at the amount of time his uncle and Hobbit Girl were spending together, trailing behind the group in conversation.

By the time they'd finally boarded the van back to the hotel, his blood pressure had been somewhere in the stratosphere. And he still had dinner to contend with, when what he really needed was more time to cram as many Tolkien facts into his head as he could manage.

Whether it was the jet lag, the pressure of playing the role of assistant, or the unending amount of information he needed to absorb, his usually almost photographic memory was failing him. The business brain that had catalogued every nuance, fashioned the business deals that had made him successful, and found niches in the market that no one else had seen had abandoned him the day Nicole walked out.

He'd clearly never had much of a brain when it came to his love life. How could he not have seen that his greatest threat lived with him?

Woke up next to him? He could tell by the twitch of an eye or the flicker of an expression when a business competitor was lying, but he'd been living with the enemy for months and had no idea.

Six months later, he still had no clue as to what had gone wrong. That was what infuriated him most of all. He was a rational man, a logical one. Some might even say cold and unfeeling when it came to business.

He'd given her everything. Funded her lavish lifestyle, showered her with gifts, introduced her to people she could only have dreamed of meeting before him. What had he gotten in return? Treason. And some bleating note about how his fiercest competitor "got her."

Stupid, stupid girl. What Richard Evans had gotten was his hands on Jackson's most fiercely guarded commercial secret. The thing that was supposed to seal his success and make him richer than Croesus when it catapulted his company to one of the most successful Wall Street offerings this millennium.

Stalking across the floor to the bed, he reached into his suitcase for a fresh set of clothes. The photo of his family tugged at him from the bedside table. Open, honest smiles. Contentment radiated from the expressions of his parents, sister, brother-in-law, niece, and nephew.

How could he have been so reckless? So

arrogant to not have settled everything for them when he had the chance? He could live with what he'd lost. It was only a matter of time before he made it all back plus some. But if the delay cost everything his parents had ever worked for, he would never forgive himself.

Picking up a folded shirt, he flicked it open with a quick shake and pulled it over his head. His fingers made quick work of the buttons before he threw the matching tie around his neck. Pulling his pants on, he snapped the belt into place and shoved his feet into black dress shoes.

He could have—should have—paid off some of the farm's debts in the months before his world unraveled. One simple little funds transfer was all it would have taken. Especially when a few bad years meant they lived shadowed by the constant threat of foreclosure. But no, he wanted to be the big man, and do it in person. Drive back into town in some flashy sports car, throwing money around like Halloween candy, rubbing it in the faces of all those people who predicted he'd come crawling back like the prodigal son within six months. Prove he wasn't the failure they all thought he was.

Never again would he be so stupid. Never again would he let any woman get past his guard, find her way into his heart. The only person he could trust was himself.

Shoving his wallet in his pocket, he pulled on his jacket as he walked back out the door. Trudging down the corridor, his fingers tugged his tie into place so it sat snug around his neck like the noose that it was. His family depended on him. He was not going to let them down again. If he could handle high-maintenance investors, he certainly wasn't going to be undone by a group of Tolkien lunatics who couldn't even separate reality from fantasy.

Jackson ran his finger around the edge of his collar as he waited in the restaurant bar for his uncle to join him. It was anyone's guess as to whether he would appear in the form of Gandalf or show up in civilized clothing. The itinerary had said suit and tie for dinner, but who knew what the Middle-earth equivalent of that was.

At least, as far as he could tell, they were dining in an ordinary restaurant tonight. Not a hobbit hole, or an Elf castle, or some other weird Tolkienesque place. He'd been afraid their first dinner would be like that scene in the first *Hobbit* movie, where the dwarves run around Bilbo's house ripping food apart with their bare hands. His borderline obsessive-compulsive tendencies had been scandalized just watching it, and he couldn't imagine having to partake in such a revolting scenario. Just thinking about it gave him the creeps.

"What can I get for you, sir?" The bartender paused in front of him.

Jackson looked down at the drinks list he held between his hands. He hadn't even had a look at it. He peered at the page, unfamiliar brand names swimming in front of him. "A Tuatara Hefe, please." He picked a beer at random. No doubt they all tasted the same anyway.

A bottle and a glass appeared in front of him within seconds and he scrawled his room number across the bill. Ignoring the glass, he picked up the bottle. He hadn't even thought to check what the old man's views were on alcohol, but he was too wrung out to care.

He looked at his watch. Still twenty minutes before everyone was due to assemble for dinner. What was the mysterious reason his uncle had wanted to meet him beforehand? He'd referred obliquely to having "something to discuss" but had given no other clues.

Rolling the chilled bottle between his palms, Jackson lifted it to his mouth and took a careful sip. Pretty good. Maybe this country wasn't quite as backward as he'd anticipated. That would be a relief, given that everything else was a nightmare.

"A soda and lime, please."

He glanced to his right to find a redhead had taken up residence a few stools over. A blue cocktail dress skimmed her curves and flared out over her knees.

She turned toward him, revealing a pert nose with a smattering of freckles and large green eyes. Light makeup highlighted her features. She looked real, which was more than he could say for the artfully painted, perfectly sculpted, surgically enhanced women who occupied his old social circuit.

A subtle scent of citrus came from her direction. There was something about her that was familiar, but that he couldn't place. But then, he'd charmed and schmoozed so many women over the last few years that they all kind of blended together.

Stop it, Jackson. He had no business thinking about the female species. They were the reason he was in this ridiculous predicament.

She caught his gaze and something he couldn't quite interpret flitted across her face before it reset to neutral. "Hi."

"Hi." He was so surprised by her opening that it was all he could manage. He scrambled for something else but came up blank. Which never happened. The old Jackson would have had a perfect follow-through. Within a couple of minutes he would have been in the empty seat beside her—

He hauled his train of thought to a screeching halt. That kind of behavior was exactly what had gotten him where he was right now.

"Tough day, huh?" She nodded toward his bottle, then took a sip of her soda.

He took another drink. "Something like that." She opened her mouth as if to say something further, but he cut her off. "Look, no offense. But I'm not really interested."

Ouch. That hadn't come out at all like he'd intended. It was abrasive. Rude.

From the way her mouth clamped shut and eyes flashed, he was guessing it was also the last thing she'd expected to hear.

What was wrong with him? The old Jackson had been a pro at making women feel amazing as he dodged their advances. He'd needed the skill to part a few lucrative divorcée investors from their money without resorting to warming their beds. He might have left the Iowa boy behind in the cornfields, but he prided himself on having a few lines he wouldn't cross.

He contemplated some form of apology, then gave up. Oh well. It wasn't like it mattered. She was just some random girl in a hotel bar in a country he never planned to visit again. With wholesome looks like that, she no doubt had guys falling over themselves—it was probably good for her to have her charms rebuffed once in a while. A good dose of rejection every now and then certainly hadn't done him any harm. He tipped his beer to himself. The men of New Zealand should really be thanking him.

"Here you are!" Thank goodness, his uncle came around the corner into the bar, saving

Jackson from the chill now emanating from three seats over. He still wore his Gandalf hat, but from the neck down was dressed in a standard gray suit, with some sort of themed tie Jackson couldn't quite make out. "Sorry I'm late. Anna packed my suitcase and I couldn't find my suspenders. Ended up being in one of those infernal inner-pocket things."

"Sorry, I should have checked if you needed help." Jackson turned on his perch and eyed the other seating available. There was no way his octogenarian uncle was going to manage to clamber up onto a bar stool.

His uncle waved a hand at him. "Not at all. Not at all." His face lit up. "Dr. Shire. Aren't you a lovely sight!" He changed direction, crossing the carpet toward the auburn-haired woman. "Not that you don't make a wonderful hobbit as well but, if an old man is allowed to say so, if I were fifty years younger . . ."

What? No. It couldn't be. Jackson almost gave himself whiplash as his head spun back to the girl who was sliding off her stool with the liquid grace of a waterfall and smiling at his uncle. "Please, call me Allie. I do have to admit that it's a relief to be out of costume on a warm night like tonight."

Sweat beaded down his back. He gave his collar a tug. He was pretty sure he was going to throw up. How had he not seen it? Admittedly the wig and the feet and the thirty pounds of padding had obscured some key features, but still. His ears buzzed. So much for some random girl he was never going to see again. Of course it had to be the one, *the one,* person he needed to win over so his Tolkien ignorance wasn't revealed to his uncle.

"If you'll excuse me, I'll leave you and Mr. Gregory to enjoy your drinks. I'll come and let you know when everyone else has arrived." She somehow managed to keep smiling while tossing Jackson the kind of death glare that would have taken out whole armies in Greek mythology. She seemed to glide out of the bar on lean legs clad in high strappy sandals, hair bouncing against her shoulders.

His uncle pierced him with wizened eyes. "What did you say this time?"

Jackson's mouth opened but nothing came out. There was no way he could come back from this. He might as well get back on a plane home right now.

Four

No offense, but I'm not really interested. Two hours later, the words still rang in Allie's head with the same clarity as if he'd just uttered them.

At least he'd had the decency to look a little ashamed when she'd returned to the bar to collect them to rejoin the group.

Maybe he'd been dropped on his head as a baby. That was about the only thing that could excuse his arrogance, his presumptuousness. Like she was some kind of morally loose barfly who had thrown herself at him.

Thank goodness she was in charge of the table seating, which she'd rearranged swiftly upon their arrival at the restaurant. She wanted Jackson as far away from her as possible in a group of nine. Louis sat to her left, at the head of the table. To her right was Spinster Sister One, then Esther in full Arwen regalia, then Jackson. Across from Jackson sat Elroy, then squabbling sister number two, then Hans, and finally Sofia, opposite her.

Allie poked a piece of steak on her plate. She hoped Jackson was enjoying the little trifecta of torment she had constructed for him, because it was going to be his dining home for the next few weeks. Maybe with the occasional spinster-sister swap to keep life interesting.

"I think it's dead now."

She looked to her side to see Louis twinkling at her. "I'm sorry?"

He nodded to her plate. "The cow. I think it's dead now."

She looked down to where her fork was repeatedly stabbing a now well-pulverized piece of beef. Oh. She put the utensil down. "Right."

"I don't know what he said, so I'm not exactly sure how bad the faux pas was, but I promise he's not as awful as he can come across." Louis nodded down the table toward his assistant. "Though, I'll grant you, he can lack a little social finesse at times."

Finesse? The guy didn't lack finesse. He lacked humility. Manners. Common courtesy. Not to mention an entire serving of general human decency. She struggled to keep her face neutral, battling the urge to resume the massacre on her plate. Apparently nothing slipped by Louis.

Breathe, Allie. He's a client. You're a profes- sional. It's not a big deal. Why do you even care?

She summoned a smile. "It's nothing. Just a bit of a misunderstanding."

"Excellent." The old man stood, pushing back his chair, and grabbed his walking stick from where it leaned against the table. He picked up his wineglass in his free hand and stepped out from his seat.

Oh, please let him be going to the bathroom

with his drink. Allie took a long sip of her water and tried to stop her gaze from following his progress, but they betrayed her.

Marching down to the other end of the table, Louis tapped Jackson on his right shoulder. "Time to swap, Jack. I want to chat with the lovely Arwen." He beamed the kind of beatific smile down at Esther that gave him an almost saintly look. He stepped back to give Jackson space to get out of his chair before settling himself into his place.

Jackson stood for a few seconds, shifting from foot to foot. He cast a despairing look at the empty spot next to Allie, and looked for a second like he might be contemplating pulling up a chair from another table and reseating himself at the head of the other end. Good. He was uncomfortable. As he should be.

Louis looked up at his assistant. "What are you still doing here? Go and talk to Sofia and Dr. Shire."

Across from her, Sofia and Hans were deep in conversation in German, while the spinsters had picked up their continuing squabble about whether they had made the right purchases at the Weta Cave.

Allie had never smoked a cigarette in her life, but she suddenly found herself with a burning desire to take up the nasty habit just to have an excuse to escape outside. Going by Jackson's finely honed physique, which his perfectly tailored suit only enhanced, she was certain there was no chance he touched the things.

"Was everything okay, Allie?" She looked up to see one of the restaurant's regular waiters looking at her battle scene of a plate.

"It was delicious as always. Sorry. I guess I wasn't very hungry tonight." She pushed it away and leaned back to give him space to clear it.

He picked up Mr. Duff's empty plate and stacked hers on top. "Dessert?"

Chocolate. That was what she needed. Chocolate made almost anything better. "The torte, please."

The sound of the chair next to her being pulled back made her flinch, in spite of it being muffled by the rug underfoot.

Jackson sat down. At some point he'd shed the jacket and his tie was now loosened, the top button of his shirt undone. He looked to his left with a resigned expression for a few seconds, as if reconciling himself to the fact that he would find no conversational sanctuary with the Germans.

He looked at Allie, his eyes seeming to plead for her to say something. She just raised her eyebrows. What? He thought she was going to help him fill in the hole he'd dug? Not a chance.

Picking up the crumpled linen napkin his boss

had thrown on the table, he smoothed it out, then folded it perfectly in half. Then in half again. And again. Running his fingers along the crease each time and checking that all corners were perfectly aligned.

Allie resisted the urge to grab it off him and crumple it back up, just to see if he would smooth it out again. Fortunately, a large piece of chocolate heaven landed in front of her before her fourteen-year-old self could be unleashed.

Picking up her cake fork, she plunged into the gooey dark chocolate torte and swiped the piece she'd sliced off through the whipped cream that sat to its side. Opening her mouth, she paused in anticipation of the decadent lusciousness.

"I didn't know it was you, okay?"

Her fork paused in midair. No. He wasn't going to spoil this moment. She closed her mouth around the cake. Chewing slowly, she waited for bliss to come. It didn't. Oh, it was nice, but nothing close to the usual moment of ecstasy that first bite of a great dessert delivers.

Unbelievable. The guy had even managed to ruin her moment of chocolate joy.

She placed her fork on the plate so she wouldn't stab him with it, and then turned her head and looked into his kind-of penitent face. "I have the same face. It's not like I was wearing a mask or something."

He blinked. "No. But the wig, the feet, the . . ." He trailed off and let his hands do the talking, waving them around in what she assumed was an attempt to communicate the padding that added an extra fifteen kilos, without actually having to say it.

"So you thought I actually looked like a hobbit? That in New Zealand we really breed actual little people with large hairy feet?"

"No." He threw his hands up. "Fine. Whatever. Don't accept my apology. Doesn't bother me."

Apology? What apology? She checked sideways to make sure no one else was paying attention to their conversation. "It's hard to accept something that you haven't even offered." She leaned toward him and ground out the words through gritted teeth. "So far all I've heard is a pathetic excuse for you being an arrogant sod who thinks that every female he so much as passes within spitting distance of is falling over herself for a piece of Jackson Gregory."

He leaned forward, closing the gap between them. He had great eyes. Bright blue, like the advertising material for some Pacific Island beach resort, which only made her angrier.

"You don't know anything about me." He forced the words out with the effort of someone holding himself back from using more colorful language.

A surge shot through Allie at the realization

that, for once in her life, she had the perfect comeback.

She leaned forward, moving so close that their noses were almost touching. "No offense, but I'm not really interested."

He deserved that. He really did. But it didn't help the way his nemesis sat in her seat with a self-satisfied smirk on her face—like it was some great accomplishment using someone's line back on them. Last time he checked, Jackson was pretty sure that was called plagiarism.

They stared at each other across their corner of the table, each refusing to be the first one to back down. He wished she did look like a hobbit. At least the frizzy hair and fat suit had hidden the fact that she had startling green eyes. The rest of her wasn't exactly unattractive either, as much as it pained him to admit it.

He set his flint face. The one that had netted him success in many a business negotiation. "Quite frankly, I couldn't care less what some tour guide in some little inconsequential country thinks."

She plunged her fork into her dessert. "Then I'm sure it won't bother you when I let it slip to your boss that you don't know the difference between an orc and a troll."

She wouldn't. Would she?

Jackson took a controlled sip of water. He

realized too late he was drinking from his uncle's glass. Ick. He forced himself to swallow. "You may loathe me all you like, but I'm still a client on your tour. Last time I checked, your company prides itself on its five-star service, even if you don't."

She raised an eyebrow and jabbed her cake-loaded cutlery very close to his face. It looked really good. He resisted the urge to take a bite.

"Actually, Mr. Duff is our client, not you. And you have exactly five seconds to tell me why I shouldn't tell him his assistant is a big fat fraud." Once again, the fork came flying so close to his face that he braced, waiting for impact.

He eyed up her weapon. "Point that thing at me one more time and you're going to lose it."

She startled, opened and closed her mouth, finally at a loss for words for a second. The fork, however, still hovered above his nose like an alien aircraft about to land. Fine. She couldn't say he hadn't warned her.

Opening his mouth, he leaned forward and hoovered up the flying torte faster than a Bugatti could reach 100 mph.

He took his time chewing and swallowed the rich morsel. Her jaw hung open as she stared at her now empty piece of silverware. Not so much as a decibel escaped from her throat.

"Delicious." He dabbed at his mouth with his uncle's napkin. "Think I might have a piece of that as well. Unless you'd prefer to keep sharing?"

Her chin snapped north again, an outraged squeak emanating from behind her mashed-together lips. A pair of very cute rosebud lips. Not that he noticed. Or cared.

Slamming her fork down, she shoved her chair out, stood, and strode away from the table, heading toward the restrooms.

Excellent. His desperate gamble had paid off. The entire incident appeared to have distracted her from threatening to rat on him to his uncle. Jackson was sure she wouldn't forget for long, but at least he'd bought time to conjure up something for the next round.

Giving in to a small smile, he picked up her fork from where it had been abandoned on the linen tablecloth and helped himself to another bite of cake. Then again, there was nothing he liked more than a challenge.

Five

Insufferable. Arrogant. Rude. Contemptible. Disagreeable. Egotistical. Discourteous. Dessert-thieving jerk. Allie struggled for more adjectives as she allowed her cocktail dress to pool around her feet and pulled on her oversize sleeping T-shirt.

Her black mood had only turned darker upon her return to the hotel and the subsequent discovery that a pipe had leaked in her bathroom, saturating the clothes she'd left puddled on the floor in her haste to get ready for dinner and forcing her to change rooms.

Picking up her dress and throwing it over the back of the armchair closest to her bed, she stomped to the bathroom, slapped some toothpaste onto her toothbrush, and started brushing her teeth. Peppermint foam filled her mouth as she scrubbed without restraint.

Who did he think he was? Calling her some small-town tour guide when he was nothing more than a glorified bag carrier. If that. So far she hadn't seen him do anything that gave him the right to call himself Mr. Duff's assistant.

She contemplated calling Kat and getting her to talk her off the ledge before she did or said something that got her fired. Allie couldn't wait to see what her best friend would make of Jackson when they met in Hobbiton. Once that girl got someone in her makeup chair, she got more out of them in fifteen minutes than most shrinks got in months.

Spitting and rinsing, Allie threw her brush down and plucked her contacts out of her eyes. She wrenched the lid off her face wash and slapped some on her face.

He wasn't stupid, though. His little dessert trick had thrown her long enough to make her temporarily forget about her threat to reveal his fakery to his boss. She just wasn't sure if he'd done it on purpose or if it was an added bonus to his uncouth ways.

Seriously, who eats with a stranger's cutlery? She could have a whole legion of communicable diseases. Not that she did, but he didn't know that!

Something about her cleanser wasn't right. It wasn't foaming the way it usually did. Glancing down, she squinted at the small travel-size bottle again. Excellent. She was cleaning her face with hair conditioner.

From the main room, her phone let out a familiar trill. Just when she thought the day couldn't get any worse. Grabbing the washcloth from beside the sink, Allie swiped it across her face while her phone kept ringing.

She wouldn't get there before it went to voice mail, but it wouldn't matter; she'd hang up and redial like she always did. Sure enough, a few seconds later her phone went momentarily silent and then started ringing again.

Padding back into the main room, Allie swiped her phone up from where she'd left it on the bedside table. "Hi, Susie."

A puff of air at the other end let Allie know how much her older sister still hated her using the name she'd been perfectly happy with until she went to university, met Grant, and "reinvented" herself.

"Allison."

Susie, aka. Mrs. Susannah Shire-Thorpe, sounded more like their mother with every passing day. The tinge of disappointment with which she managed to imbue those mere three syllables was almost pitch-perfect. Man, she missed her real sister. The one who was fun and could laugh at herself. The one she'd had before Susie hitched her wagon to a guy with political aspirations almost as high as his ridiculous bouffant hair.

She liked to think her real sister was still there, underneath the perfectly polished veneer of social perfection, but she had her doubts given how long it had been since there'd been any evidence of it.

She flopped down on her bed and pressed the phone to her ear. *Make an effort, Allie. She's still your sister.* "How are you?"

"We're great."

Allie resisted the urge to roll her eyes at the royal "we." That never would have come out of the mouth of the old Susie. It was like when she'd gotten married she'd ceased to exist as an individual and had simply become a subsidiary of a plural.

"I was calling to let you know that tonight Grant was officially selected as the candidate for Western Bays."

Allie stifled a sigh. The news was not unexpected, given that Grant and her sister had spent the last six years positioning him for selection when the incumbent retired, but she'd held on to a tiny flicker of hope that something might derail the seemingly inevitable.

Her brother-in-law would now become a member of Parliament at the next election. The seat was so safe it was a standing joke that the people of Western Bays would vote for a piece of furniture to be their MP if it wore an orange rosette.

"That's great. Congratulations. You must be thrilled." The fact that she managed to imbue the words with any tinge of enthusiasm was a credit to her finely honed acting skills.

"Of course, but honestly, it wasn't as if any other nominee could come close to Grant's pedigree. Between his distinguished career, commitment to the party, and blemish-free personal record, it really was a no-brainer."

Translation—her brother-in-law was possibly the dullest human being you could ever hope to find with a pulse. Allie was pretty sure he hadn't so much as chosen a brand of toothpaste since he was sixteen without thinking about how it would poll.

Lying back against a pillow, she waited for Susannah to get to the point of the phone call. Her sister hadn't called to chat in months and certainly not since the so-called scandal that she'd taken as personally as if Allie had caused it solely to derail her sister's social climbing.

"So we'll be having a campaign launch sometime in the next few months. And of course we'd love for you to be there." Her sister's tone clearly communicated that what they would love was anything but. "However, we were thinking that, with your history, it might be difficult for you, and we wouldn't want to put you in an awkward position, so we totally understand if you decide not to come."

Allie sat upright and wedged herself against the headboard. She would rather eat a bowl of ghost peppers while dancing across shards of broken glass than go to anything related to Grant's campaign, but she wasn't going to accept the insinuation that they were inviting-but-not-inviting her out of some kind of thoughtfulness to her.

"Oh, I don't know. It's been two years. Surely

everyone has moved on by now, even in your circles." Highly unlikely, given that some of her mother's friends still liked to bring up social scandals from the seventies, but if her sister didn't want her to come, she was at least going to make her be honest enough to admit it. "It might be good for me to be there if it fits in with my tours. Plus, I'd love to see Katie and Ed."

A sharp intake of breath told her this was not the response her sister had been expecting. "Well, you know, there probably wouldn't be much time with Katherine and Edward with all their extracurricular commitments. Katherine is taking ballet, Mandarin, and violin this term, and Edward is quite busy with piano, soccer, and swimming."

Her niece and nephew were aged four and two respectively and had been immersed in "extension" activities since their hospital wristbands were snipped off. Allie was surprised neither of them was learning Te Reo Māori. Having his kids learn the indigenous language was exactly the kind of thing she expected from her politically correct brother-in-law. No doubt an oversight that would be rectified soon.

She switched tack to keep her sister off-balance—the only way she would get anything better than a preplanned sound bite out of her. "Are you also having this same conversation with Grant's brother?" It was doubtful, considering that getting caught committing white-collar fraud had become the trend de rigueur in their circle for the last few years.

Her sister's tone turned frosty. "Simon has paid his dues for his mistakes. Whereas, last time I checked, your little indiscretion was still an ongoing court case. And given that you've hardly shown your face in Auckland since your whirlwind romance dragged the family name through the mud and made you the laughingstock of society, you can hardly pretend it's all water under the bridge."

Allie shoved down the tornado of emotions that Susannah's words stirred up. She didn't need her sister to remind her of that. Susannah wasn't the one who had lost everything. Her career. Her reputation. Her assets. Her *heart*.

Allie took a deep breath and counted slowly to three. "This is New Zealand. The country of three degrees of separation. If anyone gave a fig about the lives of the in-laws of wannabe politicians, no one would ever get elected to public office." Lucky for Grant, since her parents' dysfunctional marriage would provide some excellent fodder for anyone interested in it. "But if you don't want me there, the least you could do is be honest and say so instead of pretending it's out of some sort of concern for me."

Her sister's tone softened. "Look, of course we would love to have you there. And you know you're welcome to come and spend time with the kids whenever you want; it's just that this is a big deal for Grant and he doesn't want to take any chance of there being any distractions from the main event."

"And he thinks I'm the bigger risk of being a distraction even after what happened at the naval ball?" That event had become family legend after her mother had a couple too many cocktails and spent the evening shamelessly hitting on a poor waiter twenty years her junior.

A pause. "Well, I didn't want to mention it, but there is something else."

There always was. "What?"

"Derek will be there too."

Allie's head reared back and smacked against the top of the headboard. Her sister couldn't have stunned her more if she'd announced she was leaving Grant for the nanny. "Excuse me?"

"He and Grant ran into each other at some sort of networking event a few months ago. He's going to be helping with the campaign."

Allie opened her mouth, but nothing came out except jagged air. Her sister couldn't be serious.

Susannah read something into her silence and got even more defensive. "He'll be a great asset with his communications and marketing experience, and it'll all be behind the scenes . . ."

Allie could name many other skills Derek

possessed that were more often associated with politicians.

". . . this really isn't about you, Allie."

She was glad she'd missed the first half of her sister's sentence, since she suspected it might have tipped her over the edge. Not about her? She would stake what little she had left that this was about her somehow. Derek didn't so much as put on his pants in the morning without an ulterior motive.

"You know what, Susannah? Since you clearly know him better than I do, do whatever you like. But when it all goes bad, you can't claim that you had no idea what kind of snake you and Grant were climbing into bed with."

Her sister's outraged gasp was the last thing Allie heard before she pitched her phone across the room, where it struck the wall with a satisfying crack.

Jackson looked up as a loud snap resounded just above his head. Either the person in the room next door had hurled something at the wall or the building was about to come down. If it was the first, he could sympathize. If the second, it was probably too late to save himself, so no point in moving now.

Stretching his legs out along his bed, he pushed his laptop off his knees and onto the comforter beside him. He didn't know why he did it to himself. Between the business pages lauding Evans's company reaching a new share price high and the society pages featuring him and Nicole at some glitzy charity gala presenting a big check to the cause du jour, it was enough to give a guy an ulcer.

Especially when the check was only good because of money that should be his.

He picked up one of the cheat's guides and attempted to read a few pages on Tolkien's villains but threw the book aside after a few minutes when orcs, trolls, bolgs, goblins, and a myriad of other types of badness all merged together into one large puddle of evil. The guy'd clearly had too much time on his hands.

Folding his hands behind his head, Jackson stared at the ceiling and pondered the following day. He had to come up with a plan to keep Allison off his back. Or, at the very least, buy him more time.

It would have to be something close to reality too, since even this middle-of-nowhere country had access to Google so he'd almost inevitably get busted if he tried to manipulate the truth too much.

Rolling over onto his stomach, he typed his name into the search engine to see what the current top results were. Even after six months, he couldn't help but wince as the familiar headlines appeared on the screen. SILICON

VALLEY DARLING TUMBLES FROM FAVOR. INVESTORS LOSE BIG ON XAVIER FAILURE.

It wasn't the ones with plenty of money to throw around who haunted him. It was the people who had trusted him with their children's college funds or their retirement savings. They were the ones he would do everything in his power to repay. He never would have taken their money if he'd thought for one second they wouldn't get it back tenfold. But no, he'd been too busy dining out on his own PR to recognize betrayal when it lived under his own roof.

He was clearly going to have to tell her he'd experienced some "business difficulties" in case she Googled him, but how much was going to be required beyond that? Letting her in on the fact that Louis was his uncle? That the old man was Jackson's only chance at getting back on his feet again? That he would spend now until Christmas dressed up in as many stupid costumes she could send his way for a chance to try and right the many wrongs he'd left half a world away?

As if triggered by something divine, Skype started trilling at him. He checked his significantly reduced list of contacts and hit the button to take the call. After a few seconds, his niece's gap-toothed smile appeared on the screen.

"Hi, Uncle Jackson!" Her blond corkscrew curls bounced as half her face appeared on and then went off the screen. The girl hadn't been able to stay still since the day she was born. He could still remember her angry red newborn face in the nursery, scrunched in protest as she attempted to free herself from a blanket.

Picking up his computer, he positioned the camera so his face appeared on the screen. "Hey, Lacey Gracey." He looked at his watch and calculated the time difference. Just after five in the morning in Iowa. "What are you doing up so early?"

"Mommy said I could call you in the morning. And it's morning!"

No doubt his sister and the rest of her family were still in bed, completely oblivious to their five-year-old's predawn escapades.

"Where are you?" Her pink pajamas shimmied across the screen and back again.

"I'm in New Zealand."

"Is that near New York?"

He smiled. New York was the farthest from Iowa that Lacey could imagine. "A bit farther than that, I'm afraid."

This was so astounding that she even stopped bouncing for a few seconds. "Wow."

"I know. The plane that brought me here flew all night, and you know what else?"

"What?" She was leaning so close to the camera all he could see were her eyes and nose.

"When I left America, it was Tuesday, but when I got here it was Thursday!"

She laughed and shook her head. "Uh-uh, Uncle Jackson. You're just pickin' on me."

Probably easier to roll with that than try and explain the international dateline to a five-year-old. Even a very smart one.

"Gramma and Granddad have some new kittens."

He'd learned long ago not to try and understand the logic behind the flow of a conversation with his niece and nephew. "Really? How many?"

"Five." Four little fingers got held up against the screen. "And Gramma's sick."

Sick? How did he not know this? "Wh—"

"Lacey Elizabeth Sheldon, what are you doing up? Get right back into bed this instant!" His sister's floral nightgown appeared in the frame, followed by her half-asleep face. "Jackson, is that you?"

He saluted her across the miles. "The one and only."

"That girl is going to send me to an early grave." Beth's consternation showed in her face.

"I'm pretty sure Mom said the same thing about you more than once."

His sister shook her head, curls bouncing, and smiled. "Touché."

"Speaking of which. Lacey said she's sick. What's up?"

Across the world, he couldn't tell if what

flickered across his sister's face was a slight technical delay or something else. "You know Mom. Always putting everyone else first. I think she's just worn down. Got a cold she hasn't been able to shake."

His shoulders sagged. Yet another reminder that if he'd done right when he had the chance, his parents could be taking it easy right now instead of working dawn to dusk trying to keep their heads above water. "That's all?"

His sister gave a small shrug. "As far as I know. I think the doctor was looking at whether it's turned to bronchitis, but Mom would probably be six feet under before she'd admit to anything more than a bad cold. How's the trip going?"

"It's . . . interesting, but I'll get there." He ran his hand through his hair. "Any news from the bank?"

She shook her head. "Not since the last letter. That they've told me, anyway."

"I'm going to fix this, Bette." He wasn't sure why he reverted to her childhood nickname. "Whatever it takes."

The big-sister finger-point was still effective across thousands of miles. "Jackson, this isn't on you."

Except they both knew it was.

Six

Jackson wandered into the hotel's dining room and struggled not to yawn. Yesterday, he'd thought he'd done okay managing to get his body into a new time zone, but the morning had brought with it the feeling that a troop carrier had hit him and backed over him again.

Tipping his head from side to side, he attempted to roll out the kinks in his neck. Payback for falling asleep half-upright while trying to cram.

The room smelled like every other breakfast buffet he'd ever eaten at. The scent of over-brewed coffee mingled with those of frying bacon and mass-produced scrambled eggs. His stomach revolted at the hint of a big breakfast. Toast it would be.

Glancing around the room, he located his uncle-slash-boss sitting at a table for two by the window, a half-empty glass of orange juice in front of him. The day was blue and cloudless. Right across the road sat the national museum, Te Papa. A large sign in front advertised a T. rex exhibition. Now *that* would be a fun way to spend the day. From behind the large gray and beige building, the harbor stretched out, dotted with sailing boats and what looked like a large cruise ship coming in.

Yet another thing he couldn't wrap his head around—autumn in April. And a mild one at that. It felt wrong to be wearing shorts and a T-shirt when in Iowa his family was hunkered down in a never-ending winter.

Pulling out the chair opposite Louis, he sat and looked for a waiter. Coffee, he needed coffee. They had run out of time the evening before to cover whatever his uncle had wanted to discuss, so Louis had suggested they reconvene over breakfast, and right now Jackson was barely coherent enough to put one foot in front of another.

"Morning, Jack. Sleep well?" His uncle was wearing a navy-blue Ralph Lauren polo shirt—thank goodness there was no costume today because the itinerary involved some gourmet food tour in the morning followed by a flight north to some place he couldn't pronounce this afternoon. However, with his white bushy hair and air of excitement, Louis reminded Jackson of the rabbit from *Alice in Wonderland*. And the way his exuberance seemed to be focused in on Jackson made the hairs on his neck stand on end.

"Morning. Not bad, thanks." Jackson ordered some coffee and toast, then turned his attention back to the man who he hoped would be his financial savior. "You?"

Louis beamed. "Excellent. Most excellent. I

thought I would have trouble, but I went down like a German U-boat in the Baltic."

His great-uncle had never served in World War II, being all of five years old when it broke out, but from the way he peppered his speech with military comparisons you would've thought he'd been on the front lines the entire time.

Silence settled as Louis took another sip of orange juice and gazed out the window, apparently in no hurry to make further conversation.

Was he waiting for Jackson to say something? He knew little about his great-uncle—his grandmother's brother on his mother's side. By the time he was born, it had been decades since Louis had fled Iowa and the small stifling community they both had been brought up in. Jackson always felt an intangible sense of kinship with him, though—the two black sheep of the family who didn't want to spend their lives working the land, slaves to the vagaries of weather and a million other things you couldn't control.

The family lore centered around Louis's uncanny ability to buy land in Texas that years later would become highly sought after by oil companies, making him a very rich man. Now Jackson wondered if he also had some sort of law enforcement background or whether he was just a natural at making people squirm.

Jackson tented his fingers in front of him,

suddenly aware he had no idea what was expected of him on this trip. The whole bizarre situation had come together at the last minute and his uncle had been vague as to what Jackson's role would actually entail. The prolonged silence broke him. "So, um, I guess we should talk about what you would like me to do. As your assistant, I mean."

His uncle picked up his knife and methodically buttered his toast. He then cut the bread into four precise pieces, popped one into his mouth, and chewed at leisure. Almost as if Jackson wasn't even there, let alone asked a question.

After what felt like an eon, Louis lifted his napkin to his lips, brushed away a few crumbs, and spoke. "Oh, nothing too arduous. I'm pretty self-sufficient for an old codger. I'll let you know what I need and when I need it."

A large cup of steaming coffee landed in front of Jackson and he busied himself adding sugar and milk, grateful for something to cover up his confusion. If the old man didn't need an assistant, then why had he paid all this money for Jackson to come with him? He'd assumed Louis was killing two birds with one stone, but now it appeared one of the birds was already dead, and they could have easily dealt with any questions he had about the business plan via phone or e-mail while he was away.

His uncle peered over the glasses balanced at

the end of his pointy nose. "You're wondering why you're here."

Jackson took a tentative sip of his coffee and nodded. "Don't get me wrong, I'm very grateful for the opportunity, but yes, I guess I am."

His uncle turned his full attention to him, sliding his glasses back up the bridge of his nose with the tip of his finger. "After we met, I reviewed your business plan and my initial thoughts were favorable."

Thank you, God. Not that he still believed in one. But if he did, he would be grateful.

This was even better than he'd dared to hope. He had thought he'd be forced to suffer through much more of the tour before he got any sense of which way his uncle was leaning.

Framing his expression to be on the positive side of neutral, he waited for questions, confident he'd be able to answer to Louis's satisfaction. BabyZen was genius, the business plan solid, his connections impeccable. All he needed was the capital, which now dangled right in front of him.

Nodding his thanks to the waiter who placed a plate of five different types of toast in front of him, he surveyed the preserves selection. He didn't want his uncle to think he was too eager. Nothing scared investors off faster than appearing desperate to get your hands on their cash.

His uncle picked up his knife. "But you see, son, I believe in investing in people first and ideas second. I realize this is unusual, but it's worked well for me in the past. So while you have some good ideas, I don't know enough about you to make a decision yet."

Jackson managed to keep his expression intact while, internally, his spirits sank. He should've known there was going to be a catch. He'd been taken to the bottom of the world to spend three weeks with a bunch of Tolkienites, after all.

Louis picked up a small jar of jam that sat in the center of the table and dipped his knife in. "Obviously we're family, but let's face it, we might as well be strangers. I loved my sister, but Iowa and Texas weren't exactly locations that lent themselves to popping in for a cup of coffee and watching each other's families grow up."

It occurred to Jackson he didn't know anything about his uncle's family either. He had vague recollections from his youth of a mention of a wife at one point, maybe a couple of kids, but it was all a bit hazy. Louis certainly hadn't mentioned either.

"So you want to get to know me?" He wasn't sure whether to be concerned or not. He thought he was a pretty decent guy. His parents had raised him right. Sure, there were a few decisions they might not have approved of, but he was okay with them. He certainly rated himself as a better person than the majority of those he'd crossed paths with during his near decade in California.

His uncle spread some jam from corner to corner on his toast. "Yes, but it's a little more complicated than that. You're asking for a lot of money and, at least initially, I would be your sole investor, which I've decided requires something a little out of the ordinary."

Jackson's stomach clenched. This was not good, coming from a man who thought dressing up like a wizard for public outings was perfectly normal. "Oh?" Somehow he managed to keep his voice from reflecting that his heart pounded.

His uncle placed his knife down in perfect parallel to his toast and turned his focus back to Jackson. "That's the main reason I asked you to come with me. Being a fellow Tolkien fan was a most prodigious start and did more for your case than any fancy business plan could have. However, I'm a big believer that nothing brings out a man's true character better than being out of his comfort zone. So, over the next few weeks I'm going to be watching you so I can assess your character. At the end of the tour I'll make my final decision."

Good thing Jackson hadn't started on breakfast because at that, he suddenly lost his appetite.

Across the table, his uncle's gnarly fingers plucked up the piece of toast and suspended it in midair. "To give you a heads-up, you've already got some ground to make up."

"Oh?" How could that be when they'd barely been in the country for twenty-four hours?

"I'm going to leave you to dwell on that. Figure out what part of your behavior in the last day or so I may have found wanting. Self-reflection isan important part of personal growth." His uncle finally popped the last meticulously compiled piece of toast into his mouth.

Jackson barely managed to keep his jaw from hanging. He couldn't believe he'd signed on to try and convince the geriatric version of Tony Robbins to be his only investor. But Louis was his last hope. He'd done everything he could to tap into his contacts back in L.A. for seed funding, but after Xavier went belly-up so spectacularly, it was never going to happen. Most of them hadn't even returned his calls.

If it hadn't been mere hours since he'd promised his sister he was going to succeed, he would've been on the next plane home. Something told him all the hard work he'd done in the past in an attempt to part investors from their money for his last venture had nothing on being under his uncle's scrutiny for the next few weeks.

• • •

Allie scanned the lineup of her charges. Their overnight bags were all assembled by the hotel doors, awaiting a porter to take them to their waiting van. The flight to Rotorua, their gateway to Hobbiton, didn't leave for another hour, and it was only fifteen minutes to the airport so, for once, they were ahead of schedule.

The honeymooners were all snuggled up with arms wrapped around each other, flush from whatever had caused them to miss breakfast and show up for the morning's walking tour late and flustered.

On the other side of the coin, the spinsters hadn't stopped squawking complaints all morning. The walking was too much, then it wasn't enough. There had been too many stops but not enough. It was too hot, then too windy. Different gourmet treats they'd sampled had variously been too sweet, too sour, too bitter, too soft, too hard, too nutty, too spicy, too bland, too jammy, too chocolatey, too hot, too cold, too moist, and too dry. The one and *only* thing they hadn't been able to find fault with was the Leeds Street Bakery's famous salted caramel cookie. A bite of one of those babies and even their nitpicky little eyes had gotten round: they'd cleaned their plates faster than Gollum caught fish.

Lucky for them, because if they had complained at that point, she wasn't sure she would have been able to stop herself from banishing them from the rest of the food tour by putting them into a time-out befitting the petulant little children they were behaving like.

Legolas and Arwen, in full regalia again, now bordered on exuberant as they counted down the minutes until they arrived to their next destination. They had undertaken the gourmet tour in good grace, even though it was one of the few things in the itinerary that wasn't Tolkien related and so was automatically second-class in their world.

The only hiccup had been Esther being nabbed by an eagle-eyed shop assistant who claimed the girl had attempted to steal a *Lord of the Rings* memorabilia plate. The girl had sworn up, down, and sideways she had just forgotten to pay for it. Which might or might not have been true. Allie would need to keep a closer eye on her until she knew which it was.

Allie's gaze landed on Mr. Duff, who was chortling away to himself as he poked around in the large bag of gourmet chocolates he had purchased. Now there was the perfect tourist. Polite, unfailingly enthusiastic about everything, not a single complaint even when one would have been valid. He'd even managed to coax smiles out of the Bluesome Twosome.

Finally, Allie let her eyes stray to Jackson, who was standing a couple of feet apart from the others, hands in pockets, staring into the distance. She had no idea what was up with him today. One minute he'd been being an overly obsequious assistant, fawning over Mr. Duff, and the next he'd been so distracted he'd almost walked into a power pole. Twice.

His usual sarcastic, rude streak had definitely been absent, which left her feeling weirdly disconcerted and threw her off-kilter. He hadn't even so much as passed comment on anywhere they'd been or the foods they'd sampled. It was as though only his physical shell had accompanied them for the morning. It was just strange. Must be jet lag. No doubt his usual obnoxious self would reappear soon enough and she'd be wishing this version back.

Either way, it didn't matter to her. Her job was to deliver the tour experience the clients had paid good money for and to keep them out of physical danger, not pander to their every mood swing. That was done on a purely voluntary basis. And when it came to Jackson Gregory, he would be getting exactly what his boss had paid for and not one cent more.

Seven

Allie walked into her room at the farm-cum-boutique B and B they were overnighting at and tossed her small bag onto the bed. Three hours of freedom before dinner lay before her. One hundred and eighty whole minutes of not having to talk Tolkien, think Tolkien, or fake a deep, abiding, and eternal love for his writings.

Exactly what she needed, since by dinner everyone would be so excited by the next day's private tour of the Hobbiton movie set it would consume every conversation. It had already started. The hour-and-ten-minute flight from Wellington north to Rotorua had never felt so long as Elroy and Esther had grilled her on everything their day at Hobbiton would hold, even occasionally switching to Elvish. Whether they did this for fun or to test her, she wasn't sure. She'd passed with flying colors, of course. Actually, she'd held back to allow them to retain some pride in their abilities, when the truth was, next to her fluency, their amateur attempts were like a toddler's first sentences as compared to Shakespeare.

Back in the day, she'd applied to write her PhD thesis in Elvish with an English translation. She would have, too, if the university had been able to find three people willing and able to grade it.

Allie sighed as she tugged her boots off her feet. She was glad her thirteen-year-old self who had fallen in love with Middle-earth as the ultimate escape from her mother's never-ending disapproval and disappointment couldn't see what she had become. Who would've guessed that a job that required her to sleep, eat, and breathe Tolkien would be her undoing?

Oh, she missed academia. For all its flaws, petty politics, and the change in people's expressions when they realized she wasn't a "real" doctor, it had been a good life. Not to mention that having the impeccable timing of studying Tolkien while the *Lord of the Rings* movies were filming had resulted in the conversion of what her mother had previously deemed to be a "completely useless degree" into something that had made her not insubstantial sums as a consultant. Most of which she currently couldn't touch, thanks to the guy she'd thought was her Aragorn, but who had turned out to be more like the Dark Lord of Mordor.

The smartest girl in the room had turned out to be the dumbest in terms of the things that really mattered.

Shrugging off her traveling uniform of black pants and Southern Luxury Tours–branded shirt and jacket, she slipped into a pair of jeans and a loose-fitting top. The weather was warm but the clouds rolled above, threatening rain. Hopefully those who had decided to tour the farm would finish before the heavens opened.

Pulling her laptop from her carry-on, she luxuriated in the fact that the biggest task ahead of her was the decision as to whether to catch up on *Downton Abbey* or go really classy with *The Bachelorette.*

Flipping open the computer, she eased herself onto the cloud-like king-size bed and cracked open a Pepsi from the minibar. As she was about to select what to watch, her phone rang.

Why? How did her mother always manage to have a sense for the absolute best moments to ruin?

She stared at her phone, doing its little vibratey dance on her bed cover. There was absolutely no doubt that if she answered it, the resulting conversation was going to leave her in a bad mood. The only question was whether it would be a one or a ten on the Veronica scale.

But if she didn't, she would ring and ring and ring until Allie caved and answered.

Sighing, she swiped her phone on and lifted it to her ear. "Hello, Mother."

"Hello, Allison. What part of the country are we traipsing around today?"

"Rotorua."

"Urgh. Horrible smelly place. Don't know how

you can bear it." Said the woman who had her face plastered weekly with stuff that smelled even worse than Rotorua's famous sulfurous mud pools.

"Once you get used to it, it's really not that bad." She'd take a bit of smell over whatever toxins her mother had bubbling away any day.

"I'm sure." Her mother's tone indicated she was sure of anything but. "And how are you, dear?"

Allie's radar started blaring a big red warning siren. The only time her mother used any kind of endearment was when she wanted something. Combining it with a question about Allie's general well-being meant it was going to be something truly horrible. "No."

"No what, dear?"

Double endearment. The last time it had been used was almost two years prior, when she called to "suggest" Allie give the ring her grandmother had bequeathed her to Susannah because her sister really wanted it and Allie "didn't exactly have use for it anymore." She didn't even want to think about what her mother wanted now. "No to whatever it is you're about to ask me to do."

She wasn't usually this abrupt, but her mother had managed to have the impeccable timing to call right when Allie's well of patience had run dry. If she'd waited until after *The Bachelorette*, she probably would have found a much nicer daughter at the other end of the line.

"What makes you think I'm about to ask you

to do anything? Can't a mother call her daughter for a chat?"

Normal mothers, yes. This one? No. "Sure, what shall we chat about?"

A pause at the other end. No surprises there. Her mother could talk the leaves off the trees at a social event when she thought it was worth the effort, but when it came to her own children, she wouldn't have a clue where to start. She cleared her throat. "Actually, since you mentioned it, there was something I wanted to ask you."

Allie braced herself. *Don't react. Whatever it is, don't react. Breathe. In through the nose, out through the mouth. Whatever she says, you are Zen. You are a leaf floating on a gentle breeze—*

"How would you feel about removing your father from the board of your grandmother's trust? All it would take is a majority vote."

An expletive slipped out before Allie could stop it.

"Allison Marie!"

Allie clamped her mouth shut and forced herself to breathe through the red mist that had settled around her vision. When she trusted herself to speak, her voice came out clipped, controlled. "Mother, I'm not entirely sure what alternative reality you've decided to reside in, but he's the most competent trustee out of all of us."

Not that this was even the question. Her father's big mistake had been to be caught having an affair in such a fashion that her mother couldn't ignore it and was now punishing him through whatever avenue she could conjure up short of public shaming. And not that Allie was in any way, shape, or form pro-adultery, but she did have some sympathy for him. She imagined he would have found a warmer bed for the past thirty-something years if he'd shared it with the iceberg that sank the *Titanic*.

Not to mention she knew her mother had engaged in at least one—ahem—"liaison" during their marriage. Like that was something Allie ever wanted to think about. As far as she was concerned, the fact that one child had sprung from her parents' union, let alone two, was right up there alongside Jesus turning water into wine as far as miracles went.

Frosty silence was all that was coming from the other end. Veronica James-Shire was not a woman used to being told no.

"I am not being your piggy in the middle and Susannah shouldn't be either. You and Daddy can sort out your marriage however you like, but none of those options involve including me."

"You always take his side."

Allie stayed silent and let the accusation roll over her. Her mother didn't even want to think about what it would look like if Allie took her father's side. With the things she knew, she could write an affidavit that would make her mother's immaculate bob, blow-dried twice a week at the most exclusive salon in town, stand on end.

"Don't you care how humiliated I was? I've spent thirty-five years raising his children and supporting his career and this is what I get?"

Allie sighed. "I'm not taking anyone's side. I never have and I never will. You are both my parents and I love you equally. But this is between the two of you." She had used the lines her shrink friend, Jillian, had provided so many times over the years, they now tripped off her tongue automatically. "Now, is there anything else you wanted to talk about?"

"Actually, yes. You really upset your sister with that comment you made about Derek helping them with Grant's campaign."

What had possessed her to even ask? Done. She was done, done, done with this discussion. She reached back into the barrel of conversational tricks Jillie had provided. "That's between Susannah and me. If she's upset and would like to talk about it, she has my number."

Silence at the other end. Excellent. "Okay, well, if that's all, I need to go. Good-bye, Mother."

It took every ounce of control she possessed for her to set her phone down on her bed. It probably wouldn't survive another high-impact wall adventure. Then she picked up her pillow and held it over her face so she didn't scare the animals outside her window with her screams.

Eight

The rain had been nice plump drops when Allie marched out of her room but had turned into the stinging, pelting kind that seemed to be coming from all directions. It slapped her cheeks and hit her eyes like little needles, making it almost impossible for her to see where she was going, in spite of the fact it was only midafternoon.

After being propelled by her self-righteous fury down dirt tracks crisscrossing the farm for a while, she decided to take a shortcut across a couple of back paddocks to get back to the house. Unfortunately, her alternate route turned out to be the longest possible way to get from point A to point B, since what it appeared to lack in distance, it more than made up for in difficulty.

Everything she was wearing was soaked through. And it was all going to have to be dried again by morning. That was going to take a miracle.

Her foot skidded against the sodden grass and she only just managed to throw her body to keep herself remaining upright. Changing approach, she started sliding in her boots, the way she used to propel herself on roller skates when she was eight. Hopefully that would be more stable than her current futile attempts at walking.

She couldn't believe it. Her mother was such . . . such a . . . Her mind tried to form the appropriate words but failed. Now it wasn't just rain, but tears that blinded her. Stupid, pointless tears. They always were when it came to her mother. Veronica was never going to change, never going to be any different. Allie didn't know why she kept hoping maybe one day she would be.

She'd always played by the rules. Had always done what was expected of her. Been the quiet, reserved one who never gave her parents any trouble, head too buried in a book for her to find any attraction in the hijinks her peers were up to.

Her biggest teenage scandal had been her quitting her parents' lifeless church, where people only went to be seen by others. From her mother's reaction, you'd have thought Allie had started frequenting a street corner of ill repute.

So of course, the one time she did the unexpected, the one occasion she threw caution to the wind and followed her heart, it turned out to be her personal equivalent of the Chernobyl disaster.

Meanwhile, Susannah, who had spent her teens flitting between the wrong guys and borderline illegal activities, was now the golden girl for marrying the most boring man alive.

Her thoughts scattered as her legs flew out from underneath her and she landed heavily on her backside. Which wouldn't have been catastrophic if she hadn't managed to finally lose her footing at the top of a slope, which she was now shooting down like an Olympic bobsledder.

Oh no. No. No. No. No. No. The rain suddenly parted like the Red Sea before Moses, revealing what waited for her at the bottom. A swamp. A dark, muddy, oozing swamp.

Digging her heels and fingers into the ground, she attempted to stop, or at least slow, her flight. Nothing. If anything, her Waterloo seemed to approach even faster.

She hit the bottom, her legs plunging into the thick mud, arms whirling as she floundered for a few steps in an attempt not to go face-first into the cold, stinking mess.

The dark, thick mud slipped over the tops of her boots and down her legs. Struggling to get her legs free, she only seemed to succeed in getting them even more entrenched in their position.

There was no way she was losing these boots. Not when they were almost new and had cost her the better part of three hundred bucks. Even if she was sure what was currently filling them up contained a significant proportion of animal poop.

The more she fought, the more she got stuck. Unbelievable. This entire tour had been nothing but a disaster from the beginning.

Planting her hands on her hips, she surveyed

her surroundings. The rain had eased, allowing her to at least peer through it to see . . . absolutely no one. No one within yelling distance, anyway.

She must look ridiculous. Short redhead stuck in mud up to her thighs. She patted her back pocket. Phone was still there, though probably destroyed after her little backside ski down the hill. Not that she had anyone to call—especially since she'd neglected to load the farm's phone number into her contacts.

Ten minutes passed. No sign of anyone. Or anything. Which was the only blessing in this exceptionally ugly disguise, since she'd developed a phobia of cows on a school trip when she was five years old and one sneezed on her. To date, the most disgusting experience of her life.

Allie stared down at the mud settling around mid-thigh height. Might be time to consider relinquishing the boots and freeing them after all. Leaning down, she grabbed her right leg just above the mud line and tugged, trying to loosen her foot. Nothing. The nasty gooey mud now occupying the space between her leg and boots was as effective as a vacuum seal.

Blowing her hair out of her face, she considered her predicament. Only one option came to mind, as hateful and unthinkable as it was, if she didn't want to be stuck here for the foreseeable future.

She pulled her phone out of her pocket, half

hoping it would be broken so she wouldn't have to go through with it. But sure enough, it was fully charged and one hundred percent functional.

Scrolling through her contacts, she picked out the one she needed. The only reason she had it was the company policy requiring guides to have the mobile numbers for all customers, if they had them. Which only three had provided. The Germans—who were currently in Rotorua enjoying some cultural activities—and, of course, Jackson.

Putting the phone to her ear, she listened as the line bounced to the States and back again, and prepared to eat some humble pie.

Jackson almost didn't answer his phone, especially when he saw it was a blocked number. He maintained a general policy that if someone didn't want him to know who was calling, he didn't feel particularly obliged to talk to them.

Besides, after spending an hour wandering around the farm, pretending to be interested in the native flora and fauna of New Zealand, he was relishing the silence of an empty room. Even if it did provide way too much space for his mind to work itself into knots about what he'd already done to lose character points in the Louis tally of life.

The only reason he took the call was because it served as a valid distraction from his latest attempt at *Hobbit* cramming, which was proving to be a fruitless exercise, as the more he learned, the more he realized he didn't know. Not even Stephen Hawking could have conquered learning, in a few hours, what many people spent their lifetimes obsessed with.

"Hello?"

"Jackson?"

The voice was familiar. "Yes?"

"It's Allison."

He knew the name should mean something to him, but all neurons were obviously not firing. "Allison, hi." Hopefully whatever she said next would provide some clarity.

"I'm kind of . . . stuck."

Well, that didn't help at all—now so was he.

"Okay."

"I was walking back to the house and I slipped down a bank and I'm in some mud and I can't get out."

Things were starting to connect, but not fast enough to beat his mouth, which decided to bypass his brain. "Sorry. Who is this again? Are you sure you've got the right n—"

An icy tone he was intimately acquainted with rang down the line. "Ha ha. Don't worry about it. I knew calling you was a bad idea. I'll find someone—"

"No, wait!" Finally, it all clicked together in a blaze of light and a choir of angels singing. "Where are you?"

"In the paddock behind the house. I can see the main barn from where I am."

"And you're stuck in mud?"

"That's what I said, Einstein."

A smile slid across his face. He was probably never going to get this opportunity ever again. "Okay. I'll come, but first I need you to say it."

"Say what?"

"Jackson, please come and rescue me."

"You cannot be serious."

"Deadly."

"Fine. Jackson, please come and rescue me." The sarcasm in her voice was so thick you could have eaten it with a spoon.

He pivoted his body and placed his feet on the floor. "Hmmm, I think I'm going to need it to sound a little more genuine than that." Especially after she'd spent the entire day taking great pleasure in his misery.

A few seconds of silence, then: "Jackson, please come rescue me." If he hadn't already been sitting down, the sultry tone probably would have put him on the ground.

He swallowed, his mouth suddenly dry. "That's much better. I'll be there soon. Wait. Give me your number in case I can't find you."

She reeled off a list of digits that he scrawled down on the pad on the bedside table to put into his phone. "Okay, see you in a few."

Flipping open his suitcase, he pulled out his

running shoes, a pair of shorts, and a T-shirt and got changed quickly, throwing on a rain jacket over the top. Not even a damsel in distress warranted him rushing out to some mud pit in his nice clothes. Especially since he didn't know when he'd be able to afford more.

Walking out of the main building, he found the large barn and was over the fence into the back paddock within a few minutes. The heavy downpour that had pounded his window earlier had abated to a drizzle and he looked around, the farm boy in him automatically seeking any livestock that might take offense at his presence before he went any further. Nothing, save for a few sheep in the far corner who hadn't so much as raised their heads to look at him. The country-side rolled into the background, a patchwork of lush green that wouldn't have been out of place on any postcard.

Walking past the back of the barn, he cupped his hands around his mouth. "Allison? Allie?"

"Down here." Her voice came from a good hundred feet away.

Jogging, he crested the curve in the field and pulled up short at the sight below him. Dr. Allison Shire. Stuck in mud up to her thighs, but the top half of her as immaculate as if she were taking high tea in a hotel. At least the front, anyway.

She peered up at him, her dirt-caked hands

landing on her hips. "What? Are you just going to stand there staring?"

He let loose a slow smile and pulled his phone from the pocket of his jacket as he walked carefully down the slope. "Actually, I was thinking a few photos might be in order."

"Don't you dare!"

"Oh, c'mon, the great Dr. Shire in need of rescuing? A guy needs proof of this or no one will ever believe him."

"Jackson Gregory, if you so much as even think about taking a photo, I'll . . . I'll . . ." Her voice trailed off as she realized she was in no position to threaten to do anything. She threw up her hands. "Fine, do whatever you like. Take hundreds of photos if that makes you happy."

Well, it wasn't going to be as enjoyable now that she'd given up the fight and taken all the fun out of it. "You're a real killjoy, you know that?"

Something in her face changed. "It may have been mentioned before."

The vulnerability in her expression caught him off guard, left him unbalanced in multiple ways. He shut it down before he could dwell on why.

"Okay, let's see what you've gotten yourself into here." He looked around. The ditch running between the two small hills was probably damp at the best of times, but the rain had turned it into a fifteen-foot-wide mud pit, from which emanated the unmistakable whiff of animal poop. Wicked. "You really can't move? At all?"

She shook her head and made an attempt to lift first one leg, then the other, managing maybe an inch before the bog sucked them back. She was not helped by her heavy jeans and, he was assuming, boots of some description.

He steeled himself. This could help solve a few of the problems he was facing. He just needed to be a big enough jerk to make himself go through with it. "So I was thinking we could arrange some sort of quid pro quo. A business proposition, if you will."

A wary expression crossed her face. "What do you mean?"

He gestured to her. "Well, you need my help and I happen to need yours."

Her jaw sagged. "What kind of guy negotiates with a girl stuck in a swamp?"

A desperate one. And one who would still get her out, even if she said no. She just didn't need to know that.

Allie folded her arms in front of her, brown smearing the front of her previously unblemished cropped jacket. "Fine. What do you want?"

"Louis is going to scrutinize my every move on this trip. I need you to help me however you can. Especially when it comes to *Lord of the Rings* and *Hobbit* stuff."

She eyed him. "You really know absolutely nothing about Tolkien, do you?"

Jackson shifted on the soft ground. He had to do whatever it took to succeed at this. And there was no way he had a chance at convincing his uncle to invest in him without some serious help. And if he didn't do that, he could kiss saving the farm good-bye.

What did he care if she thought he was the world's biggest oaf, anyway? She already did, so it wasn't even a change from the status quo. "I know more than I did a few days ago. But no, you're right. Compared to the rest of you on this tour, I'm as good as illiterate. So what do you think? Do we have a deal?"

She shot him the kind of glare that could take down the grid. "If you think I'm going to help you con an old man, you can take a flying jump."

"Okay, then. Have a nice night." He turned and started walking away.

Silence from behind him. She was really going to do it. Let him leave her there. He hated to admit it, but it showed character. More than he'd seen in all of the women he'd met in L.A. put together.

He reached the top of the rise without Allie so much as breathing loudly. Glancing over his shoulder, he glimpsed her with arms crossed, not even looking in his direction.

She was calling his bluff. Loud and clear.

He turned and half slipped, half walked his way back down the slope.

Allie considered his approach through stormy eyes.

He shrugged. "Okay, fine. You got me. Even I'm not that much of a jerk."

"Why?"

"Why what?"

She flung her arms out, almost throwing herself off-balance. "Why are you even here if you don't give a pip about Tolkien? Why do you want me to help you pretend you do? Who are you? Because you're as much an assistant as I am a supermodel."

He plunged one foot into the mud, watching as it swallowed his shoe.

"Uh-uh. What are you doing?"

"I'm coming in to get you."

"Not until you answer some of my questions, you're not."

He looked at her. "What are you going to do? Fight me?"

Her face set, Allie crossed her arms. "Maybe. Want to try me?"

She probably would, too. The woman was impossible. Call a guy to come save her and then threaten to fight him when he tried. "Look, I'm trying to get Louis to invest in my business, okay? And securing his good opinion of my character is one of the hoops he's making me jump through. Being a fellow Tolkien fan seems to be a big part of that." He crossed his arms. "And you're right. I'm not an assistant. Louis is my great-uncle. His assistant quit unexpectedly and he asked me to take his place."

She turned this over for a few seconds. "What kind of business?"

Not a chance. "Sorry, that's confidential."

"Why does he think you're a big Tolkien fan?"

"Because when he was interviewing me about my business plan, he mentioned this trip. He was so excited and . . ." He shrugged his shoulders. "I guess I let him think I was a fan too, in some sort of attempt at bonding."

She studied him as if she had some sort of supernatural ability to determine if he was telling the truth. After a few seconds, her shoulders relaxed and she nodded. "Okay."

"Okay, what?"

"Okay, you can come and get me now."

How had she become the one doing him the favor? "Gee, thanks."

There was nothing around that would give him the leverage he needed to get her out, which meant there was only one way it was going to happen. And it wasn't going to be glamorous. And there was a fifty-fifty chance he was going to end up making an absolute idiot of himself.

He tucked his phone back in his pocket and zipped it up. Not that it would make much difference if he went for a swim. Though it would be a good test of the salesman's claims of it being so waterproof a navy SEAL would own it. "Okay, I'm coming in."

Taking careful steps, he watched as the cool mud engulfed his ankles, followed by calves and knees.

Wading in, he got to a couple of feet of her within a few seconds. Mud slurped around his legs but it wasn't as bad as it could be, or as strong.

"So you can't move your legs at all?"

She shook her head, wet hair slapping against her cheeks. He tried not to notice how cute she was, even when doing an impersonation of a drowned hamster. "Not beyond what I showed you."

"Well, then, there's only one way we're going to be able to do this." He wasn't planning on telling her what it was. Let her find out when it was happening. "I need you to promise to stay still, because if you move unexpectedly and throw me off-balance, we're both going to be in this stuff up to our necks."

She scrunched her nose at him, considering. "Fine."

"All right then."

Leaning over, he wrapped his arms around her backside, tipping her top half over his shoulder.

Her entire being went as rigid as an ironing

board. "Whoa, whoa. What do you think you're doing?"

Releasing his hold, he stood back up. For someone who was apparently smart, she obviously hadn't thought this through. "This is the only way I'm going to get enough leverage to get you out. What do you want me to do? Drag you like I'm a tractor?"

Allie puffed out her cheeks, resignation written across her face.

"Remember, one false move and you'll be going headfirst into this stuff." Part of him was mighty tempted.

She sighed. "Okay, I'm ready."

Leaning over again, he wrapped his arms around the tops of her legs and managed to get her into a poor imitation of a fireman's carry.

Pushing through his heels, he fought against the mud that trapped her legs until he felt it slowly beginning to give; then, with a giant slurp, it gave them up. Hardest part over. Now all he had to do was turn around and carry her the eight or so feet back to solid ground. No problem.

At least it wasn't until a high-pitched foghorn ripped apart his right eardrum. He jolted upright, and the sudden movement combined with Allie's weight over his shoulders caused him to lose his center of gravity. He tried to move back, but the mud was too thick to allow him the size of step he needed to save them both.

Realizing what was happening, he felt Allie's upper half move up and sideways as she flung herself out of his hold.

The sound of her hitting the mud was the last thing he heard before he took a deep breath and went backward into the glop, ending up in it up to his neck. Beside him, Allie floundered around, a flurry of arms and matted hair.

Getting to his feet, he looked around their surroundings, trying to work out what had caused her to scream like a dying banshee.

A large cow stood at the other side of the bog, chewing some grass and looking at them with large, curious eyes. That could not be it.

He kept turning, but nothing else met his gaze except for rolling pastures and rustling trees.

He turned back to her. "A cow? I've lost my hearing over a cow?"

She swiped a hand over her forehead, moving some hair out of her eyes and leaving a streak of brown in its wake. "I hate cows." Her gaze challenged him. "What? You don't hate anything?"

He raised an eyebrow. "Not cows." He sighed. "Give me your arm." Reaching out, he grabbed her right forearm and hauled her up to standing.

She stumbled, slamming into his chest. This time he was prepared and managed to remain upright, his hands tightening around her slim waist.

Allie blinked up at him, long lashes and green

eyes set against her dark-brown face. "I'm sorry I screamed."

"Can you say that again? I seem to have lost the hearing in my right ear."

She scrunched her nose at him. "Ha ha. Very funny."

They were standing close. Too close. His senses hummed. He still had to be jet-lagged. He grasped at the pitiful explanation. It was a hundred times better than the alternative.

The guy was a moron, but a good-looking one. Even more so close up. He reminded Allie of the plastic surgeon guy on *Grey's Anatomy* with his blue eyes and light olive skin. What was his name? Avery. That was it.

This was ridiculous. She was standing in a mud bath, in the middle of a field, being chaperoned by a cow, having weird feelings for a guy she couldn't stand.

Allie forced her eyes away from his. Solid ground was now only a meter or so away— where they'd landed, the mud wasn't as deep as where she'd been stuck. She didn't need any more of his help. Breaking his hold on her waist, she forced her feet to move.

Wading through the sludge, she was hyper-conscious of him right beside her. She made it almost all of the way when the blasted cow let out a loud bellow, causing her to scream and stumble, her hands flying out in front of her as she went face-first onto the bank. Pushing herself up, she refused to look to her side as she hauled first one leg, then the other, out of the pit, ending the whole mortifying episode with her hand slipping out from under her and flopping onto her back like a dying fish.

Jackson clambered up beside her. Out of the corner of her eye she could see him sitting down, knees up to his chest, feet planted on the ground.

He was absolutely filthy; the only part of him remaining untouched by dirt was the space from his eyebrows up. "Your middle name isn't Grace by any chance, is it?"

Allie shook her head. Then hysterical laughter bubbled up from her chest and out of her mouth as she imagined how ridiculous she must look.

Jackson stared at her for a few seconds, as if uncertain whether she was laughing or crying, then threw his head back and started to laugh as well.

It was a good laugh. The kind that came from deep inside and held nothing back. She suspected he hadn't had one in a while. Just like her.

Worst of all, something about it snagged at her heart and pulled it toward him. She slammed her mouth shut. So the guy had a small halfway decent part of him buried deep down. So what? It made no difference to anything.

Nine

"I'm sorry. We're off to do what?" The next morning Jackson stood in the parking lot in front of the farm B and B and stared at Allie like she'd asked him to strip naked and do laps. Quite frankly, he almost would have preferred that.

She smiled up at him from under her frizzy wig. Her expression held the innocence of a cherub, but the glint in her eye gave away how much she was enjoying the conversation. Little wonder since, in a matter of an hour or so, he'd look as stupid as she did, in her hobbit feet, fat suit, and frumpy dress.

He'd thought he'd read through the itinerary for the day, but obviously he'd missed what must have been a footnote in two-point font that mentioned that makeup artists and stylists would transform them into the actual characters for their Hobbiton tour. Clearly, when you had loads of money to fling around, the private extended behind-the-scenes tour of the movie set turned tourist mecca wouldn't suffice without full costumes.

Now he understood why most of the group had spent dinner the previous evening so excited they could barely manage coherent sentences. At one point, Elroy/Legolas had even teared up a little

111

and been treated to an awkward sideways man-hug from Hans. It was all a little touchy-feely for Jackson, but at least now he knew it was over more than just visiting the Shire.

He breathed in and promptly choked from the rank smell. He kept forgetting the place stunk so bad, it was like taking a bath in rotten eggs. Ostensibly because of the famous thermal sulfur pools the town was built around. He peered down at the itinerary in his hands. *Rotorua.* Every-where he looked there was another word he couldn't pronounce.

Allie interrupted his thoughts. "On the upside, you're too tall to be a hobbit."

"I'm not doing it." If the other Tolkienites wanted to make complete idiots of themselves, that was up to them, but Jackson Gregory was not going to be one of them.

Allie consulted the clipboard in front of her, although he was pretty sure that was just her cover to hide a smile for a few seconds. "I think you'll find your boss has decided differently."

Of course he had. For ten seconds he'd forgotten about his uncle and the three-week test that would determine his destiny. Okay, maybe that was a little on the melodramatic side. However, the weight of the knowledge that he had no plan B for how to get the money he needed was heavier when he woke up each morning.

So not only was he going to have to participate

today, he was going to have to pretend to be thrilled about it. It was slowly sinking in that he was going to have to spend the next two and a half weeks permanently enthusiastic, enraptured, and partaking with gusto in every single activity that came his way. Just like a true Tolkienite.

Please let him at least be a human character. With a wig of dark scraggly hair, a cape, and a sword. Maybe Boromir. He could cope with that. Especially since he spent his time on-screen perpetually with a brooding scowl. That wouldn't take much to conjure up at all. Then he died a hero and got to float off down a waterfall. All of which Jackson felt a certain amount of kinship with at this precise moment.

Just as long as he wasn't Aragorn. He'd spent the last day dodging any and all contact with Esther/Arwen, but there was no doubt he'd have no chance of that if he was trussed up as her soul mate again, on an actual part of the movie set, no less.

He looked at the minivan, where all but one of his fellow tourists sat belted in and ready to go. The only reason they hadn't left was because one of the spinsters—he couldn't tell them apart—had forgotten to take her heart medication and had to go back for it. He sighed. "Okay, who am I going to be?"

This time she didn't even bother to smother her smile. "An Uruk-hai scout."

Uruk-hai? Who, or what, on earth was an Uruk-hai? He flipped through his mind trying to come up with a face or movie scene to go with the name. The only human male he could recall other than Aragorn and Boromir was Éomer, so clearly he'd run out of luck there. Was he a dwarf? An Elf? A wizard? A monster? He directed unkind thoughts toward the long-gone J. R. R. What kind of person conjured up books with more characters than days of the year?

He carefully kept his face neutral. "Lucky me."

Her smile turned into a face-splitting grin. "You have no idea."

He should never have told her anything yesterday. He'd already spent the entire time feeling like he was trying to breathe through a straw, and yet, in a moment of stupidity, he'd dropped his guard and let her slip underneath. The one person who had nothing to lose by throwing him under the bus every chance she got. He should've left her to get herself out of the mud. Since she obviously thought she was all that, she could've just levitated or something.

"It's a type of orc." Allie spoke so quietly he almost missed it.

"Sorry?" He blinked at her. Was she *helping* him?

"An Uruk-hai is an advanced breed of orc created during the Third Age. And the scouts were the elite variety. In the movies . . ." She paused and tilted her frizzy red head at him. "You have at least seen the movies, right?"

He gave her his best death stare. "Yes, I've seen the movies."

"Just checking. Can't be sure with you."

What was that supposed to mean?

"So in the movies they were the ones that killed Boromir and kidnapped Pippin and Merry."

That rang a bell. Not that the cathedral wasn't full of ugly villains who all merged into each other. He pictured the scene from the movie she referred to and visualized the fighting that had taken place. "Tall guys, blackish, bad teeth, weird-looking ears, right?"

She shrugged. "Close enough."

"Okay." Over her shoulder he could see Spinster One hurrying out the front door.

"Your missing client is back," Jackson pointed out.

Allie turned, just in time to see the lady almost tripping over her own feet in her eagerness to rejoin the group.

"I'm fine, I'm fine," the elderly lady called across the lot before anyone could even open their mouth to ask.

"Oh, and Allie?"

She half turned and looked at him over her shoulder.

"Thanks." He forced the word out. As much as he hated to admit it, she had done him a big favor.

"You're welcome."

Though, from the look on her face, she was as uncertain as he as to why she'd helped him at all.

Allie idly watched as the blue skies and lush green paddocks of Waikato rolled by her window in a never-ending view that could star in a New Zealand tourism campaign. Behind her, the minivan was filled with exuberant chatter. Even the small frames of the usually grim Misses Barrett were almost humming with anticipation.

Glancing over her shoulder, she caught a glimpse of Jackson attempting to hold an expression she guessed was meant to be somewhere between excited and interested.

She shook her head. What had made her give him a leg up out of his hole? If it hadn't been for her, the guy would've had no clue his boss had fitted him up to be a breed of orc. Oh well, she was pretty sure he still didn't completely understand what he'd been set up for. He was going to flip out when he found out—though who knew when that would be. Most of the forty-minute journey would find them with sporadic cell coverage, which would prevent him from his practice of trying to surreptitiously get the answers he desperately needed from Google via his phone.

She hoped she was around to see it, especially following his reaction in the car park after he found out this wasn't an ordinary sightseeing trip around Hobbiton. The guy took himself way too seriously. His face when he learned he would be spending three hours in makeup and costuming —two hours longer than anyone else—would be magical!

Better yet, Kat would get to meet him. Her best friend had an innate ability to detect the true measure of a person in the time they sat in her makeup chair. She'd confirm Allie's initial reaction, and that disconcerting interlude of yesterday could be filed away as an anomaly.

Allie's gaze flitted up to the mirror she used to keep her eye on the group without constantly looking over her shoulder. Jackson had turned from the others and was peering out the window, as if immersed in the scenery. His lost expression almost had her feeling sorry for him. Almost. But this was the pit you dug when you tried to impress someone by telling them you were a Tolkien fan to get a free trip to New Zealand out of it. A little floundering would be good for him. It wasn't her job to guard his little secret. That was his problem.

It certainly wasn't her job to help him. It had kind of slipped out before she realized. And when had he started calling her Allie? She wasn't sure what bothered her more: that he had, or that something in her had liked the way it'd sounded coming from him, American accent and all.

She was going to have to get him back to "Dr. Shire," or "Allison" at the least. "Allie" was too close, too friendly, too familiar. And being any of those things with Jackson Gregory was out of the question.

Forcing her eyes off him, Allie looked around at the rest of her charges. There were no big surprises regarding what everyone else had chosen, especially when Tolkien didn't provide a wide range of heroines to choose from. Esther and Elroy—well, a deaf and blind man could guess their picks. Ditto with Mr. Duff. Ethel was going to be a hobbit, Mavis a Rohan villager, which made Allie happy since she would be able to tell the sisters apart for a day. Sofia was a perfect Éowyn with her fair coloring. For some reason, Hans had chosen Lord Celeborn. Not exactly an obvious pick, given that his hulking physique was about as far from lithe and Elf-like as you could get; they'd had to get his costume specially made.

She wished he'd chosen one of the trolls. He would have made a perfect troll, and at least then Jackson wouldn't have found himself alone on the side of evil. Not that it mattered to her. Just because the guy had pulled her out of some mud and made her laugh for a few seconds didn't mean she gave a fig about anything to do with him. Not even the seed of a fig. If they even had seeds.

In fact, now that she'd enlightened him as to

his destiny today, she was pretty sure she could consider the debt paid. They could return to their respective fighting corners and all would be right with the world again.

Letting Jackson Gregory get under her skin was not an option. Not when she was only months away from finally starting to reclaim her life.

"So." Kat picked up a small brush from her extensive collection and dusted its bristles against the back of her hand. "Time to spill. Who's the hottie?"

Allie looked over the group for a couple of seconds. Two hours after the group's arrival at the Green Dragon Inn and taking over the function room, Hans and Elroy had been transformed and costumed and the rest were well on their way. She made her gaze skip over Jackson, who sat in a folding chair, his face coated in goop, halfway to becoming an Uruk-hai. She turned back to her friend. "Who?"

Kat raised her blond eyebrows at her. "Okay, let me clarify. Who's the hottie you keep forcing yourself not to look at?" Her Australian accent grew more pronounced as she drew out the latter half of the question.

"I have no idea what you're talking about." Hopefully her frilly collar would hide the tell-|tale blush she could feel starting at the base of her neck.

Trust Kat to spot the weird tension that had been bouncing between her and Jackson all morning. And it was all her fault for helping him; it had thrown the whole foundation of their hate-hate relationship off-kilter. Now they seemed to circle each other like two boxers in the ring, each waiting for the other to make the move that would define the next round.

Kat tucked some strands of blond hair that had fallen out of her ponytail behind her ear. "Allison Shire. How long have we been working together now?"

"Almost five years." They'd originally met on the set of *The Hobbit*, just before Allie had moved to England to finish her PhD. Now SLT used Kat's company for all their Hobbiton days. When the makeup business was slow, Kat sometimes came in as a temporary co-guide for longer tours like this one. The gypsy-style life of a tour guide didn't leave a lot of room for the nurturing of friendships. So Allie was grateful for this one.

"Don't use too much base—she doesn't need it," Kat instructed the artist working on Esther, then cast a critical eye over the activities of the other two members of her team before turning back to Allie. "That's right. And in that time you've showed up with a few cute guys on the tours. Not many, I'll grant you, but a few."

"And your point is?"

Kat jabbed the makeup brush she was holding in her right hand toward Jackson. "My point is, I've never known you to so much as look at any of them twice, let alone struggle to stop yourself from looking at one."

Allie forced herself to look at Jackson, who was sitting, face frozen, under strict orders not to so much as twitch a muscle as the third layer of goop dried.

"The only thing going on between us is that we can't stand each other. Mainly because he is the world's biggest pain in the behind." Her conscience flinched a little at her words. The guy had saved her yesterday. She could probably be a little kinder.

Kat eyed her up. "Uh-hmmm. And what makes him any different from all the other high-maintenance people you've had on your tours? Like the guy who wanted to fly with his sword?"

Allie groaned. "Don't remind me." Six months earlier, one of her German tourists had tried to get on a plane with his sword stuffed down his pants.

She'd thought the paperwork for dealing with an injury was bad, but it was nothing compared to what was required in trying to extract a client from airline security.

"So what's he done that's got you doing this weird little 'can't look, won't look, even though I really want to' thing?" Kat picked up a pot of something brown, dipped her brush in it, then tested the color on her arm.

Allie gave in a little. "I don't know. We grate on each other. It's been that way since the moment he walked off the plane and opened his mouth. He's rude and arrogant and condescending and then I get a glimpse of something more and it just throws me."

Kat compared two brushes in her hands. "So basically you have *Ten Things I Hate About You* chemistry. It's about time you had that with someone. I was beginning to worry you were only going to be good for a convent after Derek."

Allie almost choked. "Firstly, we don't have that kind of chemistry. At all. Secondly, even if we did, I'm *married*." She forced the last word out under her breath. Just having to say it brought all the shame and humiliation of her predicament rushing back.

Kat rolled her eyes. "C'mon, even you have to admit that's debatable. How have the courts not unmarried you yet anyway? Janine!" She stopped a passing assistant and handed her the brush and pot. "Use this one under Gandalf's eyes."

Allie waited until the girl had moved on before she answered. "He keeps fighting me. Every single step of the way." While she slaved away to pay off the tens of thousands of dollars of debt he'd somehow started racking up in her name before she'd even walked down the aisle. He'd especially outdone himself in the three months and five days between the day they'd pledged till death did them part and the day her entire world had publicly imploded.

"Eight tailor-made designer suits at over twenty grand." She mumbled the words half to herself. Eight. *Eight*. Who needed eight tailor-made suits when they didn't even have a real job?

"I still can't believe you didn't take a scissors to them." Kat tightened and retied the black apron wrapped around her slender waist, its large pockets stuffed with the tools of her craft. "Anyway, I need to go back to turning your guy into an orc."

"Uruk-hai." She corrected Kat without even thinking about it.

Her friend rolled her brown eyes. "I know. I did work on hundreds of subtypes of the nasty things every day for three years of my life. I'm pretty sure I know the different nuances of pike-men, swordsmen, crossbow-men, berserkers, sappers, and scouts better than even you, Ms. Tolkien PhD."

Allie winced. "Sorry."

"I know, I know. You can't help it. At least you don't correct my grammar."

No point telling her she used to be that

annoying person too, until it resulted in an unfortunate run-in with a professor who started deducting marks every time she did it.

Her eyes followed Kat as her friend headed back to work on Jackson—who was looking less and less like himself and more like a hideous monster with every brushstroke. A change she was appreciating more with each passing minute.

Jackson's face felt like it was coated in a combination of plaster of Paris and PVA glue. It was not a pleasant feeling. More than anything else, it itched like he'd been attacked by a swarm of mosquitoes. He clenched and opened his hands by his side, trying to distract himself from the irritation.

"Don't move." The blond makeup artist was so close to his face he could feel her breath on his cheek, even through all the layers of stuff they'd been piling on for the last couple of hours. At least it sounded like her, but he couldn't be sure since he could barely see a thing through the two minuscule slits they had left him for eyes.

"CanIhavesomewaterplease?" He tried to ask the question nicely while not moving his mouth, but the words all mashed together like a bad car wreck.

When they'd arrived, the rest of the group had been herded off to the café for coffee and refreshments, but he'd been whisked straight to this chair of torture. Now, after two hours in a warm room, he felt like he'd been lost in the Sahara for weeks.

Allie's unexpected fit of helpfulness hadn't extended so far as her warning him that being turned into an Uriki, or whatever it was, was going to be an experience only slightly more enjoyable than traversing Dante's nine circles of hell.

"Here you go." A straw materialized against his lips and he gulped down the cold liquid. How she had interpreted his request, he had no idea, but he was grateful.

"Thanksh."

Almost as if she had read his mind, the girl spoke. "After doing this for four years, you get to be an expert at deciphering what words sound like when people can't move their lips."

Having emptied the vessel, he settled back in his chair and closed his eyes. He wasn't sure which was worse—the stuff being slapped on him or the interminably long time the whole exercise gave him to think. There was literally nothing else to do when you weren't allowed to move and couldn't even hold a conversation.

He wasn't a thinker, he was a doer. That was what had made him successful—doing. Not thinking about doing. The world rewarded the risk takers and the movers. The people who took chances. Until it didn't.

All this time to poke around in the cobwebby closets and dark corners in his own head—it wasn't his thing at all. It gave his subconscious way too much space to bring up things that weren't helpful, like how Nicole had constantly harped on at him about how she wanted to spend more time together. Or how, even when he was practically rolling in money and at the top of his game, there were moments when it all felt alittle bit pointless. Or why flailing in the mud yesterday afternoon with some girl he couldn't stand had been the most fun he'd had in years.

"Make sure you keep your eyes closed." Something prodded and scraped around them and another layer got added. He couldn't help flinching a little.

"No moving. If I hit your eyeball while I do this, you won't be having fun." The edge of something pressed up against his eye socket while something sharp scraped across his eyelid. The sound of material flaking off and hitting the bottom of something else reached his ears.

"Okay, done. Open your eyes."

He opened them up, then blinked at the burst of light when his lids lifted all the way for the first time in hours.

His vision cleared and he jumped at the sight of the blond makeup artist leaning down and peering at him so closely their noses almost touched. "Relax, I need to make sure there's nothing in your eyes. Blink again."

He did and by the time he opened them again she was nodding. "Perfect. If I do say so myself. Now your mouth."

Her gaze went to his lips and he found himself struggling not to lean back to create some distance as she got far more in his personal space than he was used to. Or comfortable with.

"Oh, for goodness' sake. Relax." She poked his bottom lip with something. "If I thought you'd be as bad as Allie, I would've done your mouth first when you couldn't see."

He wasn't sure what to make of that cryptic comment and didn't dare ask. The idea of having anything in common with her was not welcome. He was here for one thing, and one thing only. The money. The tour guide was only of use to him as a means to an end. She had to be.

Ten

Finally, they were ready. And, with the exception of Hans, who was never going to look like an Elf without losing a hundred pounds and being blasted with the ray gun from *Honey, I Shrunk the Kids*, they all looked like they'd stepped straight off the movie screen.

Especially Jackson, who looked so ferocious, Esther had let out an ear-piercing scream when she turned around and found him looming behind her.

Allie was also sure that the fact that he could barely talk through his restrictive mask and makeup was going to increase the enjoyment factor of the day a hundredfold—for her, at least. Between the makeup, the balmy late-summer temperatures, and his heavy costume laden with armor, he was going to be sweltering in his own personal sauna.

"Thanks. Your team did a great job as always." Allie helped Kat fold up the director-style chairs everyone had been sitting on.

Kat smiled. "We don't exactly do it for free."

"Well, the company is hardly about to go down the financial gurgler either." Anything but, if the new Porsche the company's CEO had acquired recently was any indication.

"So, you going to give your handsome orc a chance?"

Allie shook her head. "At what? Even if I wanted to, *which I don't,* he's here for three weeks. The only thing I'm less interested in than a romance is some kind of stupid holiday fling." She grimaced. "Wouldn't that be something for him to go home and brag to his frat-boy friends about? Got a trip to New Zealand and hooked up with the tour guide as a bonus. No, thank you."

"I don't think he's like that."

Allie raised her eyebrows. "And you know this from all of three hours with him during which the guy couldn't even talk?"

Kat shrugged her slender shoulders. "I'm just saying. Just because Derek turned out to be a lying, cheating scumbag, it doesn't mean you should consign every guy to that basket. One mistake in your entire life does not a destiny create."

Easy for Kat to say. With her spotless romance record and perfect boyfriend. "Say hi to Dan for me."

Kat snapped one of her large black makeup cases shut. "I know what you're doing. And we will be picking this up down south. I'd put money on you singing a different tune next week."

Allie had forgotten for a second that Kat was joining them for the next leg of the tour. "Bet away, my friend, but get ready to lose." Ha. Like anything could change that much in a week.

• • •

A trickle of sweat dribbled down Jackson's back and joined the pool that had started at the waistband of his pants. And they hadn't even stepped outside yet.

"Okay, everyone, ready to go?" Allie had turned from her conversation with the makeup artist and addressed the group who milled around the room, half of them still enraptured with the images of themselves reflected in the full-length mirrors or busy posing for selfies.

He had to admit, they had done a great job. Allowing for things that couldn't be changed—like height and weight—everyone looked remarkably Tolkienesque. Even him. Especially him. He'd even given himself a fright the first time he'd seen himself in full regalia. He hated to think of the effect he was going to have on any unsuspecting small children out roaming the place.

"I knew you'd look magnificent." His uncle appeared beside him. Though only half the height of Gandalf, Louis had all the wizard's attitude.

"I'm not sure whether to thank you or maim you." He kept his tone light as well as he could, given his restricted ability to speak.

Keep the eye on the prize, Jackson. Eye on the prize.

"Louis, could you help me tie this?" Spinster

Two appeared in front of his uncle, dressed as some kind of villager and holding the ends of her apron strings.

His uncle gave a half bow. "It would be my pleasure, Mavis."

The old lady, who up until this moment had been one of the whiniest people Jackson had ever met, giggled—*giggled*—as she turned around. And if he wasn't mistaken, his uncle took much longer than necessary to tie the two ends into a snug bow.

Louis finished tying the bow with a flourish, and Jackson's mask was the only thing that kept his jaw in place as the guy finished the move by giving her a pat much closer to her behind than to her waist. "Is that okay?"

Mavis turned back around. "Perfect. Thank you." Oh man, the lady was simpering as she fluttered her sparse eyelashes. Good thing he'd missed out on morning tea with the others, because old people flirting was a bit more than his usually ironclad stomach felt like it could handle.

Though maybe he should encourage anything that might have the potential to distract his uncle from him. They both watched as Mavis threw a glance back over her shoulder as she walked away. "What was that?"

The guy looked up at him with wide, innocent, geriatric eyes. "What?"

"Never mind." There was no way he was going to have a conversation with an eighty-year-old about whether he was putting the moves on another retiree. As far as he was concerned, that sort of thing finished at fifty. Max.

His stomach rumbled, reminding him that while everyone else had been enjoying a leisurely coffee and morning tea, he hadn't eaten since the ridiculous predawn hour they had been evicted from their beds. The rooster had started crowing as they were eating breakfast. It wasn't right.

"Jackson!" The impatient voice cut through his culinary wishes. "Coming?"

He returned to Middle-earth to see that he was the only person left in the room and that Allie was holding the exit door open with a harried look on her face.

"Sure, sorry." He lumbered toward her, feeling about twenty pounds heavier than usual.

Allie had already turned her attention back out the door. "What is she doing?" She muttered the question under her breath, then her whole body stiffened. "Esther, stop! Leave that letterbox alone!"

Jackson froze, ears hurting. For such a small person, she sure knew how to pack some serious volume.

"Catch up!" She flung the words at him over her shoulder as she took off at a run, her ugly floral dress and frizzy wig streaming out behind her like the plume behind a fighter jet. He watched with something akin to awe. It took skill to run in prosthetic feet about four sizes too big; even he could admit that.

Hopefully whatever the Arwen-wannabe had gotten up to would keep the group too distracted for a while for them to notice his prolonged absence. He certainly wasn't going to operate at anything faster than a very slow stroll to rejoin them.

Trudging outside, Jackson took in the vista. His eyes roved over the stone bridge, rolling hills, and pastureland that formed the basis for Hobbiton. Into the hills were dotted the familiar round colorful doors that even he recognized from the movies. In the midmorning sun, it looked like one of the magical lands that might have appeared at the top of *The Faraway Tree*, one of the Enid Blyton books he loved as a kid.

Sucking in the fresh country air, he let his gaze idle on the picturesque lake in front of him. He might have been here under false Hobbit-loving pretenses, but even he could admit this was pretty cool. It wasn't every day you got to spend hours roaming around a globally famous movie set. And being separated from the incessant chatter of his merry band of Tolkien lovers made the moment that much more enjoyable.

Speaking of which . . . He looked around to see if he could spot them. He should probably at least keep track of where they were so he could find them if he needed to.

After a few seconds, he spied them across the bridge, gathered in front of a Hobbit house a couple of hundred feet or so away. Someone, who he assumed to be their official guide for the day, stood in front gesturing wildly. Allie stood a few feet back from the group, her hand up to her ear as if on a phone call. Perfect.

Movement in the corner of his eye caused him to turn his head back toward the lake. A child—or possibly a little person; he couldn't be sure from where he was—stood near the edge of the bank. Jackson looked around to see who the person was with, but there was no one else nearby.

The little person turned and he caught a glimpse of his face. Definitely a child. At a guess, around three or four. What was wrong with people? Where were his parents?

He lumbered down the hill and over the bridge as the boy started getting closer to the water than Jackson was comfortable with.

Then he broke into a run as the child slipped, his arms windmilling around as he tottered at the edge of the lake. Jackson reached out and grabbed the child's arm just as he started to fall toward the water. Digging his heels into the soft ground, he tipped backward to counterbalance the weight of the boy. He so wasn't going into the drink for a second day in a row.

He lifted the boy up in front of him and scanned him for any sign of injury. "Are you—"

His words were cut short by blue eyes bugging and a look of complete terror storming across the kid's chubby face. Then the boy opened his mouth and let loose the kind of bloodcurdling scream that would've done any D-class horror flick proud.

What was his problem? Then Jackson registered his own brown-black leathery-looking arm and remembered what he looked like. Oh. No wonder the kid was howling like a hysterical banshee.

"It's okay. I'm not really a . . . a . . ." His mind went blank. For the love of all that was good, he couldn't remember what he was dressed up as. Meanwhile, the little banshee not only kept screaming but started thrashing around, arms and legs going everywhere.

"Hey!" The shout came from behind him. "What do you think you're doing? Get your hands off my son!" The last sentence was punctuated with a few words that weren't familiar, but which Jackson assumed to be a choice selection of the local cursing vernacular.

He dropped the boy back onto the ground and turned to the angry father. "I—" This time his sentence was cut off by a large fist barreling into his face and sending him flying backward.

Allie had no sooner dealt with the fallout from her resident sticky-fingered tweenager attempting to steal Bilbo's mailbox as a Hobbiton memento when a gut-twisting child's scream split the air from down below.

The entire group turned toward the sound. Time seemed to pause as she realized Jackson had not, in fact, caught up.

In that split second she knew—*knew*—she was going to turn and find that the screaming somehow involved him. Lord, give her strength.

She stayed in position for the amount of time it took to take a breath and start counting to three. Except she never made it past two, as the entire group suddenly let out a collective gasp that had her spinning around faster than a grade-five tornado—just in time to see some guy in a red T-shirt punch Jackson in his Uruk-hai face and send him flailing backward into the lake.

She took off running. Again. For the second time in ten minutes, she tried to outwit her stupid fake feet that threatened to send her face-first into the ground with every step.

First thing she was doing that evening was writing the stupid things up as a health and safety hazard. If she still had a job, that is. Because at this rate, it was entirely possible she might do bodily harm to at least one of her clients before it was time for lunch.

She made it about halfway down the hill before the inevitable happened. One fake foot snagged on the ground and she went down and over, and over a few more times, until she reached the bottom of the hill—her shoulders, behind, and pride all throbbing equally.

Staggering to her feet, she made it to the lakeside in time to see Jackson wading through the waist-deep water toward the bank like some kind of Middle-earth swamp monster.

His face was half gone. The browns and blacks Kat had meticulously painted on dripped off in patches, revealing pieces of rubber work underneath. A piece of lake weed was draped over his shoulder and across his torso like a pageant sash. His wig of matted black hair was gone; she caught a glimpse of it floating in the water a few feet behind him like a large water rat.

"What did he do?" She addressed her question to the shaggy-haired guy who'd thrown the punch and was standing on the bank, one fist clenched, the other arm holding a young boy with dark hair and big blue eyes.

"He touched my boy, is what happened." The man didn't take his eyes off Jackson's slowly approaching form, his six-foot frame tensing as if readying himself to take another swing.

"I saved him from falling in the lake, you stupid idiot!" Jackson shot the words out, the visible portion of his face set in the grimace of the robot cop from *The Terminator*.

The guy's expression turned from menacing to something less certain.

"You stopped his son from falling in the lake?" Allie wanted to check what she was hearing.

"Yes." Jackson splashed to a stop at the edge of the bank, as if reluctant to get out of the water. She couldn't blame him. "I was up there"—he gestured in the general direction of where she'd left him—"and I saw him down here by himself. And so I came down to tell him to stay away from the edge and find out who was supposed to be watching him. By the time I got here, he was about to go in."

And for his trouble, he'd gotten smacked in the face. Now that he was closer, Allie could make out a trickle of blood tracing a path from beside his left eye down his cheek. Even through the remaining makeup, she could see his eye already starting to swell. Ouch.

"But he screamed." The guy took a step back and shook his head.

"Of course he screamed." Allie snapped the words at the errant father. "He's, what, four years old? One second he's falling into the lake and the next he's being grabbed by an Uruk-hai. I would've screamed too."

Paperwork. Oh the paperwork this was going

to require. SLT demanded a treatise if a client got so much as a bee sting.

She stepped toward Jackson as he hauled himself onto dry ground. "That's like two hours and a few hundred bucks' makeup and costuming you've just destroyed there, buddy."

Jackson peered down at his running makeup and dripping costume, trying to smother a grin. Apparently he'd just realized his dress-up day was over before it had even really begun. For some reason this just made her madder.

"Is that what happened, Alex? Were you going to fall in the lake and this guy grabbed you?" The kid looked at his father, then at Jackson, and gave the smallest hint of a nod.

Awesome. She'd taken a tumble down the hill for some moron who couldn't keep track of his own child and decked the guy who saved him. Her shoulder was killing her. "Where were you? What were you doing letting him so close to the water unsupervised? If it hadn't been for Jackson seeing him, he could have drowned!"

The man opened his mouth, but she wasn't finished with him yet.

"And him." She jabbed a finger in Jackson's sodden direction, now incandescent on his behalf. "He's wearing almost ten kilos of armor. What if you'd knocked him out? He would've gone down like an anchor, and I'm guessing you wouldn't have jumped in to save him." She didn't even want to think about that. A client dying on her watch was unfathomable. Even an arrogant, annoying one who needed to close his mouth. Jackson's jaw was hanging so low it was an open invitation to the native bug life to make themselves at home.

Mr. Punch-'Em-up Father of the Year at least had the decency to look ashamed. "I just lost track of him for a second. One second we were in the Green Dragon and the next time I turned around, Alex was gone."

She raised her eyebrows. A second, huh? She wasn't unfamiliar with how fast little people could move, but they were a decent distance from the inn.

The guy turned to Jackson. "I'm sorry. It seems I owe you an apology and a thank-you. I was out of my mind with worry and when I heard his screams and saw you holding him, my mind jumped to the worst. No hard feelings, I hope?" He held out his hand.

Allie waited for Jackson to come back with something biting to cut the guy down to size. Instead, he took the guy's hand and gave it a solid shake, lake glop spattering on the ground as he did. "No hard feelings. I know I must've given the little guy one unforgettable scare."

He turned to Allie and opened his mouth to say something but paused, his brow creasing into little ridges. "What happened to you?"

Man, his eye was really puffing up bad. "What do you mean?"

He gestured at her, lips quivering as though fighting a losing battle against a large grin. She bristled. What was so funny?

"Why are you covered in grass?"

Jackson was one happy man. With the exception of the right side of his face, which felt like it had borne the brunt of a two-by-four, he felt great. The wonders of a hot shower and being allowed to wear proper clothes again. Even the fact that he probably wasn't going to be able to see out of one eye for a few days couldn't ruin his fantastic mood after getting out of spending the day as an orc-thing.

And that was without taking time to relish what he was certain had been a glint of approval in his uncle's eye as Allie relayed the tale to the group.

"Ow!" He couldn't help the yelp as Allie dabbed the cut on his face with antiseptic, the piercing sting bringing him back to reality in the private dining room at the Green Dragon Inn.

"Oh, don't be such a baby." She was crowding his personal space. At some point, she'd lost the wig, but her hair was still pulled back, a few errant flyaways dancing around her jawline. A faint hint of citrus wafted around his nose.

"That's not a nice thing to say to someone who saved a life." He meant it as a joke, but somehow it came across petulant and patronizing.

She snorted. "Stay still, Hero Boy." Her green eyes squinted as she tended to his cut. He wasn't going to mess with her, no sirree; the little spitfire had given that father a dressing-down. The guy was probably going to have nightmares about it for the rest of his life.

As long as he lived, Jackson would never forget the sight of her decimating a man who had six inches and a hundred pounds on her, while covered in grass clippings from the top of her frizzy wig to the toenails on her fake feet.

"Why do you do this?" The question slipped out of him. Allie could hold her own in any boardroom he'd ever been in. The more he knew about her, the less the tour guide gig fit.

"Do what?" Something undecipherable crossed her freckled face as she stepped back, threw the cotton ball into the trash can, and rummaged in the medical kit on the table beside her. She pulled out a slim packet and ripped it open. "These should do."

Picking up a pair of tweezers, she plucked a slim sterile strip out of the packet. "Don't move. I need to put this over the cut."

Hmm. He might be wrong, but he was pretty sure she was evading the question. Interesting.

"What's your PhD in?"

"English literature." She smoothed the strip down.

He waited for more, but nothing else came. Even more interesting. He'd met a lot of people with doctorates, and every single one of them would happily talk for hours about their beloved field if asked. Even if the topic was the most boring and obscure thing you could possibly imagine. "Wh—"

"One more should do it." She leaned forward, then suddenly jerked back and covered her mouth just as an enormous sneeze shook her small frame. "Sorry. Stupid grass."

It was one of the spinsters who'd told him Allie had taken a tumble down the hill hurrying to get to him. Oh, how he wished he could have seen it. He struggled to contain his smile.

She sighed and paused mid-placement of the next strip. "What now?"

"I've heard of falling head over heels, but you've taken it to a whole new level. I'm flattered, though."

"Yes, you're a regular Casanova," she deadpanned. Stepping back, she studied his face. "That eye's going to hurt tonight. Take this." She held up a bag with ice cubes. "And make sure you get a fresh one before we leave."

A grimace crossed her face as she slapped the ice pack into his hand. He realized that he'd never checked to see if her little tumble hadn't resulted in anything more than great comedy. "Are you okay?"

She paused and rolled her shoulder a couple of times. "It's nothing. I dislocated my shoulder in the fall, but it popped right back in so I'm sure it'll be fine."

Whoa. What? He sprang up, almost knocking her over in the process.

"What are you doing?"

He pulled a chair out. "What am I doing? What are *you* doing? Why aren't you at the hospital? That needs to be checked out. Put in a sling. Strapped up. Sit down. I'm going to find someone to call a doctor. Or someone . . ." He trailed off. He was in a strange country in the middle of nowhere. He had no clue how to get her seen to.

She glared at him. "I have eight people to look after. Two of whom have already created a whole lot of extra paperwork for me tonight." She gave him a pointed look. "I don't have time to get it checked out. I told you, it'll be fine."

"Are you out of your mind? What's wrong with you?"

"What do you care?" She made a point of looking at her watch. "It took you over an hour to ask."

Touché. "I'm sorry. I . . ." He ran out of words. Because there were none. She was right. He'd been a self-absorbed jerk who thought the whole thing was a great joke. He hadn't considered for a second that she might have gotten hurt.

A smile cracked her face. "Gotcha."

"What do you . . ." Realization dawned. "It wasn't."

"You're not the only one who can be funny around here."

"That wasn't funny. That was mean." He sucked in his breath as he realized that somehow, in the last few seconds, things had gotten borderline flirtatious.

So, because inside he was still a thirteen-year-old boy, he stuck his tongue out at her.

Allie raised an eyebrow. "Oh, that's real mature."

"I'm rubber and you're glue. Whatever you say bounces off me and sticks to you." What was that? He hadn't heard that saying in years—let alone said it to someone.

"What are you? Twelve?" But she was smiling. And Jackson didn't like the effect it had on him. At all.

Alex's dad had hit him pretty hard; he probably had a minor concussion. That was it. Now that he thought about it, he did have a bit of a headache and felt a bit dizzy. Classic concussion symptoms after a blow to the head. That was it. That was all of it.

Eleven

Allie rolled her head and listened to her vertebrae crack. First thing after this tour, she was going to make an appointment with her chiropractor. Her entire body felt jolted out of alignment. She peered out the window of the Green Dragon Inn and checked her watch. Almost two. The group should be on their way back to the inn for a late lunch. They were going to have to eat fast and get a move on to make their flight south back to Wellington.

Between Esther and Jackson, she was sure she'd lost a good decade off her life today. Probably more. Thank goodness there was nothing on the itinerary for this evening, because she really, *really* needed a break from these people.

It had been a bad morning. She'd decided that as she'd stood in a steaming hot shower back at the farm and tried to scrub all the dirt and grass off.

Nothing shook your faith in your bad opinion of someone like them saving the life of a child. Actually, that wasn't even it. She was pretty sure the only type of person who wouldn't rescue a small child would be a sociopath. Or a serial killer. Not exactly a high bar.

It was more that then he had to go and be all *nice* to the father who'd given him a shiner when the Jackson she'd thought he was would've been a condescending git about it. And then, *then,* as she was struggling not to notice his ridiculous blue eyes or the fact that he hadn't shaved for a few days and looked like a rugged movie star, he had to go and be all . . . she didn't even have a word for it. Normal? Kind of flirtatious?

What mattered was that the day had altered the foundations of their mutually disdainful relationship that had been working so well.

Plus, she knew he knew she'd tried to deflect his questions about her. Bad idea. She should've spun him a couple of good stories, but she hated lying—which was good, because she was also terrible at it.

She preferred to tell the truth—but leave large chunks of detail out. She was sure that if there was anything that would kill the weird vibe between them, it would be the words *I'm married*—even though that wasn't the whole truth.

The only highlight was that she'd had to return to the farm to get her backup hobbit dress— yes, she had two—which gave her an excuse to send Jackson to rejoin the tour without her once she'd finished fixing his face.

"Interesting morning, Dr. Shire?" Gandalf had snuck up on her. For an old guy, Mr. Duff could

147

sure move with stealth, especially considering the inn's wooden floors. Where had he even come from? She looked around for the rest of the group but couldn't see them.

"That's one word for it."

The older man let out a bit of a chuckle. "I have to say, when I saw you rolling down the hill I was sure we were going to be needing a new tour guide."

Allie summoned up a smile. "Oh, they breed us pretty hardy here. You can't get rid of me that easily."

"Excellent."

"Did you enjoy the rest of the tour?" Thank goodness Hobbiton had been able to lend someone to supervise the group while she tended to Jackson.

He beamed. "Oh, it was brilliant, just brilliant. The level of detail they thought of is genius . . ." And he was gone, rattling off his favorite parts.

Allie envied him. She wished she could return to the days when she'd had the same passion for the books, the movies, all of it. When she'd earnestly believed there wasn't a problem in life you couldn't find an answer to in the works of Tolkien. Oh, and the Bible, of course.

Unfortunately, neither of them seemed to have a passage for what to do when you found yourself an accidental bigamist married to a lying, cheating, bottom-feeding, sorry excuse for a man.

And those were his good points.

"Okay, I'm sorry. It wasn't me. I didn't mean to. I'll never do it again." Jackson interrupted her thoughts, hands held up as if in surrender.

Where had he come from? Why was no one using the front door? "What?"

She looked around. Mr. Duff had disappeared into thin air. It was like the guy was actually a wizard.

"You looked like you were about to hit someone or something. Thought I should get my apology in before I lose use of my remaining eye."

He wasn't wrong there. In the two hours since she'd last seen him, his right eye had swelled almost shut, showcasing some beautiful shades of purple.

"You're a real comedian today, aren't you?" As hard as she tried, she couldn't keep the laughter out of her voice.

A smile tugged at the side of his mouth. "I like to think it's one of my many, many talents." She was glad he was only operating at half strength, because having only one of his blue eyes staring at her intently was unraveling something inside of her.

Get a grip, Allie. Every other compelling reason why nothing could happen with Jackson aside, developing a thing for a guy who was only in the country for three weeks was romantic stupidity.

"I'm sure you like to think so." Oh man, what she had meant to come out as cutting had somehow come out as teasing. She had to get this back onto appropriate neutral ground. Maybe they were too far gone to find their way back to mutual disdain, but at the least, she had to keep it strictly professional.

The sound of her phone buzzing cut through her muddled senses. A welcome interruption, for once.

She swiped the call on without even looking at the screen. "Hello, Allison speaking."

"Ah, my darling wife. It's been a while." The smooth British accent had always been able to send chills down her spine. Except now the reason for them had changed.

Trying to maintain a calm exterior, she mouthed "Sorry" to Jackson before forcing her feet to walk away. Fast.

"Don't call me that." She didn't even bother to ask how he'd gotten her number. She'd bet a hundred bucks he'd palmed her sister's phone when Susannah wasn't looking.

Opening the front door of the inn, she stepped outside and headed for a nearby bench from which she could see anyone approach. This was one conversation she couldn't have overheard.

"Why not? It's what you are."

She took a seat on the cool wooden slats. Her body still throbbed from the tumble down the hill and now this. At a rapid rate, today was turning into a cataclysmic combination of disasters and suffering. She should warn people not to travel on the same plane as her this evening. Her life was obviously doomed.

"What do you want, Derek?"

"Nothing." He pretended to sound hurt. "Can't a guy call his wife to say hi?"

She let out an unbelieving laugh. "Normal guys, sure. But we both know you aren't that."

"Ouch. That's not the sweet Allie I knew."

"Yeah, well, she's long gone. Thanks to you. Disappeared the day she discovered she'd been conned and her marriage was a sham." Why was she talking about herself in the third person? That was just weird.

"C'mon, Allie." He pulled out the slick, charming tone that had worked so well at getting him whatever he wanted in the past. "You're the only girl for me. How many times do I need to tell you the whole thing with Julia was a stupid drunken mistake? That I honestly thought it had been annulled."

Allie looked across the lake surrounded by hills dotted with multicolored hobbit-hole doors. She tried to fight the memory of the time she and Derek had stood in this very spot. One of the most magical days of her life. Blissfully newly-wed and convinced she'd snagged the perfect man. No idea the truth was that Derek had snagged her for money to escape mounting gambling debts to people who extracted late payment with their fists. Or worse.

She blew out a breath and forced herself back to the present. "We're not talking about this again, Derek. I don't want to hear it." She'd long since stopped trying to make sense of the lies he spun to explain his way out of his web of deceit. "Look, we both know that sooner or later you're going to run out of stalling tactics and the court will rule in my favor. Why do you keep throwing away good money? Let it go. Let's move on already. We could part as . . ." Her sentence trailed off. Part as what? Friends? Not in this lifetime.

"Except I don't want to. I want to stay married. Build a life with you." He paused, as if granting her a split second to say something.

She said nothing. She had learned long ago that the only voice Derek had any interest in listening to was his own. Sure enough, he kept on going.

"Seems ironic, doesn't it, that I'm the one fighting to save our marriage while the so-called Christian is the one trying to destroy it?"

She clamped her mouth shut, forcing back the desire to scream at him that one couldn't destroy something that had never truly existed in the first place. Her gut twisted. He was right, though. If—when—the annulment came through, it would legally be as though they had never married in the first place, but a court ruling would do nothing to change all the other regrets she would have to live with for the rest of her life. The ones that snuck up on her and placed her in a choke hold at moments when she least expected it.

If she'd listened to the internal nudging she'd felt telling her to tread cautiously and keep her eyes open when it came to Derek, she wouldn't be in this mess. Instead, she'd let herself get swept away by the fairy-tale romance, only to wake up and discover she'd drunk from a poisoned chalice.

Her hands gripped her phone so tightly her fingers hurt. "Don't call me again. If you've got something to say, send it through the lawyers." And with that, she hung up. Whatever the purpose of his call, one thing had been achieved: the noose of her past was still tied firmly around her neck.

Twelve

Allie looked about as thrilled as if she'd taken a call from the tax man. Not that it was any of his business. Not that he cared.

Jackson stared at the ceiling of his hotel room, his face throbbing. Putting a tentative finger to his cheek, he winced. He wouldn't be surprised if the guy had fractured his cheekbone.

The last time he'd had a black eye, it had been the result of a brawl at a frat party. One he'd inadvertently started after the president had taken exception to Jackson chatting up his girlfriend. Not that he'd known she was.

See. Right there. Girls. Causing Jackson Gregory nothing but trouble since he was five, when Mandy Larson had tattled on him for drinking out of her juice box.

He closed his good eye and groaned as Allie approached. She'd spent the rest of the afternoon reserved, going through the motions. Didn't even crack a glimmer of emotion when little Miss Light Fingered got busted trying to pilfer a special-edition mug from the inn, only to find out they were each being given one as a memento.

At least they had the night off. After flying back to Wellington, he'd been relieved to discover there was nothing planned for the evening. His uncle had accepted an invitation to dinner with Ethel. Or maybe Mavis. Jackson really needed to figure out how to tell them apart. Anyway, the upshot was that the other spinster looked like she was about to have a stroke and Jackson was free for the evening.

He logged onto Skype and checked his watch: after midnight in Iowa. His sister was a bit of a night owl, but it was probably a little late to call, even for her.

As if connected by telepathy, his computer screen started ringing. He looked up, expecting to see his sister's family on the screen. Instead it was a somber-looking man in a suit. What was George doing calling him now? It was late in L.A. Whatever it was, it couldn't be good.

He hit the answer button. "What's wrong?" No point bothering with social niceties when the guy charged by the minute.

The liquidator's grainy face peered back at him. "Mr. Gregory. Where are you?"

"I'm in New Zealand."

The guy looked at him as if he'd taken a shuttle to Pluto.

"I sent your secretary an e-mail." Jackson tilted the laptop screen so he could see a bit better. "How is winding everything up going?"

"We're getting there. Looking at about twenty-seven cents on the dollar once expenses are taken out." He gave as close to a smile as Jackson suspected accountants could. "Your car did well at auction."

"Thanks." His Corvette Stingray C7 had been his pride and joy. The day he'd driven off the lot with that baby, he'd truly thought he'd made it.

George cleared his throat, pushed his glasses back up his nose. "I wanted to give you a heads-up that some of the investors are talking about coming after you personally."

"Me? Why? What for?" Not that he had anything anymore worth them coming after— unless they literally wanted the clothes off his back.

"They seem to have formed a view that either you were negligent in some way or the product was never as close to market as you claimed."

Opening the minibar, Jackson passed over the hard liquor in favor of a Coke and snapped the can open with a satisfying crack. "Well, they're right on the first point. If you can call not considering your girlfriend in cahoots with your biggest rival negligent."

"Your refusal to go after Ms. Thomson for corporate espionage isn't helping anything."

"How could I? She wasn't an employee. She was my girlfriend. And you know as well as I do that trying to sue her would cost far more money than the company has."

He hadn't breathed a word about Nicole to anyone. However, it didn't take a genius to figure out that when the girlfriend of one businessman shows up on the arm of his closest rival at the same time the first man's company goes bust, there might be a connection.

"Meanwhile, Rob is raking in the millions from your stolen property."

Jackson sighed. "I know that. You know that. He knows that. Nicole knows that. But how could I ever prove it? The guy is clever. I guarantee he falsified stuff for months to make it look like the system was something his company had also been working on."

He took a long pull of his soda. "Do I have anything to worry about?"

The guy shrugged. Must be nice to have a job where you could earn four hundred bucks an hour to do a shoulder workout. "Who knows? This is America. People have been sued for way less. I told them that even if they went after you personally, there's nothing there. You're the first company owner I've ever worked with who sold all his assets to make sure there was something to be distributed to investors."

"What was I going to do? Drive around in my fancy car and enjoy my flashy condo while they got nothing?" He might have been far from perfect, but he still had a good grasp of the Ten Commandments, and he was pretty sure that fell under "Do not steal." In spirit, if not in law.

"Um, yeah. That's kind of how it usually works.

Do you not know how much the higher-ups at Enron pocketed while driving the company into the ground?"

"Yup. And I have no idea how they live with themselves. So what's my share?"

George consulted something off the screen. "Once you clear off the secured debtors and pay me and the taxman, you get fifty-one percent of the remaining amount." He scrunched his face as he did some mental arithmetic. "Don't quote me, but I think that would be about thirty grand right now."

"I don't want it." There was no way he could take any of the money before a few critical investors had their money back. The ones who had trusted him not with their excess, but with savings they really needed. "Can you give it to some of the others?"

"Well, if you officially decline it, then I have to evenly distribute it among everyone according to their entitlements. But if you have certain people you'd like your share to go to, then put it in writing and I'll arrange for the checks to get cut to them."

"I'd like to split it three ways between the Slatts, the Mortans, and the Wades." Ten grand each wasn't going to come close to paying back what they'd invested, but at least it was something.

"So what's the remaining debt add up to?"

"Four point six million, give or take fifty grand."

Add his parents' debts on top and he needed a nice even five mil to make good with everyone he needed to. Improbable, but not impossible.

"Thanks, George. I'll drop by in a couple of weeks when I'm back. Let me know in the meantime if anyone decides they do want my pants."

The man's brow furrowed. "I'm not sure a court would literally award them your clothes."

Sarcasm. Lost on 99.9 percent of all accountants.

Jackson closed his laptop screen. Just what he needed on top of everything else—a potential lawsuit.

Five million bucks. He rolled the figure around in his head. There was a number to focus the mind. Unless the spunky but inconvenient redhead had stacks of cash sitting around, it was time to focus on what he was here for. And it wasn't her.

Allie slouched back in her chair at the hotel bar, nursing her lime and soda. It had taken her the best part of an hour to write the report for the head office detailing Jackson's newfound occupation of lifesaver.

If only he'd dodged the punch, she would've been able to justify not writing the report, on the basis that no one had been hurt. But any injury was a mandatory form 44, and even she couldn't pretend he didn't have any of those when half his face was the color of an eggplant.

She blew out a breath and tried to stop her mind from playing the image of him striding out of the lake like he was some kind of Middle-earth version of Colin Firth's Mr. Darcy.

Then, because she was clearly a glutton for torment tonight, she'd Googled Derek and discovered that in the last two years, he had reinvented himself as some kind of PR maven. He even had his own website, with enough schmancy photos of him to fill a fashion catalogue.

She almost threw up a little in her own mouth when she read on his "About" page that he was "happily married to his lovely Kiwi wife."

She stared at a Google montage of images of him with the who's who of Auckland. How could they all be so stupid?

Allie took a slug of her soda and tried to pretend it was something stronger. She even contemplated asking for a table in the restaurant and ordering the entire dessert menu.

"Penny for them?"

She looked up at Louis, who was leaning against the back of the chair beside her. She hadn't even realized he'd been standing nearby. "Pennies aren't legal tender in New Zealand, I'm afraid."

He smiled. "True. And from the look on your face, they were the kind of thoughts that would be worth a lot more, anyway."

Flagging down a passing waiter, he ordered a black coffee, then came around the chair and sat down across from her. "The heart isn't always wrong, you know."

Her head jolted. "I'm sorry?"

"My wife. She left me. Took our two kids and disappeared when I was on a work trip. It was years before I saw them again." He leaned back in the chair and folded his hands behind his head like he was talking about the weather.

"I'm so sorry."

"It was a long time ago. The sixties, when the world got a bit too drunk on the concept of free love and doing whatever 'felt' right. I blamed myself. So I decided that because I had such poor judgment of character when it came to her, I could never trust myself again."

Allie took a long sip of her drink, because she didn't know what to say. The man clearly had some intel on her, but she wasn't planning on offering up anything more if she could help it.

"The truth was, I was right to blame myself, but not because of that. I was so busy making money, building my empire, that I neglected my family. That was the real reason she left. I was just too pigheaded to see it." He tipped some sugar into the cup that the waiter had placed in front of him and gave it a stir.

"I'm sorry." Again. For the third time. What else was there to say?

He propped one ankle up on the other knee. Not bad flexibility for an old guy. "My biggest regret is that since then, I've met a number of wonderful women. Many of whom I'm sure would have made me very happy. But I never allowed myself to open up to any of them because of what she did. And so here I am. An old man with a lot of money, but no one to share my life with."

She opened her mouth to offer a feeble attempt at disagreement, but he shook his head as if knowing what she was going to say.

"It's probably too late for me. But it's definitely not for you."

"I don't understand."

Louis gave her a long look. "So you fell for a scumbag. It happens. Don't spend the rest of your life punishing yourself for it. Just because your heart was wrong once doesn't mean it's always going to be. I'm not saying don't be careful. Do your due diligence. But there are plenty of good guys out there, Allison. Give them a chance."

"I . . . I don't even know if I'm free to." She gripped her hand in her lap nervously. "There are lawyers and a court case, and it's all a big never-ending debacle." Her greatest fear clawed at her. What if, at the end of it all, she lost and the court sided with Derek? Then what?

"I know." He responded to the question that was obviously written across her face. "I have a private investigator check out the people I deal with." He leaned forward in his seat. "But, unless your lawyers are incompetent, one day it will all be behind you. A distant memory."

They better not be, given how much they charged her if they so much as thought in her general direction. She swirled her straw around her now empty glass, the remaining ice clinking in the bottom.

"Tell me, Dr. Shire. What do you think about God?" He took a tentative sip of his coffee.

She startled. Now there was a question she hadn't been asked in a long time. "Honestly, I try not to these days. I'm pretty sure He doesn't think much of me."

Not that she could blame Him. He'd given her enough blazing signs not to marry Derek, an astronaut could've seen them from outer space—but no, she'd had to bowl on through them all. Choosing to believe her own naïve, foolish heart over all the warnings and people telling her she was making a mistake.

One side of his mouth lifted up. "Oh, I know you're wrong about that. Trust an old man who has seen a lot. God always has a way of working things out if we step back and let Him. He's especially good at the ones that appear impossible, because that's when we usually give up trying to fix it ourselves."

She almost laughed. Easy for him to say when he was crazy rich and returning from what had clearly been a successful dinner date with one of the spinsters. She had lost everything. And so far God didn't seem to be going out of His way to help her out with any of it.

"Well, I'd better turn in. I'll be praying for you." He stood, knees cracking.

As much as she resented his assumption that she needed him to, knowing that he would be felt kind of nice.

"Oh, and Mavis has bluer eyes."

"What?"

He gave her a wink. "That's how you can tell her and Ethel apart."

What was the guy, a mind reader? Oh well, at least that was one problem fixed. These days she'd take whatever crumbs she could get.

Thirteen

Jackson was pretty sure this had to count as one of the longest days of his life. It was mid-afternoon and they'd been on the go since early morning, traipsing after some new guide to obscure places all over Wellington that had allegedly been *Lord of the Rings* or *Hobbit* film locations. Judging by the enraptured expressions of everyone else in the group, he was the only one who thought hammering a tent peg through his forehead would be more enjoyable than this.

He'd managed to show an appropriate amount of enthusiasm hour after hour. They'd been shown the locations where Aragorn was washed ashore after being attacked by another evil thing whose name he couldn't remember, the Gardens of Isengard, the site of the orcs felling the trees, where the hobbits hid from the Nazgûl, and a bunch of other places he had zero interest in, but now he'd officially lost the will to live.

Even the knowledge that his uncle, if he was paying attention, would be able to tell Jackson wasn't exactly an ardent fan wasn't enough motivation to continue on with the charade— especially since his banged-up face throbbed like it had its own pulse.

The best part of the entire day had been when Elroy and Sofia had an altercation because Sofia questioned Elroy's credentials as a true Tolkienite. Something about how if he was a true fan, then he wouldn't have visited the Helm's Deep location, as the Elves were never there in the book, it was made up for the movies. Allie had moved in to smooth the waters just as it started getting interesting by pointing out that if people only went to the same locations their characters were in the books then everyone would miss out on half the tour.

At least they were at the last stop—Rivendell, aka Kaitoke Regional Park—so the torment would be over soon. They had to get back to the hotel to pack their bags and fly to the South Island first thing in the morning.

Jackson stifled a yawn as the film location guide warbled on enthusiastically in the background. The group moved forward, but he lagged behind, flapping his Boromir cloak in the breeze, feet treading on lush green grass.

"Blah blah Elves blah blah hobbits blah blah one ring to rule them all." Jackson muttered the words under his breath.

"What did you say?" Allie's voice cut through his thoughts. She was in a new hobbit dress today. A blue one. He hadn't thought it possible, but it was even uglier than the green dress. It must have been smaller, too, because the fat suit was gone. And the feet. The horrible frizzy hair was back, though.

Her face was scrunched: most likely, she was offended by his lack of appropriate reverence for her imaginary best friends. Hmm, this could be fun.

He looked down at her and smirked. "I said blah blah oh look there's a bunch of trees that were in the movie for less than a second! Oh wow—if you stand on one leg and tilt at exactly twenty-seven degrees with one eye closed you can see a rock that was part of Helm's Deep!"

It wasn't like she could deny it. It had been over a decade since *Lord of the Rings* was filmed. Foliage had grown and land had been acquired for other purposes.

"C'mon," he continued. "Even you have to admit the guide's enthusiasm for a few things was way over the top. Trees. And hills. And a river. And rocks." He leaned forward and whispered: "Just between you and me, I'm not sure if you noticed, but they all look the same. You can tell me. You guys just point to any old thing and tell people it was in the films, don't you? It's not like they'd ever know."

The fact that he didn't even pretend to be interested seemed to grate against something deep inside her. He could practically see a fierce protectiveness rise up within her at his blatant derisiveness.

"You realize you are talking about some of the greatest movies of all time? Seventeen Oscars. And that's just the *Rings*, not the *Hobbit*. Eleven for *The Return of the King*—making it tied for the most Oscars for one film ever!" She was almost spluttering with indignation and outrage. Jackson imagined he had just done the equivalent of telling a new mom her baby was ugly.

He raised an eyebrow. "True. But excuse me if I'm skeptical of the Oscars as a way to judge a film's worth. I remind you that one of the other films that also has eleven gold statues involves Leonardo and Kate making out on a sinking ship and the worst pop song of all time."

She flinched. *Ah.* He smothered a smile. He'd bet good money teenage Allison had had Jack and Rose posters plastered all over her bedroom wall and that her CD player had blasted Celine Dion on replay. Not that she'd ever admit it.

Allie seemed to regain some equilibrium. "So you're saying you didn't even like the movies?" She looked at him like he'd said he didn't believe in gravity, or the sun, or Double Stuf Oreos.

Jackson shrugged. This was the most fun he'd had all day. By a very wide margin. "Look, clearly we are polar opposites on this, but I'm not sure why they matter anyway. I mean, they're just a bunch of really loooong books and movies. Don't get me wrong, they're not bad, but deserving of all this madness?" He waved his hands in the general direction of the entire universe. "I don't get it."

She didn't even attempt to restrain her outraged expression. "You can't be serious."

Maybe if he got her mad enough she wouldn't speak to him for the next two weeks. Better yet, she'd avoid him as much as possible. That would be ideal. Let him get on with why he was here rather than remain distracted by her feisty nature and general pocket-size cuteness. "Dead serious. So a bunch of little people save Middle-earth. Big deal. It's not like that plot isn't the same as those of thousands of other books and movies. I mean, it's all very nice and cuddly and feel-good, but not exactly life changing. Except I guess for the people who made their squillions out of it."

Her fists clenched at her side; he bet she itched to give him a matching set of black eyes. Too late, he realized that he'd miscalculated—that in his desire to do whatever it took to stop Allie from getting any further under his skin, he hadn't considered that razzing the one person on this tour he needed on his side would be a really bad idea. And now he was in too deep to try and retreat.

"You are so, so . . ." She trailed off, as if there

weren't adequate words in the English language to describe him.

"Right. And you know it." He'd been intending to say something placatory, but the even more inflammatory words just slipped out. Why didn't he just take a spade and dig his own grave? There was no way she wouldn't rat him out to his uncle after this. And part of him didn't blame her.

Allie's face turned an interesting shade of red and she stood on tiptoe in an attempt to get in his face. In her flat shoes, she barely came up to his nose.

"You know what? I feel sorry for you, because the only reason you can possibly not get why Tolkien is so great is because he writes about themes that are sooooo far outside of your frame of reference. It's like your brain flashes a big red 'Cannot compute, cannot compute.'"

"Really? Well, since you apparently know me so well, why don't you enlighten me?"

"Like honor and sacrifice and valiance and doing something bigger than yourself for the greater good. Like struggling with your own doubts and fears and frailties and coming out stronger—"

She was still ranting, but Jackson was having trouble concentrating. All of his efforts were going into not focusing on how cute she was when she was mad. Her petite frame was fairly bursting with indignation and disgust.

He had to admit that as pure entertainment, Tolkien was definitely up there. There were even a couple of moments during the movies he'd felt a twinge of something, not that he would ever admit it to her. But since he'd already cast his die, it was way more fun getting her worked up over her beloved author. Where would the joy be in letting her think he might even be finding his way to a begrudging admiration of the guy?

A sharp poke brought him back to earth "Ow!" He rubbed the tender spot on his left side where she jabbed him. "What was that for?"

Allie glared at him. "You aren't even listening to me."

He struggled to keep the smile off his face. "You know why?"

She threw her hands up. "Why?"

"You're pretty cute when you're mad."

Where that had come from, he had no idea, but apparently he couldn't have said anything to throw her more off-kilter if he tried.

She stumbled, grabbing onto his arm to stop herself from falling. She blinked up at him. Once. Twice. "You are such a . . . such a . . . man!"

And with that, she spun around and stormed away, hideous dress flapping in the wind behind her.

What was wrong with him? What did he think she was going to say? *Oh wow, thanks. Well then, that changes everything. You're not a total moron after all.*

Stupid, insufferable man. Too bad she hadn't done her thesis on Jane Austen. One of Austen's heroines would have had the perfect line to describe him. Probably Lizzie Bennet, since she seemed to have gotten the monopoly on good lines when it came to insufferable men.

Instead, she'd studied a guy who wrote real heroes, whose characters said things like, *"All you have to decide is what to do with the time that is given to you."* Who battled dragons and orcs and took three arrows in the chest but still kept fighting. Jackson might have been dressed up as Boromir, but Boromir would sooner have died than said something so ridiculous as *"You're pretty cute when you're mad."* So would Aragorn. Or even naïve, bumbling Sam for that matter.

She tried to ignore the thought tugging at her underneath the surface as she stormed after the rest of the group. So what if Jackson thought she was cute? The words held all the meaning of those of some drunk guy hitting on her at a bar. He hadn't even meant it. He'd said it to throw her off-balance. And it had worked perfectly.

What was wrong with her? Why did she keep letting him get under her skin? What did she care if he didn't recognize the genius of Tolkien? Why hadn't she told his uncle the truth about him? The guy was an arrogant, obnoxious moron who probably aspired to marry someone off *The Real Housewives of Orange County.*

She was such an idiot. After yesterday, she had actually thought there might be more to him than she'd originally thought, but she was no better than some girl starring in some teenage rom-com thinking she could convert the bad boy. Convinced that underneath that tough exterior was really a sensitive caring soul that would find its way into the sun if given some tender watering.

The only kind of watering she wanted to do with Jackson Gregory involved holding his head under some.

Before she knew what she was doing, her feet had turned themselves around and she was marching back to where he still stood. "Were you brought up by the state?"

"Huh?" He wielded his fake sword at her and made some large slashing motions with it through the air.

She tried to ignore his forearms flexing as he completed a figure eight and rested the weapon on his shoulder—the same way she'd been trying to ignore how good he looked in his costume all day. *Focus, Allie. Focus!*

"You know, in foster care. Did your father beat your mother? Did your puppy die when you were little and you're still grieving? Were you bullied for being fat in high school? Did a girlfriend cheat on you? Do you have some sort of mental illness?"

His mouth hung slightly ajar at her onslaught. "What?"

"I'm trying to work out if there's some legitimate reason why I should give a nit on a monkey's behind about you, or if you actually are just a total jerk for no good reason."

"Oh. Well in that case." He scrunched up his face. "To answer your questions. No. No. No. No. Yes. No."

She stared at him. Five nos. One yes. Only problem was that in her outburst she couldn't remember the order she asked the questions or even what all of them were. Except she was pretty sure the mental illness one was last and that was a no. Thank goodness. Because that would have been beyond mortifying.

"And no." He was grinning down at her, perfect white teeth gleaming.

"No?" Another no?

"No, I'm not going to tell you which one I answered yes to. You're a smart girl, Dr. Shire. You work it out."

He sauntered away, then paused, looking over his shoulder back at her. "Let's clear one thing up, though. Jackson Gregory has never been fat."

Argh! If she didn't need this job so bad it would be worth it to smack him in his smug purple face.

This was meant to be a low-stress day for her. Someone else had been paid to be the primary entertainment, allowing her to zone out and worry about a myriad of things that could go wrong early tomorrow in the attempt to relocate nine people and a ridiculous amount of luggage over the Cook Strait.

Instead, she was standing in the middle of a park in the back of beyond, more steamed than a Chinese dumpling.

"Jackson Gregory was never fat." The man was unbelievable. What kind of person said that? No doubt it was true. He had the confident bearing of someone who had never gotten a day's grief about his physical appearance in his life, but still.

She tried to ignore the way the smile he tossed back over his shoulder had made her heart kick up a notch, and not out of anger, either. For some completely insane unknowable reason, the guy was growing on her.

Not to mention the glint in his eye now had her wondering how much of his Tolkien-hating had been real and how much had just been him messing with her. And she'd walked straight into it.

Nothing to worry about, Allie. They had less than two weeks left on the tour. Then he would be gone, back to America, back to his life. Whatever that held. Who cared what it held? Just as long as it had nothing to do with her.

Fourteen

Allie peered up at the evening sky as the minivan pulled in to a spot on Wellington's wharf. The occasional cloud waltzed far above and the air still held the remnants of the warm day. The lights of Eastbourne sparkled in the distance across water as flat as her mood. At least the weather was perfect for the evening cruise. Thank goodness. Late April could go either way, and it wasn't the same on a cold, rainy night.

She studied the boat sitting alongside the wharf. This whole dinner cruise on the harbor was a new addition to the itinerary. In the past, this night had been designated for a low-key quiet dinner at the hotel for people to order room service or do whatever they liked, since they were exhausted from another big day and needed time to pack for the flight the next morning.

But nooo. Someone had to go and complain that they hadn't come all the way to New Zealand and paid through the nose for a luxury tour to be left to eat in the hotel and—ta-da!— here they were.

Her suggestion that she would happily organize dinner out for anyone in the group who wanted it had been met with a determined silence from the head office. The updated itinerary now came with a price increase that more than covered the cost of the cruise.

She sucked in a breath, stared out the front windshield, and tried to pull herself together. Derek's phone call still had her shaken up. The guy always, *always,* had an ulterior motive. It unnerved her not being able to figure out what was behind yesterday's call.

And now, she had to spend the evening stuck on something she ordinarily avoided at all costs—a boat. What a fitting end to a stinking couple of days.

Good grief! She dug around in her handbag, trying to sift through the contents in the dim light. She'd totally forgotten to take her seasickness medicine before they left the hotel. Oh, this was not good, not good at all.

"Are we here?" Elroy's voice called out from the back.

"We are indeed." Twisting open her bottle of water, she liberated two pills from the packet of Kwells and knocked them back. *Please act fast. Please act fast.*

Swallowing another gulp of water, she put the lid back on and turned around. "All right. Everyone ready?" It wasn't really a question, so she didn't wait to hear any answers. Opening her passenger door, she dropped onto the pavement and slid open the back door, holding out her hand to help Mavis—thanks to Louis's little tip, she could now tell the two sisters apart—then Ethel, down the awkward step and onto the ground.

"Oh, we've been so looking forward to this. We're going to head right up to the stern, if that's okay with you." Ethel beamed up at her. Hobbiton seemed to have breathed new life into the spinsters. They'd been virtually brimming over with enthusiasm ever since visiting it.

Allie summoned up a smile. "Of course."

Sofia popped out next, followed by Hans's lumbering form, which appeared in the door-way. How the man managed to squash his bulk between the seats was beyond her, but he had claimed the second-row window seat from day one, leaving poor Sofia perched precariously on the seat beside him. Every time they turned a corner, Allie half held her breath, expecting the long-limbed girl to fall into the aisle.

The German dropped to the ground with the grace of a buffalo and grabbed his wife's waist. "Such a beautiful night. So romantic. We like you, Dr. Shire. But we are going to have some alone time before dinner. Okay?"

"Sure. Great. The boat is all ours. Just remember, dinner will be served at eight." The last thing she needed today was to have to find them and interrupt their canoodling.

"Yes, of course." He nodded and grinned at his wife.

"The board is set, the pieces are moving." Sofia offered up the cryptic Gandalf quote with a mischievous smile. What was that about?

Allie stepped away from the door before Jackson could appear. Leading the group toward the boat, she chattered away about the harbor, the boat, city history, anything she could think of to fill the air and keep her mind distracted.

Walking up the gangplank, she half listened to everyone chatting as she checked in with the captain and made sure everything was set. At least on a boat she didn't have to worry about losing anyone.

Everyone boarded and scattered around the deck to take in the views. Two waiters walked around trying to find people to disperse drinks and nibbles to. There seemed to be a ridiculous amount of food for only nine people.

Their minivan still lingered on the wharf, so she gave Marge a thumbs-up to signal she could go. The driver returned her sign but made no move to leave.

Oh well. As long as he was back for them when the boat docked at nine-thirty, it wasn't for Allie to worry about what their driver did in the interim.

Walking around the prow of the boat, she almost collided with Elroy coming from the opposite direction. "Everything okay?"

"Great. Great boat. Lovely view. Looking forward to an unforgettable night."

Everyone was far more enthusiastic about this than she had been expecting. She had thought they'd be dead on their feet by now.

She put a hand to her stomach. So far, so good. The Kwells must be doing their thing. Usually she was feeding her breakfast to the ocean within a few minutes of being on the water. Relieved, she snagged a couple of rice paper rolls from a passing tray. With all the drama of the day, she hadn't had much to eat since breakfast.

"How's the shoulder?"

Jackson stood beside her, chicken wing in hand, the lights of Wellington arranged around his head like a halo.

Be civil, Allie. He's still a client. "Much better than your face, if it feels anywhere near as painful as it looks. Can you even see out of that?"

He raised a finger to his purple, puffed-up eye and winced. "A little." He moved his hand to his mouth to smother a yawn. "Sorry. I'm beat. Can I apologize in advance if I fall asleep face-first in my potatoes?"

She couldn't help but laugh at the same guy she'd wanted to choke a few hours ago. "Only if you forgive me the same thing."

The boat gave a slight shudder as it pulled away from the dock. She looked around. "Where's Louis?"

"He said he was going to the little boys' room."

She couldn't see anyone else. It was a ridiculously large boat for so few of them. She'd have to tell the head office that the exclusive use for their group was a tad over the top—not that they listened to her opinions.

"I need to go and talk to the chef." She was pretty sure the spinsters came up with dietary restrictions just to mess with her. When they were getting in the van to drive to the boat, Ethel had announced that her personal psychic had told her to abstain from red food for the rest of the week. Why? Had the woman seen choking on a tomato in the elderly lady's future?

Walking around the side, she saw their van was still parked there. And . . . She stumbled, clutching at the railing in an attempt to remain upright. No. They didn't. They couldn't have.

"What are you doing?" She yelled the question across the thirty odd meters at her seven charges lined up along the dock waving merrily at her.

"What's going on?" Jackson was beside her.

"We're going on that boat!" Esther yelled with a grin as she pointed with both arms and her body to a luxury launch tied up a bit further up.

How weird that the first thing that went through her mind was that at least now she wouldn't have to worry about the little thief stealing anything off this boat. Then she realized she had much bigger issues.

"You two have fun!" Hans's grin practically took up his whole face—they'd have nowhere near as much fun as he was planning to have, she would bet.

"Tell the chef sorry about the red-food thing!"

Allie turned to the sailor guy standing by where the gangplank had been. "You turn around and take us back there right now!" She hissed the words at him.

"Sorry, ma'am. No can do. The old guy promised to double this if we continued the sailing as originally planned." And he opened his fist to reveal a thick, folded-over wad of hundred-dollar bills.

She turned back to see them all walking toward the launch, except for Mr. Duff, who stood on the wharf. Seeing he had her attention, he gave a big smile and offered up a salute.

She was going to kill them. All of them.

He was going to kill him. Rich old man who held his destiny in his hands or not, his uncle was a dead man.

"Is this one of my character challenges? Am I supposed to jump off and swim?" Jackson yelled the questions at the top of his lungs, the distance between him and Allie and the wharf rapidly increasing. Like he hadn't already had enough experiences with New Zealand's aquatic life.

The old man held a hand to his ear, pretending

he couldn't hear him. Giving them another salute, he turned and headed toward the other boat bobbing on the water.

"Unbelievable," Jackson muttered under his breath, sucking back the few choice words he wanted to add. There was no way this was a character test, when the old guy wouldn't even be here to observe it. At some point, Louis had turned into a full-throttle matchmaker. With very deep pockets. If Jackson had had any idea this was part of what he was signing up for, he would've been on the first plane home.

At least he wasn't alone in his anger. Allison couldn't have looked more horrified if she'd somehow mistakenly found herself in the cast of *The Bachelor*.

His pride hurt a little. So they didn't exactly get along like a house on fire, but he'd thought, after the last couple of days, they'd at last found their way to some sort of truce. Okay, until he riled her up so bad today that she hadn't acknowledged his presence the rest of the afternoon. Though, as far as he could tell, she hadn't given the game up to his uncle yet. Right now he just wasn't sure whether to be grateful or wish she'd put him out of his misery.

"So how long are we stuck on this thing?" He directed his question straight ahead to the enormous expanse of ocean and sky that was now their vista.

"Two hours."

She muttered something under her breath that sounded like a mumbled reference to having to explain her runaway tour to the head office.

"C'mon." He quirked a smile at her. "It's not that bad."

"Says the guy who's never met my boss."

"Was that who was on the phone yesterday?" It was none of his business, but after the phone call, she'd seemed on edge the rest of the day. Jittery.

Something crossed her face. "No." She ran a hand through her hair, tousling her updo. Staring at the receding wharf, she groaned. "As if I don't already have enough paperwork to do tonight."

He shrugged. "So don't tell them. This is hardly your fault."

"That's not what they'll think." Allie bent over and rested her head on the metal rail. He tried not to notice how perfectly the bodice of her green cocktail dress hugged her curves. Unfortunately, that would entail jabbing himself in the onegood eye he had left.

Allie tipped her head sideways and her green-eyed gaze slid up to his face. She looked at him in silence for a couple of seconds, lips pursed as if she were deciding whether to deign to continue speaking to him. "So what are we going to do?"

"Have dinner? I'm starving."

"Fair enough." She pushed herself up from the railing. "Especially since I don't have wads of hundred-dollar notes on me to buy our way back. Do you?"

He made a show of pulling his empty jacket pockets inside out. "Definitely not." What was his uncle up to? And how and when had he gotten everyone else to sign up for it?

Allie walked ahead of him toward the dining room, the full skirt swaying in the breeze. Wisps of hair that had fallen from her pulled-back do danced in the light breeze around the nape of her neck.

Stop it, Jackson! Done with women, remember? Done with women. He tugged at his shirt collar. Man, it was a warm night. In spite of it being autumn in April, he still couldn't get his head around it.

Allie opened the door and stepped in. He followed, only to find she had stopped right inside the doorway. Smacking into her back, he caused her to stumble, and his hand leapt out to snag her around her waist before he could think about it.

"Are you—" His language skills failed him as he saw what had caused her abrupt halt. Little sparkly lights were strung around the entire room, a female singer crooned from some-where, and by an expanse of windows in the middle of a sea of dining isolation sat a table for two. Complete with candles, roses, and a bottle of champagne on ice. Like something staged straight out of the world's most clichéd dates.

A groan escaped Jackson's lips before he could stop it.

Allie cast him a scathing look. "You mind?"

Huh?

She jabbed her chin toward where his hand still rested on her waist, and he dropped it faster than a scalding iron.

Letting out something that sounded like a cross between a whistle and a sigh, she strode forward to their table, blew out the candles, picked up the ornate candelabra, and dropped it into a trash can in the corner of the room. Returning to the table, she picked up the roses and delivered them, vase and all, to the same trash can.

On the final trip, she plucked out the bottle of vintage Moët from the ice bucket standing beside the table and waved it in his direction like a club. "You want any?" From the tone of her voice, there was only one acceptable answer.

She wasn't going to be getting it from him. There was no way he was letting a bottle of expensive champagne get thrown away.

"Easy, tiger." Walking toward her, he pried the champagne from her fingers. If Allie kept shaking the bottle around like that, it would explode like a fountain when opened. And he, for one, could use a glass.

Pulling the foil off the top, he twisted the cork, holding his breath for a second as it came off the top of the bottle with a pop.

Half filling the two wine flutes on the table, he placed the bottle back in the ice bucket, handed one glass to Allie, then tipped his toward her. "To Louis. For at least stranding us with a great bottle of champagne."

She just looked at him.

"Oh, come on. You can't not return a toast. It's practically unconstitutional."

"New Zealand doesn't have a constitution." But she gave in to a small smile as she clinked her glass to his. Pulling out a chair, she sat down, her full skirt swooshing out around her. "On the upside, at least I don't have to suffer in these for the next couple of hours." She used the toe of one shoe to dislodge the other from her heel, kicked it off, then repeated the process with the other foot. This time the stiletto spun through the air before landing on the carpet upside down.

Taking a sip of her wine, Allie surveyed the table, now naked save for the cutlery and salt and pepper shakers. "That's so much better."

Jackson pulled out his seat across from her and sat down. "Nice work. Much less awkward."

She scrunched her face at him. "You think it was awkward? I just thought it was tacky. It only would've been awkward if we were on an actual date, and it's not like that's ever going to happen."

It was like getting stabbed in the eye with a poker and trying to pretend he didn't feel anything. "True." Thankfully the single word came out calm and controlled. The opposite of the unexpected tangle of emotions churning in his chest, which wasn't helped by the constant subtle but noticeable rolling of the boat.

"Don't get me wrong. I'm super impressed they managed to pull it off, even if it was all for nothing. And I'd love to know how your uncle managed to get Esther to go along with it, given she's had dibs on you since the Aragorn costume."

He groaned. "Please tell me I don't have to wear that thing again."

Allie laughed as she pierced a piece of feta from their just-delivered antipasto platter with her fork. "That depends entirely on you."

Jackson scowled at her. He had enough on his shoulders without some tweenager chasing after him, especially since it was becoming clear that at some point in the last three days, the feisty redhead sitting across from him had gotten under his skin in a very big way.

She pushed the platter toward him and he speared an olive. Her nose wrinkled as he popped it into his mouth and bit down on the salty morsel.

"You can have all of those."

"Not an olive fan?"

She shook her head. "Not at all. Nasty little

things. The first time I had one I thought it was a grape. Put me off for life." She pulled some hairpins loose and ran a hand through her now free hair. He tried to ignore the desire welling up inside him. What was wrong with him? Four days ago he'd sworn off women for life, and now he was sitting here struggling to keep his eye on the prize.

"Loosen up, Jackson. Get rid of your jacket and tie. You look like you're suffering almost as much as I was."

He grimaced. "Probably more." Thankfully, she would never know he wasn't talking about his clothes.

Candles, roses, and champagne. The romance trifecta. For a split second, Allie had wished the floor would open up and drop her into the ocean. The long swim back would have been far preferable to dinner with Jackson chaperoned by fairy lights, sultry background crooning, and the aroma of rose petals.

Then she just got mad—mad at her stupid life and this stupid job that had her stuck on this stupid boat. Mad at Derek for ruining everything. Mad at her naïve self for ever falling for him. Mad at the whole group for stranding her with the one guy she was desperately trying not to be attracted to. Mad at Jackson for daring to be more complex than the arrogant self-absorbed prat she'd originally pegged him as. Hotter-than-the-surface-of-the-sun livid.

Dumping the candles and flowers in the rubbish bin had made her feel a whole lot better than thousands of dollars of therapy had ever managed.

Allie almost wished her mother could have seen it. It might have been the only time in her life she would've been proud of her. The woman was like a cross between Anna Wintour and Martha Stewart. In fact, Martha had found more favor with Veronica after the whole insider-trading fiasco.

And Allie's unseemly temper tantrum had worked. Exceptionally well, if the gaping hole where Jackson's mouth ordinarily resided was anything to go by. By the time she'd renounced the whole shebang as tacky, rather than awkward, he'd looked like he swallowed his own tongue.

And that would be Allie a gazillion points to Jackson's two.

She took another sip of her champagne and placed the flute on the table. There was only one flaw in her cunning plan: the guy sitting across from her. Thanks to her genius suggestion, he'd taken off his tie, undone a couple of buttons, and shoved his sleeves up to his elbows, revealing a pair of muscular forearms.

Why on earth had she thought that was a good idea? He'd been attractive enough all dressed up in his suit. Now all relaxed and slightly rumpled, he looked good enough to eat with a spoon. Somehow, the smashed-up face even managed to add to his appeal. How? She had no idea.

"Do you really not like anything to do with Tolkien, or were you just getting a kick out of making me mad today?" Since they were trapped here, she might as well ask the question that had been bugging her since their little altercation at Kaitoke.

A smile played on Jackson's lips. "I can't deny a little of the second may have come into it."

"You're pretty cute when you're mad." His words kept playing in her head, despite her attempts to pretend they'd never been said.

"But, I will admit that I'm hardly in a position to take any kind of educated stance on the matter."

She seized on his words. She could talk about Tolkien all night; it was a safe topic. Well, safer than anything else that came to mind. "So, what do you want to know?"

Jackson seemed to think for a second while he speared a pickle. "Who's your favorite Tolkien character?"

"That depends. Are we talking about the books or the movies?"

"Are they that different?"

She almost choked on the last of her drink. Were they *that* different? Were the sun and the moon different? Pepsi and Mountain Dew? "It depends on the character. But yes, it would be fair to say that Peter Jackson and his team took a lot of creative license with some."

"Like how?" Jackson actually looked interested.

Allie thought for a second. No point telling him about the major characters like Glorfindel who had been cut completely from the movies; they wouldn't mean anything to him. "Like Aragorn. The movies make him look weak, both when it comes to Arwen and his role. In the screenplay he loves her but makes no real effort to securetheir future. It was all on her to give up her immortality. He is full of fears and self-doubt, and unwilling to embrace the destiny. He doesn't take up his forefathers' sword until nearly the middle of the third movie, when Elrond brings the reforged blade to Dunharrow."

"And in the books?"

How to sum it up succinctly? "Arwen's father's terms were that she could only wed the man who had become king of both Gondor and Arnor, and this was a driving force for him. Tolkien writes Aragorn as a man of singular destiny for which he is prepared by Elrond and toward which he labors throughout his life. He bears the sword wherever he goes, even when it's in shards. He's not afraid to fight for what he wants—Arwen."

Which was what every girl wanted. Part of what

had had her tumbling head over heels for Derek was his unwavering pursuit of her. And look what that had brought her. Allie picked up her fork and stabbed a piece of prosciutto.

Jackson seemed to sense her change in mood and didn't pursue it any further. Dipping a breadstick into some sort of pesto, he leaned back in his seat and took a bite. "Mmmm, this is good."

Reaching out, he went to dip the stick back in. Before she even thought about it, her hand flew out and slapped it away. The breadstick flew from his hand like a miniature baton, landing on the carpet about six feet away.

"Hey!"

"Didn't your mother ever teach you not to double-dip?"

"What?" He looked at her like she'd started talking Elvish.

"That"—she pointed at the breadstick—"went into your mouth. You don't go dipping it again in something other people have to eat. It's uncouth."

Oh dear. That was, word for word, exactly what her mother had said more times than she could remember. She even *sounded* like her. The compulsion to go and pick the breadstick up from its lonely spot on the carpet followed—the legacy of being raised by a woman who once rang the police to find out where she could buy the plastic booties worn at crime scenes.

A slow smile crossed his face. "You're telling me you've spent your entire life denied the pleasure of having more than one helping of salsa on a tortilla chip?"

When he said it like that, it sounded pathetic. But he had never met Veronica.

"You think it's funny, but you're talking to the daughter of a woman who once slapped the prime minister's hand at a cocktail party when he went to double-dip."

His mouth dropped. "You're joking."

"I wish I was."

"So are you telling me in— What's your mother's name?"

"Veronica."

"That in Veronica's world"—he pulled out a new breadstick, dipped the end in the pesto, and waved it at her—"after I've bitten off this end, that's it? I have to suffer the boredom of a plain breadstick for as long as this breadstick shall live?"

"Yes." It came out uptight and prim.

Actually, now that she thought about it, he could flip it around and use the other end. Bit late to work that out now when she'd already slapped the guy.

"Allison Shire." He was doing a terrible job of smothering his grin. "I dare you to live a little. Indulge in a breadstick that has pesto on every bite. Double-dip. Triple-dip, even. I, as the only other person sharing this dish, give you permission."

"Don't be stupid."

"If you don't, then I'm going to eat all the rest of them like this." He bit off the pesto end and chucked the rest of the breadstick over his shoulder. Picked up another one, dipped it, and did the same.

She had to curl her hands around the bottom of her chair to stop herself from getting up and scuttling around, picking them up from the floor. "Do what you like." She reached out and took a sip of water. "I don't have anything to prove to you." The words came out defensive.

He stopped suddenly, breadstick number four halfway to his mouth. "No, you don't. I'd imagine you're the one person who doesn't have anything to prove to anyone."

From the look in his eyes, they weren't talking about something stupid like baked goods or double-dipping anymore. She opened her mouth to come back with something flippant, something to get them back on safe, neutral ground. But somehow her brain forgot to instruct her mouth because what came out was "Except I ruined my life trying to prove my mother wrong."

Her whole body felt like she had shoved her finger into an electrical socket. What on earth had possessed her to admit that? To *him* of all people. What was wrong with her?

Her mind went into a meltdown, trying to work out what she was going to say to his logical follow-up questions. Why? How? When? What happened?

"I've ruined a whole lot of peoples' lives trying to prove my entire town wrong." As Jackson's words hit the air, his whole body froze, and she got the sense he had the same hysterical questions running through his mind.

She could breathe again, struck by the realization this was probably one of the most honest conversations she'd had since the day Julia showed up at her lecture and made her life a public sideshow.

"What happened?" Her fingers twisted around themselves, performing an intricate dance on the tablecloth. "Sorry, it's none of my business. You don't—"

"My company collapsed." A sardonic smile crossed his face. "Quite spectacularly, after my girlfriend stole my most closely guarded intellectual property and gave it to my biggest competitor." Bitterness steeped his tone. "I developed a logistics supply chain program that will revolutionize retail. The IP was what everything was built around,what was going to take us big. I was the only one who knew how everything fit together. And Nicole, it turned out. After she turned over my files, instead of propelling our Wall Street listing the company had to fold, taking with it some of my investors' retirement funds and college savings for their kids."

"I'm sorry." The boat dipped into a swell, pushing her back against her chair.

"Me too." He picked up his water glass, then put it back down. Pushed it around in front of him. "It was six months ago and I can still hear the sobs of one father asking me how he was supposed to tell his son he wasn't going to be going to his dream college after all." A tornado of vulnerability, misery, and regret stormed across his face at the admission.

He stared at something over her shoulder. "If I can't convince Louis to invest in my new business and find a way to pay them back, I don't know how I'll ever be able to live with myself. I'm supposed to be passing some kind of character test and somehow I've ended up starring in some kind of matchmaking scheme in Tolkien land. What am I supposed to do with that? No offense." He looked trapped. Exactly how she felt. "I mean—"

"The phone call. Yesterday." Allie's soft words interrupted his litany of regrets, compelled by a force stronger than her own fear.

Was she really going to go there? She sucked in a deep breath. Ignored that her insides were performing moves like they were auditioning for *So You Think You Can Dance*. She could solve this for Jackson right now. Tell him the truth. He'd tell Louis and whatever he was up to trying to matchmake the two of them would be over. Allie tried to find the words to explain her sort-of marriage. "It was m—" Suddenly her stomach let out the kind of roll usually reserved for roller coasters at Six Flags and her hands flew up to her mouth as she cut herself off mid-sentence. Then she was up and running. Heading to the rubbish bin.

A retch and then a . . . Oh dear. A shuddering heave, her entire body arching over as she puked all over the roses. And her own feet.

So much for Kwells.

The last time Jackson had rubbed a girl's back while she puked violently had been . . . never.

Not once. Not his sister. Not a cousin. Not a single girlfriend. And he had the type of fearless stomach that survived eating street food in India, so his own personal experience was of zero help.

So he dug deep and tried to remember what his mom had done the couple of times Beth had the stomach flu. He came up with vague memories of back rubbing and soothing noises.

Here he was, on a boat in the middle of the harbor, awkwardly rubbing Allie's back while she emptied her stomach for what had to be the fifth time. He'd quit with the soothing noises after he decided they weren't so much calming but sounded more like some kind of animal in pain.

The only good news in the whole scenario was that there had been enough of a break between the first and second round for him to grab another trash can, since the first one was already full of the flowers and candles.

Jackson looked up to find the waiter hovering at his elbow. "Is there anything I can get for her, sir?"

Allie pulled her head out of the trashcan and just managed to croak out, "Dry ground," before shoving it back in.

Jackson looked at the young guy. "How long?"

"We've turned around already, so another five, ten minutes, maybe?"

"Okay. Can you arrange a cab? I need to get her back to the hotel as fast as possible. Oh, and do me a favor and put all that stuff in a bag or something?" He nodded to Allie's sick-coated shoes on the floor, her purse, his jacket and tie. From the state she was in, he was betting he would be carrying her off the boat.

The guy still hovered.

"What?"

"Um, the chef wanted me to check it wasn't anything she ate."

Allie shook her head and mumbled something

that echoed around the tin can that he translated as she got very seasick.

What was she even doing on a boat if it made her that sick?

He looked at her, practically folded in half, clutching her vomit receptacle like it was the last lifejacket on a sinking ship. This was definitely not the moment to be asking that question.

He squatted in front of her. "Allie." He kept his quads poised, ready to move if they hit another swell. She'd already almost toppled off her seat once, and had been saved only by him grabbing the back of her dress and hauling her back up.

There was no response. "Allison!"

Her head lifted, glazed eyes appearing over the gray rim.

"We're going to dock soon. Do you think you can walk?"

She looked at him like his words were coming at her from the far end of a very long tunnel. After a few seconds, she gave the world's smallest nod.

"Are you sure?"

A few more seconds and an even smaller head shake. For the first time, he noticed most of the ends of the front half of her hair had been caught in the puking avalanche. Poor girl. The decision to release it from her updo had definitely not paid off.

A change in the vibration of the engines and then the feel of the boat nudging up against something. Finally.

The waiter appeared with a bulging plastic bag and an empty trash can. "There's a cab waiting for you on the wharf."

"Okay, thanks." Taking the clean bin, he pried the half-filled one from Allie's grasp and replaced it with the new one.

He handed the used one to the guy, who looked less than thrilled. Not that he could blame him. The thing stunk. Bad.

"Allie, we're here. Time to get off now. Can you stand up?" He half stood and looped his arm around her back, tucking his fingers around her rib cage.

Making a valiant effort, she struggled to her feet, the material of her full skirt rustling. To her credit, she did still know what mattered and kept a very firm hold on the bin.

Tugging her arm across his back, he tried to take a couple of steps, but he was pulling deadweight. Oh, this was hopeless. It would take them until tomorrow to get off this blasted boat.

"I'm picking you up. Don't fight me. Seriously." Nothing.

With a swoop, he swung his free arm under the backs of her knees and lifted her into his arms, the bin balancing perfectly in the L shape made by her legs and torso.

"Can you take that down to the cab for us?" He nodded at the plastic bag. "Having only one good eye and all, I need to concentrate on getting her off without dropping her in the water."

Given the last few days, he wouldn't be surprised if he did. And in her current condition, the poor girl would probably sink like a rock.

The guy nodded. "I'll get the door." Striding across the room, he held open the door to the deck.

Jackson hoped he didn't think he was getting a tip, because he had no money. And they were about to catch a cab with a driver who'd expect to be paid. *Didn't think that one through, Jackson, did you?* Fingers crossed Allie had some money in her purse. If not, he hoped his uncle was back at the hotel to foot the bill. It would only be fair, given that this whole debacle was his fault.

He adjusted his hold and Allie mumbled as he resettled her, trying desperately not to notice how perfectly she fit or how good she felt curled up against his chest.

He tilted his head down. "What was that?"

"You smell good." She nestled further into his chest, too out of it to notice his heart had just stopped.

Fifteen

Little gremlins were taking sledgehammers to the inside of Allie's skull. Her mouth was as dry as Arizona in August. And her whole body about as hot.

"Allie." The word echoed around in her head, like someone was trying to communicate with her from another planet. "Allie, you need to wake up."

Wake up, which would require opening her eyes. Way too hard. She hadn't had a migraine this bad since she was fifteen and her father had decided to take the family sailing around the Bay of Islands. She'd spent the entire time feeding the fishes.

Ocean. Boat. Sailing. Sick. Little snippets of recall started rising to the surface of her consciousness, stringing themselves together.

Stranded. Roses. Jackson.

Her eyes flew open. No. That couldn't be right. "Welcome back."

Except the man himself was standing in her hotel room, looking down at her.

She screamed. The volume took even her by surprise. He jumped, stumbled back into the ottoman, and went over, legs flailing in the air like those of a dying fly.

Shooting upright, she swung her legs over the side of her bed and froze as she saw bright green splotched with stains.

Why was she still wearing her cocktail dress? And what on earth had happened to it?

A tsunami opened in her mind. The rest of the group sneaking off the boat. Eating dinner with Jackson. Talking. *"The phone call yesterday. It was—"* The next memory she had was of her running to be sick. Very, very sick.

She groaned.

"You okay?" He was back on his feet but keeping a safe distance. Looking very refreshed in jeans, a T-shirt, and some trendy casual shoes.

She scrunched up her face, tempted to close her eyes to try and hide from the mortification overtaking every sense. "How bad was it?"

He kind of opened his mouth, but nothing came out.

Allie buried her head in her hands, then peeked out between her fingers. "That bad, huh?" It must have been downright horrific for him not to be taking the opportunity to give her grief about it.

Jackson shifted on his feet. "Let's just say I didn't know it was physically possible for one small human to expel that much in such a short time."

"How did we get back here?"

"We caught a cab. Sorry, I had to use the money in your purse. I didn't have any."

She only half heard him, accosted by a hazy memory of snuggling into someone's arms. Mumbling something. Mumbling what?

"Did you have to carry me?"

He nodded. "You were pretty out of it."

"I'm so, so sorry. I haven't been on a boat in years. I had hoped maybe if I took something it wouldn't be too bad." She ran a hand through her hair. It snagged on something at the end. She held a lock up in front of her face, and the smell of sick wafted under her nose. She'd thrown up on her own hair? In front of *him?* It was almost more than she could bear.

"What are you doing here?"

He unfurled a slow smile at her. The kind that put a slow burn in her stomach. "You asked me to stay."

"What?" She hadn't. Oh please, please let that not be what she had mumbled. She wasn't that girl. She was so not that girl. She took a quick inventory of her person. Vomit coated. Yes. Disgusting. Very. All clothing present and accounted for? Yes, yes, and yes.

Whatever mortifying things she might have said in her stupor, she could live with. At least she hadn't done anything that was going to haunt her forever. She was already overloaded with baggage in that department.

"Just joking." He grinned his "gotcha" grin.

Her ramrod posture wilted, a breath she hadn't even known she was holding rushing out. "I . . ." If this had been night one, she would've known there was no way she would've ever said such a thing. No matter what her state. But something had changed in the last few days that scared her and made her feel like whenever Jackson was around, gravity had changed.

Something in his face shifted. "Sorry. That was in bad taste." Leaning over, he tilted her chin up with the tip of his finger and looked straight in her eyes, causing her breath to suddenly come out staccato. "Just so we're clear. I know you're not that girl. And I am many things, but I am not that guy."

Thank goodness. She could breathe a bit easier. "So what happened?"

"It was all very proper, I'm afraid. I carried you up here. You got angry at me for trying to put a blanket over you. Told me to leave you alone. I escorted myself next door to my own room, had a very refreshing night's sleep, and here we are. Me, all ready for another exciting day of hobbit adventures, and you . . . well, probably about to start moving really fast any second now."

The way he said the final sentence triggered something. Hold on. Hold on. "What time is it?"

"Just after seven."

She was on her feet. "We have a plane to catch in like an hour." They could not miss that flight. Not when there was a packed schedule waiting for them at the other end. Everything would collapse like dominos if they were delayed.

"I know. That's why I'm here. I figured you might need a wake-up call."

Her mind was speeding. Ten minutes to have a shower and get dressed. Fifteen to round everyone up and get them in the van. Ten minutes to the airport. They might be able to make it.

Grabbing a pair of jeans and a fresh SLT-branded T-shirt out of her suitcase, she threw them on the bed and started throwing everything else back in.

There was only one thing that was less desirable than missing their plane: dwelling on the disturbingly pleasant memory of being in Jackson's arms.

What on earth had made him say that? His father would've given him the look he used ever since Jackson had gotten too big for him to turn over his knee.

"You asked me to stay." It had fallen out of his mouth, a joke, but the way her face had collapsed and her eyes been overwritten with fear was far from funny. Even now she remained unbalanced, bouncing all over the room like a careening bowling ball.

"Allie, stop." Grabbing her wrists, he forced her to a halt. "I've got it. I'll get your stuff together. You go get cleaned up."

She looked at him, uncertain.

"Go." He turned her toward the bathroom door and gave her a gentle prod in the small of her back. "I'll get everything out here together and meet you downstairs. Everyone else has eaten breakfast. They're meeting us there in ten."

"Okay. Thanks." She grabbed her clothes from the bed and disappeared into the bathroom. He heard the sound of the water turning on.

Stop it, Jackson. Focus. The last thing he needed to think about was Allie in the shower. He'd already been enough of a cur for one morning.

Tossing her spare room key—which he'd taken, suspecting she might need a personal wake-up call—onto the bedside table, he got to work. Checking the wardrobe and drawers, he shoved clothes into her suitcase and zipped it shut.

He turned his attention to the papers and documents strewn over the desk, accordioning them into a pile and shoving them into the satchel on the chair that contained her laptop.

He stole a glance at the clock. After quarter past seven already. If they were in the States, they wouldn't have a snowball's chance of catching an eight-thirty flight, but obviously things worked on a different timetable in New Zealand.

Her phone on the nightstand vibrated, doing a little dance across the surface. He let it go to voice mail. Then it started up again, continuing its rumba toward the edge of the table.

Hmm. Maybe it was something urgent. When the phone started up a third time, he snatched it up. Blocked call. Running his thumb across the screen, he put it to his ear. "Allison's phone."

A pause.

208

"Hello?"

"Who's this? Where's Allie?"

"She's . . ." His brain caught up with his mouth before he finished the sentence with *in the shower* and possibly got her in a lot of hot water. This guy could be her father, her *boyfriend*. He suddenly realized he'd never considered for a second she might be in a relationship. "She's not here right now. Can I take a message?"

"Yes. Tell her Derek called. I'll try her again later."

Something about the way the guy issued his directive sent a spurt of uneasiness down Jackson's spine. "Okay. Will do." Ending the call, he dropped the phone on the bed.

Turning his attention back to closing up the satchel, he realized that the white noise of the shower had stopped. Time to get out of here. The last thing he needed was to have to talk to a fresh-faced and clean-smelling Allie.

He tapped on the bathroom door as he walked past. "Allie. Derek called. He said he'd ring you later."

Then he opened the door and hauled her stuff into the hallway. Maybe she did have a boyfriend. That would help solve this little problem of not being able to shake the feeling of holding her in his arms. Because if there was one place Jackson Gregory would never go, it was near a woman who was already spoken for. Not ever.

Sixteen

"You've got to get it together, Allie." Allie muttered the words to herself as she realized she'd been staring at the same piece of paper for minutes and not seeing anything.

The group had spent their first two days in the South Island taking in some of the best it had to offer after her bacon had been saved by a flight delay of seven minutes. For once, no one had complained about taking a couple of days away from Tolkien. Not exactly a hardship when their "days off" revolved around indulging in wine-tasting in rolling vineyards, kayaking crystal-clear waters, and a road trip to the picturesque coastal town of Kaikoura to go whale watching.

It was one of her favorite parts of the tour. However, this time it was lost in a blur of trying to recover lost memories from the boat night, attempting to rein in her unease over Derek's continued attempts to make contact, and trying to squash her ever-rising awareness of Jackson.

She could not be off her game today—not when letting her tribe loose in the New Zealand countryside was involved. And definitely not when Kat was back on board. Her friend would spot that something was off in a heartbeat and badger her with all sorts of uncomfortable questions Allie didn't have the energy to evade.

"Miss Allison. Can I talk to you for one moment?" The gray cloak of his Lord Celeborn outfit flapped behind Hans as he walked up to where Allie was standing in the lobby of Hotel d'Urville.

"Sure."

"Sofia. She is not able to join us today."

"What's wrong?" The beautiful unlikely Tolkien nerd had grown on Allie.

He made some indecipherable gestures with his hands. "It is . . . how do you say . . . the women's time?"

The women's time? Oh. "Is she okay?"

"No worries. She take some pills and stay in bed today. Very disappointed to miss out on today, but like this." He clutched at his stomach and pulled a face that made him look like a cross between constipated and under the influence.

"Okay, tell her I hope she feels better."

She turned her attention back to the list for the day. Well, this threw a spanner in the works. Everything had been carefully orchestrated around eight participants—four duos—and now there were seven.

Chewing on her bottom lip, she pondered the problem. They could still do three groups of two and a soloist. Jackson and Hans were the only solo contenders. There was no way she would let any of the others go alone.

Mr. Duff with Esther, Elroy with Mavis, Hans with Ethel, and Jackson by himself. That could work. Jackson would probably even be grateful, and she certainly owed him after the boat debacle.

Done. Standing back, she triple-checked the four rucksacks in front of her. GPS locators, check. Emergency flares, check. Water, check. Snacks, check. First-aid kits, check. Everything they could need as they competed against each other in an orienteering challenge in the Kahurangi National Park—home to a number of filming locations.

Not that there was really any chance of them needing any of it apart from the water and snacks. The high-tech GPS and emergency beacon system ensured she would know everyone's location at all times, and each drop area had been especially chosen to mitigate as many natural hazards as possible. As a backup, there were the set of emergency flares. It would take just one group of lost, dead, or badly injured wealthy tourists for SLT to watch its business go down the gurgler. So on this, the company spared no expense.

Of course, the inclusion of an exclusive wilderness "adventure" across the land used as filming locations otherwise inaccessible to the public helped to justify their high tour fees.

Today, her charges would journey just like the Fellowship, except with helicopters, compasses, and a gourmet picnic lunch at the end of their leisurely hike.

"All sorted?" Kat, whom she'd snagged as her co-guide for the week, was back from checking that everyone's chosen costume was terrain- and weather-appropriate. No scantily clad Arwens catching pneumonia on her watch, thank you very much.

Allie walked along, zipping up each backpack. "Yup, except Sofia's unwell, so she isn't coming. I was thinking of maybe sending Jackson off solo."

Kat raised an eyebrow. "You think it's wise sending someone off by themselves? If something were to happen to him . . ."

Her hackles went up. She'd been doing this for two years while Kat flitted in for a few days at a time when there was a lull in the makeup business. "Nothing has ever happened to anyone on one of my tours."

Kat held up her hands. "Chill, Allie. I'm just asking. Have you ever sent someone off by himself?"

She had a point, not that Allie would ever admit it. "He'll have a GPS and emergency flares. And if something was going to happen, I'm pretty sure neither of the sisters would be able to prevent it, and he would have been teamed up with one of them if Sofia were coming."

Kat shrugged. "It's your call; I'm just the assistant."

Too right she was. Allie smoothed down her green Woodland Elf outfit. Elroy and Esther would no doubt hate it, but Arwen was already taken, Kat with her Cate Blanchett looks made the perfect Galadriel, and there was no way she was spending another day in a hobbit outfit.

She tried to ignore the little voice at the back of her head chiming in that it didn't exactly hurt that the outfit was about a hundred times more flattering than a frumpy floral dress. And she got to carry a bow and arrows, which was cool. Even if completely unnecessary, given that the closest she'd get to killing anything would be unpacking the ham sandwiches for lunch.

"I think everyone's gathered." Kat pointed to the corner of the lobby where they'd instructed everyone to meet.

"Great, let's go." She picked up the backpacks and walked toward the group. "Morning, everyone."

They all stopped chatting. "I'm sorry to say Sofia isn't well today and won't be joining us. So, we were thinking . . ." She paused and caught Jackson's eye for a second. ". . . of proceeding with three teams of two and one soloist. That is, if you don't mind going alone, Jackson."

"Fine with me." He looked relaxed, a smile playing at the edges of his lips. She turned her attention away before she could linger on how good he looked in his Boromir outfit.

214

"Um, I'm not sure I'm okay with it." It was Ethel. "What if something happens to him?"

"You'll each have GPS tracking with an emergency beacon, and everyone also has emergency flares in their backpacks."

"Which are hardly going to do him any good if he's at the bottom of a ravine, unconscious!" Mavis decided to chime in.

Good grief, you would've thought they were sending them out into the Alaskan wilderness, not some beautiful, but not exactly difficult, New Zealand countryside. The worst that could probably happen would be that someone might stumble into a wasps' nest or somehow fall into a gorse bush.

Allie shifted the bags in her hands. "I assure you, he would have to be a long way off course before there would be any chance of him falling down a ravine."

Jackson folded his arms in front of him, impressive forearms crossing over each other. "I was an exemplary Boy Scout. I'll be fine."

Allie caught a look passing between the twins and saw a scheme coming like a runaway train headed right toward her. They wouldn't. Not again.

Mavis turned back with a small smile playing on her lips. "Why can't *you* go with Jackson?"

And there it was. Allie opened her mouth to start listing the many, *many* reasons why that wasn't an option, but at the last second she made the mistake of looking at the guy and something shot between them that short-circuited her brain. In that moment, she would've trekked through the Sahara in a swimsuit if he suggested it. "Sure. Why not?"

There was nothing for a second, everyone knocked off-kilter by her surprise agreement.

Esther finally broke the silence. "The chopper guy can drop you and Jackson somewhere harder, farther away. Since you already know where we're going."

Over her dead, Elf-costumed body. "That's really not necessary."

"What do you think, young lady?" Ethel turned her steely eyes to Kat. "Should they get a harder option?"

Allie turned laser eyes on her. *Do not even think about—*

Kat flashed a megawatt grin at her. "I have just the thing." Kat reached into a sheaf of papers she was holding and pulled out a route envelope marked VERY DIFFICULT. Allie stared at it. It had never been used. Ever.

Gandalf clapped his hands. "Right, well, that's settled then. So Jackson and Allie don't have an unfair advantage, they'll be dropped off somewhere different than usual."

She looked at Jackson. His face had leached to the color of photocopy paper. She was going to hazard a guess he hadn't exactly been paying attention during the Introduction to Orienteering course they'd attended the previous day, and she couldn't navigate her way out of a paper bag.

They were stuffed.

Jackson liked to think he was in pretty good shape, but apparently hours hitting the weights and treadmill in the safety of a gym had nothing on grappling with good old Mother Nature.

This little orienteering quest was going to kill him. Or maim him for life. He was certain of it. And they'd only been going all of about fifteen minutes. After being ditched by a smirking chopper pilot, they'd decided to climb the nearest hill to try and get their bearings. Easier said than done.

"When I say, 'Watch out,' that does actually mean, 'Watch out.' " Allie offered the advice from over her shoulder after he yelped as a tree branch flicked back and struck him in the middle.

Easy for her to say. She operated much lower to the ground than he did and was clad in the easy-to-move-in robes of a Woodland Elf. She made a very cute Elf, which he was trying very hard not to notice. He was also trying not to read anything into her unexpected capitulation to being partnered with him. He'd failed miserably—on all fronts.

He'd spent the last couple of days trying not to notice things about her and not succeeding. And the more attention he paid to her, the more intrigued he became. At least she seemed oblivious that since their night on the boat, he felt like an awkward teenage boy around her.

Finally breaking through the scrub, they scrambled over some rocks to find a plateau about three-quarters of the way up the hill-slash-mountain they were climbing. Pausing, they surveyed their surroundings.

It's only the two of you out here, Gregory. Try to get it together and not make an idiot of yourself.

"Okay." He pulled the topographical map Kat had handed him out of the handy pocket inside his cloak. "Should we take a look and see if we can figure anything out from here?" He unfolded it and looked around for a flat spot on the ground on which to spread it out.

"Don't look at me."

"You mean you don't know how to read this thing?"

Allie shrugged as she twisted her hair back, pulling it into a messy ponytail. "Why would I need to? Before today all that was required of me was to drop people off at their designated spots, then wait for them at the destination with a massive spread for lunch."

Excellent. Allie was as useless as he was when it came to the great outdoors. Possibly even more so.

He held the map up in front of him and turned it ninety degrees and then another ninety, trying to look like he had a clue as to what he was doing. He scanned the scenery spread out around them, hoping for something—anything—that would make sense of the paper in his hands.

She groaned. "I didn't even eat breakfast. I was planning on kicking back with a nice sandwich while the rest of you found your way."

"Tough life you lead." He tucked the map under his arm, pulled the compass out of his pocket, and tilted it at her.

She shook her head. "No clue."

"Seriously?"

She crossed her arms. "Look, buddy, you're the one who went on the little map- and compass-reading course yesterday, not me. You just go ahead and bust out those Boy Scout skills you were bragging about and get to it."

"Yeah, about that."

She stared at him. "You weren't a Boy Scout, were you?"

"Not even for a single minute. Though I have used a magnifying glass to start a fire before."

"So how were you planning on finding your way to lunch, oh great solo one?"

He shrugged. "Well, I figured it would either be so easy a blind man could do it, or that if anyone didn't show up on time, one of you would come find us with your magical little GPS thingy."

She shifted on her feet.

"So which was it?"

She sighed. "A little of column A, a little of column B."

"What does it look like anyway?"

"The GPS?"

"Yeah."

She dug around in the backpack. "Nothing exciting. Black, digital screen. Red button to set off the emergency beacon." She started digging a bit more. Then she knelt on the ground and started pulling stuff out of the bag. Water, food, first-aid kit.

"Oh no. I can't find it." Her expression had lost some of its nonchalance. "I took it out in the chopper to check it. I'm sure I put it back though." She upended the bag and shook it. A few more things tumbled out, but nothing that looked like a GPS.

"You're joking, right?"

"Yup." She flipped her wrist and held up a small black object in her palm. "Catch."

Before he had even processed what she'd said, Allie flicked her hand and the thing flew through the air to his right like a discus.

He launched himself sideways and watched as the disc flew through his outstretched hands and then disappeared over the side of the hill they were standing on.

Allie scrambled to her feet and came to a

skidding halt on the edge of the drop. They both watched as the GPS rolled, bounced off some rocks, and eventually disappeared into the foliage below.

"I'm guessing you were about as good at baseball as you were at Scouts, huh, Slugger?" Allie dusted off her brown leather pants and faced him. "If Kat was watching her tracker, we should see a chopper any minute now, because she just watched our altitude drop like a rock and will think one of us has taken a dive off a cliff."

"What about the emergency beacon—could it have set that off?"

Allie shook her head. "Unlikely. It has a cover you have to flick back so you can't set it off accidentally."

They both watched the horizon for a few seconds, waiting to see if their ears could catch any hint of the *thwack-thwack-thwack* of a chopper engine. Nothing, except rustling trees, the sound of birds chirping, and the wind blowing.

Jackson got to his feet and brushed himself off. "Worse comes to worst, we could stay here and wait for them to come get us."

Allie gave him an incredulous look. "One, you may have no pride, but I do. Two, for all we know, that thing has shattered into a thousand little pieces on its little journey down the cliff and is no longer functional. And three, aren't you here to pass some kind of character test?"

Oh yeah, that. For a few blissful moments, he'd forgotten about that.

"Now, I may be wrong—it has happened once before—but I'm guessing you sitting on your behind waiting to be rescued isn't quite what your uncle has in mind." Allie looked up from where she was stashing the supplies back into the backpack. "So we're going to have to find where we're going or die trying." Zipping the pack shut, she picked it up and handed it to him.

He took it and swung the canvas bag over his shoulder. "Who knows what he had in mind? Nothing makes sense about this whole thing."

She tilted her head. "How so?"

How so? What was there that made sense about being at the bottom of the world, at the whim of an octogenarian who wouldn't give any details about how he was going to decide whether he was going to fund Jackson's latest venture or not?

Jackson shrugged. "Well, I don't even know what he's looking for. Was the night on the boat part of the test, or was he just messing with me? No idea."

It was the first time either of them had referred to that night since leaving Wellington three days before. He wasn't even sure if she remembered the part of the conversation where he'd lost his filter and let his guard down.

She twisted an errant lock of her hair around her finger, then bit her bottom lip for a second.

"I can't remember if I said it in the middle of my charming puking and all, but thanks for looking after me that night."

"Anytime." He resisted the urge to palm himself in the forehead. *Anytime?* What did that even mean?

A wry grin appeared on her lips. "Hopefully not."

"Right, of course." The bumbling teenager was back. Wicked.

She opened her mouth as if to say something else, then abruptly turned and started walking, her bow and arrows bouncing against her back.

"Where are you going?"

"To the top. Like we agreed. We can't work out anything from down here, where we can only see one-eighty degrees. If we're going to figure out where we are, we need to be able to see all around us." She nimbly climbed up a rock and then scrambled up another steeper set.

He followed, trying to keep pace. "So where are you from, anyway?"

"What?"

He shrugged. "We're going to be stuck with each other, what? A few hours? Figured since I've swept you off your feet twice now, we should at least get to know each other a little."

She paused and scrutinized him for a second. "Auckland. I grew up in Auckland. My family have been in New Zealand forever. If you heard my mother, you'd think we found the place."

Auckland was New Zealand's largest city, if he recalled the guidebooks correctly, toward the top of the North Island.

"Did you like it?"

She shrugged. "Can't really complain about growing up here. What about you?"

"Iowa. A little town called Pennington. The population might sneak over ten thousand if you counted a few four-legged friends."

A glimmer of a smile. "Can't say I picked you as the rural type."

"Farm boy. Fifth generation."

"And you don't know how to read a map?"

Whoa, talk about a jab to his man-pride. "I can read a real map just fine. What we've got here is closer to hieroglyphics." Plus, in the concrete jungle of L.A., his GPS told him everything he needed to know. It was time to change the subject from his wilderness inadequacies. "What about your family?"

"My father's an investment banker. My mother . . ." She trailed off. "I was about to say my mother's just Veronica, but that wouldn't mean anything to you. My mother is kind of what you would get if you crossed Martha Stewart with Margaret Thatcher."

"Sounds like quite a force."

She grimaced. "Like a category-five hurricane."

"So what does she think of this?" He gestured at her outfit and the surrounding wilderness.

Allie burst out laughing. "Oh, she loves it." A deaf person couldn't have missed her sarcasm. "What about your parents?"

He thought of his parents and smiled. "They've been married almost forty years. Pretty much the definition of salt-of-the-earth types. They love each other, love their family, and work as hard as you can imagine."

"You the only boy?" She skipped over a fallen tree trunk.

"I am."

"Heading back to take over the farm one day."

She managed to get him right where it hurt. "I'm not really a farm guy. I'd be a terrible farmer. Thankfully, my sister married a guy who is through and through." He knew his parents still harbored hope he would return home one day and take over. But the truth was, short of a Saul of Tarsus kind of transformation, it wasn't going to happen. Just the thought of spending the rest of his life stuck in a small town, subject to all the uncertainties of farming he'd watched his parents suffer under his whole life, made him break out in hives.

Time to change the subject. Not that he hadn't revealed far more personal stuff on the boat, but now not knowing if Allie remembered any of it was starting to bother him.

"So, apart from it making your mom so happy, what do you love most about *Lord of the Rings*?"

225

That should be safe. Get them back on track. And maybe even provide some useful insights into what his uncle might be wanting from him.

Allie didn't say anything—for a few seconds, he thought she might not have even heard his question. Then she paused, turned back, and studied his face. "The unlikely heroes. Hobbits— they don't have anything of what the others do. They don't have the immortality or wisdom of the Elves. The brute strength of the dwarves. The bravery or history of man. The wisdom of the wizards. Yet, it's the humble hobbit who is chosen for the mission of saving Middle-earth. It reminds me that we all have the capacity to be greater than we think we can be."

"But Frodo almost gave in to the power of the Ring." He might not know much about Tolkien, but even he hadn't missed that detail.

Allie tilted her head. "He did. That's another part of Tolkien's genius. There's not one character in the books whose exploits are possible on their own. Who is without flaw or failing. Frodo can't complete his mission without Sam. And it's Sam's words that we remember when everything feels lost to us, 'But in the end, it's only a passing thing, this shadow. Even darkness must pass. A new day will come.' " The words slipped from her tongue as easily as if she'd been reading them from a page.

"Can you quote all of the books like that?"

"Just the parts that resonate the most." As Allie said the words, her face shuttered, as if she'd said too much, and she started to walk again, leaving him to ponder her back.

One thing was certain, his arms still resonated with the way she'd felt in them. The citrus smell of her hair, how she'd burrowed into his chest like a trusting child. The memories refused to diminish, as much as he'd spent the last three days trying to scrub them from his mind.

He was saved from his disruptive line of thought as the climb suddenly got steeper. He focused now on the need to climb up boulders, scramble through undergrowth, and dodge low-hanging tree branches.

After about ten minutes, he felt like he was about to have a heart attack, while Allie skipped on ahead of him like they were going for a gentle stroll through a meadow.

Just as he thought he was going to have to tamp down his pride and beg for her to slow down, they got through some dense bush to find themselves almost at the top. Allie stopped so fast he nearly found himself eating a bunch of arrow tails.

"What are you doing with these, anyway?" He tapped her quiver. "Planning on catching us dinner?"

She looked up at him. "You joke, but I happen to be a crack shot."

"The same way you're a great throw?"

"Look, Butterfingers, don't even try and blame that one on me." Allie walked a few steps and unshouldered her bow. Pulling an arrow out, she examined its tip. "I should paint this red."

"Why?"

"Gondor used red arrows to summon its allies in times of need." She smiled. "There's some random Tolkien trivia for you. Now, where were we? Oh, that's right, you were questioning my archery abilities." She fitted her arrow onto the wire.

"What are you doing?"

She shrugged and started to pull the string back. "Talk is cheap."

That thing was pointed way too close to him for his comfort. And the wire appeared to be pulled pretty taut. And she didn't even seem to be looking.

"Do you mind? At least give me a chance to—"

The word had barely left his mouth when a few things seemed to happen at once. A sensation of air moving at his side, a sound of a *thunk* right behind him, and the realization that Allie's bow no longer held its arrow.

He tried to turn to see where it had gone, only to find himself caught on something. Twisting around awkwardly, he caught sight of the arrow, its shaft still vibrating where it had impaled the end of his cloak on a tree.

● ● ●

Allie sucked a breath in through her lips. It felt wispy and thin, as if she couldn't get enough in to fill her lungs, and not just because they were at high altitude. She'd been centimeters away from turning the guy into a shish kebab. She didn't even know what had happened. One second she'd been messing around, about to admit she didn't have a clue what she was doing when it came to using a bow and arrow. Then the next . . . Well, one-half of the pair was gone, Jackson's cape was nailed to a tree, and he had the shell-shocked facial expression of someone who knew he'd just come very close to meeting his maker.

Slinging her bow over her shoulder, she tried to keep her expression bored, as if she shared DNA with William Tell or something.

Jackson looked at his clothing pinned to the tree, then back at her. He opened his mouth, but nothing came out. He tried again. "Please tell me you did that on purpose."

She lifted an eyebrow.

He studied her face for a second. "On second thought, I don't want to know." Reaching down, he pulled the arrow out of the wood and fingered the gash in his cloak. "Mind if I keep this as a souvenir?" He held the arrow up.

"Be my guest."

"I've never met anyone quite like you, Allison Shire."

It could've been meant in a hundred different ways, but the manner in which his eyes darkened and his gaze seemed to linger on her lips sent a sizzle through her body.

She had to say something to neutralize the situation. Nothing good could come of indulging in her growing attraction, especially not when they were alone in the middle of nowhere with hours before anyone would come looking for them. She forced herself to laugh. "You've never been to New Zealand before, Jackson Gregory. I promise you, I'm nothing special." So she'd been told plenty of times.

He opened his mouth as if to argue, but then closed it. Even he couldn't fight her on that. Yet why had a small part of her hoped he would?

Turning, she grabbed the map from him. "Come on, let's work out where we are. Otherwise, at this rate, they really will have to send search parties out to find us."

At least Kat had been kind enough to mark where they needed to get to on the map. And the pilot had marked where he had dropped them off. So how hard could this be, really?

She pointed to where X marked the spot. "Okay, so we landed about here, and we've been tramping about twenty minutes or so, but most of it was uphill, so we can't have gotten far. I'm pretty sure the closer the lines are, the steeper the terrain."

Jackson leaned in, getting close—way too close—as he studied the flimsy paper. His breath fanned down the side of her face. She fought the crazy desire to rest against him. "So do you think we're here?" He pointed to one spot where a number indicated a peak. "Or here?" He pointed to another close by to the right. Both were in the general direction of where they wanted to be heading. At least that was encouraging.

She looked at the scenery surrounding them, trying to overlay what she was seeing onto the lines on the map in front of them, but it might as well have been in Arabic for all the sense she could make of it.

"No idea. If I had to make a guess, I would go with that one." She stabbed at the peak on the left. "But that's ninety percent finger-in-the-wind kind of stuff. Please tell me you gleaned something of use from the course yesterday."

He stood up with the compass and turned around slowly, stopping when he was facing away to her left. "Okay, this is north. So now we should orient the map."

Allie spun the map until the arrow at the top was pointing in the same direction. "So we want to be heading northeast." She jabbed at the left-hand peak. "If we're on top of this, our destination is over that hill." She pointed at a hill that appeared to be a couple of kilometers away. "But if we're on this one"—she pointed at the peak on the right—"our destination is over that one." She pointed at a hill farther east, then leaned back on her heels. "No pressure."

She handed him the map and stepped away, the closeness of his presence unnerving her.

"That one." He pointed to the left.

"You sure?"

"Of course I'm not sure," he snapped. "Give a guy a break. I'm a farm boy turned IT entrepreneur. I've never even held a compass in my entire life, let alone used one to navigate across a mountain range dressed in a flipping medieval costume."

It was disconcerting how much more attractive he became when he had his grumpy face on. Brow furrowed, eyes flashing.

"Cool down, Slugger. Just like to know what I'm dealing with." She unscrewed the bottle of water in her hand and took a slug. "Want some?" She offered the bottle to him. He took it and knocked back a few gulps.

Unzipping the backpack, she put it back inside. "We're going to need all our limbs free to get down from here."

"Do you believe in God?"

"Huh?" Where did that come from? Allie looked up to see him gazing across their surroundings. "Yes. Though I can't say we're on the best terms at the moment." What would a God who created something so vast, so great, want with her? Especially when she'd managed to stuff up her life so monumentally by disobeying Him. "You?" She couldn't say why his answer mattered, but suddenly, it did.

He ran a hand through his hair, leaving it standing on end. "My family are big believers. Me, not so much. But then you see something like this and it's kind of hard to believe it's a fluke. That we're all here, that this"—he waved his hands around—"exists because of millions of years of pure dumb luck and complete randomness."

Allie stood and looked, really looked, at the beauty surrounding them. On one side, the majestic Tasman Sea stretched as far as the eye could see, the kind of blue you saw in movies and tourist brochures reflecting back at them.

On the other side, rocky mountains, grassy meadows, deep-green forests, and long plains stretched down the South Island. It was pretty incredible. Very incredible.

"I know what you mean." One of the things that had first drawn her to Tolkien was the way he weaved in such amazing themes of faith. Redemption. Hope. Good overcoming evil. Right from the beginning in *The Silmarillion*, where the story of the creation of Middle-earth was an incredible allegorical retelling of the Creation and Fall in Genesis.

For the first time she realized how much sense

it made that when her own faith was so frail and fractured, even her beloved Tolkien felt distant. A shadow fell over her, though she was standing in sunlight.

"You okay?"

She hadn't been okay for a long time, but for some reason Jackson's presence made the ache that much bigger, wider. "We should get going." She turned around, dodging the question. "Lead on."

Jackson took one final look at the map and nodded toward his right. "This way." Lifting up the map, he started to fold it, but then a big gust of wind ripped it out of his hands and sent it tumbling across the rocky ground.

No. No. No. No. No. No.

They both ran. Allie made a mighty leap to jump on it, but her toe missed the edge by a millimeter as the wind picked it up and sent it flying into the air like a paper airplane.

Jackson leapt, his fingers scraping the side of the parchment, before it danced out of reach. And out, off the side of the mountain. They both stood, frozen, watching as it wafted away. Gusts of wind made it seem like angels were using it to play chase: it landed only to be picked up and blown again. Slowly, it disappeared into a tiny line far below.

"You have got to be joking." Jackson spat the words out, the clipped sound of them suggesting he was restraining the words he really wanted to say. He looked at her. "Why are you smiling?"

Why was she smiling? And when had being lost in the middle of nowhere with this guy become the most fun she'd had in ages? "Because that one cannot be blamed on me."

Lost. They were bone-numbingly, exhaustedly lost. No GPS. No map. Just two people wearing *Lord of the Rings* costumes wandering in the wilderness.

Allie's face bore a long scratch from a branch that had flung itself at her, and Jackson was limping after rolling his ankle on some loose rocks. To say they made a sorry pair was an understatement.

They had been walking for hours and had learned the hard lesson that things were often much farther away than they appeared.

"They'll be looking for us by now, right?" Jackson checked his watch. Almost three. Way past lunch. As if on cue, his stomach rumbled.

Allie looked back over her shoulder. "There are some muesli bars in the pack. Have one."

"I'm good." He wanted to conserve whatever they had in case worse came to worst. He'd eaten a good breakfast and wasn't in danger of starving anytime soon.

A sense of futility swept over him. According to whatever measure his uncle would be judging him by today, he'd failed. Not only that, but they might actually be in real trouble if the gathering dark clouds above them turned nasty.

At least the walking was a bit easier at the moment as they traversed a ridge devoid of plant life. "We need to get higher—somewhere we can let off the emergency flares and be seen. They're all we have left."

Allie looked at the sky and scrunched her nose. "I don't think those clouds are going to break soon, and we still have a good four hours of daylight left. I'm sure we can find our way before dark."

Was she more nuts than a jar of Jif? "We have no idea where we are. We have no idea what direction we should be heading in. All another four hours is going to get us is even more lost."

Not to mention there was no way he was taking the chance of them being stuck here overnight. He'd read that there weren't any really dangerous animals in New Zealand, but he preferred not to find out for sure.

Plus it got cold at night. And neither of them was dressed for that. Staying warm would require getting very cozy . . . On second thought, an overnight adventure was suddenly looking appealing . . . *Whoa.* He reined his thoughts back in.

Allie's top teeth worried her bottom lip. "I'm

not going to be responsible for you having to quit because I'm a bad throw."

How could this girl not think she was anything special? Her statement had been bothering him for hours. Though not nearly as much as the fact that he hadn't been able to find the words to explain how wrong she was.

"We wouldn't be in this situation if I was either a decent catch or could read a map and compass. Do we really want to keep going and take the chance they call in search and rescue for us, if they haven't already?"

She groaned. "Can you imagine? Oh my gosh, it would probably make the papers."

"Why?"

She gestured at them. "Look at us. Two people lost in the bush, dressed as *Lord of the Rings* characters, with basically nothing to get us through the night. If search and rescue have to come find us, I'm so fired."

He looked down at her. How was it possible that, with her hair all tangled from battling with scrub and her outfit streaked with mud and foliage, she was cuter than ever?

"You're not getting fired, because we're going to hike back up there and let the flares off." He pointed back up the peak they'd just scrambled down.

"Come on, Jackson. Give us another hour. If we're still lost by then, we can climb that one." She pointed to another hill in the distance.

"Allie." He got right in her space to try and make her listen, attempting to ignore the way his senses lit up at being so close to her. "Whatever my uncle is judging me by doesn't matter. All that matters is getting you out of here safe." Without his permission, his hand reached up and brushed a stray hair off her cheek. "I wouldn't be able to live with myself if we kept going any longer and something happened to you." She looked up at him from under long lashes, and the chemistry between them was undeniable.

Keeping his eyes locked on her wide green pools, he ran his hands down her arms and entwined his fingers in hers. Tugging her close, he leaned down and rested his forehead on hers. "Don't fight me on this, Allison Shire, because this is one fight I will win."

Her body leaned into his for a second and the *thwack-thwack-thwack* of his heart pounding in his ears drowned everything around them out.

Allie jumped back, eyes springing wide open. "Do you hear that?"

Jackson jolted. "What? Hear what?"

"That!"

He heard it. What he'd thought was his runaway heart was in fact the sound of a chopper approaching. The one that now hovered above them, Kat waving at them from the front window.

If only he could tell them to go away.

Seventeen

"I'm com— Argh!" Allie tripped over her laptop cord and barely missed clocking herself on the bedside table as she tried to get to her phone before it went to voice mail.

She'd always had some klutzy tendencies, but since her day traipsing around the wilderness with Jackson, it was like what little coordination she did possess had gone on strike.

Walking into doors, pouring juice into her lap, dropping stuff—you name it, she'd probably done it.

She reached up from her prone position on the carpet, grabbed her phone off the bedside table, and answered the call without even looking at the screen. "Hello?"

Too late, she realized her mistake. *Please don't be Derek.* That was the last thing she needed when she was still trying to navigate her train-wrecked emotions.

"Hello. Is this Allison Shire of Southern Luxury Tours?"

"It is."

"Ms. Shire, it's John Prescott here, from the Museum Hotel."

"Oh, hi. What did one of them leave behind this time?"

An awkward silence, then a clearing of the throat. "Well, it's not so much what someone left behind, as what seems to be missing."

She pressed her head back against the carpet. Of course it was. "Another robe? Just add it to the charge for the room and we'll sort it out." It still surprised Allie that so many wealthy people seemed to have a thing for nicking hotel robes. It was why they had a standing order with all the hotels they stayed at to add any onto the bill.

"No, I'm happy to report all robes are accounted for."

Allie pushed herself up off the floor and leaned against her bed. What now? So far the best she'd had was when a guest had stolen all the lightbulbs out of every room he'd stayed in. "Okay. Give it to me."

"A lamp."

Allie almost fell back over. "Excuse me?"

"One of the bedside lamps."

It didn't beat the lightbulbs, but it was up there. Especially if her memory served her right. "But aren't they quite large?"

"They are."

Well, she had to give a certain tweenager points for creativity. "Let me guess. Esther Johnson's room." Allie didn't even want to know what other ill-gotten souvenirs she might have stashed in her bright-pink suitcase.

A hint of a smothered laugh came down the line. "Correct. I realize this is a little awkward, but we'd quite like it back if possible."

Allie sighed. Given what hotels charged for pre-loved robes, she didn't even want to think about what a designer lamp would be billed at. "I understand. I'll take care of it."

They closed their conversation and Allie added *find stolen lamp and courier back to Wellington* to her mental to-do list.

She'd just gotten to her feet and put her phone back on the table when it rang again. There was more? "Yes." The one word came out exasperated. Harassed.

"Hello. Is this Dr. Allison Shire?" The accent was English. Male. Proper. Older. Her posture suddenly got better without her even thinking about it.

"This is she."

"Dr. Shire, it's Dr. Everett here. You may not remember me, but I was one of your thesis markers."

No, it couldn't be. "As in Dr. Lance Everett?" Not remember him? How could she not remember the man many considered to be the world's foremost Tolkien expert?

He chuckled. "That would be me. I'm not sure if you're aware, but I've recently become head of the English faculty at Oxford."

"No sir, I wasn't." The man was a legend. She

241

had attended a multipart lecture by him once where he'd recited the entire *The Hobbit* verbatim; there was nothing the man didn't know about Tolkien and his works.

She pulled her phone away and looked at the screen to see if she was being pranked by one of the few people who knew her well enough to come up with such a joke. An international number flashed up at her.

She cleared her throat. "How can I help?" Not the smoothest of responses, but better than what could've fallen from her mouth: *Do you know who you're calling? Are you sure you've got the right number?*

"Well, I'm hoping you might be able to assist me."

Huh?

"I have an opening in my department for a full-time English-literature lecturer in the next academic year with a strong focus on Tolkien. Our usual lecturer is going on maternity leave in September, and I need someone who can take two or three courses. The university hasn't been able to keep up with demand since the first *Rings* movie came out. We thought it would abate after the last *Hobbit* movie but it just hasn't let up. Anyway, I was going through some CVs that the department kept on file from previous job applications, and yours was in there."

Allie was momentarily struck dumb. She'd applied for a job that was way out of her league over a year before. Having never heard anything back, she'd assumed it was the Oxford version of laughing at her stupidity for even trying. Just like with the twenty-seven other lecturing jobs she'd applied for all over the world and not gotten. Academia was a very small world. "I see."

"Yes. Your credentials are excellent and your thesis was first-class. I contacted Auckland University and the department was kind enough to give me access to some of your lectures online. They were excellent, so I was just calling to give you the details in case you would like to consider applying?"

Her breath had stalled. "For a job? Lecturing at Oxford?"

"If you are the successful candidate, yes. I need to be clear though. It will be a fully competitive process. I'm just selfishly making sure we have the best possible pool of candidates to select from. It would be a twelve-month contract initially, starting late September. No guarantees of anything beyond that."

She struggled to formulate a coherent thought over the sound of her brain turning to white noise. "You know I haven't been in academia for a couple of years?"

"Yes. I understand you've been getting some real-world Tolkien experience, which I think is

243

most advantageous. Too many lecturers have never left our hallowed halls and experienced life from the great outside. Obviously, if you did apply and were selected for an interview, the panel would have some questions about your sabbatical."

That was an overly generous way of describing it. "Okay." She hadn't been in a lecture hall since the day it had been strongly suggested she take some unpaid leave until the Derek situation blew over. Apparently one of your lecturers being publicly accused of bigamy wasn't the kind of attention the university was interested in. It hadn't exactly helped that her lecturing skills had also fallen apart after her husband's other wife told her in front of two hundred students they were married to the same man. Fighting a panic attack every time you stepped into the lecture hall did not exactly help your teaching ability.

"So would you be interested in the role?"

Would she be interested? In going back to the country where she'd gotten her PhD? In getting to work in academia again? In never having to lead another tour? In finally having direction with what to do with her life? Um, yes. Then she heard the words, "Can I get back to you?" coming out of her mouth.

"Of course. I realize this was unexpected. However, we will be acting with reasonable haste on this. Applications will be closing end of next week. You can find the details on our website. Feel free to contact me if you have any further questions."

"Of course, I understand. Thank you."

He reeled off his e-mail address and phone number, which she managed to jot down before he closed with a cheery "Good day, Dr. Shire. I look forward to hearing from you."

She tossed her phone onto her bed in a daze.

"Can I get back to you?" Two years ago, this would have been a dream come true. More than. It would have been the dream she didn't even dare to dream coming true. So why hadn't a resounding *yes* come out of her mouth?

A possible escape hatch had opened up right in front of her. An answer to all the prayers she hadn't had the audacity to even think. Why on earth would she be hesitating to walk through it?

"What's going on?" Jackson nudged Allie with his elbow as they stood in line to order coffees for the group, who were all happily situated at a large table in the bustling café.

In a couple of hours they would be relocating to Christchurch. Even he'd heard of the largest city in the South Island after watching the news about a devastating earthquake in 2011 that had killed and injured hundreds of people. It was also the second-to-last stop on the tour. He couldn't believe it had only been two weeks since the day Allie had marched into his life in her ugly hobbit outfit. Nothing in him could grasp that, in less than a week, their paths wouldn't have any reason to cross again. Ever. Unless he created one.

Allie gave no sign she'd heard his question. Maybe it had been drowned out by the loud coffee machine and staff yelling orders. He tried again. "Is everything okay?"

The girl had been operating like a zombie all morning and this was the first chance he'd had to find out what had happened.

"What do you mean?" She barely glanced at him, her glazed eyes flickering for a split second before she faced the back of the person in front of them again.

"I mean, you may be present in body, but

you are most definitely not in spirit. What gives?"

The line inched forward and Jackson craned his neck, trying to see what was taking so long. The girl at the till ran her fingers through her hair, looking flustered as she jabbed at buttons.

Good, the longer this took, the longer he had Allie to himself. He turned his attention back to the cute redhead at his side.

A breath puffed out of Allie's parted lips. "I had a phone call this morning. A job opportunity. I think. Sort of."

Jackson tried to pretend his heart hadn't changed rhythm at her words. "Cool. Where?"

"Oxford."

He racked his brain. The name sounded familiar and his knowledge of New Zealand geography had progressed markedly in the last couple of weeks. "That's down south, right? Near Christ-church?"

That got a reaction from her. Even if it was a frosty glare that could have frozen fire. "Oxford University."

His mind struggled to process what she was saying. "As in *the* Oxford? In England?"

"Yup."

He tried to frame his next question in a way that wouldn't be offensive. "So um, how did your name come up?"

She rubbed her forehead. "I applied for a job there a while ago. He said they'd kept my application on file."

It was in moments like this he realized how far his feelings for her ran ahead of what he actually knew about her.

"Hold on. Where did you do your doctorate?" The line suddenly leapt forward. They were next up to order. Seriously? It had picked right now to get moving?

"Cambridge."

"As in *the* Cambridge?"

She looked at him. "Yes, *the* Cambridge. Also

in England. On a full scholarship for what it's worth. Where did you think I got it from? Bought it off the Internet?"

His mouth opened but nothing came out. From the heat rising from his neck, he was pretty sure he was turning as red as a traffic light.

She looked at him with incredulity. "Seriously?"

"Um, to be fair, the first time we met it was at the airport and you were in a hobbit outfit holding a sign with my name on it. That doesn't exactly scream doctorate from one of the world's most prestigious universities." Too late he realized how bad that sounded. "I mean, you must be the only tour guide in the world with . . ." He trailed off, realizing he was digging his verbal pit of doom even bigger. *Stop now, Jackson.*

She looked at him. "So you think tour guides must be dumb?"

He held his hands up. "Never said that."

Her face contorted. "Yeah, well, I may be *just* a tour guide, but at least I'm not trying to leech money off an old man under false pretenses because of poor taste in girlfriends."

Ouch. Her accusation hit him with the sting of a scorpion's tail. "Tell me how you really feel, why don't you, Allie?"

Her eyes widened, her face looking about as stricken as he felt. "I—"

"Hi, what can I get you?" The person in front of

248

them had gone and the girl at the register was smiling at them. Then she seemed to realize she'd found herself in the middle of something and looked down and started straightening up the jars of cookies lining the counter.

He couldn't believe only a few seconds ago he had been trying to work out how he could pursue whatever it was between them. "You know what, I think I need some air. I'll get Hans to help you with the coffee."

He turned around and walked away, heart thudding against his rib cage, fists clenched by his sides. What did he care what she thought anyway? How could he have been so stupid again? Let a woman in and she turned around and smacked him in the face with his vulnerability. Never again.

Eighteen

Two days and two locations later, Allie still felt nauseous over the spiteful, vicious words she had spewed at Jackson. He'd been avoiding her ever since. Switching places at tables to not sit near her, never speaking to her, even avoiding eye contact—not that she could blame him.

". . . *because of poor taste in girlfriends."* The words still echoed in her head, as fresh as the horrid moment when she'd heard them hit the air and realized what she'd said. They would've been bad enough if she were Jane Doe average.

But no, they'd come from her, the girl who'd been so blinded by a guy, she hadn't for a second entertained the notion he was marrying her for her money and ability to get him a New Zealand visa—all to escape a very big hole he'd dug himself in regard to some unforgiving people in the UK.

She buried her head in her hands. The cynical part of her thought she should be glad she'd irreparably shattered whatever it was between the two of them. Her cruel words had certainly uncomplicated something that had been quickly getting out of control. If it hadn't been for that helicopter—by sheer chance, it turned out—finding them just in time, she knew what would've happened next, and she hated herself for it.

It would've been tempting to leave the situation unresolved—they only had five days before the tour ended. Except for the quiet voice inside telling her every second she would never forgive herself if she didn't try and mend this. If she didn't tell him the truth—even when it meant there could be no getting back to the possibilities that had remained between them.

Allie had been lingering by the elevator doors for an hour, waiting for him to come downstairs. Finally, the doors dinged open and Jackson walked out. Bolting out of her chair, she practically launched herself across the lobby to him before she could change her mind.

"Jackson."

Cold blue eyes didn't even meet hers. "Dr. Shire."

"Please, can we talk?"

"I'd prefer not to." He started walking toward the dining room with long strides, leaving her, with her shorter legs, to scuttle after him like a crab.

"Please." The one word was so obviously drowning in desperation he actually stopped and looked at her for the first time in two days, rather than above her, around her, or through her. "Two minutes."

He sighed. "Fine."

They took a couple of chairs in the otherwise empty bar area. Jackson pulled out his phone and tapped across the screen. He flipped it to face her, and she saw he'd set the timer for exactly two minutes. He placed it on the table in between them, hit START, and leaned back in his chair.

The seconds were ticking and she was wasting them. She cleared her throat, trying to get something—anything—out. "I'm sorry. What I said was cruel and unfair. I've spent the last two days trying to work out what made me say something so horrible and I don't know. And I'm ashamed I am responsible for saying something so ugly." Her words tumbled out over each other. How much time had she burned already? Thirty seconds? Less? More? The screen had gone blank.

"I, of all people, have no right to be casting aspersions on anyone's relationship. Especially when I pretty much hold the gold card when it comes to being used. And so I'm sorry. I'm sorry for saying such hateful things. Sorry I ruined our . . . friendship. You told me the truth and I used it against you. I know it won't change anything, but I need you to know I get it." She sucked in a deep breath. Time to tell him about Derek. He deserved at least that. "I w—"

The buzzer cut her off before she could finish. Not that she'd known exactly how the ugly truth was going to come out. She'd had a well-rehearsed speech and the entire thing had flown from her brain faster than an M16 fighter jet after her first *"I'm sorry."*

Jackson was already standing. Reaching down, he silenced his phone and shoved it back in the pocket of his jeans.

"Wait. You don't have anything to say? Nothing?" She sounded needy. How mortifying. But she wasn't prepared for this. She thought she'd prepared herself for every possible reaction, but not for *nothing*.

He looked down at her, face as blank as a hotel sheet, and shook his head. "Not to you."

And he turned and walked away.

Allie looked like he'd struck her. Jackson forced down the temptation to second-guess himself as he strode into the dining room. Setting the timer on her had been a bit harsh, but if he hadn't, he would've gotten sucked right back into those green eyes. Don't look back. If he had to look back and see her face all crumpled and hurting, he knew he wouldn't be able to keep his distance.

He needed to walk away more than anything. There was something about that girl that swung him way off-kilter and made him question everything about what was important in life. He couldn't afford that kind of distraction. The game plan was set; he just needed to see it through. He could convince his uncle to sign on the dotted line—for the sake of his family and all the people who had trusted him with their money.

No girl could compete with that, no matter what kind of inconvenient feelings she stirred up in him. Even when he was out-of-his-mind angry with her, he still had to fight the urge to pull her into his arms to see if she would mold into him the way he imagined she would.

Walking into the dining room, he bypassed the buffet and headed straight for the coffee. He poured himself a cup of strong black stuff from the pot and pretended not to see Elroy waving at him from across the room as he picked an empty table for two by the window.

Taking a tentative sip of the steaming brew, he tried to convince himself he'd done the right thing. So her degree was from Cambridge—so what? So she might apply for some fancy-pants academic job back in England—what did it matter to him? In less than a week, he'd be back in the States, laying the groundwork for his new business. He'd have more than enough to keep him occupied. Satisfied. In a matter of days, this whole ridiculous trip would be a distant memory. All going well, a mere stepping-stone to his destiny.

The more he tried to convince himself, the

bigger the sailor's knot in his gut seemed to grow. So he turned his mind to more important things. Like the look on his parents' faces when he unyoked them from the massive burden of debt they'd been dragging around his entire life. Girls came and went, but family—now that was for-ever. *Right, God?*

He startled at the unexpected thought. Where had that come from? Coffee sloshed over the side of his cup, scalding his fingers. Grabbing a napkin, he wiped his hands, then dabbed at the stain on the white tablecloth.

What did he care what God thought? Not that he was convinced there even was one. Yet another thing that made him the black sheep of the family. Everyone else knew there was a God with the same certainty as they knew autumn was harvest time.

"I'd offer you a penny for them, but from your face, they're worth a whole lot more than that."

Jackson jolted. How long had his uncle been sitting at the other side of the table? The old man took a sip of orange juice as he regarded him with knowing eyes.

"Anything I can help with?"

Jackson shook his head. "No. Thanks." Then changed his mind. He'd probably already blown whatever chance he had anyway so he might as well ask. "Actually, yes."

"I'm all ears."

"Why did you set Allie and me up on the boat that night?" It had been bugging him since that evening. What was the point?

Louis picked up a piece of toast. "Did you know I have a wife and three kids?"

Where had that come from? "No, sir. I didn't."

"Ex-wife, actually. We've been divorced forty years and I still struggle to say it. Even though she got remarried back in seventy-eight."

"I'm sorry."

Louis leaned forward. "Here's the thing, son. Money comes and money goes. I lost almost everything in the crash of eighty-seven and spent years trying to get back on my feet. But want to know my biggest regret?"

"Sure."

"When I was your age, I was so obsessed with building my business I let it cost me what really mattered. I have more money than I will ever need, and for what? I don't have a wife to share it with. I haven't seen any of my kids in a decade. Never met my grandchildren. I wasn't a bad husband or father. I was just an absent one. So busy making money so they could have the right stuff, it never occurred to me all they wanted was me. That was why my wife left. She told me it was too hard being in love with a ghost."

Jackson stared at his coffee mug, unsure of

what to say. When he looked back up, he found himself pierced by his uncle's intense gaze.

"I set you up that night because you'd have to be blind, deaf, and dumb not to see what exists between you two. And it's something that many people spend their entire lifetime trying to find. I'm an old man, with a lot of money, and not a lot to spend it on. So"—he shrugged his shoulders—"I figured, why not?" He looked at Jackson closely. "Can you look me in the eye and tell me you wish I hadn't?"

Jackson couldn't find the words for a few seconds. He wouldn't trade that evening for anything. Not even given how mad he was at her now. "No. I can't."

"Don't be like me, Jackson. Don't end up a rich old man who has built an empire and then discovered it's completely worthless without anyone to share it with. I would give anything to go back and have a do-over. I would live in a trailer if it meant Lorraine was there with me."

Jackson mulled his uncle's sermon over for a few moments, not sure what to do with the unexpected dump of personal information. "So you're saying it doesn't matter if my parents lose the farm or if I can never pay back all the people who trusted me and I let them down?"

His uncle shook his head as he swallowed his toast. "No, I'm not saying that at all. I'm saying they're not the only things that matter. And, while they're important, they're definitely not what matters most. What matters most are God and family."

Interesting. He hadn't pegged Louis as religious. For some reason, he'd assumed he shared his own skepticism in the existence of God.

"Why do you believe in God?" He wasn't even sure where the question had come from, but for some reason he really wanted to know the answer. Weird Tolkien obsession aside, his uncle was a very switched-on old guy who wasn't the type of person Jackson would think needed some kind of religious crutch to get by.

His uncle pondered for a few seconds. "For me it's not so much about why. The truth is, I always knew there was one. I just didn't want to admit it because I was afraid of what that would mean."

Jackson rolled his uncle's words around in his head. They resonated somewhere deep down, but he didn't have time to think about it now. His uncle wasn't the one who would have to live with himself if his parents lost the farm that had been in their family for five generations. And so far God had been zero help in that department.

His parents were the most faithful people you could imagine. If anyone deserved God's favor, it was them. Instead He'd stood by, inattentive, as they battled droughts, floods, and crop disease, never able to catch a break. The few times they'd had a good harvest and been able to get their heads above water and breathe, something bad always happened to put them back under.

Jackson was the only one they had to solve this—not some uncaring invisible divinity. His shoulders sagged as his attempt at righteous anger rang hollow. For all he railed against someone who might not even exist, Jackson had had the opportunity and the money to provide his family with at least a couple of years of not having to worry about how they were going to pay their debts, but he'd blown it.

And that was all on him. He let out a breath. And Allie was right. If he hadn't made a few poor choices, he wouldn't even be here.

Which made how he'd just treated her even worse. He pushed his chair back. "Can you excuse me for a few minutes? There's something I need to do."

Nineteen

This was ridiculous. Allie tried to stem the tears that wouldn't stop coming. Why did it even matter? Why did his snub hurt so much? In a week, they wouldn't even be in the same country anymore. There would be no reason for them to cross paths ever again.

She'd been a guide for people with terminal illnesses who had been given months to live, who were taking this trip before they became too sick to enjoy it. Young, previously healthy people with everything to live for. She hadn't cried like this over any of them. So why now? Why *him?*

She sucked in a breath, stared at the hotel's floral carpet, and tried to pull herself together.

"Is it eight-thirty we have to be back in the lobby?" Sofia's heavy accent came from behind her, cutting through Allie's melancholy.

"It is indeed." Her attempt at perky was a bit on the shuddery side, but passable. She swiped her hands across her cheekbones, knowing, even as she did, it was a pointless maneuver. If anything, she'd probably just smeared her mascara even further.

How embarrassing. How unprofessional. Nobody paid thousands of dollars to be confronted by their tour guide having a meltdown. Hopefully Sofia had gotten all the information she needed and wouldn't come any closer.

Light footsteps and Sofia's long slender legs appearing beside her killed that wish. "Can I tell you something"—Sofia's brow rumpled as she tried to find the words she needed—"in secret?"

"Sure." Allie turned her body to be able to look up at Sofia without craning her neck.

Sofia lowered her voice. "Hans, he is not good with horses."

"He's scared of horses?"

Sofia shook her blond head. "No. He like them. He just think he good rider, but bad rider. Very bad. He look like this." And the slender woman jumped up and down and flailed from side toside. "So would be good if you could give him old horse. Slow horse."

Allie managed a genuine smile at that. "And you?"

"Oh, I'm a great rider. I do equestrian. I ride better than Arwen with Frodo."

"Great."

"Are you okay?" Sofia peered at her face.

Allie summoned up a smile. "Oh, just a few allergies."

She got an unconvinced look in return. "Thinking that you don't want to know the end because how could the end be happy?"

Allie blinked at Sofia's paraphrase from Samwise Gamgee. "I don't think happy endings are my thing." The honesty slipped out before she could stop it.

Sofia smiled. "Frodo and Sam thought the same, climbing Mordor. Remember, all great stories are filled with danger and darkness." Sofia's words were from the same exchange Allie had quoted to Jackson the day in the wilderness. But even Samwise Gamgee couldn't help her now. Nothing could help her now.

Thankfully, any further probing was cut off by Hans appearing in the doorway to the dining room.

Sofia tossed her a wink as she waved at her husband. "Remember, I said nothing."

"Your secret is safe with me. I have the perfect horses for both of you." Allie made a mental note to swap Hans's and Jackson's horses as she turned and sagged back in her chair. She had been planning to give Jackson the oldest, slowest horse of the bunch as a joke, but that had been before her big mouth destroyed everything.

Heavy footsteps sounded behind her. Knowing her luck, probably Hans asking to make sure she gave him the fastest, most spirited horse of the herd.

And then Jackson appeared and took the same seat he'd grudgingly sat in only twenty minutes or so ago.

She stared at him, keeping her mouth clamped shut. She didn't trust herself to speak this time. Had no idea what might come out if she did.

Why did he have to be so attractive? All smoldery and broody and unshaven and tousled. So not her type. Soooo not her type.

And she was clearly insane, even thinking such things about a guy who couldn't stand her. Who she couldn't stand. Oh, who was she kidding?

Allie jolted to. She'd been so lost in her internal monologue that she'd missed him saying something. And she had no idea what it was.

Get it together, Allie. Seriously.

He cleared his throat. "So, um, yeah. I'm sorry."

She blinked. Was he *apologizing?* When he'd just sat in the same chair and shot her apology down faster than she could blink?

He sighed and ran a hand through his dark hair. "I think I was more angry because I knew you were right. I've made some choices that, with the benefit of hindsight, I'm not proud of. Letting Nicole move in was one of them."

Because she stole his IP?

He seemed to hear her unspoken question. "Not because she stole my work. That was an added bonus. It just . . ." He seemed to flounder for words. "It wasn't how I was raised. I knew it wasn't right, but in the end it was easier to give in than try to explain what was just a gut feeling. I never even told my parents we lived together because I couldn't face their disappointment. So your words hit a bit of a sore point."

"I'm sorry. I shouldn't—"

He held up a hand, smiled. "I'm pretty sure you've already apologized plenty." His brow furrowed as he studied her face. "Have you been crying?"

She swiped her hand across her cheek. "Allergies. Must remember to take some more meds before we go today."

He studied her face for a second, then seemed to accept her answer. "I'm sorry I was such a jerk before."

"It's okay." She'd deserved every word of it.

He stuck out his hand. "So, friends?"

She placed her hand in it, where it was swallowed by his much larger palm. "Friends."

Friends. The problem was, everything in her wanted much more than that.

Twenty

He was in serious straits. Jackson unfolded the pamphlet he had folded with exacting precision and stared again at the images it contained. He breathed in and then out, attempting to find some equilibrium. As much as was possible anyway, given that the rutted road they were traveling on had him bouncing around like a popcorn kernel over heat.

A sharp bend threw him into Hans before he could grab something—anything—to prevent it. "Sorry."

The large German grinned at him from his two-thirds of the backseat of the SUV they were traveling in. How Jackson had ended up with him, instead of his wife, in the chaos of getting everyone into cars, he still had no idea. Those two were usually stuck as close together as Merry and Pippin.

Jackson crumpled the pamphlet and tossed it onto the floorboard. Of all the important details about this tour, how had he overlooked this one? To be fair, the place where "Rohan riders' journey to the Pellannor" had been shot was just one of a long list of film locations they were visiting over three days. Residing innocently between the sites of "Gandalf's ride to Minas

Tirith" and "Rohan refugees trek to Helm's Deep," it didn't exactly jump off the page flashing red lights of doom.

He wasn't even sure if he'd read the whole list, let alone given it any thought, since none of the explanations meant anything to him anyway. He'd still have been clueless if not for Esther throwing a fit about not being allowed to wear her Arwen outfit because it didn't meet safety requirements.

He ran his hand through his hair, only half taking in the beautiful rugged scenery. Maybe he was worried about nothing. It had been twenty years, maybe even longer, since his last encounter. He might have grown out of it. People grew out of irrational childhood phobias all the time.

And there was no way he could let Allie see even a hint of his fear—not after the grief he'd given her about that stupid cow. After everything he'd been subjected to on this trip, this would be more humiliation than he could bear.

And then there was his uncle. Jackson didn't even want to know how many nails were in his coffin, but he was sure this would be the final one. Who would entrust millions to a guy who changed the channel at *Mr. Ed* reruns?

It wasn't even like he had a good reason. No traumatic childhood experience. No knowing someone who'd once been in some sort of serious horse-related incident. Nothing. Horses had just scared the pants off him his entire life.

He closed his eyes and tried imagining himself walking up to his chosen companion, giving it a pat on the nose. Feeding it a carrot. Riding off into the sunset like the man from Snowy River. His stomach lurched. Maybe not.

He was thirty-two years old, for crying out loud. He'd grown up on a farm and stared down plenty of scarier things in his life.

All the rationalizing in the world was no competition for his breakfast, which was trying to fight its way to the surface.

The SUV skidded to a halt in a lush pasture, in the middle of absolutely nowhere. If it hadn't been for a cheerful "Here we are" from the driver and the other cars pulling up beside them, he would've thought they were lost.

Opening his door, he unfolded his legs from their wedge-shaped position and exited the car. Breathing in the crisp air, he cast his gaze around the green rolling hills, guarded by towering snowcapped mountaintops. At least if today was going to be his last, it was in one of the most beautiful places he'd ever seen.

Doors flew open as the rest of the group tumbled out in various states of enthusiasm. Esther appeared to have gotten over her sulk as she was chatting with Mavis, hands flying in all directions.

Movement across the meadow caught his attention. Three men and two women were walking toward them, each leading two or three horses. His chest tightened.

So much for his hope they would be small, docile creatures closer to the pony end of the horse spectrum. These were the Hulk versions of the equine kingdom. Even from fifty feet away, he could see the powerful muscles rippling underneath glossy coats. Lips flapped open to showcase enormous white teeth that could no doubt chomp a man's arm off, if they were so inclined.

He watched them approach, fighting the urge to step behind Hans and hide like a turkey in the third week of November.

"You ready?"

It was Allie. The woman could move with the stealth of a ninja when it suited her.

He was not even close to ready. "Of course. Horses. Great. Me and horses, we're like that." He held up two fingers crossed over each other. Then his brain caught up with his runaway mouth and he realized how wrong that sounded. "I mean . . . I um . . . like horses." This time his voice came out an octave higher than normal. He might as well shoot himself now.

She gave him a weird look that matched the strange vibe charging the air between them. "Ooookay." She opened her mouth, as if to inquire further, but then closed it again. After two days of arctic-chill silence on his end, he couldn't blame her for not stretching out the conversation.

"So which one is mine?" *Please let it be an old nag. Please.*

Allie scanned the lineup, then pointed to the largest one of the bunch. "That one. Her name's Tinkerbell." She gave him a mischievous smile. "I think you'll make a great team."

He forced himself to keep his expression neutral as he stared at the enormous, dark brown thing. He'd need a ladder to be able to mount her. As if she knew she was being talked about, "Tinkerbell" looked their way, flared her nostrils, and tried to tug the reins from her handler.

Jackson snorted out a semi-hysterical laugh. At least when he got thrown off and trampled to death, it would probably be over fast.

"Would you like me to swap you for something a little more . . . sedate?" Allie looked up at him innocently, the golden highlights in her hair glistening under the morning sun. "Like maybe Chaos." She pointed to a smaller, dapple-gray horse that stood serenely, making no attempt to move, even though her reins were dangling free and no handler was nearby. He had to give the Kiwis points for having a good sense of irony when it came to animal naming.

He sucked in some crisp mountain air. "I'm

sure Tinkerbell and I will get along fine." He was surprised he could even get the words past the scrambled eggs trying to climb back up his throat. It was a small miracle that they came out sounding close to nonchalant.

"Great. I've got to get the others sorted." She threw him a smile that left him short on breath before striding away. Her perfectly fitted cropped jacket, jodhpurs, and knee-high boots did nothing to alleviate his sudden light-headedness.

Steady, Jackson! He forced his gaze away. Sucked in some more air. It was just the high altitude affecting him. Plus his impending date with doom. Nothing to do with Allie. Allison. Dr. Shire.

Something inside him groaned at his lame attempt at self-deception. He'd clearly gotten rusty at the art of lying to himself over the last few months. He wasn't sure if that was a good thing or not.

He did know that falling for his tour guide was definitely *not* a good thing.

Allie had almost told the guy to plant his butt on the ground and put his head between his knees, he looked that gray. Hopefully he hadn't eaten anything dodgy for breakfast. The last thing she needed was to deal with some kind of food-poisoning debacle.

Holding her wind-whipped hair back from her face, Allie tried to maintain some equilibrium against Esther's continued whines. ". . . Arwen if I'm not allowed to."

"Unfortunately, New Zealand and Middle-earth have slightly different health and safety regulations." Truth be told, there was no law in New Zealand that specifically forbade a whiny, preteen girl from riding a horse in Elf regalia. They were a lot more vague than that, but she had neither the inclination nor the energy to justify her call.

The whining continued and she tuned in only enough to hear snippets about Liv Tyler.

Allie finally snapped. "Liv Tyler had a stunt double. Last I checked, you don't. If Jane shows up anytime, I'll be more than happy to let her roam the countryside dressed as Arwen. But you are not. End of story. If you don't like it, I'll have one of the drivers take you back to the hotel."

She wished she could take the words back before they'd even left her mouth. The girl might be a pain in the behind, but she was only twelve. Over Esther's shoulder, she watched as Elroy fought against an imaginary foe with his sword, which he would also be leaving behind if he wanted to get on a horse.

"Who's Jane?" The girl's voice was so soft, Allie almost missed the question.

She softened her voice. "Jane Abbott was Liv Tyler's stunt double. Look, I'm sorry I snapped at you, but it's my responsibility to keep you from hurting yourself. And when you're not an experienced rider, having you in clothing that could get caught or tangled up isn't safe."

"Okay." For a second, the difficult preteen vanished and Allie caught a glimpse of the young, insecure girl behind the facade.

Allie rocked back on her heels. This was the first crack Esther had shown. The girl hadn't so much as flinched when Allie had asked her to hand back the lamp without a fuss, just returned with it under her arm and handed it over with a mutinous look. Her father hadn't been any help at all, cracking a joke about kids being kids.

Might as well ask. She had nothing to lose. "So, what's with all the stealing?"

Esther looked at her. Tugged at her long, dark braid. "My parents are splitting up. That's why my dad took me on this trip. They think I don't know."

Oh. The pre-divorce guilt trip. It wasn't the first. "I'm really sorry."

"I've been super good for months, but it hasn't made any difference. Since that hasn't worked, I guess I thought if I got in trouble then maybe Dad would stick around." She offered up a wobbly smile. "I know that doesn't make any sense."

Ahhhhh. Allie's heart broke. Poor kid. She crouched down so she could look the girl in the eye. "I'll be praying your parents can work things out. Maybe having some time apart will help. But I do know one thing. You getting in trouble or being perfect isn't going to save their marriage. I promise. Only they can do that."

Esther heaved a sigh almost bigger than she was. "I know. I haven't taken anything since the lamp."

Allie wasn't sure what to say. *Thanks? That's great?*

"So what's up with you and Jackson?"

Allie startled at the sudden change in direction. "What?"

Esther shrugged. "I answered your question, so I figured I get a question too. And mine is, 'What's up with you and Jackson?' "

"Um . . ." Allie stalled, lost for a response.

Esther cast a look over Allie's shoulder. "I mean, he's no Aragorn, but he's probably the next best thing."

"It's complicated." Why was she justifying her nonexistent love life to someone who wouldn't even know what Hammer pants were?

Esther gave Allie a shrewd look. "As complicated as Aragorn and Arwen?"

"Um, no." She couldn't claim that her dramas trumped having to give up immortality.

"Well, he likes you and you like him. I can tell."

Allie restrained the urge of her inner twelve-year-old to ask how Esther knew Jackson liked her. She wasn't so good at squashing the tingle that went through her at Esther's confident statement.

Esther held up a hand, shading her eyes against the sun. "If Aragorn and Arwen can make it work, so can you."

Kermit and Miss Piggy also made it work for a while, but no one was using that as a basis for arguing that frogs and pigs should date. Maybe because none of them were *real*.

"Esther?" One of the handlers came up to them. "I've got your horse ready."

The inquisition had ended. Thank goodness. Esther followed the guy toward Buttercup, and Allie got to her feet, turning to see Jackson mounting Tinkerbell nearby. Swinging his leg over the saddle, he sat atop the huge horse with all the comfort of a man sitting on top of a large cactus with no pants on.

Allie grabbed the reins and handed them up to him while the handler adjusted his stirrups. She tried to banish the feelings Esther's words had unleashed inside her. It didn't help that, even clearly out of his comfort zone, the guy sat up on his horse looking hotter than the Sahara.

"Thanks." The word croaked out of Jackson's mouth.

"Are you okay?"

He let out such a violent sneeze that Mildred, the horse beside Tinkerbell, startled just as Ethel was being helped onto her.

Allie peered up at him. He really didn't look so good, his torso kind of weaving on top of the large horse. There was a higher pollen count than usual for this time of year. Maybe he got hay fever too. "Do you need an antihistamine?"

He swallowed. His eyes started bugging and a hand grabbed his chest. "Can't . . . breathe." He rasped the words out with the bad theatrics of someone doing their first show way, way, way off Broadway. Like she was falling for that.

"Ha, ha, very funny."

His eyes bugged some more and he made a noise like he was trying to suck air through a small tube.

She stared at him, waiting for him to burst out laughing, enjoying thinking he'd fooled her.

Instead, the guy tumbled over, toppled off the horse, and landed in a pile at her feet.

Twenty-one

"What is wrong with you?" Allie's eyes were so wild and wide it seemed entirely possible they might defy all laws of human physics and explode from her head.

"With me?" The oxygen mask muffled his words, but she clearly managed to interpret them, given the next thing he felt was her shaking him. Clearly her parents had never taught her about being nice to invalids.

"Yes, you!"

He could now see her pacing out of the corner of his eye. He tried to turn his neck to watch, but the pain rocketing up into his temples put a stop to that pretty quickly. Where were they? What had happened?

"I could have lost my job because of that stupid stunt you pulled. You put everyone at risk—most of all yourself. You could be dead right now! Did you even think about that?"

He closed his eyes. Dead would mean he wouldn't be able to feel every atom in his body screaming at him. Dead would mean a hefty life insurance payout and his parents being able to pay off the farm. On those terms, it actually sounded fairly good.

He tried to pull his thoughts together. The last

thing he remembered was climbing on the monster horse. After that, everything turned blurry. Very blurry.

Pleading ignorance was probably the only thing that might get her down off her high and mighty ledge. "I didn't—"

A finger jabbed into his face. "Don't you even try it. I saw your face when you saw those horses. Stupidly, I thought maybe you hadn't ridden much or weren't a big horse person. It didn't cross my mind that anyone, not even you, would be stupid enough to get up on one when they were deathly allergic."

His muddled brain couldn't even begin to unravel if that was meant to be a compliment or a smackdown. He was going to guess at the second.

Hold on. What had she said? He was allergic?

She was still ranting. ". . . EpiPen, never would've gotten you down on time. Had to call a rescue chopper. Do you have any idea what kind of paperwork that means?"

He tried to gather enough force to project his questions past the mask. "I'm allergic? To horses?"

She tased him with her eyes. "Don't try and play dumb with me, Jackson Gregory. I know you're a farm boy."

He leaned back in against his pillow, too tired to find the words to try and explain that farms and horses didn't necessarily go hand in hand like ketchup and fries. Though, now that he thought about it, horses had always made him sneeze. Could he have been allergic this whole time and the years of not coming into contact with any just made it worse?

"I hope you've broken something." Her voice bounced off the sterile hospital room walls as she paced. At least that's where he guessed they were. "I hope you have to be laid up for the rest of the tour in a hotel room. No more schmoozing your uncle. Just you all by yourself with bad daytime TV."

He followed her movements. At some point, she'd shed the cropped jacket and her SLT-branded top had come half-untucked. Her hair was pulled back in an off-center haphazard ponytail. She looked undone and out of sorts. Because of him.

He managed to lift a hand, nudging the oxygen mask off his mouth. If nothing he said was going to calm her down, there was always a bit of fun in making her even madder. "Why are you so mad at me?"

"Seriously? Seriously!" She appeared by his side. "Have you not heard a word I've been saying? You could have died. Tinkerbell could've been hurt if you'd spooked her. I could lose my job. The whole group is being inconvenienced because you're an arrogant, entitled schmuck who couldn't get off his prideful pedestal and admit he was allergic to horses."

"So when did you realize you like me?" He wasn't sure where the words even came from, but they hit the room with the force of a ballistic missile.

Allie staggered back. "What!"

He managed a feeble shrug. "No one gets this worked up over someone they're indifferent to. So I was just wondering when you fell for me?"

"Argh!" If eyes could flash fire, he would have been so incinerated it would have required dental records to identify him.

He steeled himself for the slap he could sense coming. That should take care of the one remaining part of his body that wasn't hurting.

Instead there was no resounding pain against his cheek. Worse. Her hand froze in the air and she stared at him, shaking her head. "He's not worth it, Allie. Not worth it." The words were muttered under her breath; she might not have even been aware she was saying them out loud, but they slashed through him like they'd been boomed across the universe. She'd finally worked out the one thing everyone else already knew.

Allie shoved the door to Jackson's room open and stormed into the hospital corridor. A power-walking nurse wheeling some medical machinery swerved to avoid her, a wheel just missing Allie's toe.

"Sorry!"

The woman was out of hearing before the word was even out of her mouth.

What was wrong with her? Not even with the rudest, most chauvinistic, sleazeball clients had she ever come close to indulging in her desire to give them a good slap. And some of the situations they'd put her in had been a lot more deserving of one. Lecherous smiles, wandering hands, outright solicitations for services not listed in the com-pany brochures. She'd managed to extricate her-self from all of them without ruffling any expensive feathers.

Instead she'd lost it over what? Some meaning-less goading from a guy trussed up in a hospital bed who couldn't even move?

He was right, though. If it had been any other client, she would have been oozing sympathy. To come on the tour, people had to sign the world's longest and most exhaustive waiver imaginable, and broken limbs were nothing new. Plus they paid through the nose to be coddled and madeto feel okay in events such as this—even if they'd come about their injury in the most ridiculous way imaginable.

Sagging against the hallway wall, she blew out a breath. What was it that made Jackson Gregory get under her skin like nothing else? He was wrong, so wrong. She didn't fancy him, couldn't fancy him, but she was far from indifferent.

When had she fallen for him? The question

kept repeating in her head. Haunting her every breath. She could try and rationalize things in her head until the Second Coming, but there was no denying the way her emotions had gone into meltdown when she'd realized he was having a severe anaphylactic reaction. Or the desperation in her prayers during the moments after she'd stabbed him with the EpiPen and waited for the epinephrine to kick in.

Desperation that went far deeper than if it had been any other person from the group crumpled on the ground.

Allie breathed in the universal hospital scent of antiseptic and body odor. She had to find her way back to the cool, professional exterior she'd maintained at the beginning. That had worked. She was a guide; he was just another client.

Except at some point along the line he had turned into anything but.

She hoped he hadn't broken anything. Despite what she'd said, having to deal with someone with a broken limb was a nightmare at this point on the tour. The paperwork would be horrible. The incident reports, the re-litigating of hazards, the write-up for the head office. Hours on top of hours of extra work. And that was before she even started dealing with unraveling his travel insurance if he couldn't fly home when he was supposed to.

Sirens sounded and trolleys rushed past her.

People shouted orders across the beds. A few hours ago that had been Jackson.

Why couldn't he have just said he was allergic? There was no shame in it. It would've been a bit of a boring day for him while the others went off to ride, but it would have been better than this.

The last guy who had made her this mad was Derek. Not that she'd stuck around long enough to show it. No, she'd called the lawyers, changed the locks, packed her bags, and moved out before he'd even gotten home.

Running away. That she was good at, which made the possibility of Oxford even more tempting. Except she'd promised herself she wasn't going to run again—not until she reclaimed her life.

Twenty-two

Five hours later, Allie trudged into the hotel lobby. Unbelievable. The man was unbelievable. It had taken all of her willpower not to leave him at the hospital and let him find his own way back. Instead, she'd had to put up with his insufferable smirking during the entire cab ride.

"You still mad?" He spoke from where he hobbled beside her on a pair of crutches. Nothing broken, thank goodness. Just a badly sprained ankle and a lot of bruising.

She slid a glare to her side. Even almost more infuriating than his aura of smug calm was the fact that he didn't look even the slightest bit ruffled, let alone like someone who had taken a tumble off a horse and spent the better part of the day in Accident & Emergency.

Meanwhile, she was caked in mud down one side from where she'd taken a slide across the field in her haste to get to her first-aid kit. To make it worse, the quick glimpse she'd had in the hospital bathroom mirror had revealed a dirt-smeared face to match hair that looked like it had taken a roll on the forest floor.

"I'm not mad. Just tired." That much was true. The only good thing about this day was that it was over. Done. Finished. Kat had left a voice mail to say she would be fine taking the others for dinner solo, and in a few minutes, Allie would be in her room, listening to the sound of glorious hot water filling up her very large bath. Where she intended to soak until she was as wrinkled as a piece of fruit left in the sun for too long, followed by room service and some terrible TV.

Her spirits lifted at the thought.

"Allison." Every neuron in her body jumped, like she was at the receiving end of a lightning strike.

It couldn't be. It wasn't possible. There was no way.

"Allison, over here." The same voice, just a little louder. Though of course not loud enough to qualify as "raised." Because Veronica James-Shire never so much as raised her voice, let alone yelled.

Allie turned, and sure enough, there was her mother, rising from a chair in the lobby like a wraith rising from the mist. If a wraith came with perfectly coiffed caramel highlights, clad in a custom-made black pantsuit.

It was at moments like this she knew there had to be a God. A neutral universe wouldn't have such a warped sense of humor.

Her mother glided toward her like a model on a runway. She must've had a recent round of Botox, because the only sign of dismay her face could register at her daughter's appearance was a slight flaring of her nostrils.

This was, after all, the woman who believed no occasion or outfit was complete without a set of pearls, including her biweekly yoga class.

"Mother." Allie's voice finally found itself. "What are you doing here?"

Her mother smoothed her tailored jacket needlessly with her perfectly manicured nails. "I was in town, so I thought I'd drop by and see if my daughter was free for dinner. Though"— she struggled to arch her eyebrows—"obviously not in that state."

Obviously.

Her mother's eyes flickered to Jackson. "Where are your manners, Allison? Aren't you going to introduce me to your friend?"

A very unladylike phrase shot through Allie's head. From the moment she had heard her mother's voice, she had completely forgotten about Jackson standing beside her, observing this entire car wreck of a scene.

She forced her tone into neutral. "Mother, this is Jackson Gregory, one of my clients on this tour. Jackson, this is my mother, Veronica James-Shire."

"Lovely to meet you, Mrs. James-Shire." Jackson moved with surprising grace for someone on crutches as he shook her mother's hand, holding it a second longer than strictly necessary.

Her mother preened. "It's actually just Ms. James now, but please, call me Veronica."

Allie wanted to sink into the floor at her mother's simpering. She was so busy being mortified by the way Veronica was sizing up Jackson like he was some kind of calorie-free, carb-free dessert, she almost missed her mother's announcement.

"Wait, what? Just James? Does this mean . . ." Oh, please let it be so. Please, after years of public show and private dysfunction, let her parents finally be getting divorced.

Her mother flashed her left hand, which still held the very large diamond her father had been badgered into giving her for their twenty-fifth wedding anniversary. "Darling, Mr. Gregory doesn't want to hear about our little family tiffs."

Jackson shifted on his feet. "Well, I'll let the two of you catch up." The man was smart enough to take the chance for an exit when one presented itself. "Thanks for everything today, Allie."

Turning, he hobbled toward the lift as fast as he could manage. Even though she knew her mother was watching her, Allie couldn't stop her eyes from following him.

"Now, I've made a booking for us at Rata." Her mother glanced at her diamond-studded watch. "It was for eight but obviously you won't have enough time to clean up by then, so I'll change it to eight-thirty."

No way. "I'm sorry, but I don't have time for dinner at Rata. In case you didn't notice the crutches, I've got a ton of paperwork that needs to be sorted tonight."

Her mother opened her mouth as if to argue, and then something indecipherable flickered across her face. "Okay, I can cancel Rata. How about somewhere quick? You have to eat."

"I was planning to grab a burger from Ferg's." Unless it was a canapé ferried to her on a silver platter, her mother viewed any food requiring the involvement of hands as beneath her.

"Sounds great."

Allie stared. Who was this woman? More importantly, what did she want?

Her mother shooed Allie away with her hands. "Go get changed. I'll wait here for you."

Jackson turned the scene he'd witnessed in the lobby over in his mind as he tried to maneuver down Shotover Street in search of some dinner.

It was crass of him to even think it, but Allie's mother reeked of money, from the tips of her immaculately cut and colored golden-brown bob to the toes of her pointy stilettos.

Unfortunately, all the riches or cosmetic work in the world couldn't change the brittle edge to her voice or the hard-edged expression on her face that told of someone who had spent a lot more time in her life frowning instead of laughing.

287

She was about as far from Jackson's down-to-earth, fun-loving mom as you could get. His parents might never have had the kind of money Veronica wore on just one finger, but from the disapproving way she'd sized Allie up, he was sure he'd gotten the better end of the parenting deal.

Allie's comment on the hike about not being anything special made more sense now. It was going to haunt him even more now that he hadn't managed to say something, anything, to convince her otherwise.

Jackson eyed up the row of cafés and fast-food places lining the road. Set against a backdrop of towering snowcapped mountains, Queenstown was easily the most beautiful city he'd ever been to. It was nice to be able to absorb the majesty of it all at his own slow pace.

He hadn't been able to get hold of his uncle, so the group must be out for dinner by now. Which suited him fine. After the ridiculous amount of effort it had taken to navigate showering and getting dressed with his dud foot, he was starving. As nice as all the fancy food was, after today what he really wanted was a huge burger. Or pizza. Something large and loaded with carbs.

Gritting his teeth, he tried to ignore the pain radiating up from his foot. He had to be able to find something close by. Surely. As if God himself had heard him, he stopped in front of a place with a steady stream of people entering and exiting with paper bags that emitted such amazing smells his stomach rumbled.

The people sitting outside were eating some of the most tantalizing-looking burgers he'd ever seen. Perfect.

Hobbling inside, he managed to navigate the crowd to order a burger, fries, and onion rings and find a spot by a window at one of the long tables.

Balancing his crutches beside him, he propped his throbbing foot up on the empty chair across from him. As much as he'd fought it at the time, thank goodness Allie had ignored his protests and gotten his prescription for painkillers filled. By the time he managed to limp back to the hotel, he was definitely going to be in serious need of some.

Unscrewing the top of his lemonade, he took a gulp and breathed in the smell of meat and grease. Heaven.

"Here you go." The friendly girl who'd taken his order and noticed his crutches placed a tray down in front of him and disappeared before he could even say thanks, let alone give her a tip.

Selecting an onion ring, he crunched into the battered goodness. He closed his eyes in bliss, picked up the bag, and ate a second, then a third, barely pausing for breath in between.

Forcing himself to put them down, he unwrapped

his burger and took a huge bite. Beef, bacon, and barbecue sauce joined together in the food version of Handel's *Messiah*. He almost groaned with joy. Oh, this was so much better than some microscopic serving of fine dining.

Another bite and another, punctuated with a mouthful of salty, crunchy fries. By the time he paused for breath, his meal was half gone.

". . . being so difficult." A cultured voice, so out of place in a burger joint, cut through his buzz.

"After everything we've done for you, all we ask is this one small thing." The woman continued from somewhere to the left, her voice becoming increasingly familiar.

It couldn't be. He snuck a glance sideways. It was. On the other side of the window, sitting at one of the outdoor tables: the same golden helmet of hair, ramrod-straight posture. Blinged-out finger tapping the tabletop. And Allie, a picture of misery as she sat slumped across from her mother, breaking a fry in half, then in half again.

He couldn't help himself. He ducked even farther behind the folding window frame that partially obscured him from their view. Though all it would take would be for Allie to look up and slightly sideways and he'd be busted.

"This debacle has carried on too long, Allison. Does the reputation of the family not mean anything to you? How are we supposed to hold our heads up with this hanging over us? Derek's assistance with campaign fund-raising has proved invaluable, so your pathetic attempt at smearing him to Susannah has proven to be completely off the mark. He also feels badly about this whole misunderstanding between the two of you."

Derek. The name was familiar. Wasn't that the guy who'd called the morning he was in her room?

Allie pushed her food away and said something he couldn't quite hear. Picking up a sheaf of papers resting by her elbow, she tried to hand them to her mother.

Veronica pushed them back toward her, leaving Allie to put them down in the middle of the table, anchored by a bottle of soda. "I can't believe I raised such a selfish daughter. You've never lived up to your sister, but I have to admit, I thought better of you than this. Are you truly so ungrateful after everything I've done for you?" Her lashing tongue whipped through him, and he didn't even know the woman.

Allie opened her mouth, but nothing came out, a lone tear speaking louder than any words ever could as it traced a trail down her cheek.

Okay, he'd had enough. Compelled by a force he couldn't deny, Jackson pushed up from the table, grabbed his crutches, and swung himself out the front door and around the corner to stand beside their table.

Allie looked up at him, face draining to the color of Cool Whip.

He captured her gaze for a second and then turned to her mother. "I'm sorry. I realize this is none of my business, but you obviously don't know your daughter. I've spent every day of the last two weeks with her and I'm not sure who you're talking about, but it isn't Allie. She is kind and funny and smart. She manages eight of us with our quirks and demands and, yes"—he gestured to his ankle—"as you can see, occasional lapses into stupidity. She is about as selfish as I'm vegetarian. So whatever it is you're asking her to do, there's a good reason why she won't."

His own audacity stunned him, but he wasn't sorry. He held his breath, hoping he hadn't made everything worse.

Veronica stared at him, her expression brittle. "You're right, Mr. Gregory."

Had he actually made the woman see the truth? He glanced sideways to see her daughter's chin lifted, a flicker of hope appearing in her eyes.

"This is none of your business." She waved her manicured hand at him like he was a pesky fly.

Across the table, Allie's whole body deflated like an old balloon. And the way it felt as if someone had ripped open his chest and clenched a fist around his heart told him loud and clear it was time to stop kidding himself about his feelings for her.

Twenty-three

Allie sighed as she positioned herself on her couch, placed her bare feet on the coffee table, and clicked on her laptop to open up the incident report form she was going to have to file. The first thing in the trees' worth of paperwork Jackson's little tumble was going to generate.

Jackson. She couldn't even process everything that had happened today. This morning, he hadn't even been talking to her. Tonight, he'd been her most gallant defender. And in between, he'd managed to jam in a rescue chopper ride and a trip to the emergency department.

Outside her window, waves lapped against the shores of Lake Wakatipu, reminding her of yet another thing on her to-do list. A write-up of the new hotel they were staying in. Not that she could complain, since she'd been given an executive suite. Though it was disconcerting having so much space after being used to small hotel rooms. What was she supposed to do with two bedrooms, two bathrooms, a chef's kitchen, and a dining table for eight?

It accentuated her solo status, if only to herself. All the empty chairs, unused crockery, and echoing silence accused her—as if waiting for the nonexistent people for whom they had been created, the conversations and laughter that weren't happening. So much so she'd suggested Kat ditch her room and join her for the rest of the week, and Kat had agreed.

Focus, Allie. This was exactly why she avoided seeing her mother. Because not only did it inevitably end in tears, but it always left her melancholic for days.

Her emotions tumbled around like they'd been stuck in a blender. Unable to forget for a second the way Jackson had stood up to her mother. No one had ever stood up for her like that. Ever. Certainly not to Veronica. Their parting had been chilly at best when her mother left to catch her flight. Mostly because of Allie's refusal to work things out with Derek, who'd somehow managed to convince her mother the small issue of his other marriage was just a little "misunderstanding." However, Jackson's intervention certainly hadn't helped matters.

Not with her mother, and certainly not with Allie's now ludicrous attempts at denying how she felt about him.

What was she meant to do with her growing feelings for this guy who so aggravated her one second she wanted to clock him with the nearest blunt object, then the next looked at her like he could see through all the barriers she put up to keep herself safe?

Her lips turned up at the memory of him telling off her mother, totally unaware of the big smear of barbecue sauce across his chin. It was a good thing she'd been sitting, otherwise the heady combination of adorable and downright sexy would have probably knocked her off her feet.

When—how—had Jackson Gregory managed to tunnel his way into her heart and take up residence there?

Running her hands through her hair, she huffed out a breath. *Don't be so stupid, Allie.* It was nothing more than a bit of unexpected chemistry. It would be nothing more than a vague memory within a week of the tour's end. She was pretty sure he'd forget about her the minute he limped onto his plane home. Especially now, since he'd probably heard enough to work out that she was the last person in the world he should want anything to do with.

She pushed her glasses up the bridge of her nose and turned her attention back to her screen. Tapping it awake from its slumber, she navigated her way through the opening pages, then honed in on the detail. The forms that would be pored over by the risk-averse wonks at HQ to make sure she had struck the perfect balance between covering the company's butt and showing appropriate respect to the client—regardless of how much of the blame they deserved.

Reason for accident? Her fingers flew. *An astounding level of stupidity by the most amazing guy I've ever met.*

And there it was. The oxymoron of how she felt about Jackson in black and white. She hit the delete button until it disappeared from the screen and dutifully typed, *Client allergic to horses. Did not declare either on booking or indemnity waiver, or to guide.*

She sat and pondered her next sentence, remembering how Jackson had sneezed with such violence it had even freaked out Mildred, who was ordinarily as highly strung and prone to sudden reactions as the average cabbage.

Knock knock knock. Allie's fingers paused over the keyboard.

Must be someone at the suite next door. There was no one with any reason to be knocking on her door at—she checked her watch—almost nine-thirty. Kat and the group were doing a degustation menu that should take them until ten to get through.

The sound came again. This time there was no mistaking it had come from her door. Sighing, she tilted her screen down so it couldn't be read, leveraged herself up from her seat, and padded toward the entranceway.

What could it be now? Nothing would surprise her after today. The entire day had felt like the universe was throwing everything at her. It had clearly decided it couldn't possibly let the final hours go to waste.

She peered through the peephole, and her breath caught. What was Jackson doing here? For a second, she contemplated not answering, afraid of what she might do or say. But the way he'd left her mother speechless for the first time Allie had ever witnessed—meant he deserved better than that.

Turning the deadbolt, she swung the door open and peeked around. He was in a pair of well-worn jeans and a fitted gray T-shirt, a five-o'clock shadow creeping across his jaw. The visual was all sexy and rumpled—like something out of a men's magazine shoot. Her breath stalled.

Jackson had been attractive enough already, but there was something about adding the standing-up-to-her-mother factor that upped it a hundred-fold. If she'd known Iowa produced farm boys that looked like this, she would've found her way to the great corn state years ago.

He leaned on one crutch; wedged against his torso was a stack of . . . pizzas?

Words. Need to speak. "Hi?"

"Hi. I think you might still have my phone in your bag from the hospital. And my drugs." He nodded to the four pizza boxes that emanated a combination of enticing smells. A plastic bag dangled from the hand gripping the handle of the crutch. "You barely touched your meal so I brought a ransom payment."

It was true. Any time spent with her mother did have the effect of killing her appetite. She'd barely managed a bite of her burger, even though Veronica uncharacteristically had managed to restrain herself from her typical passive-aggressive commentary on her daughter's diet and dress size. Hints of cheese, tomato, and herbs wound their way up Allie's nose, and she almost drooled.

"Thanks, but I'm fine." Her stomach let out a rumble that outed her as the liar she was.

Jackson raised an eyebrow and the hint of a smile plucked at one side of his mouth. "Uh-huh."

She stood in the doorway. Wavering. The sensible thing to do would be to leave him there and go get his stuff and trade it for a pizza. She'd get fed, he'd get his phone and drugs, and whatever this weird chemistry was between them would get left alone. No harm, no foul.

And then what? Eating pizza in a huge empty suite with only paperwork and her own depressing thoughts for company? That appealed even less.

Fingers curling around the cool, metal door handle, she pulled and stepped back as the door slid all the way open. "Come in."

"Thanks." He hobbled through the doorway and past her, stopping a few feet inside.

The door swished against the plush carpet as she closed it. She moved around him and started back down the hall. "Let me go check my bag." She was hyperconscious of his presence following a few feet behind her. At least being in a suite made the situation a bit less weird. A hotel room would have been a bit too confronting, too *intimate*.

The accumulating smell of cheese and pizza dough caused her stomach to do an anticipatory flip, dragging her thoughts away from the disturbing direction they had started to head.

What was with the food? He could've just knocked on her door and asked for his phone and painkillers. Or, even more sensibly, rung her from his room. Though, at some point, they'd catapulted over the border that delineated sensible.

Allie grabbed a glimpse in the hall mirror on her way to the kitchen. Her hair was pulled up into a straggly, crooked ponytail and desperately needed a wash. Ugly reading glasses—why, oh why, hadn't she left her contacts in? She'd stripped all her makeup off, revealing blotchy uneven skin, and her eyes still bore evidence of the crying jag she'd had over her mother as soon as she walked in the door. Again.

Her bag sat where she'd dropped it on the kitchen counter and she walked toward it. Anything to distract her from the fact that he smelled of some kind of masculine soap and that she hadn't been alone like this with a guy who scattered her emotions in years.

"Where should I put these?" He said the words easily. Like there was nothing weird about this at all. Like they were friends who ate pizza together all the time. "I didn't know what you liked, so I got a mixture."

"Um . . . anywhere will be fine." She gestured around the large open-plan kitchen and turned her attention to finding his stuff. *Thunk.* He dropped the precarious pile onto the bench next to her, moving the plastic bag to sit next to them.

Her hand grasped around a rectangular object, and she fished it from her bag. Sure enough it was his phone. She held it up in her palm. Next followed the brown paper sack holding his painkillers. "Sorry."

He glanced up from where he was pulling containers out and lining them along the granite countertop next to the pizza boxes. "No problem."

Her stomach let out an unladylike gurgle. "What exactly do we have?"

"Um, hold on a sec." He turned, facing her full-on, barely a hand's width between them. She involuntarily took a quick breath as she found herself staring at his broad shoulders. She tilted her head, her gaze traveling to his chin, lips, nose, eyes. Her toes curled. This guy was far too sexy for his own good. Actually, he was far too sexy for *her* good. This was bad. Very bad.

She quickly took a small step back to overcome the sudden overwhelming desire to reach up and run her fingers through his hair and down his arms and— *Whoa, Allie. Don't even go there.*

It was getting hot. Her face suddenly felt like she'd been out on a summer's day with no sunscreen. *Get busy. Unstack and open boxes.* Hopefully if Jackson noticed her blush, he'd put it down to the warmth of the pizza boxes as opposed to the very inappropriate series of thoughts zapping through her brain.

"Here you go." Their fingers brushed as he handed her a long receipt so she could see what he'd ordered.

Zap. Another thought. Another two degrees. The heat of pure attraction rampaged through her body. She was going to have to lose a layer soon. She didn't remember Derek ever having this effect on her. The two of them had had pizza many times over the years and not once had she needed to remove any items of clothing in his presence to cool down her internal furnace simply because his fingers brushed hers while handing over a receipt.

Allie glanced at the white piece of paper. "One thin-crust vegetarian pizza with no cheese. No cheese? Why would anyone want to eat pizza with no cheese?"

Jackson shuffled his feet. "I just thought maybe you were one of those girls who didn't like to eat carbs and dairy and stuff."

Ha! Not likely, when her jeans were a size

larger than she'd admit to. "We've eaten together for two weeks. At which point did I impress you as the kind of girl who doesn't eat carbs and dairy?" She held up her hand as he opened his mouth. "Don't answer that. It was purely a rhetorical question."

She looked back at the list. "One chicken, cranberry, and brie pizza. One spinach, pepperoni, feta, mushroom, and tomato pizza. One super supreme pizza with barbecue sauce. One serving of lemon-pepper wedges with sour cream. One chicken and avocado salad. One spaghetti carbonara. Two slices of chocolate mousse cake. Two slices of passion fruit cheesecake. One Diet Coke. One regular Coke." She refused to look at the dollar figure at the bottom.

He shrugged. "Okay, I might have gone a little overboard, but I wanted to be sure I got something you liked—especially after what I put you through today, and then . . ." He trailed off, clearly not wanting to put into words the obvious about her mother. Instead he just looked down, ocean eyes drilling into her.

She placed the paper on the counter. "You really didn't need to. All part of the job. You'd be amazed at the stupid things I've had to deal with." The last sentence came out a bit more harshly than Allie had intended. "I mean, this is great. Thank you." She gestured at all the food covering the surface. "I just wasn't expecting it."

Derek would never have bought out a pizza joint's menu because he wasn't sure what she might feel like eating. He was definitely a more budget-restrained kind of guy. Or so she'd thought—until she discovered that was only with *his* money. With *her* money, he was a pro at making extravagant gestures, like the bachelor party for which he'd "borrowed" her credit card and racked up almost five grand.

This was too much; it was all too much. "I—" Her voice caught in her throat and before she knew what was happening, a tear rolled down her cheek, and then another. She attempted to stem the flow with her sleeve, but they kept coming until there was a torrent pouring down her neck, pooling around the edge of her top.

She tried to pull them back in, shove them down. Shires didn't cry. She definitely didn't cry.

"Hey. Hey. It's okay. It's all going to be okay. Come on."

She had to stop crying. He couldn't see her like this, but the gush refused to slow. She couldn't even talk. Shuddering breaths squeezed from her shrunken lungs. She looked at the floor, the wall, the bench—anywhere but him—as she attempted to blink away the tears.

Warmth surrounded her. She'd been scooped up in his embrace, her head on his chest. Her arms wrapped themselves around his torso almost as if they had a will of their own, and she buried her face in his soft, lemony-smelling T-shirt. One of his arms was around her waist while the other stroked her back. It was everything she had imagined it would be. And more. He felt safe. She'd never expected that.

"Shh. It's okay, Al." His ragged, whispered words feathered down her face and straight into her heart. No one had ever called her that before, but Jackson could say it a million times and it wouldn't be enough.

For the first time in a long while, she even believed things might actually work out.

They stayed entwined for a few seconds—if only it could be a few centuries. Lucky him: drop by to get his phone and be accosted by an emotional wreck. Allie loosened her arms and stepped back slightly. Tilting her head up, she found his blue eyes boring into hers filled with concern . . . and something else she couldn't identify. He was so close that, when he exhaled, she could feel his breath on her lips. All it would take would be the slightest tilt of her toes to kiss him.

Bad idea. Very bad. She might not have been the sharpest needle in the haystack when it came to relationships, but even she knew only bad could come from kissing one guy when you might still be married to another. She quickly raised her sleeve up to her nose and wiped it in the most unladylike way possible before she did something to add to her list of regrets. A flicker of something crossed Jackson's eyes. Relief maybe? He loosened his arms as she stepped back a bit more.

To burn the bridge once and for all, she reached over, plucked a tissue from the box on the counter, and proceeded to blow her nose loudly. Nothing cooled the flames of passion more efficiently than expelling large amounts of snot in front of the object of one's affection.

Not that he was— Oh, this was seriously messed up.

Sure enough, by the time she looked up, Jackson was cracking open the remaining pizza boxes.

"I'm sorry about that. It's just . . ."

He stopped and gave her his full attention.

"It's just been a tough week," she finished. Wow, that wasn't lame. Not at all. She turned her attention back to opening the pasta container.

"You want to talk about it?" Jackson's arms wrapped around her waist from behind. "It's completely up to you."

The bottom of his chin scraped against her hair and, almost as if it had done so a hundred times before, her whole body relaxed into his. A perfect fit. His warm breath grazed the side of her face as her hands came to rest on top of his. He spread his fingers, slipping them through hers.

His next breath caressed the space between her collar and the curve of her neck, setting fire to every cell from the tip of her spine to the arches of her feet. She tilted her head, and the next breath traveled across the side of her mouth, leaving her lips tingling in its wake. God help her, she wanted to kiss this guy more than she had wanted to do anything in her life.

And then what? The thought somehow cut through her haze of longing, breaking the spell for a split second. When the kiss ended, all she would be left with was an even bigger mess than the one she was already in.

"Food. I need food." She practically leapt from his arms as she reached out and grabbed the closest slice of pizza to her. She shoved it into her mouth, now safe to turn to face him. After all, she couldn't kiss someone with a mouthful of pizza.

What was she *thinking?* She was married. Maybe. Sort of. Or was she? Until Jackson had shown up and thrown her world into chaos, it hadn't even been a question she'd been forced to confront, and Google didn't seem to have any guidance as to what the moral code was when you married someone who was *already married to someone else.*

A smile creased his face. "That one's got . . ."

Urgh. The salty putrid taste of olives assaulted all of her senses.

"Here." Laughter lined his voice as a napkin materialized in front of her face. "Spit."

Not a chance. She waved the napkin away, almost retching as she forced herself to swallow the foul taste. Nasty, nasty things.

"I'm impressed. I can't believe you ate that." Eyes twinkling mischievously, his arm reached around her and grabbed a slice of the same pizza. His other hand rested lightly on her waist, his thumb brushing against a millimeter of bare skin between her T-shirt and pants.

"I can't believe you got one with olives!" Allie moved along the bench on the pretext of getting a slice of something else, though she really just needed to get outside of his personal space before her resolve melted.

"Sorry, I happen to love the little suckers. And . . ." He gestured toward the other side of the pizza. "I did actually get it half no olives."

Of course he did, because what she needed right now was something else to make him even more appealing. Placing the remains of the slice on a napkin, she reached for the drinks, twisting the lid off the Coke. Grabbing a couple of glasses, she poured a large one for Jackson, then turned her attention to opening the Diet Coke.

After a couple of seconds of struggling with the cap, she looked at him in frustration. "So are you going to offer to help me or just indefinitely amuse yourself with my inability to open a soft drink?"

Jackson raised an eyebrow. "Now there's a

moment to savor: Allison Shire admitting she needs help." He took the bottle from her, twisted the cap off with the flick of his wrist, and poured her a glass.

"Thanks."

His crooked smile sent her heart rate up a few more beats. He picked up his own glass and took a slow drink. "So, Dr. Shire. Does this mean I get my phone back?" His long lashes swept up like a wave during the final seconds before it broke.

She blinked. What had she even done with it? The last thing she remembered, it had been in her hand before she had gotten, ahem, slightly distracted.

She looked around her kitchen, filled with enough food for ten people, and caught sight of his phone sitting beside the cook top. "Oh, I don't know . . ."

He unfurled the kind of smile that almost made *her* need crutches to stay upright. "I'm not sure I have another trip to the pizza place in me. Is there anything else I can offer?"

Her breath stalled. Somewhere in the back of her mind a red flashing sign was screaming *Eject, eject!* as she wavered on the brink between the safe and rational and the far more desirable.

His gaze flickered down to her lips, the tantalizing promise of possibility hanging in the mingled breath between them. A tilt on her toes, and it was no great mystery what would come next. Her entire being thrummed at the thought, almost overriding her sensibilities.

What was she doing? Only a few hours ago, she'd almost tripped over herself denying his assertion she was falling for him, and now what was she about to do? Throw herself at him?

Not to mention the *m*-word hung over her like a scarlet mist. She had to tell him. She wasn't sure why—he'd be long gone before the mess with Derek would be sorted out—but she knew with every passing second, her conscience flogged her even more for continuing to allow her secret to hover between them like a dark shadow.

She dropped her eyes, stepped back. "Jackson, I need to tell you about Derek."

He shook his head, put a finger up against her lips. "Al, I don't need to know about your ex-boyfriend. Not right now."

She pushed his hand away. She had to tell the truth even though it would ruin everything. "No, he's—"

A loud knock at the door interrupted her. What was going on? She usually had as many surprise visitors as a mausoleum and suddenly tonight it was Grand Central Station.

Jackson smiled as he tilted his head toward the door. "Popular lady." He turned, picking up his slice of pizza as though the last thirty seconds hadn't happened.

Pulling her scattered senses back together, Allie moved back to the door and peered through the keyhole. Kat stood there, shifting on her feet.

She pulled open the door. "Hey."

"Hey." Kat stood there for a second, then said, "You going to let me in?"

Allie registered the small suitcase by her friend's side. Oh. She'd totally forgotten she told her friend to come stay. "Of course." Allie stepped back. "Sorry."

Kat brushed past her, pulling her suitcase behind, and headed down the hallway before Allie could get anything else out. "Man, that group is great, but what a handful. And since when do Louis and Mavis have something going on?"

Allie hurried after her, but not fast enough.

"How was the hospital? Anything to report between you and the h— Oh!" Kat came to an abrupt stop as she rounded the corner into the living area. "Hello."

How the girl managed to cram so much insinuation into five letters Allie didn't know, but it was impressive.

"Look at that. The man himself."

Jackson leaned against the counter, the remains of the pizza crust in his hand. "That would be me."

Kat pulled out her Cheshire cat smile. "Fancy that." She surveyed the array of food. "Mind if I have some? I'm starving. Fine dining is all very lovely, but not exactly filling."

She addressed the question to Jackson, not Allie.

"Go for it." Jackson grabbed another piece of pizza, shoved his phone and medicine into his back pocket, then levered his crutch back under his shoulder. "I was actually about to go."

He hobbled around the island bench and paused for a second in front of Allie, capturing her gaze. "Thanks for the phone. And everything else today." He tilted his head and gave her the kind of smile that did absolutely nothing to cool her out-of-control internal furnace.

"No worries." She tried to keep her voice steady, conscious of Kat's triumphant gaze, but failed miserably.

What had just happened?

Allie didn't even follow him down the hall; she was frozen like a Narnia statue while he struggled for a few seconds, trying to balance pizza slice, crutch, and opening the door.

He paused and unfurled the lethal smile at her again. "Night, Al. See you in the morning."

He really needed to leave. Now. "Night, Jackson. Thanks."

She didn't so much walk as float back to the kitchen in a daze.

"Oh, I am so good!"

Allie jumped at the sound of Kat's voice, slamming her foot into the side of the breakfast bar. For a second, she'd forgotten Kat was even there. "Ow." She hopped up and down, clasping her foot with both hands while attempting to stay upright on her good foot. "I think I broke my toe!"

She looked up to see her friend now seated on a bar stool grinning at her with a forkful of pasta almost at her lips. "If you have, you and Jackson could get matching crutches. That would be super-cute."

Allie pulled out the bar stool next to Kat, slumped onto it, buried her head in her hands, and groaned. The sound bounced off the granite counter.

Next to her, the sounds of Kat hoovering up pasta continued. "This is really good. Want some?" She poked the corner of the plastic container through the gap in Allie's arm.

"No, thanks." She reached down and rubbed her throbbing toe, which was already beginning to swell. "Look at this. I'm probably not even going to be able to walk in the morning."

"Oh, it'll be fine! You bruise if someone breathes heavily near you." Kat didn't even blink as she finished the last bite of pasta and reached for a slice of chicken pizza. "So spill. You've got some explaining to do. Sorry if I interrupted something, by the way." From the smirk on her face, she couldn't have been less sorry. "Though now I understand why you didn't pick up my call earlier."

"No, that was because of my mother."

"What did Veronica do now?" Kat had met Allie's mother twice. First at her engagement party, then at her wedding. It would be fair to say they were not members of each other's mutual admiration society.

"She showed up."

"She's in town?"

"Yup. She just appeared in the lobby. I was walking with Jackson from the hospital. Tangent —his ankle is just sprained, not broken. Anyway, she convinced me to have dinner. So we went to Fergburger."

"Sorry." Kat held up a hand. "Veronica James-Shire went to Fergburger?"

"I know. Oh, and apparently it's just James now. Anyway, of all the places, Jackson was there and overheard her having a go at me because I wouldn't sign some papers. He stood up for me. And then he showed up with all this . . ." She waved her hands around at the food spread across the surface.

Kat took a bite of her pizza and chewed. "So, just so I've got this straight. Jackson took on Veronica. Then he showed up here with enough food to feed the whole hotel."

"Yup."

"And you didn't kiss the guy until he was blue in the face?"

"Of course not!"

313

Kat laughed, the sound bouncing off all the top-of-the-line stainless steel appliances. "Sorry, but judging by the way you two looked when I showed up, I'm guessing 'of course not' is a slight overstatement."

Busted. "Oh, Kat, what am I going to do?" Allie buried her head in her hands as the memories of the evening washed over her. How could she be attracted to him? Worse, how could she have almost acted on it when she wasn't free to?

"So do we like him now?"

"I don't know." Allie let out a groan. "Half the time I want to kill the guy, but then he goes and does things like this and . . ." She trailed off, unable to find words to express the myriad of conflicting emotions rocketing around.

"Have you kissed him?"

"No." Though only just. The thought filled her with shame. Married women didn't go around kissing other men. Even thinking about it—no matter how much of a sham marriage they might have.

"But you do like him."

Allie groaned again. "Yes."

"A lot?"

"Apparently so."

"As in, you want to see him again soon?"

"I see him every day." Allie pulled a piece of pizza toward her and picked off a slice of pepperoni. She *really* didn't need any more complications in her life. "Most importantly, I'm not free."

"Does Jackson know that?"

She shook her head. "I was about to tell him and then . . ."

"But then you look into his eyes, your knees buckle, and your little heart goes pitter-patter, and he makes everything seem okay, and you forget all of those things?"

Well, that and the fact the person sitting next to her had chosen that exact moment to knock on the door.

Allie sighed. "Something along those lines, pathetic though it may seem." Especially when he was looking at her with those heavy-lidded eyes.

"It's not pathetic. Derek put your heart in a blender and chopped it up into little bitty pieces and then he—"

"I know. I *was* there."

"Sorry. Anyway, for a start, it's no surprise you're emotionally vulnerable right now. The combination of Derek drop-kicking your self-esteem to the moon, then showing up for Grant's campaign, and an unexpected Veronica visit is quite a combination."

Since when did her usually blunt friend start talking like a shrink?

Allie cracked one eye open to make sure this wasn't a weird dream in which Kat had been replaced by Dr. Phil. As far as she was aware, Kat had never used the words *emotionally vulnerable* in a sentence. It was kind of scary.

"But, putting all that aside, you and Jackson have something real. Seriously. Everyone can see it."

"You're not hearing me, Kat. I can't have anything with anyone. Real or not—not until the court decision comes through and assuming it's in my favor."

Her friend pursed her lips. "You need to give your lawyers a rocket. What's it been—two years?"

"Next month."

"That's ridiculous. They're billing you for doing absolutely nothing."

"Derek and his lawyers keep delaying everything."

"Call them. Tell them to fight back. Hard. I bet you a squillion dollars they could have this sorted within weeks if you threatened to take your business elsewhere. Instead, you've probably got some little pimply intern sitting on your file charging you a couple of hundred bucks every time they write you a letter about another delay."

"You're probably right." She was. She'd call them in the morning; it was ridiculous.

"You know what else I think I'm right about?"

"What?"

"I think you like the delays. They give you something to hide behind because as long as you're still technically 'married,' you don't have to take a chance on another guy. You have an excuse not to grapple with putting your heart back out there."

Seriously? Kat thought she wanted to live in limbo? "You think I like this? You think I like being legally attached to a guy who cost me everything? I can't even touch my own bank accounts because he and his lawyers convinced some stupid judge I might pilfer the so-called marital assets."

"I'm not saying you like it, but I think you've grown used to it, even comfortable, and I definitely think it's less scary than the alternative." Kat reached forward and pulled the tub of mousse toward her. "The rest of your life is a long time to be afraid of getting hurt. At some point you're going to have to take a chance again, Allie. And sure, you might get hurt. But you also might find the love of your life."

"I'm pretty sure Jackson isn't the love of my life." He couldn't be. Who fell in love in two weeks? That only happened in cheesy Hollywood rom-coms.

"How sure? Sure enough to not tell him the truth in all its miserable glory? Sure enough to let him leave and not spend the rest of your life wondering if you missed out on something that could have been great? Tell him the truth. Tell him the scary, ugly truth, and let the chips fall where they will. Nothing good ever comes out of hiding stuff this big."

"I tried to tell him. You showed up!"

Her friend raised her perfectly plucked eyebrows at her. "What about all the other times you could've told him when I wasn't anywhere near you? Correct me if I'm wrong, but weren't you guys lost together, just the two of you, for like six hours?"

She was right. Again. It was like getting pummeled by Yoda. "I'll tell him. Tomorrow. I promise."

"Um, if I say something, do you promise not to get mad?"

"What?" What else could there possibly be?

"Have you ever thought maybe you're never truly going to get past this until you confront Derek?"

She felt her whole body flinch. Absolutely not. She was never going back there. Running away had worked fine so far.

Twenty-four

Jackson's senses were still spinning as he limped back into his hotel room. What was that? He leaned against the wall of his room to take some weight off his screaming ankle. He knew one thing it was: a world record for the number of almost-kisses in the space of fifteen minutes.

What was happening to him? The last couple of hours felt like they'd been lived by someone else. He wasn't even familiar with this guy who ordered half a pizza menu for a girl he wasn't even dating. It wasn't like he even needed his phone, and he could've managed overnight on the Advil in his travel bag and gotten the stronger stuff in the morning.

And then when she'd broken down—the vulnerability in her face had sucked him in like a black hole . . . The memory of how perfectly her body fit into his arms, molded into him, was enough to make him contemplate finding a glacial lake to jump into to cool down. Thank goodness Kat had shown up before he could get himself in some serious trouble. Every instinct told him kissing Allie would have been undoable. No going back.

He rested his head against the cool wall of the entranceway, trying to order his scrambled thoughts by inserting some logic into the equation. Everything that was rational and sensible was screaming at him there was only one way this crazy thing, whatever it was, could go. Total disaster.

From the moment he walked off the plane, Allie had thrown him off-balance. Nothing should have surprised him by now, and yet the day's revelations had him questioning everything he thought was important. The whole reason he was here seemed to be fading into insignificance.

He couldn't let that happen; too much was riding on his success. Not just for him—for his family and the people back home he needed to make good on his word that he would get their money back.

And yet, sitting in that burger joint, watching her take hit after hit from her mother, none of it seemed that important anymore. All he wanted to do was sweep her up in his arms and make her feel safe, protected. *Loved.*

The final word bounced around in his head, ricocheting like an emotional bullet. Sure, he believed in love theoretically. His parents had it. Nick and Beth too. He just never really thought of it applying to him. Not like that. Not in a way that meant he suddenly felt compelled to give up everything to pursue it.

He'd never said the *l*-word to anyone. Not even Nicole. He'd been determined he wasn't going to say something he wasn't sure of. His relationship with Nicole had initially been mutually beneficial and fun, and sure, there had been moments when he thought he might love her, but in a purely abstract kind of way.

The truth, if he cared to admit it, was that when she left he'd been angry, yes. Humiliated, yes. Betrayed, sure. Heartbroken, even. But that was over losing his business—not Nicole. The hole in his life when she left hadn't been nearly large enough for their relationship to be close to the real thing.

Hobbling over to the couch in his small living area, he threw down his crutch, collapsed onto its edge, and pried off his one shoe. The generic white hotel ceiling stared down at him. He tried to reconstruct his life around these overwhelming feelings by first imagining telling his uncle the truth. That he didn't care about Tolkien at all. That he'd only come because he wanted the financial support for BabyZen. He tried to imagine calling his parents and telling them he had given up on this new business idea because he'd met a great girl and was sorry if that meant they lost the farm.

And then what? She lived in New Zealand; he lived in America. What was he going to do? Marry her? The idea seemed so ridiculous he laughed out loud, until it started settling into the crevices of his soul—even reaching down and transforming into images of waking up beside her every morning. Of getting to fight with her for the rest of his life. Of cute, auburn-haired, green-eyed children— *Stop it, Gregory!*

He lurched up off the couch and started hopping toward the bathroom. A cold shower—that would be a good place to shock him back to his senses, which clearly he'd left behind in the paddock when he fell off that blasted horse. Of course. That was it. He'd taken another blow to the

head; the second in two weeks. An undiagnosed concussion was what was wrong with him.

His shoulders relaxed. That had to be it. He didn't have feelings for Allie—not real ones. He just had a few neurons that had gone AWOL on him, shaken loose in the fall. A shower and a good night's sleep would get them back in line.

Despite his best attempts, the sad excuses dropped away hollow. He didn't have a head injury. He was just flat-out crazy about the girl.

Limping into the bathroom, he opened the shower door and twisted the cold tap on full. Time for a dose of reality. Sure, he was attracted to her. Sure, he liked her a lot, but that was it. Nothing more, nothing less. Going to the other side of the world for a few weeks and finding "The One" wasn't reality. It was fantasy. In a few weeks' time, it would just be a memory. As long as he didn't step out of line and do something that would load him with even more regrets.

He let the door swing shut. Propping himself up against the bathroom sink, he stared at himself in the mirror. He looked haggard—evidence of the sleep he hadn't gotten since his fight with Allie.

He didn't want to be that guy he'd been with Nicole ever again. The one who squashed what he knew to be right in the name of convenience and pragmatism. He wanted the next girl he kissed to be more than something. He wanted her to be everything.

God, help me. The three words wound their way up from somewhere deep, quieting his troubled thoughts. He'd made such a mess of his life at this point, it would actually take divine inter-vention to make the crooked paths straight.

I was afraid of what it would mean. His uncle's words came back. That pretty much summed it up: he liked to be in control. He operated by logic, what he knew and could see. Relinquish control of the steering wheel? Even if he wanted to, he wouldn't know how.

You've spent the last decade in control and where has it gotten you? The question bounced around his head, its truth striking at him.

I do believe. Help me overcome my unbelief. The words echoed up through the decades. Ones from a Bible story that had made no sense to his eight-year-old self, but now captured him.

The sound of his phone ringing split the moment and jerked him back to reality. Beth's ringtone. Turning off the water, he grabbed his cell from his pocket. One day he'd tell her about how her little brother went to New Zealand and almost lost his mind. She'd love it.

"Hey, sis."

"Hey." Her voice was tense. "You somewhere you can talk?"

"I'm in my room. What's up?"

"Actually, it would be better if we Skype. Can you do that?"

"Sure. Just give me a couple of minutes to get set up."

Exiting the bathroom, he hopped back across the bedroom using the backs of furniture for support. He pulled his laptop out of his bag and hooked it up to the hotel's Wi-Fi.

They must have received the foreclosure notice. That had to be it. He looked at the date. May 12. Surely not. Andrew, the bank manager, had gone to school with his parents. He promised he'd give them until at least the end of May.

His hands roamed through his hair; there had to be a way to buy them some more time.

The familiar sound started trilling and he hit the button before it could squawk out more than a few notes. It took a few seconds for the video feed to flicker onto his screen but when it did, he saw four people scrunched into the screen. His sister and parents up front, with his brother-in-law in the back, the top of his head cut off by the edge of the screen.

Beth's eyes were red rimmed. His sister would be taking this hard. She loved the farm with every atom in her being—in a way he never understood.

"Surely we can convince them to give us more time." The words were out of his mouth before he even realized it. "I mean, the economy is bad, there are farms for sale all over the place. There's no way they'd get for it what they want. We'll convince them it's in their interests to hold off for now."

The faces on the other side of the screen registered a combination of confusion and understanding.

His father spoke first. "Son, this isn't about the farm."

"Then wh—"

His question was drowned by his sister bursting into sobs, then clasping her hands over her mouth.

"I'm afraid your mother has some bad news."

"Wh—"

Suddenly he knew without any of them saying anything. The big C. All of his grandparents had died of some form of it.

"No." He shook his head. "No. No." Like maybe if he said it enough, it wouldn't be true. The pizza churned in his stomach.

She was only in her late fifties and lived the epitome of a healthy life. She'd never smoked and rarely drank; she exercised and ate well. She wouldn't touch anything marked *diet,* adamant it wasn't "real" food.

"What kind?" Jackson forced himself to ask.

"Ovarian."

The same as his grandmother. "Can't they just . . ." His voice trailed off. It wasn't the kind of question a son ever wanted to ask his mom, but surely doctors could take them out? It wasn't like she needed them anymore.

Assuming they'd caught it before it had spread further, but even if it had, they had gold-plated health insurance. That was the one thing he hadn't failed them on. He sent them a check every year to pay for it; it would cover the best treatment there was.

"Has it spread? Where have they referred you to? Do you have a treatment plan yet?" The questions tumbled out of him. "I'll get online right away, do some research as to the best places. I'm sure I know some people who could make recommendations."

For a second the silence coming from the other end of the connection was so eerie he wondered if someone had accidentally hit MUTE.

"Hello?"

His mom shook her head. "We're sorry, Jackson. We're so sorry." Her voice shook.

"Sorry? For what?"

"There were some bills that needed to be paid and . . ." Her voice cracked and then broke.

"I don't understand."

His father, normally a man of few words, was now one of none. It was Beth who finally managed to pull herself together enough to talk.

"The last check for insurance you sent . . ." Then she broke too, but not before what she was trying to say started seeping in.

He looked at his parents. "You didn't pay it? You don't have health insurance?" He could barely force the words out.

"We . . ." His father looked away for a second and swallowed. When he turned back, his face appeared to have collapsed on itself. "We have some. We just downgraded."

"You *downgraded*." He repeated the word stupidly, still not able to absorb it. He had chosen that package specially—had it tailor-made even, back when he had an insurance broker to make sure the policy would cover not only this exact scenario, but all the others that had seemed most likely. An accident on the farm. Heart problems, which also ran in the family.

"Does it cover *anything*?"

His father's face seemed to collapse even more. "It did. But between all the tests and the specialist visits and everything else, it'll be maxed out soon."

"What do you need for treatment?" He couldn't even bring himself to ask what the so-called urgent bills were that might end up costing his mother her life. If it turned out the money had gone to call the vet or fix the ancient tractor again—when he'd tried to buy them a new one last year—he might lose his mind.

"We—"

"What will it cost for treatment?"

His father's face seemed to drop even lower. "Almost a hundred thousand. At least."

Maybe they could send her to India. Or some other second- or third-world country. He was sure he'd read an article somewhere about how cancer treatment was much cheaper in some places because the government wouldn't let the drugs be patented.

"Jackson, I'm not going to India. I want to be here, in my home, with my family. We've placed it in God's hands."

He hadn't even known he'd been speaking out loud until his mother's voice cut through his thoughts.

"Did you consult God before you decided to spend your health insurance money on something else?" His words came out demanding, harsh. He wanted to reach across the ether and pull them back. "I'm sorry, Mom."

"It's okay. You have every right to be angry."

He stared at the screen. His sister and brother-in-law were now partial figures in the background.

"When?"

His mom shook her head. "Jackson, it's okay. You can't—"

"When would you need it by?"

His father sighed. "The doctor said to have the best chance of success, she would need to start treatment within the next month."

"Okay, then."

This was his fault. If he'd done right by them, they never would have been put in the position where they felt they had to make the choice they had. His family would've had enough money to pay for the stupid vet bill, or electricity, or fertilizer, or whatever it was.

If he'd sent them even a quarter of the money he'd squandered on designer suits, buying a nice condo, and being seen at the right places to woo more investors, this wouldn't have happened. Instead he'd justified it all as an "investment" so he could eventually write one big check and cure all their financial woes, instead of just helping them keep their heads above the water.

He was going to fix it.

No matter what it took.

Twenty-five

Quiz night. The night on the tour when everyone's true colors inevitably revealed themselves. In Allie's experience, not even the most introverted and shyest of participants could hold back when their reputation as a true Tolkien aficionado was on the line.

The two teams sat around tables that had been set up in the private function room at the hotel, replete with after-dinner snacks and drinks. At the table to her left sat Team Frodo—Louis, Ethel, Sofia, and Elroy. To her right was Team Sam—Jackson, Mavis, Hans, and Esther. It was her policy to split up people traveling together as much as possible. In her experience, it only stoked the competition and made for a much more interesting night.

Of course, everyone was fully costumed for the event.

For her part, Allie wore the same Tauriel outfit she'd worn for wilderness day. It was her little slice of rebellion, since the true believers would hate it.

As a group, they'd spent the day on some more traditional Queenstown tourism activities. Everyone had taken to the Shotover Jet with gusto. Even though she must have done it fifty times, the childlike thrill of being ricocheted at high speed across the rushing water and the craggy canyons never dimmed. Though how Duchess Kate had managed the entire thing on the royal tour without so much as a hair getting out of place was beyond her. Then she'd taken Louis and his harem wine tasting and for a gondola ride while Kat took Elroy, Hans, and Sofia bungee jumping and skydiving with Esther tagging along to watch.

She tried to catch Jackson's eye. The poor guy had opted to spend the day in his room with his foot up and looked to be in a bit of a funk about it. She had spent the day trying to rid her mind of the memory of his arms around her and being cradled against his chest.

"All right, everyone, all phones and electronic devices in the box." She pointed to the container sitting beside her and watched while everyone walked up and deposited their various devices in the box—a policy instituted three months previous after a quiz night had turned into a brawl over accusations of cheating.

Stacking her question cards into a neat pile, Allie gave them a good shuffle in front of everyone, the unbending cardboard digging into her palms.

"So this is how it works: I'll ask a question. Questions have different point values, depending on difficulty. A team has fifteen seconds to agree to an answer. If a team gets it right, they get the points. If they get it wrong, it passes to the other team for a maximum of two attempts each. We alternate who gets the first attempt. First team to fifty points wins. Each person from the winning team gets to choose their prize from the memorabilia brochure on your table."

She'd deliberately split the wilderness winners, Louis and Esther, to make sure as many people in the group as possible had the chance to win something.

Elroy looked like he was about to start asking questions, so Allie hurried on.

"Before anyone asks, the questions and answers have been vetted by well-qualified Tolkien experts who all agree the answers are correct. Needless to say, where books and movies conflict, books always trump. Judge's decision is final, and no correspondence shall be entered into."

Louis raised his hand.

"Mr. Duff?"

"We were wondering if we could make this a true head-to-head?"

"In what sense?"

"Well, you still score to teams, but instead of the team answering it, we should go individual-to-individual. That way you can score both by team and individual so there could be not just a winning team, but also an individual champion. No extra prize, just pride."

Allie looked around the room. "What do you all think? Everyone would have to agree for it to happen."

Louis's table, where everyone had obviously already been prepped, let out an enthusiastic roar, while Team Sam paused to contemplate, Jackson's face losing color.

Hans spoke first, his heavily accented English filling the room. "I accept the challenge."

Esther spoke in Elvish. "I am confident in my abilities."

Allie fought the urge to roll her eyes. "One more rule—since some people in the room aren't fluent in Elvish, official answers in English only."

She looked at Mavis. Given that both sisters had spent most of the day simpering over Louis, she was pretty sure what her answer would be. Sure enough, she nodded. "While I don't claim to be the expert, it would certainly be interesting."

"Jackson?"

Jackson's face bore the look of someone who had shown up at a funeral, only to discover it was his own. Little beads of sweat glistened on his forehead, and he licked his lips. As if he had any choice now.

He looked at her with desperate eyes and she sent him a mental shrug. What did he want her to do to save him?

"Sure . . . why not . . ." His voice jittered.

Oh dear. It was going to be like watching an

unarmed man get sent into the Coliseum to take on the gladiators.

What was the name of the German blimp in the 1930s that had burst into flames and plunged to the ground? The *Hindenburg*, that was it. It was like Jackson was on his own personal version of that, watching the fire creep nearer and nearer, waiting for the moment when he went down in a ball of hot fury.

It was made a hundred times worse by the sympathy that folded Allie's face; she was the only other person who knew what was coming.

He steeled himself. He couldn't afford to let her affect him at all. In any way. Not when there was now so much more at stake.

At his table, Hans and Esther had both assumed what he took to be their competitive poses—hunched over with focused faces—while Mavis sat serenely. It wouldn't surprise him if one of the sisters blew them all out of the water. In his experience, it was always the quiet, unassuming ones who were the real threat to be reckoned with.

At least Allie structured the questions to start with the easier ones—maybe then he'd have a chance of at least getting a couple right before his pride, dignity, and chances of getting the money from his uncle went up in smoke.

The draw had Sofia against Mavis first, then

him facing Elroy, Louis battling Esther, and then Ethel against Hans. A question to each.

The fellowship, in their wisdom, had also decided competitors had to stand in front of Allie, so there was no chance of their team helping them.

"Okay, for an easy one point. Sofia, what does the 'J. R. R.' stand for in J—?"

"John Ronald Reuel." Sofia fired the answer out before Allie had even finished the question.

"Correct."

He let some breath leak from his chest. That wasn't so bad—even he could answer that one. A little light of hope found a spark.

No one from the other team so much as murmured approval as Allie scored a point next to Sofia's name on the board.

"Mavis. Where was J. R. R. Tolkien born?"

No hesitation from Mavis. "South Africa."

"Correct."

It sounded familiar. He might have gotten it.

Sofia and Mavis returned to their seats. His legs felt like logs as he stood and walked to face off against Elroy, who had a smug, all-knowing look on his face.

"Jackson, one point. What is the name of the region in which the Hobbits live?"

His brain stalled. Seconds ticked by. He had read this somewhere. He knew he had.

"You have got to be kidding me." Esther's weedy voice echoed from behind him.

"Five seconds, Jackson."

Elroy's face was a study in disbelief; he was clearly unable to fathom how Jackson hadn't already spat out the answer.

A word suddenly flashed before him on a page. He didn't have time to question it. "Eriador."

One side of Allie's mouth lifted in a half smile. "Correct."

"Elroy, one point. What is the name of the tower that holds the Eye of Sauron?"

"Barad-dûr."

He hobbled back to the table. One round down.

The rest of the round passed in a blur. Everyone else got everything right. No surprises there.

Two rounds later, he managed to pull another rabbit out of the hat and was now matched against his uncle. His team was down by two points after Hans had gotten the answer wrong to a question Jackson didn't even understand.

Allie looked at the question card and then at him, her eyes trying to tell him something, but he had no clue what. "Jackson, which female character did J. R. R. Tolkien introduce in *The Hobbit*?"

There was a rumble of discontent from the other table. "That can't be two points. That's a gift," someone muttered.

He knew this one, he knew he did. He looked at Allie's outfit and the name flashed into his mind. "Tauriel." He said it loudly, confidently. Not only had he not made an idiot of himself against his uncle, he'd get his team back in the game thanks to the feisty leader of the Woodland Elves.

Allie visibly winced as a chill settled across the room.

"That is incorrect. Louis?"

His uncle looked at him with pity. "It's a trick question. There are no female characters in *The Hobbit*, except a couple of passing references to Belladonna, Bilbo's mother."

"Correct."

No. What were the chances he'd be able to convince his uncle the painkillers had muddled his brain?

"We want to trade." Esther's voice rang out. "He's a fraud."

Tauriel. Of all the characters he could've chosen, it had to be her.

Fans had only just managed to reconcile themselves to Arwen's prominence in the films, and she at least had been a creation of Tolkien's, appearing in the appendices to *Lord of the Rings*.

Tauriel had been a hundred times more controversial. Not only because she was entirely invented by Peter Jackson and his writing team for the sake of the movies, but because the actress Evangeline Lilly said in an interview that people who knew Elvish had "too much time on their hands," which had gone down like a sack of cement with those who considered themselves true followers.

It was the look on his face that had almost undone her. For a second, he'd truly believed he had the answer and had managed to get his team back into the game. His whole face had been transformed.

Then the way it had crumpled when Louis had delivered the real answer . . . She'd have to have been heartless not to feel sorry for him, especially after little Miss Arwen added her jibes to his humiliation.

She looked down at her cards. After another three rounds in which the other team had pulled even farther ahead, Jackson stood in front of her again with Ethel, looking defeated before she even opened her mouth.

They were now into the three-pointers. The questions only people who had pored over the books and appendices would have a chance of being able to answer.

She looked at Ethel. The dark horse who had so far gotten everything right and was in the lead. Everyone else had gotten a question wrong at some point—even Sofia, the walking Tolkien thesaurus.

"Gandalf was revealed as a keeper of one of the three Elven rings. Who was it that gave him this ring?"

The woman didn't even pause to think. "Cirdan."

"Correct."

Allie flipped to the next card and looked at the question. *In what battle was Fingolfin killed?*

She pulled in a breath. Jackson wouldn't even know who Fingolfin was. Turning to him, she created a question and hoped he would remember their passing conversation. "What token was used by Gondor to signal urgent help was needed from allies?"

He looked at her. The seconds ticked over. He didn't remember. Then an odd expression passed over his face. "A red arrow?"

She blinked. He had. "Correct."

Behind him, his table erupted into cheers.

She made that question up just for him. He would've been suspicious anyway, but he knew it for sure because he caught a glimpse of the word *Fingol* on the card she was holding, which was neither in the question or the answer to the one she'd asked him.

His team had still lost, but he was okay with that. Winning would have felt too much like cheating, especially after his Tauriel debacle.

Across the room, Allie was chatting with Sofia, but her gaze would occasionally wander his way and a smile played upon her lips that made him want to kiss her senseless.

Which made the ankle and the crutches a blessing in disguise. It also made him feel like the world's biggest heel for what he was about to do, but having spent the day stuck in his hotel room, staring at the gorgeous view while pondering his options, he didn't see any other way.

This is what I have to do, right, God? His attempt at a prayer was clumsy. It had been a long time, but despite the news from home last night, he'd woken up in the morning with a disconcerting certainty he needed to at least give the faith thing a shot. It couldn't possibly make things any worse than he'd already managed on his own.

Finally wrapping up her chat, Sofia left the room and Jackson hobbled toward Allie.

She met him halfway.

"Hi."

"Hi."

"Thanks for the question." His palms were clammy. He was stalling, trying to delay what he knew he had to say.

She arched an eyebrow. "I have no idea what you're talking about."

Gosh, she was so beautiful. Her hair was done in some kind of elaborate side braid, which was all very nice, but it was the knowing smile on her lips and the mischievous gleam in her eye that undid him. She had the power to make him forget about Nicole, the farm, his mom's cancer, all of it.

Suddenly he realized he had been staring at her when it was his turn to speak. "About last night—"

"So, there's something—"

They both spoke at once, their words piling on top of each other.

Usually he would be all "ladies first" but not this time. If he didn't speak now, he might not say it at all.

Allie stopped talking and stood waiting for his direction. He shifted on his crutches. *God, please let there be another way.* He threw up one last urgent prayer. He'd been doing variations on it all day, but so far no divine intervention had shown up.

He sucked in his breath. *Do it, Gregory. Just get it over and done with. Like ripping off a Band-Aid.* "About last night. I um . . ." He wound his fingers around the plastic handles and gripped them tight.

Allie tucked a strand of stray hair behind her ear. "Jackson, there's something I need—"

"Allie, please, I kind of need to say this."

She stilled. "Okay. I'm listening."

He forced the lie out. "I think I may have given you the wrong impression last night."

She tilted her head. "How so?"

She wasn't going to make this easy, was she? "I, um, may have given you the impression last night I'm interested in you. As more than

341

friends." He fumbled the line worse than a kindergartner playing his first football game.

No kidding, dude. And what might have given her that impression? The fact you could barely keep your hands off her? Or that if Kat hadn't shown up, you would've kissed her and you both know it?

He waited for her to verbally tear him into bite-size strips, as she was so proficient at doing.

Instead she just looked at him, a collision of emotions playing across her face. "And you're not." It was a statement, not a question.

"No." He managed to choke the single syllable out. Barely—since every atom in his body was calling him out as the big fat liar he was.

"Okay."

Okay? That was it?

"That's it?"

Her brow furrowed. "Um, thanks for the clarification?"

Awkward silence.

"So, um, you had something you wanted to say?"

She shook her head. "Nope. Not now. Need any help with your stuff?"

He tried to search her expression for a hint of disappointment or hurt, but he got nothing. Either she had missed her true calling as a world champion poker player or he'd totally misread things and had never been out of the friend zone.

Given that he'd spent the entire day agonizing

over what to do, he should've been thrilled. Instead, as she flicked him a wave over her shoulder as she left the room, it felt like she'd taken his heart with her.

"He said what?" Kat almost spat out her apple juice.

" 'I may have, um, given you the impression I am, um, maybe interested in you as more than friends.' " So, she might have thrown in a couple of extra ums, but if she didn't try and make light of the conversation, she might cry.

Allie propped her moccasin-clad feet up on the coffee table, then realized she'd assumed the identical position she'd been in the night before when Jackson knocked on the door.

Twenty-four hours and another lifetime ago.

She'd worn the Tauriel outfit partly because she sensed he liked it. How pathetic was that? At least he'd barreled ahead and gone first before she could tell him about Derek. Because that wouldn't have been awkward at all. *Hey, so, just thought I should mention I'm married. That's nice, because I don't fancy you at all.* Ack.

Kat put her glass down, broke a line of chocolate off the block of Berry & Biscuit they'd torn open, then passed it to her. "I hope you were like, 'Dude, guys buy me out a pizza joint all the time. Why would I read anything into that?' "

Allie laughed for real this time.

Kat snapped off a square and popped it in her mouth. "Do you think he meant it? Sounds like his ex did a bit of a number on him. Maybe he just freaked out. I was there. He was not looking at you with just-friends eyes."

Allie snapped off a row for herself. "Well, whatever eyes he was or wasn't looking at me with last night, his vision has obviously cleared today. I can't believe I even rang the lawyers this morning."

"Good girl." Kat held her hand up for a high five. "What did they say?"

"Just that they were expecting a ruling any day now." They'd been saying that for months, but she'd decided to go glass half-full and give them the hotel's address just in case they were right this time. "Probably cost me two hundred bucks to open my file."

She popped the chocolate into her mouth. Left it on her tongue to dissolve into creamy soft goodness.

She should be feeling relieved. Problem solved. What had been starting to become very complicated was now uncomplicated.

It didn't matter if he meant it or not or what his reasons were. It never would have worked. For fifty thousand reasons.

So they'd shared a few moments. A bit of chemistry. She'd had that before and look where it had gotten her.

A box of tissues appeared under her nose. She pushed it away. "I'm fine. I'm good."

The tear trickling down her cheek betrayed her. She swiped it away and got angry. "What is this? I don't even know why I'm crying. I've known the guy for two weeks. Seriously, what is this?"

She looked across to see Kat grinning at her with chocolate-coated teeth.

"Why are you smiling?"

Kat tried, and failed, to wipe the smile off her face. "I'm sorry. I know I shouldn't be, but it's like you have 'ta-da, breakthrough' flashing above your head in big neon lights."

"Have you been drinking? Like, a lot?"

Kat reached over and grabbed her hands. "Allison Shire, you know I love you like crazy, but I have spent the last two years with a shadow of the Allie I know. It was like the day Julia walked into your class, you shoved real Allie somewhere deep down and put a lid on her. Do you realize I have never seen you cry over Derek? Not once. You find out your husband is already married and not a tear. So as far as I'm concerned, hallelujah, praise the Lord for Jackson Gregory. I may plant a big kiss on him when I see him tomorrow because that guy has finally managed to crack the freaking nuclear bomb–proof barricade you've been hiding behind."

Allie didn't dare tell her friend this was the second time in less than twenty-four hours the guy had reduced her to tears. For two opposite reasons.

"I cried over Derek." She had—the day Julia had showed up and shattered her world with the same ease a wave destroys a sandcastle. And then she'd packed her bags, changed the locks, called the lawyers, and hardened up. She was a Shire. And Shires didn't show weakness. Veronica had drilled that into her children since before they could walk.

Her best friend was right. She'd spent the last two years trying to ignore the hurt and pain. And all it had gotten her was feeling like she'd swallowed an entire weather system and was just waiting for it to unleash its fury.

Reaching over, she plucked a tissue from the box and tried to stem the river now cascading down her cheeks. She was afraid that now she had started crying, she'd never stop.

Twenty-six

Vudu Café was packed. The noise of the people crowded around tables bounced off the ceiling and walls. A long cabinet ran down the center of the restaurant, holding a range of food that made Jackson's mouth water just looking at it. He'd asked for the best place to get coffee in Queenstown and the hotel receptionist had not steered him wrong.

Jackson tried to navigate through the fast-moving throng on his crutches, scanning to figure out which line was for people ordering takeout and which for people waiting for a table. He could wait. It wasn't like he had anything else to do this morning, since the others were off visiting the last set of location sites, and they weren't crutches-friendly.

Maybe the bustle and some good food and coffee would distract his conscience from how he'd ignored Allie the day before. There didn't seem to be any middle ground with her. Either his heart was out there or it was barricaded behind a wall of seeming indifference. He was sure a shrink would have a field day with that one.

He was so sure he'd made the right decision, except everything in him screamed that it was wrong.

He blinked and there she was. At the table right in front of him. Sitting at a table for two. On her own. Her attention captured by the packet of sugar she was carefully stirring into her coffee.

Just as he was about to turn away, she looked up and saw him staring at her. A wary look crossed her face. Not that he could blame her.

"Hi." He spoke first. "What are you doing here?" It came out more accusation than question. *Great start, Jackson.*

She lifted an eyebrow. "Even tour guides are allowed the occasional day off." She looked at his crutches, then around the buzzing room. "Do you need a seat?" It was the kind of polite, halfhearted offering made with the expectation the other person would say no. He opened his mouth to fulfill his end of the unspoken deal, but what came out was, "Sure, thanks."

Jackson sat down, balancing his crutches against the table. Shrugging his jacket off, he hung it over the back of his chair.

What were the chances of them being in the same café at the same time? Maybe there was a bigger plan in play.

He looked down at the table. Picked up a packet of sugar and spun it between his fingers. "I'm sorry I've been a bit of a jerk the last couple of days."

He looked up to see her studying him over the rim of her coffee cup.

"I found out my mom has cancer. It's . . . advanced." He didn't know where the words came from. Hadn't known what he was going to say next, but that wasn't it. *Good one, Jackson, be that pathetic guy who plays the sympathy card.*

"I'm really sorry." Allie's fingers reached over and covered his and he found himself blinking back tears. What was wrong with him? He didn't cry. Ever.

He breathed deeply, forced back the betraying moisture. "I need this money. Like, really need this money. My parents, they downgraded their health insurance. And their plan won't even begin to cover what she needs for treatment." *And it was all my fault,* his conscience tacked on at the end.

"I can't afford any distractions. I have to do whatever it takes to convince my uncle to invest in this idea. If I don't . . ." His voice trailed off. He didn't even want to think about any other scenarios.

A smile played on her lips. "So I'm a distraction?"

He couldn't look away. Trying to deny his feelings any longer was futile, like trying to catch a hurricane with a butterfly net. "You're a bit more than that." It was like once the words started, he couldn't hold them back. "Allie, you undo me. When I'm around you, I forget about everything else. And it scares me more than anything ever has."

Her mouth parted. "It scares me too."

His blood thrummed in his ears as he saw in her eyes what he knew was reflected in his. Then a shadow crossed her face.

"Jackson, there's something I really need to—" Her words dropped over a verbal cliff as she stared at a blond, preppy-looking guy who'd appeared beside their table. "Derek?"

Derek? As in, the guy whose call he'd answered? The guy Allie's mom had given her a hard time about? Ex-boyfriend Derek?

As Allie gaped up at Derek, something in his gut told him reality was a whole lot more complicated than that.

The guy smiled, but it didn't come even close to reaching his gray eyes. "Hello, darling wife. Hope I'm not interrupting anything."

The words hit Jackson's ears like a whip. His *what?* Almost as if carried by the force of them, his head swung back to Allie. She was still staring at Derek, all color draining from her face. Her hand jerked, knocking her purse from the small table, change clanging against the floor as it fell and scattered around feet and under chairs. She didn't even look or seem to notice.

One look at Allie's wide, panicked eyes told him he hadn't misheard. She looked between the two of them. "Derek, what—Jackson, I—"

"Is it true? Are you married?" She couldn't be. It wasn't possible that, after everything, he'd gone and fallen for a married woman. Or that, in all their time together, Allie hadn't so much as given a hint she was someone's wife.

Her mouth tried to form words, but nothing came out for a few seconds. Her face was a hurricane of emotions. Finally, a defeated "I don't know," fell into the space between them.

He almost laughed. She didn't know? How could you not know if you were married or not? It was a pretty straightforward yes or no question.

"Well, if she doesn't know, I can tell you. Yes, she is."

His fist itched to punch the smug look off Preppy Guy's face. Feel the cartilage of his nose shatter the way Jackson's heart had. Instead, he forced himself to his feet, shoved his crutches under his arms, and stumbled across the café, pushing through the people crowding the counter in his haste to get to the door.

Fresh air. A deep breath. His fingers clutching the hard metal of the handles of his crutches. A cool wind against his bare arms. His coat was still inside. Abandoned on the back of his chair.

Then it was around him. Hands draped it around his shoulders. The hands of a woman with a *husband*.

"How could you? How could you do this to me?" The words falling to the cement pavement, laden down by their own weight. He didn't, couldn't, turn. He couldn't look at her.

She was worse than Nicole.

"I'm so sorry, I . . . Please let me try and explain. I was about to tell you."

Sure, she was. That's what all liars said when they were caught.

Her shoes now stood in front of him. Blue Skechers blocking his view of the cracked pavement.

"You're married." He directed his words to her feet.

"It's been in court for two years. It's complicated." She sounded like she was choking back tears.

"You're *married*." He looked up, staring over her left shoulder at the top of a nearby mountain.

"Jackson. I . . ." Her voice cracked with anguish, or maybe it was giving up after telling so many lies—he couldn't quite tell.

"Were you really ever going to tell me?" He clenched his fingers. "Did you get some kind of kick out of making a complete idiot out of me? Was this some sort of revenge for how things were at the beginning? Were you ever going to get around to saying, 'Oh, and by the way, Jackson, I kind of have this thing called a husband'?" He spat the words at her, his anger finally breaking through his numbness. He wanted to push her to say something—anything—to try and hurt her as much as he was.

"I'm sorry. I never meant—"

"To hurt me. Yeah, yeah, I know the script, Allie." It was the same lousy one he'd read on the note Nicole left him.

"Please, let me explain. Derek and I, we, he . . ." Their looks collided, hers pleading with his to give her a chance to explain. "Please don't hate me. I was going to tell you. I swear. I tried, but we kept getting interrupted."

Hate? He felt a lot of things. Betrayal. Confusion. Relief. Sadness. The anger that a few seconds ago had been choking him receded like a fast-changing tide. "I don't hate you. I just . . ." His teeth tugged at his bottom lip.

She studied his face for a second, as if looking for something. "I'm sorry. I . . ." She ran her fingers through her hair. "You're the last person who deserves this. Any of this. I'm never going to forgive myself."

He looked at her. The copper hair. The perfect eyebrows. The eyes that, a few minutes ago, he'd wanted to find himself in forever. *Nothing*. Whatever had once drawn him to her was gone. He set his face like marble. "Just go, Allie. Just take your lies and go back to your husband. I hope the poor guy knows what he's got in you." He couldn't stop the bitterness that imbued his final words.

Hurt flashed across her face, but she stepped

back. "I'm so sorry, Jackson. It isn't what you think, but you're right, I should have told you." And with that, she headed back to the café. Back to her husband.

She'd thought after she found out about Derek and Julia it wasn't possible for her heart to be more broken—turned out she was wrong, because she didn't remember anything hurting as much as the vise currently clamped around her entire being.

Maybe it was because this time she was the one causing the pain. Last time she'd been the victim; there was a certain amount of comfort that came with that.

She walked back into the café, the image of Jackson jumping up from the table as if he'd been struck with a flaming poker seared into her mind.

Where Jackson had been, Derek now sat. The guy who'd once captured her heart and then made a fool of her in front of everyone she loved, everyone who mattered. He was the reason she'd spent the last two years of her life living like a nomad instead of lecturing in the halls of academia.

She'd hoped never to have to see Derek again as long as they both should live. Lord knew she'd paid her lawyers enough to make it so. What on earth was he doing here?

Her eyes skittered over him. His sandy blond hair was a little longer than she remembered, touching the top of his collar; his body as lean as it had always been.

Derek looked up as she approached. "I'm sorry if that was awkward." His face held a hopeful, almost beseeching, expression. His eyes implored her to speak.

If he'd been anyone else, she would have fallen for it. But she'd fallen too far, been hurt too much, wavered before that expression too many times to ever be so stupid again.

She looked down at the table, seeing not her so-called husband but Jackson. His stricken expression morphing into incredulity when she said she didn't know if she was married. Not that she could blame him. It was an unbelievable thing not to know.

It was all her fault. Why hadn't she told him earlier? Found a way to slip "Oh, and by the way, I might be married" into a casual conversation? Or better yet, "So, funny thing, I got married to this one guy, but it turns out he already had a wife."

She pulled out a chair and slumped into it. "What are you doing here, Derek?" She didn't bother asking how he'd found her. It didn't matter. Not now.

"The courts have ruled my first marriage isn't valid." He lifted a shoulder. "Something about the paperwork not being filed correctly in Vegas. So you, my dear Allison, are still my wife."

She didn't even look at him. "I don't believe you." Her fingers gripped her seat. It couldn't be true. There was no way this had dragged on for two years—cost her thousands of dollars—only for that to be the answer.

He pulled some papers out of the pocket of his jacket. "You may not want to believe me, but you have to believe these."

She glanced down and saw the seal of the High Court. Not that that meant anything. Derek had proven himself to be capable of the most far-reaching of deceptions. She wouldn't be surprised to discover document forgery was another of his hidden talents.

"I'll believe it when my own lawyers tell me."

"Can you look at me?"

She turned, emotions threatening to overwhelm her as she looked her betrayer full in the face for the first time since she'd fled their home. Her home.

He leaned over and touched her hand. She snatched it away.

"I'm sorry. I know I hurt you more than I could even begin to imagine. But please, I'm desperate. I can't give up on us. Why do you think I've fought it so hard for the last two years?"

Well, that was a pretty easy one. M-O-N-E-Y. Namely, hers. An annulment would have left him with nothing. A divorce? Who knew what he'd gain from that. And that was before they even got to his questionable visa status, since it had been granted on the basis of their relationship.

He lifted his hand and grazed a finger across her cheek.

"Don't touch me." She spat the words out through gritted teeth, slapping his arm away.

They couldn't still be married. It wasn't possible. He was married—had been married—to someone else, the day she walked down the aisle. All naïve and innocent, thinking she'd met the love of her life when instead she'd fallen for the world's biggest con man.

She looked up to find tears in his eyes.

"I'm so sorry, Al."

"Don't call me that." He'd never called her that before. The only one who had was Jackson. She wasn't going to let Derek take that too.

Derek took a breath, as if trying to gather himself. "I'm so sorry for everything. I know I don't deserve one, but, now that the court stuff is done, I'm here to ask for another chance to make it up to you and prove I can be the man you thought I was."

Her whole body jolted, as if plugged into a live socket. *What?* This was not part of the plan! She was getting over this. Over him. Finally able to contemplate returning home, to her old life, without overwhelming humiliation making her want to find the biggest hole she could and bury herself in it.

Sure, she wasn't quite there yet, but she almost was. But the plan did not include *this*—him showing up here. Or the court finding in his favor.

Looking at him stirred dormant emotions, and memories came rushing back. Memories she had been trying to forget. Of how he'd been the first guy to make her feel like she was really seen, known, *loved*. How he'd proposed by creating a literary treasure hunt, leaving clues in books that she was using to write her thesis. Of finding love notes in the middle of piles of marking. Of how good things had been in her naïve ignorant world before it all came crashing down.

They swirled around inside her, crashing up against what she'd been feeling just a few minutes previous for another man. The guy she had imagined for all of thirty seconds she might have a future with, until the past came slithering through the door and wrapped itself around her neck.

Twenty-seven

Married. She was married. Jackson's head spun as his feet hobbled down the path back toward the hotel.

One crutch caught in a crack in the pavement, almost throwing him onto his face. Of all the times to not be able to make a quick getaway.

For a few seconds everything had been perfect. The freedom of finally opening himself up, taking a chance. The look on her face said he wasn't alone—only for it to all lie ruined around his feet, mocking him with the futility of it all.

His face burned. He had sworn he would never be that guy—the kind that got involved with a married woman. Some things were sacred.

With his ankle screaming, he sank onto a bench overlooking the picturesque lake, buried his head in his hands, and gulped in mouthfuls of cool air. How could he have been so stupid? He had cast all reason, logic, aside—beguiled by her openness and seeming honesty.

Clearly, from the way her face collapsed and the tension between the two of them, there was more to the story than he was privy to, but married? She couldn't have found a way to drop that into conversation? When he'd told her about Nicole would have been a good start. A simple

"Ironic that I'm married and in a big court fight with my husband."

He sucked in a shuddering breath. It was okay. He was used to betrayal. It wasn't even like this was a big one in the scheme of things. He'd known her less than three weeks. It wasn't a big deal. In a couple of days he'd be back on a plane to America, leaving her and her drama behind.

It just proved his gut instinct to keep his distance from her had been right all along. In fact, everything would be fine right now if he hadn't walked into that coffee shop and been struck by thirty seconds of temporary insanity. What had even possessed him to do that?

It wasn't like it was ever going to work. They were from two completely different places, living completely different lives. What kind of idiots thought they had fallen in love after less than a month anyway? People on reality shows was who. And look how that usually worked out.

Yes, he'd been attracted to her. Yes, he'd liked her a lot. But it wasn't the end of the world. If anything, it was further proof of what he'd known when he walked off the plane into this stupid country: the only person he could trust was himself.

In the whirlwind of all this insanity, he'd allowed himself to forget that for a few days. At least he'd found out the truth before he was really invested.

His head kept saying all the right platitudes, but his heart was thundering like it wasn't getting enough blood.

There were only two days left on the tour. All he had to do was keep his distance. It would take a miracle, but he was desperate enough to ask for one.

God, help.

They were the only two words he managed to offer up before he felt Allie settle beside him, her distinctive perfume wafting on the morning breeze. He shifted away—as far as he could get without falling off the bench.

"Will you at least let me explain?" Her words were soft, so quiet he barely caught them, even though she was only inches away.

He looked up into her pained profile that stared straight across the mountain vista. She had also positioned herself between him and his crutches, so it wasn't like he could get up and walk away.

He shrugged his shoulders. "It's not like I can stop you."

It was the flat disinterest in his tone that cut deeper than anything else. If he'd at least been angry, she would have known it mattered, but it was like he'd closed down every human emotion and was about as human as Michelangelo's David.

Curling her fingers around the cool seat of the

stone bench, she tried to think. Where to start? What to say?

Obviously anything between them had been shattered, but Jackson at least deserved to know the truth: that she hadn't been playing with him, that what was between them was . . . well, as real as it could have been.

She closed her eyes for a second, gathering her composure to tell the story she hadn't told anyone outside of her lawyer. And that was only because she had to. She kept hoping that if she didn't think or talk about it, she could escape the stranglehold of humiliation that engulfed her.

"I met Derek in my final term at Cambridge. At a petrol station of all places." In the middle of writing almost 24/7 to finish up her thesis, it was one of the few places she'd ever gone. He was using the fuel pump on the other side of hers.

It had been the definition of a whirlwind romance, given a helping shove by her own insecurities. She was boring, academic Allison. She never had guys falling over themselves finding her attractive or interesting. So when, suddenly, dashing Derek appeared on the scene, she'd fallen as easily for his charms and perfect salesman pitch as Pooh Bear for honey.

"We got engaged fast. Faster than a lot of people thought was wise. But I was in love. Or thought I was." Before she'd known it, there had been a rock on her finger. Turned out it was fake, which her sister would have picked up on in a split second flat. But no—naïve, gullible Allison had fallen for that as well. Along with the fiction of how it had been his mother's, who with her dying breath had made him swear he would save it for his one true love.

She couldn't believe she'd fallen for it all. His whole story had basically mashed together the tragic components of twenty romance novels. It made her sick just thinking about it.

Not for one second had it ever crossed her mind that he knew exactly who she was. That she was the target of Derek's perfectly executed campaign to both get out of the UK and set himself up for life. That her so-called soul mate had a gambling problem and was neck-deep in debt with the kind of guys who didn't send letters requesting payment for debts, but rather broke legs.

She'd returned home with the PhD, a fiancé, and a great lecturing job lined up at the University of Auckland. She refused to listen to her parents and their reservations about a short engagement, or to her own conscience giving her grief about marrying a man who didn't share her faith. She'd just plowed on ahead with destroying her life.

"My family has money; it turns out he knew that. He knew before we'd even met who I was. I was just a pawn in his plans to set himself up for life and get a New Zealand visa." Derek denied it—or, more accurately, his lawyers did, but they weren't the ones left paying off the thousands of dollars he'd put on her credit card without her knowledge or trying to explain the tens of thousands that had just disappeared out of her accounts.

"Three months after we were married, I was giving a lecture. A woman showed up, Julia. Claimed she was Derek's wife. She said they'd gotten married in Vegas a few years before." She chanced a look sideways. Jackson sat, face set like a mask, no indication he'd heard a single thing she'd said save for a slight twitch in his aw.

"I've spent the last two years in court fighting for an annulment. Derek told me they've ruled and I've lost. I'm so sorry. I have no excuse. I should have told you when things . . ." She trailed off. She had no idea how to finish the sentence. So she stopped talking and waited for him to say something, anything.

Silence for a few seconds, then Jackson shifted on the seat. "Okay, I let you explain. Now may I have my crutches please?"

Lifting them up, she handed them to him. He used them to push himself up to his feet then put them under his shoulders.

He looked down at her, face written with so much hurt it could fill a novel. "I trusted you. After everything, I trusted *you*. You knew about Nicole, all of it. And you still didn't tell me."

"I'm so sorry." She could say those words for eternity and it wouldn't be enough. And they both knew it.

He leaned heavily on his crutches, weighed down by her deception. "It's a bit late for sorry. I just can't do this. Whatever it is. Whatever you're asking of me."

His words cut through her like lava through a mountainside, stripping her of her ability to speak. All she could do was nod.

Twenty-eight

Allie looked at the papers spread across the table. They'd been waiting for her when she walked back into the hotel. It was true: Derek was telling the truth. She was married. To him.

She'd spent the whole afternoon staring at the thin pile. Reading and rereading the ruling. Praying the words would somehow miraculously change to *We find in favor of the plaintiff.* But no—they remained what they'd been the first time she'd read them. *In favor of the defendant.*

She'd even put in a call to the lawyers just to make certain it wasn't a terrible mistake, only to find out the partner whose name was at the bottom of the page had keeled over from a heart attack that very same day and the office was closed for his funeral!

She looked at the date for the thousandth time. The court's decision had come out the day she'd last rung the lawyers, the morning after Pizzagate. If she'd called a few hours later, it would've been waiting for her.

The irony of her life knew no bounds.

"I don't understand." Kat sat next to her, reading through the papers. "How can they find in his favor?"

"A technicality. Something about the papers not being filed correctly in Vegas."

"And that took two years for them to work out?"

"And thousands of dollars."

"What are you going to do?"

Allie pressed her hands against her temples. "What can I do?"

Kat studied her face. "You aren't seriously thinking about going back to him."

"I said vows, Kat. In front of two hundred people. In front of *God*. I meant them. If the court has decided I'm married to him, I have to at least give it a try. Maybe he's changed." Even to her own ears, the last sentence sounded like she was trying to convince herself. So it was no surprise when Kat snorted.

"You never liked him."

Her friend ran her fingers through her hair.

"I never thought he was good enough for you, Allie, that's true. He was too smooth, too polished. What about Jackson?"

Just the sound of his name made her want to curl in on herself. "Jackson wants nothing to do with me. Not that I blame him."

"Yeah, well, bit of a shock to find out the girl you've fallen in love with is already married, I'd imagine."

"He's not in love with me." She couldn't let herself go there. It was bad enough trying to deal with knowing he'd had feelings for her. *Had* being the key word.

"If it makes it easier for you to believe that, go for it, but the guy looks at you like you hung the stars in the sky."

She couldn't even think about that. Thank goodness nothing had happened between them. Well, nothing physical. The way her heart felt like it was being pummeled and repeatedly rolled through a pasta machine made it clear the same couldn't be said in other ways.

She rolled her fingertips over her temples, trying to work away the building headache. "For better or worse, for richer or poorer—that's what I vowed. I have to at least try to believe we've gone through the worst."

Her phone vibrated on the table. What now? An international number flashed on her screen. Her stomach contorted. In all the madness of the last couple of days, she'd totally forgotten she put in a call to Dr. Everett with a couple of questions about the job opportunity—not that his answers mattered anymore. She couldn't leave New Zealand before sorting out this marriage mess, one way or the other. And that was going to take a whole lot longer than Dr. Everett had.

She couldn't believe it. After spending the last year applying for every vacancy in academia for which she was vaguely qualified and getting nowhere, she was giving up a chance at her dream job.

Picking up the phone, she took a breath and answered the call. "Allie speaking."

"Dr. Shire, Dr. Everett here. I have the answers to your questions about the position." The British accent was as clear as if it had been coming from across the room, rather than the other side of the world.

Might as well confront this head-on. Get it over and done with before she could overthink it. "Dr. Everett. Thank you for returning my call. I'm so sorry but I've just had a family situation unexpectedly come up. I'm not sure how long I'm going to be tied up with it and I would hate to waste your time. So unfortunately, I don't think it's going to work to apply for the position. Thank you for thinking of me, though. I really appreciate it."

Kat had stopped reading the papers and was staring at her.

"I'm disappointed to hear that, Dr. Shire. Would you like me to keep your CV on file if anything arises in the future?"

Her throat closed for a second. First Jackson and now this? She was sacrificing so much for a marriage she didn't even want to a man she didn't even love. "Yes. Please. Thank you, sir."

"You're welcome." He cleared his throat. "I hope your family situation resolves itself."

Not half as much as she did. "Thank you."

Ending the call, she leaned back and closed her eyes.

"What was that about?"

The only person she'd told about the job was Jackson, foolishly hoping he would be the one giving her a reason not to take it. "A possible lecturing job at Oxford."

"And you turned it down."

"You can't turn down what you haven't been offered. I was just asked if I was interested in applying. I probably wouldn't have gotten it anyway." Better to assume that and not even allow herself to think about what might have been.

Kat muttered something under her breath.

Allie opened her eyes and looked at her friend. "What was that?"

"If Derek hasn't changed, I'm going to kill him."

Allie tossed her phone back onto the table. "You won't have the chance, because if Derek hasn't changed, *I'm* going to kill him."

Kat tapped the papers with her nails. "I still can't believe it."

"Can you manage the last couple of days?" She'd already told Derek to book her a ticket on the last flight to Auckland. At least that way if she couldn't make it, it would cost him something for once.

"You mean you're going to go tonight?"

"I can't stay here. I'll tell the head office there's been a family emergency." She couldn't face Jackson and see the hurt and betrayal flashing across his face. Didn't trust herself with what she might say—or do—if she saw him again. It was better that she just leave.

She'd have to go without saying good-bye to everyone on the tour—that would be tough. She'd never had to abandon a tour before. She felt like a mother hen abandoning her chicks.

"Are you sure this is what you want to do?"

"It's what I have to do." What she *wanted* to do was find Jackson and tell him she'd fallen for him. Ask him to forgive her. Beg him to give what they had a chance. Serve Derek with divorce papers, offer him whatever he wanted to not fight it.

"Why? Why is this what you have to do? You don't owe him anything. Not another chance. Not a single solitary thing."

"Shires don't get divorced, okay?" The words burst out of her and hit the room. "My parents have the most miserable marriage known to man built on that one principle. So I have to try. I know my family isn't exactly the Brady Bunch, but they're all I have. I can't face them if I don't give my marriage a chance."

Kat curled both hands around her shoulders. "Is that what this is about? Not besmirching the family name?"

"She doesn't try, Kat. My mother has never tried. My whole life I have never seen her make any effort to make it work with my dad. I have to be better than that. The court says I'm married to Derek, so I'm going to be different and at least give it my best, even if it makes no sense to anyone. Even if it's the last thing I want to do. I need to try—for me, even if it all ends badly, so I can look myself in the mirror and know I gave it a shot. So I can at least try and clean my slate with God and make this right somehow."

Kat bit her lip. "Allie, God doesn't want your clean slate. He just wants you."

No one had ever wanted just her. Allie bit her bottom lip. She had nothing left to say. No other words to explain the compulsion to open the door of her life, her heart, back to Derek.

Allie could see the fight go out of Kat's eyes. "Okay. I'll be praying for you."

There was a knock on the door. "That'll be him." Her husband. She couldn't even think the words without feeling like she was going to suffocate. *God, help me.*

Kat stood. "I'm going to go to my room— otherwise I might slug him."

"I'll come say good-bye. I'm almost packed." She'd call Susannah from the airport. She hoped they didn't already have a houseguest residing in the spare room.

Another thing to add to her to-do list: contact

the property manager and find out who was living in her house and when their lease was up. Allie and her sister hadn't shared a roof for more than a few nights in over a decade; it was probably best if they kept it that way.

If there wasn't any room at her sister's, she'd book herself into something nice and fancy until she knew what the situation was with her house. Maybe the Hilton. Now that the court ruling was out, the freeze on her assets would be lifted, so she might as well spend some of it before Derek did.

Stop it. If this thing was going to have a chance, she couldn't think like that.

"You don't have to do this." Kat broke her chain of thought by putting a hand on her friend's shoulder, as if knowing a hug would break her.

Allie pinched the bridge of her nose. No tears— especially not in front of Derek. "Except I do."

Twenty-nine

Jackson limped into his hotel room. He was testing out his ankle without crutches, since he had to return them to the hospital the following morning.

At least the shards of pain spiraling up his foot kept him distracted from the epic disaster his life had become. He hadn't even thought that was possible when he'd agreed to come to this blasted country—turned out he was wrong! Like he'd been about everything recently.

The whole day was a blur. He'd gone down to breakfast, steeled himself to see Allie and feel nothing, only for Kat to tell the group that Allie had a family emergency and wouldn't be back. He hadn't missed the sympathetic glance Kat sent his way.

He'd then spent half the day trying to dodge writing in the card one of the twins had rustled up for the group to send to Allie. He'd failed, but had managed to get away with just scrawling his indecipherable signature.

The rest of the day was spent avoiding his uncle, who gave him knowing eyes every time he looked his way.

Thankfully, his ankle provided the perfect

cover to miss a few activities and sit around and stew in his own septic funk instead.

He couldn't believe she was gone. Just like that.

He didn't even bother trying to convince himself he was fine about it—not when his entire being felt like it had been swallowed by a black hole.

Married. How could she be *married?* It was like the punch line to a really bad joke.

Hopping into the bathroom, he popped a couple of the codeine pills he'd been prescribed and washed them down with a glass of water.

He checked his watch. Right on time to talk to Beth. Hopping back into the main room, he flopped onto the queen-size bed and opened his laptop.

Sucking in a breath, he tried to find some sort of equilibrium. *Time to get some perspective, Jackson.* What his parents were dealing with was way worse than anything he was going through.

He opened up his Skype screen and checked to see if his sister was already online. Her icon flashed green on his screen, so he hit the VIDEO CALL button. It only got out a split second of the calling tone before the little *schwoop* sounded. However, instead of his sister's face, his parents appeared.

They looked . . . relaxed? He rubbed his eyes and maximized the screen. No, he hadn't been mistaken; some of the stress shadowing their faces the last time they'd talked was gone.

Something lifted inside him—maybe they'd had some good news from the doctor and things weren't as bad as they'd first thought.

"Hi, Mom. Dad."

"We've sold the farm!"

He blinked. Tried to process what they'd said. No hello, nothing. "What do you mean you've sold the farm?"

His dad wrapped an arm around his mom's shoulder and gave it a squeeze. "Well, we don't have the cash yet. We settle next week, but it's all locked in."

"I don't understand."

His mom smiled. A real genuine grin. "We got a good offer. A more than generous offer. Enough that we can buy a smaller place a bit closer to town with enough money left over to fund most of my treatments."

Had the entire world gone mad? "But the farm's been in our family for five generations. You've put everything into that land."

His dad leaned forward, his nose and lips taking up the screen. "You're right, son, but not everything is meant to last forever, Jackson. We've loved our life here, but things change. Nick and Beth have their own place to look after and you don't want to be a farmer. I'm sixty years old. It's time to let it go."

He wished he could rebut his father, but his dad was right. There was not a single atom of Jackson that wanted to be a farmer. Not even to keep the farm his great-great-great-grandfather had won in a poker game in the family.

"Your mom's illness has been a blessing."

Jackson blinked, unwilling to accept what he'd heard. Stage-three cancer a blessing?

Another shoulder squeeze. "Not knowing how much time she may have left has made us prioritize the important things in life. Spending time together, enjoying Lacey, Dylan, and Baby Bean. We want to travel and spread our wings a little. We may even come and visit you."

"But I was going to get you the money . . . I was going to find a way . . ." His words trailed off. He couldn't promise that. The odds were at least fifty-fifty Louis wouldn't invest in him. And if that happened, he had nowhere left to turn.

His father leaned forward. "Son, I need you to listen to me. We appreciate everything you've done for us. We truly do. But we never asked you to rescue us, Jackson. That's not your job. Never has been. Never will be. I'm not sure how you got the idea this was your burden to bear."

Because he'd left. Because he was a disappointment. Because he figured if he didn't want to be a farmer, he at least had to redeem himself in other ways.

"At the end of the day, Jackson, it's only dirt. Lots of dirt. Has it been in our family a long time? Sure. Will I miss it? Of course I will, but it's not everything. I'm a husband first, then a father, then a grandfather. Those God-given roles are way more important and mean far more in eternity than the ground I till."

"Are you sure this is what you want?" He didn't even know why he asked the question. It wasn't like he could conjure up a better solution out of thin air.

"It's an answer to prayer." His mother's gray bob bounced as she nodded. "More than. We prayed that if God wanted us to sell, He would send a buyer to offer at least enough for us to pay off our debts and buy a new place. What He's provided is one who is paying far, far more."

Jackson studied his parents' faces. They were both terrible liars and there was no sign they were trying to put on a brave face for his sake. No, they looked genuinely happy. Relaxed, even.

"Well, then, that's great. I'm glad it's all worked out." It was the best he could manage in his still shell-shocked state. "When will you be moving?"

"Even though we settle next week, the new owner isn't in a hurry to take over. His lawyer said he's happy for us to stay until we've found a new place if we still run the day-to-day operations.

He'll take over paying the staff, utilities, everything."

It all sounded too good to be true. Well, as good as it got in the circumstances. But if there was anyone who deserved to be the beneficiaries of such good luck, it was his parents.

"That's great." What was he killing himself for? The farm was gone, his parents didn't need money for his mom's treatment. The idea of getting his investors their money back no longer drove him mad like it had before. What was the whole point of this? Allie was gone. It was all for nothing.

He realized he couldn't even remember when he'd last thought about Richard and Nicole. Or the anticipated thrill of building up a new business out of the ashes. He didn't miss his old life in L.A. a single bit.

He didn't even care about getting back into business; it was just a means to an end. An end that no longer existed.

What was he going to do now?

Thirty

Jackson dropped their two carry-on bags beside some spare armchairs in the airport lounge. The lone perk of traveling with someone who had a seat at the front of the plane while he had seat 56J to look forward to. Maybe thirteen hours with his knees up to his nose would distract him from the feeling of his heart being ripped out of his chest and fed through a shredder.

Slumping in his seat, he tried to untangle his thoughts. Three weeks ago he'd been in this very airport, willing to go to almost any lengths to convince Louis to fund his next venture. Now, he wasn't sure he wanted it.

The only thing monopolizing his thoughts—his every breath—was that he'd somehow managed to fall for a married woman. And he had no idea how he was going to get over her.

He looked up to see his uncle beside him, a cup of coffee and a cookie balanced in his hand. "Let me get that for you." He took the cup and saucer and placed them down on the table between their seats.

"Thanks." His uncle lowered himself into the opposite armchair, propping his cane up against the arm. The man was incapable of masking the smile that kept taking over his face. Jackson was guessing it had everything to do with the sneaky kiss he'd caught the guy planting on Mavis before they left their hotel in Queenstown. The tour had produced a full-blown octogenarian romance. Who would've guessed that was in the cards three weeks ago?

"You okay?" Even though he tried to arrange his face into something bordering on serious, his great-uncle's lips twitched.

Jackson sighed. He needed to tell his uncle the truth and let the chips fall where they may. He didn't even know what Louis had decided, but he didn't want it on his conscience that he'd initially taken this trip under false pretenses. "I need to tell you something."

"Shoot."

"I haven't been honest with you."

His uncle leaned back against the plush leather and steepled his hands. "I'm listening."

"I'm not a Tolkien fan. I never have been. Before the flight over here, I'd only seen one of the movies. I haven't read any of his books. I don't know an orc from another bad guy. They all pretty much look the same."

His uncle didn't even blink. "I know. I've known all along."

"I'm sorry?"

"I was pretty sure before we even left, but I was certain in Wellington when I threw you for a loop with Gollum."

"I don't understand."

"I probably owe you an apology. The truth is, I didn't even really need an assistant. But I'd been asking the Lord for a chance to spend some time with family, and then you showed up. I figured it might be a bit weird, a great-uncle you didn't know from Adam asking you to go on vacation with him, and my assistant did happen to quit, though he wasn't coming on this trip. It was the best I could think of, so I went with it."

Jackson tried to think of something to say, but nothing came.

Louis picked up his cookie, broke it in half, and put one piece back on his saucer. "I did think about putting you out of your misery a few times, but it was too much fun watching you try and maintain the facade."

Jackson's mind finally started processing the information, his mouth working again. "I don't understand."

"I told you this was all about your character. You not being a Tolkien fan was even better as far as I was concerned. I figured plenty of opportunities for you to show your true character would present themselves."

Jackson rubbed his forehead. "Like how?"

"You told George to redistribute your share of the proceeds to other investors. That shows integrity."

Jackson's mouth almost hit the floor. "How did you know that?"

His uncle took a bite of his cookie, chewed a couple of times. "I'm a very well-connected man. You were prepared to put Allie's safety over completing the wilderness challenge. That shows you don't get so set on the goal you lose sight of what's really important. And you just told me the truth when you didn't know if it would affect my decision to invest in you. That makes you a man of principle."

Jackson shrugged. "But does it? The main reason I wanted the money was to help my parents out with the farm, but my mom's sick and they've sold it."

"I know."

Was there anything he didn't know?

Louis tipped some sugar into his coffee and gave it a stir. "I bought it."

Jackson stared at him. "You bought our farm."

Louis gave a slow nod. "It's been in your family for five generations. Couldn't let it go to any Joe off the street. Especially with the market at the moment—they wouldn't have been able to get close to what it's worth."

"What are you going to do with it?"

His uncle shrugged. "Honestly, I hadn't really thought much about it. That's the joy of getting to be this old and having as much money as I do. Sometimes you get to do something because you want to and think about how it will work later. I'll probably hire in a manager to run it in the short term and keep on whoever your parents had as help and go from there. I've asked my guy on the ground to ask your father for any recommendations."

"Okay." He didn't know what else to say. It was all too much.

"I'm sorry about your mom, by the way."

"Thanks."

"Is that what's been hanging over you the last few days, her diagnosis?"

"Yes. No. That was part of it."

"And the other part?"

"Allie's married."

Louis picked up his cup. "Actually, she's not."

Jackson stared at his uncle, barely able to hear above the sound of his own pulse drumming in his ears. This conversation had just gone from the surreal to the impossible. He was tempted to slap himself to make sure he wasn't dreaming. "But I met her husband. She told me herself."

Louis took a sip of his coffee, acting like he hadn't dropped the verbal equivalent of the bomb that leveled Hiroshima. "You may have met Derek, but he's not her husband. The court found in her favor and annulled the marriage. He's still married to the girl he shacked up with in Vegas in a haze of bourbon and stupidity."

Jackson's body thrummed with pent-up incredulity. Was this how someone felt before they spontaneously combusted? "But he told her the court had ruled against her and upheld their marriage."

"Yup, he's a slippery character. Never underestimate the lows to which desperate people will stoop. His visa is due for renewal and I understand immigration have been asking a few pointed questions about his relationship status. Plus he's about as broke as you are. Not to mention, he has a few not-so-nice friends back in the UK who still hold a few grudges about some debts he took a while to pay."

Jackson was on his feet. "I need to go find her. Tell her."

"Jackson." His uncle leaned forward, laid a hand on his arm. "She's a smart girl. She'll figure it out. God has a way of making sure the truth always come to light."

"But—" Jackson couldn't say it. The thought of her around that sleazeball, thinking she was married to him, made him want to put his fist through a wall.

It's okay. I've got it. The words came out of nowhere, wrapping around his fledgling faith. The peace that encompassed him made no sense, but nothing did right now.

He forced himself to sit back down, but he couldn't stop one leg from bouncing like it was on a pogo stick.

"So here's what we're going to do." His uncle pulled something out of his inner coat pocket and opened it. A checkbook.

He started scribbling. "This"—he held up a check for two hundred grand—"should be enough to get the Mortans, Slatts, and Wades back up to about two-thirds of what they invested in your company. But I'm giving it to you on one condition—that after this, you're done. You consider their debts repaid."

Jackson stared at the seven loopy zeroes on the rectangular piece of paper.

"But it was their college and retirement funds. They need all of it back."

"It was, which they *chose* to invest. I'm sure you were a great salesman, don't get me wrong. But you didn't cheat them out of it, you didn't con them out of it, you didn't take advantage of them. They chose to give you that money. And they knew there would be an element of risk. I'm sure they are nice people, but they also got greedy and shouldn't have invested what they couldn't afford to lose." His uncle placed the piece of paper between them. "Agreed?"

Jackson picked up the check. Stared at it. He couldn't guarantee he'd ever be able to match it, let alone give them more, especially now that he had more important matters to consider. "Agreed."

His uncle tapped his pen on his checkbook.

"Here's the deal, Jackson. I don't know anything about apps, but you passed all the character requirements I have, so I'm happy to keep my end of the deal and invest in your next venture. But first, I have just one question for you."

"Okay."

"Is this what you really want to do?"

Jackson studied the glass top of the coffee table trying to really think over the commotion going on in his heart and head.

Was this what he really wanted to do? There was no looming foreclosure on the farm for him to worry about. The investors he cared about were getting most of their money back. He had nothing holding him to L.A. All of his worldly belongings he could pack into a couple of suitcases and a few boxes. Did he really want to start a business again from scratch right now? He knew what it felt like to have money; it hadn't made him happy. He'd found what made him happy. And she couldn't be bought.

He shook his head. "No. I don't think it is." As he said the words aloud, he knew they were true. He didn't care about getting revenge on Richard and Nicole or rubbing their faces in his next success. He couldn't care less if he never owned a nice condo or drove a flashy sports car again.

"Do you know what you want?"

"Allie." She wasn't married. He was still

having trouble processing the concept. He wasn't convinced he shouldn't walk out of this airport and find her right now and tell her. It would be a lot easier if he hadn't deleted her number off his phone in a fit of fury.

His uncle smiled. "Well, I can't help you with that one, son. Want my advice though?"

"Sure." Why not? The man clearly knew everything.

"Once she finds out about Derek, she's going to need a bit of time to find her footing again and work things out for herself. Rushing in there like a knight on a charger will probably not go so well. So be patient. Trust God. If it's meant to be, He'll give you a good kick when it's time to make a move."

Jackson blew out a breath. He wasn't good at being patient. If he had a clue where she was, he probably wouldn't still be sitting here. "I'll try. But what . . ." He trailed off, unable to finish the sentence. The horrible possibilities were too numerous to contemplate.

"Don't worry. I'm keeping an eye on it. Allie's already been burned once, so she has her eyes wide open. If need be, I've got people on my payroll who can give things a little hurry along so she finds out sooner rather than later."

Jackson stared at the old guy, with his innocent face and twinkling eyes. Was he actually Gandalf? It was either that or else he was really high up in the mafia with his "people" and information flows.

He decided it was better not to ask. Just in case "a little hurry along" involved Derek, concrete boots, and some deep water, all of which sounded like an excellent idea right now. "Why do you care so much about us?"

His uncle leaned back in his seat. "Jackson, I would do it even if you hadn't gone and fallen for her. I like Allison a lot. Which makes it important to me that she finds out the truth. And, like I've said before, when you're an old man with a lot of money, one of life's luxuries is that you can indulge whims that might not make a lot of sense." His uncle picked up his cup and took a sip of his coffee. "What about everything else? Do you know what you want to do next with your life? Besides spend it with a certain redhead?"

Jackson contemplated for a second the idea that had been knocking about for months, but that he'd written off as being impossible. But since he'd heard about his parents selling the farm, it had gotten louder, more insistent. "Yes, I think I do."

Thirty-one

She had forgotten something. What could it be? Allie scanned the groceries she'd placed on Susannah's kitchen counter one more time, trying to calm the nagging feeling she'd missed a vital ingredient somewhere along the way.

It had been an okay day. It was weird being back in Auckland—the city she'd avoided for so long. She and Susannah were cautiously navigating sisterly ground, and, with the family all out for dinner, Allie had offered to dust off her much neglected culinary skills for dinner with Derek.

She glanced at the clock: 6:16 p.m. He'd said he should be over by around seven. Her sweaty running clothes stuck to her. Shower or start dinner first? She lifted up an arm for a whiff. Not too bad. Best to start dinner and then get ready. Besides, she was the world's messiest cook and would inevitably end up with pasta sauce in the most unlikely of places, no matter how careful she tried to be.

Her stomach gnawed itself. What was she even nervous about? Derek was her husband. And he was the one trying to earn his way back into her heart and life, not the other way around.

Jackson's face flashed up in her mind and she forced down the foolish wish that it was him she was cooking dinner for, that he was the one walking through the door. In a couple of hours, he would be on a plane back to the U.S. Their paths would never cross again. Which was a good thing. For there to be any chance of making this marriage work, Jackson couldn't be anywhere near it.

She turned her attention back to the book that sat open in front of her. The chicken and pasta recipe looked okay. She'd never tried it before, and had chosen it solely because it was the first recipe she'd found that seemed to only contain ingredients she actually knew and didn't seem too threatening.

Step 1: Chop the onion into fine pieces and then sweat for approximately five minutes.

Sweat the onion? What on earth was sweating an onion? Allie scanned the page for more explicit instructions on what would make an onion sweat, but the book remained mute on the topic. She flipped to the back looking for a glossary. Nothing. How on earth could a book called *1-2-3 Cook* not have a glossary? What did they expect? That people were born with innate knowledge of how to sweat an onion?

Her concentration was broken by the front door opening. She glanced at the clock. Six twenty-one. Weird. She was sure Susannah had said they were going to go straight to dinner after she'd picked Katie up from ballet.

Footsteps sounded in the entryway, but not the raucous sounds that always accompanied her niece and nephew. Susannah must've popped back to pick up something. Oh well, it would be nice to have some distraction while she prepped, even if just for a few minutes. For all her initial misgivings, her sister had turned out to be far more human than she'd anticipated. All she required of her unexpected houseguest was that Allie never ever call her "Susie" ever again. Though for some reason "Suz" was deemed acceptable.

"I'm in the kitchen." She turned around and pulled open the knife drawer. It was time to do battle with the onion. A few seconds later, she heard steps walking up the hallway. "What did you forget?"

Where was the chef's knife? She was sure she had seen it in there this morning. The footsteps entered the kitchen. *Aha, found it.*

"Hey, Suz. Do you know what it means to sweat an onion?" Allie wrestled with assorted tableware to get to the knife.

"No clue, sorry." It was not her sister.

The knife came loose and she spun around, wielding it not unlike some crazed psycho killer in a horror movie.

Derek quickly took a few steps back, cowering behind a large bunch of bright flowers he held in his hands, although they were separated by a wide kitchen counter. What did he think she'd done—become a skilled knife thrower in the last two years?

"Derek?" For the love of all things good, what was he doing here already?

He waved a hand weakly. "Hi."

His face was pale and he looked like he was about to hurl. And she had mopped the floor only this morning.

Speaking of things to hurl. Allie put the knife down, slowly. The guy still brought up such strong emotions in her, she ricocheted from hate to something-not-hate in a millisecond. She didn't trust herself not to throw the knife at his head if he made the wrong move or said the wrong thing.

She glanced down. Great. Why did she never get to be the one looking glamorous? "Nice of you to knock." Her voice came out a lot harsher than she'd intended.

He winced. "Sorry. I did. You mustn't have heard me. And the door was unlocked, so I figured someone was home." He slowly walked forward, pulled out a bar stool, and plonked himself down on it as if he belonged there.

Allie's finger's curled around the edge of the counter. What did he think he was doing? Sitting down like nothing had changed, when everything had. *Be nice, Allie.* The whole point of this was to try and see if this could work.

She had stood up in front of hundreds of people and promised for better or worse till death did them part, but if she'd had even an inkling of how bad the "worse" could be, she never would've walked down the aisle in the first place.

He held out the flowers to her. A huge bunch of lilies. They'd been one of her favorites her whole life. The flowers he'd brought her on their first date. That she'd carried in her bouquet. He had no way of knowing that the sight of them now only brought pain. She took them, the paper rustling in her arms, and placed them on the counter.

"I know I'm early. I just needed to see you." His eyes didn't quite meet hers.

She swallowed back the urge to tell him he had long since lost the right to *need* anything from her.

The thought of the last couple of years had her fingers itching to find the nearest blunt object. Out of a desire not to get a criminal record, more than a concern for his safety, she crossed her arms over her chest. "So talk."

He formed a triangle with his fingers, resting his chin on the point. "I can understand how angry you still are with me."

She highly doubted that. Not when she herself was still shocked by the waves of fury that occasionally overtook her. If he did, he would not have waltzed in here and voluntarily sat down.

He would have been standing at the door ready to run at a moment's notice.

He would have shown up *on time* after she'd had a chance to give herself a pep talk before their evening began.

She stared at him, her heart doing strange things at the sight of the guy she had once loved sitting in her sister's kitchen like he belonged there.

"I missed you, Allie." His eyes bore into hers.

I'd stopped missing you.

The truth in the thought took her breath away. She hadn't thought about it—hadn't let herself think about it—since the day she'd found out about Julia. She'd told herself she couldn't possibly miss someone who was the opposite of what she'd believed, all while ignoring her persistent longing for him. But it was the truth. At some point, she'd stopped missing him—so much so that seeing him sitting there just felt weird.

"I'm so sorry for what I did to you. I would do anything to change it, I hope you know that." He held her eyes with his. "I know we can make this work." He leaned forward, as if about to reach for her hand. She took a step back.

This time it didn't feel like a hole had been ripped out of her heart, but out of the floor. This wasn't happening. This was the stuff of fantasy and cheesy movies. How many times in the early days had she dreamt of something like this? Of the whole stupid thing being a huge mistake and them finding their way back together? But now that it was happening, she didn't feel happy or even relieved. She felt nauseated.

The truth was, none of it had been a mistake. Just because the court had decided not to uphold his previous marriage on a technicality didn't change the fact that Derek had lied about more things than she could count and broken her heart in more pieces than there were numbers.

"Say something." His voice was pleading.

"What do you want me to say?" Her voice was totally controlled. Unlike her hands, which were spasming. She was having some kind of fit. She clasped them in front of her, nails digging into her palms.

"I don't know. Just something. Anything."

"You honestly think you can do what you did, waltz into the house, tell me you miss me, that you're sorry, and I'm going to throw myself at you?" The harshness of her words startled even her. *Simmer down, Allie.* She had agreed to try and give things a chance, after all.

"No, of course not." He placed his hands flat on the countertop. "That's not what I thought at all. I know I have a long way to go to prove to you I've changed. I still can't believe you've given me a chance to try and show you. I promise I'm not going to take it for granted."

She sighed. The guy was trying. She had to give him that.

"Are you at least going to sit down?" He pulled out the stool next to his.

She looked everywhere except into his eyes. She'd always had a weakness for his slate-gray eyes. If she let herself gaze into them, she was going to be in big trouble. She gestured at her attire. "I have stuff to do, Derek. I need to get changed, cook dinner. We have plenty of time to talk later."

"You look fine." At least he didn't say *great*, which would've been a big, fat lie, and she was done with those.

He stood up, walked around the counter until he was standing right in front of her. Tipping her chin with his fingers, he forced her to look into his eyes. "I need you to know this before one more second passes. I don't want a divorce. I don't want us dancing around in some kind of 'maybe we'll try to work it out, maybe we'll get divorced' thing. You're the only woman I've ever loved. Please." He took a deep breath. "I love you, Allie. I am still in love with you. I'll do whatever it takes to prove it to you. Give you however long you need. To make this, us, work again."

"Whatever it takes?" She repeated his words again. She didn't know this Derek. This contrite, humbled guy. He was saying all the right words, but her heart still held too many scars from the searing hurt he'd wrought to be able to let it go.

"I couldn't live with myself if I allowed what we had to be thrown away without fighting for it. For you."

"I didn't throw us away, Derek. You did, remember? When you married me after you had already married *someone else*." Whatever the court had ruled, that was a fact. When she'd walked down the aisle, he hadn't known whether he was still married or not. If Julia hadn't hunted him down because she'd learned there was no record of their annulment, he never would have been caught.

"How do you pick up the threads of an old life? How do you go on, when in your heart, you begin to understand, there is no going back? There are some things that time cannot mend. Some hurts that go too deep . . . that have taken hold." Frodo's monologue from the end of the movie *The Return of the King* rolled across her.

"I know, Al." She flinched. Why did he keep calling her that? The only man she wanted to hear that from was the one she was never going to see again.

". . . I can't ever give you an adequate explanation. I just . . . I knew if I told you, it would hurt so badly and probably destroy us and I couldn't do it."

So instead he turned her into an accidental bigamist. Charming.

He stared at her, all troubled gray eyes and earnest expression. "I thought I was ready to let you go, if that was what you wanted. But seeing you again in Queenstown brought it all back. I forgot how good we were together. How much I love you."

Against her better judgment, her heart started to hope. All she wanted to do was tell him it was okay and they could fix this. That it was going to be all right. The man was her husband, after all—for better or worse.

Her face obviously betrayed what she was feeling because his eyes lit up.

"Allie."

All of the air had been sucked out of the room. She felt like she was suffocating. He said her name exactly the way he used to when he was kissing her—like all his hopes, dreams, and desires had all come true in her.

Except this time they didn't have the same effect they used to. Instead, everything in her yearned for a different guy. The one with ocean-blue eyes she could happily drown in and a smile that made her knees buckle.

The one who never wanted to have anything to do with her ever again.

Placing a palm against Derek's chest, she stopped him before he could come any closer.

"I'm going to get changed. There are plenty of drinks in the fridge."

Ducking around him, she forced her legs to walk out of the kitchen and up the stairs to her room.

She closed the door behind her and sank down on her bed. *God, I can't do this. It's too hard.*

She didn't love her husband anymore. Maybe she never even had. Maybe she'd just been blinded by his charm and attention. By the guy every girl wanted, wanting her.

She didn't want Derek, but she didn't want a divorce. It was like the beginning of a bad joke.

Taking a deep breath, she tried her prayer again: *God, all I want is to be free of Derek, so if making this work is Your will, then I need Your help. I can't do it on my own.*

She was a different person from the one she had been two years ago. The only way they had a chance at making this work was if she believed he was too. He'd promised he would come to church with her. The old Derek wouldn't have gone near the place, so that was a start.

Sliding her bedside drawer open, she stared at her wedding ring that lay nestled in its box. She had meant those vows. Pledged them before God.

Closing the drawer, she stood up and lifted a blue wrap dress from her closet before padding toward the guest suite.

Time to let go of Jackson Gregory. She was a

married woman and was going to do everything in her power to make it work because it was the right thing to do.

Half an hour later, Allie returned to the kitchen, hair blow-dried, makeup on, the bottom of her dress swishing around her knees.

The room smelled like an intoxicating blend of onions, garlic, and basil. Pausing in the doorway, she took in the scene. Derek stood over a simmering pot of pasta sauce, a glass of water beside him. Water, not beer. That was different too. He even wore an apron, and there seemed to be the hint of a hum above the boiling and chopping.

In spite of her reservations, her spirits lifted.

Looking up, he broke into a smile when he saw her. "You look amazing."

She couldn't help but smile in return. "Thanks." She walked toward him. "What can I do to help?"

He waved his hand toward the fridge. "Grab a drink. Sit. I've got it all under control."

She turned on the oven for the bread as she walked toward the fridge. Taking out a bottle of apple juice, she poured herself a glass and added a few sprigs of mint from the plant sitting on Susannah's windowsill.

Turning around, she found him staring at her. "What?"

"I'd forgotten how beautiful you are."

It was all a bit overwhelming. She busied herself with returning the juice and grabbing the items for the salad out of the vegetable drawer. She stayed for a couple of extra seconds, allowing the coolness of the interior to sweep over her.

Her shoulders loosened. This could be her life. There were plenty of girls who would give their right arm for this.

Bumping the door closed with her hip, she laid the pile of ingredients onto the countertop and removed a chopping board from the rack. Locating another knife and a salad bowl, she started dicing tomatoes.

The two of them worked in companionable silence for a few minutes, and with every passing second her frayed nerves relaxed.

"What kind of pasta did you want to do?" She looked up to see Derek lifting the lid off a boiling pot of water.

"There's some fresh fettuccine in the fridge." Allie turned to open the door and get it out, just as Derek's hand also closed over the handle.

There was no denying something arched in the air between them. His fingers wrapped around hers and she looked up, finding herself caught in his gaze.

She forced herself to hold it, tried to shove away thoughts of the blue eyes she really wanted to be looking into.

"Allie, I . . ." His words faded as he reached up and caressed her cheek, then tugged some hair behind her ear.

All she had to do was move the smallest distance, give him the slightest indication, and it was clear what would happen next. Everything churned. Did she want this?

The churning kicked up a notch, but it wasn't desire. So much for divine intervention. There was only one guy she wanted to kiss and it wasn't her husband. "Der—" The sound of her phone ringing cut her off—not that she even knew what she planned to say.

She tugged her hand out from under his and walked to the sideboard, where her phone lay. Her heart thundered.

She picked it up and swiped, thankful for the excuse to gather her thoughts and quiet her emotions. "Hello?" Out of the corner of her eye, she watched Derek pull the fettuccine out of the fridge and head back toward the pot now threatening to boil over.

"Hi, can I speak to Allison Shire, please?" The woman's tone was cultured.

"Speaking."

"This is Deborah Moore. I'm an associate at White, Smith & Thompson. I'm so sorry it's taken me so long to return your call. We've been trying to work through Mr. Kilpatrick's files since his passing and it's taken longer than we would've liked. And your message had us a little confused, so I wanted to double-check everything before I called, just in case there'd been a mistake on our part and we'd sent you the incorrect information."

Her hands tightened around the phone as she turned her back to Derek. "Oh? How so?"

"Well, your message referred to papers you received from us notifying you of the court's decision to decline your annulment petition."

"That's right." Something propelled her to walk farther away from her husband. Rounding the other end of the island counter, she watched him as he turned down the gas and dropped the pasta into the water, seemingly oblivious to her con-versation.

"That's not correct. On the thirteenth of May, the court granted your petition on the basis of Mr. McKendrick being already married. We sent papers to you on the fourteenth to that effect."

Granted your petition on the basis of Mr. McKendrick being already married. The words echoed in her head.

"So I'm not . . ." Her words trailed off, her mouth failing to form them.

"Married. No, legally you never have been. Would you like me to resend you the papers?"

"Actually, I'll come in and collect them, if that's okay."

"Of course. I'll leave a package for you at

reception. We're still in the process of unfreezing your assets, but that shouldn't be more than a couple of weeks away. Your banking and investment accounts are all done. You should be receiving confirmation regarding them any day now. The house will probably take the longest because of all the paperwork involved."

Allie struggled to process the information coming at her. She had money again. *She wasn't married.* "That's fine. Thank you."

"I'm very sorry for whatever the misunderstanding was that occurred."

Misunderstanding. Whatever there had been, a misunderstanding was not it. "Thank you. And thanks for calling."

Pressing the END CALL button on the phone, she placed it carefully down on the sideboard. She was free—free! It had all been a lie, again. Somehow, Derek had gotten her copy of the papers and substituted them. For what?

Ice washed over her as she stared at her not-husband's back. Had he already intercepted her new bank cards? Emptied her accounts? It wasn't unthinkable, given that he must have somehow accessed the papers from her lawyers and replaced those with false ones.

Derek turned around and smiled. "Pasta will be done in a few minutes."

She looked at the man who had almost brought her to ruin, again. Whatever memories, wistfulness, and wishful thinking had existed a few minutes before had disappeared like a vapor. "How long?"

His brow crinkled. "Three, maybe four minutes?"

He was still talking about pasta while she was watching her life unravel. Again. But this time she wasn't going to run away. "No, how long did you honestly think you had before I would find out the truth? I mean, surely even you knew there was going to be a limit to how long you could intercept my mail and whatever else was required for me not to find out."

He looked at her and with slow, deliberate moves turned around and twisted the knob for the pasta pot to the off position. She battled the urge to grab the metal container and dump its boiling contents over his head.

Turning back, he wiped his hands on a dish-cloth and shrugged. "I figured I'd play it for as long as it lasted."

His eyes were cold, his face hard. The facade of the repentant, besotted Derek from a few minutes ago well and truly gone.

"Why?"

"C'mon, Allie. You're not that stupid. Why would a guy like me bother with a girl like you?"

All her internal organs started twisting around each other. "I'm going to take a flying guess your visa is due for renewal sometime soon and you need me for that . . ." She trailed off. Why did he want to stay in New Zealand so badly? Was there yet more she didn't know about him? Some big reason he didn't want to go back to England?

Her hands gripped the back of the bar stool he'd been sitting on. Then she remembered it wasn't her problem anymore. *Thank God.* "And did you really think after everything, I'd let you near my money anytime soon? Even if I did think we were married?"

"I would've found a way. It had all been too easy so far."

"Too easy . . ." She repeated his words stupidly.

He let out a laugh ringing with scorn. "Nothing to it. Once I found out what hotel you were staying at, it wasn't too hard to flirt your room number out of the receptionist. I used that to pick up your mail, swap the papers out, and give it back pretending to be another guest who'd gotten your mail by mistake, then sit back and watch you swallow it hook, line, and sinker."

The guy standing opposite her might be incapable of genuine human decency but she had to admit he was fully deserving of the Oscar for Best Actor.

He picked up his jacket. "When I met that Jackson guy, I thought he might actually pose a challenge. An unexpected complication." His face turned smug. "But even dispatching him wasn't a problem. I almost felt sorry for the guy. He actually seemed to care about you."

Everything started buzzing at the mention of Jackson.

She swayed, her grip on the stool the onl thing holding her upright. This could not be happening. *This is not happening, God.*

"Oh dear. Don't tell me I disrupted the path of true love. Don't worry, Al." Seriously. If he called her that one more time, she was going to punch him.

". . . I'm sure given much longer, he too would've worked out you're nothing special." His expression, tone, everything, openly mocked her. The guy was a sociopath. *She'd had a lucky escape.*

The thought cut through all of her confusion and panic. Her mind suddenly cleared and an eerie calmness flooded through her.

"Get out." She managed to force the two words out.

He opened his mouth, but she held up her hand.

"Get. Out." She took a few steps backward before she started looking for things to start throwing.

He walked toward the door. Pausing, he turned back and smirked. "It was always a long shot. I can't believe I almost got away with it. Twice. How stupid can one person be?"

Suddenly, she was across the room, two years of pent-up rage and betrayal channeling through her fist and into his face. Derek's expression spun through emotions like a roulette wheel as he stumbled back, hands over his nose.

Getting his balance back, he took his fingers away for a second. Enough to glimpse that they were covered in blood.

Not a single atom in her was sorry.

She shook out her throbbing hand, opening and closing her fingers. The movies never showed you how much actually punching someone hurt. The guy had one heck of a hard face; she'd give him that.

Derek glared at her. "If it's broken, I'm going for assault." His words were muffled through his hands.

Allie took another step so they were almost toe to toe. "I'd think pretty hard about that. You make me lawyer up again and I'll be coming after you for fraud, theft, and whatever else they can come up with. Now that I have all my money back, I need something to spend it on. Now, get out. Now!"

Derek spat some blood onto Susannah's hardwood floor. Adrenaline surged through Allie's body at the undisguised loathing on his face. She fought the impulse to back down, put distance between them. For the first time it struck her that maybe now was the time to be afraid, not feisty. But she was done with being afraid.

After one last glare, Derek spun around and

stormed out, the echo of his feet detailing the path of his departure.

Allie let out the breath she hadn't even realized she'd been holding, her head whirling as the vibration of the door slamming echoed through the house. The whole thing had been a lie. Derek was gone. Forever. It was over. Finally.

Her legs buckled, and she hit the shiny floor.

Allie's whole body heaved against gravity as it was swallowed into an ocean of grief. One with no shoreline in sight.

This was not how her story was supposed to end.

The light outside grew dimmer until darkness tiptoed through the windows. So many things spun through her head, she couldn't even finish one thought before another interrupted, clamoring to be heard.

She waited for the much-talked-about "peace that passes all understanding." For some kind of epiphany that would make things better or at least bearable, but nothing came. Just the big, gaping chasm.

She'd tried to do the right thing, but in doing so, she'd destroyed what she had with the guy she loved to be with the one she was married to. She'd turned down the opportunity to apply for her dream job. All for nothing.

Thirty-two

"All right, enough. Time to move on out." Susannah's very loud voice accompanied bright sunlight flooding Allie's nice dark cave, also known as Susannah's spare room, which she hadn't moved from since Tuesday night, except for the bare necessities. It was now Friday. Or maybe Saturday.

For all of their differences, her big sister had proven to be more than adept at dealing with the mess of a human she'd come home to after Derek had stormed out. It turned out that nothing accelerates the reformation of sisterly bonds quite like one of them needing to be scraped off the kitchen floor.

"Up. Up. Up!"

Noooo. Allie groaned and burrowed farther under the covers. She'd handed in her notice and still had a couple of days before she was due to return for her final tour.

Her sister was determined. Sheets and blankets were ripped back. Allie scrunched her eyes shut against the glare. Who knew sunlight could be so painful? She rolled over and buried her head under her pillow. Maybe if she ignored her, Susannah would go away. Actually, scratch that; it had never worked before.

"I. Am. Not. Getting. Up."

The pillow was ripped from her grasp. "Yes. You. Are."

Lifting her head up, Allie looked at her sister through blurry eyes. As per usual, Susannah looked immaculate in a blue sweater and cargo pants, her hair pulled back in a ponytail. She also looked insanely cheerful for what had to be some obscene hour of the morning.

"Susannah, I'm heartbroken. In fact, let me rephrase that. I am heart-shattered. Into a gazillion tiny pieces. I've spent the last three days bawling my eyes out."

Her sister looked at her and raised an eyebrow. "Actually, *darling* . . ."

Definitely more than a hint of sarcasm in "darling."

". . . you've only spent part of the last three days bawling your eyes out. You've also spent part of it watching every chick flick I own"— she gestured at the pile of DVDs on the floor— "eating the supermarket out of every cheesecake and tub of ice cream they have in stock, and reading far too many trashy magazines." Her foot nudged the precarious pile at her feet.

Allie glanced around the room. Hmm, there were a lot of empty ice cream containers scattered around the place, now that she mentioned it. It also smelled a little like a gym bag had been left to fester in a corner somewhere.

She sat up and crossed her arms. "Yeah, so?" She scowled at her sister. "I think I've earned the right to a few days of self-pity. Don't you? Now if you'll excuse me." Reaching over, she grabbed her pillow from Susannah's arms. "I am going back to wallowing. Feel free to open the window as you close the curtains on your way out."

Susannah sighed and sat down on her bed.

No. Don't do that. You're going.

"Bug, I love you, and if I thought floundering in your misery would help you get over it, I would leave you to it, but it's not. All it does is give you way too much time to rehash Jackson-and-Allie memories and second-guess every-thing you ever said and did. It's a beautiful Saturday morning. It's time to reenter the real world. Because for a start, if you don't get your backside on that plane tomorrow, you might not have a job left to show up to."

Like that was such a big loss. "I don't care." Allie moaned, throwing herself back on the bed and burrowing her head in her arms.

The bed shifted as Susannah reached down. The sound of pages turning filtered through. Allie peered at her sister over her arms. Why was her sister always right?

Susannah held up a couple of magazines. "Look, most of these headlines are about famous women getting dumped. It happens to the most successful women in the world. You're in great company." She pointed at one cover. "I mean, it's not like your husband had an affair or you got ditched on national television."

If only. "Look at all those girls. We both know in a couple of months they'll all be back on the cover with some hot new guy while I'll still be here alone and heartbroken." She looked at all the ice cream containers around her. "And faaaaat."

Susannah stood up. Finally. Thank goodness, she was going to give in and let her stay in bed. She turned around as she reached the door, perfect ponytail swishing. "I'm sorry. I really didn't want to do this but you've given me no choice."

Huh?

A few seconds later her sister returned, holding Ed waaaaay out in front of her.

What was going on? A second later her nostrils were assaulted by the smell of something between mustard gas and a cowpat she'd once had the misfortune of falling into. "Good grief. What is that?" She pinched her nose, but to no avail.

Susannah grimaced. "That is my darling son. Check this out." She turned him around to reveal a slimy brown stain seeping down his pants. Allie retched, eyes watering. "Here, hold him a sec."

Before she could refuse, Susannah shoved the little stink bomb into her arms and disappeared.

Allie adopted an identical pose—holding her nephew as far away from her as possible. It wasn't easy, when he wasn't exactly the world's most petite toddler. "Hey. You can't leave him here. Where are you going?"

Her smelly nephew grinned. "Stinky poop!"

She couldn't hold him any longer so she lowered him to the floor. "Aren't you supposed to be toilet trained by now?"

"Nappy is gross!"

"Yeah, no kidding, pal."

Susannah marched back into the room dragging Ed's activity table behind her and chucked it into the corner closest to the bed.

Allie caught a glimpse of the evil plan her sister had brewed. Oh no, she didn't!

"Right." Susannah spoke through her own pinched nose. "Here's your choice. You can stay here as long as you like. Weeks, in fact. But he stays in here with you."

Over her dead body. Which, judging by the potency of his nappy combined with the small size of the bedroom, might well be sooner than she had imagined.

"Aw, come on, Susannah. That's cruel and inhumane. In fact . . ." She paused to try and wipe her watering eyes on her T-shirt-clad shoulder. "I'm pretty sure it could be classified as biological warfare."

Susannah took her son from her hands and

serenely carried him toward his toys. "Be that as it may, I've given you your options. Outside with the world, or in here with Mr. Stinky. Your choice."

Allie looked around her Laura Ashley–inspired cave and then over at her nephew grinning up at her. With every second, the smell grew even more gag-worthy. No way she could stay in this room with that. She was depressed, not suicidal.

"All right. I give up. But it'll be all your fault when Ed doesn't have cousins. You've put me off of ever having children." As if it was even a remote possibility anyway, right now.

Her sister glanced at her son and grimaced. "Well then, poor Ed's going to be stuck with just his big sister, because he's put me off having any more children as well. Now, you've got thirty seconds to decide what big move you're going to make to change your life. I know we have our differences, but we are Shires. When we get knocked down, we get back up. End of story. You are scary smart and beautiful, and you are too good to waste any more time wallowing over a guy who was never worth you. Twenty seconds."

Her sister's words powered up something inside her. She was better than this. Derek had taken all he was going to get. God had not given her breath so she could waste one more of them on him. "Can you pass me my phone?" She gestured to where it sat on the armoire.

Susannah picked it up and tossed it to her, underhand style. Picked up Ed from where he'd wrapped himself around her legs.

Allie scrolled through her contacts. Please let her have saved it. Please. The name lit up her screen, and she hit it before she could second-guess herself.

"Dr. Everett."

"Dr. Everett, it's Dr. Shire here."

"Dr. Shire." He sounded surprised, but not in a bad way. "What can I do for you?"

"My family situation has changed since we last spoke. I was wondering if the applications were still open for the position we spoke about."

"They are." She could hear a smile in his voice. "But only just. They close in four hours. That is, they close today, but we didn't specify a time, so I'm assuming we'll be accepting them until midnight."

It couldn't have been more an answer to prayer if an enormous divine finger had appeared and painted GO TO ENGLAND on the wall.

Blowing out her breath, she managed her first genuine smile since the second before Derek had shown up in the café and shattered everything. "You'll have my application by then."

"I look forward to it. Good night, Dr. Shire."

The dial tone left her with an uncontrollable grin on her face.

"What was that about?"

She stared at her screen for a second, then up at Susannah. "I'm applying for a lecturing job at Oxford."

Her sister's eyes widened. "When did this all happen?"

Allie didn't respond, a stark realization seeping into her. She couldn't go to Oxford, or really move on with her life, until she at least tried to make amends for one of her biggest failings.

Allie looked at her sister. "I need to find Jackson. I can't do this until I make things right. In person."

"How are you going to do that?"

Given that she'd wiped his number from her phone the day she'd decided to give Derek another chance, there was only one way she could think of. "I'm going to Iowa."

Her sister high-fived her. That hadn't happened in a decade. "Oh yes, you are." She dropped Ed onto Allie's lap. "After you change one nuclear nappy."

Thirty-three

FOUR WEEKS LATER

Allie hadn't been this terrified since she defended her thesis. Twenty-eight hours from Auckland to Des Moines, via L.A. and Chicago. Then another three hours on the road to Pennington.

Driving in the wrong side of the car on the wrong side of the road with a brain that had completely given up on trying to compute miles instead of kilometers.

Her phone trilled on the seat beside her. Kat. She tried to flick on the indicator so she could pull onto the shoulder but turned on the wipers instead. They emitted a loud screeching sound as they swung back and forth over the dry windscreen.

Navigating the car onto the dusty side and slowing to a stop, she swiped on her phone. "Hey." They'd last talked on her Chicago stopover when she'd bought a donut just for the brown bag to breathe into.

"So how's Iowa?"

Allie looked at all the fields lining the sides of the rural road. Green stalks rose as far as the eye could see, a few perspicacious ones reaching taller than her car. "Corny."

"You far away?"

"I think I'm about twenty minutes."

"How are you doing?"

"I've been traveling for more than a day. I'm sticky and stinky and scared out of my senses. What am I doing, Kat? I've lost my mind."

"Maybe a little. But it's the best thing that's happened to you in years. What's the worst that can happen?"

"That Jackson's told them all about me. That they hate me for what I did to him. That they won't tell me where to find him."

"In which case you're no worse off than you are now. And at least you tried."

A thought suddenly struck her. "Oh my gosh, Kat. His mother has cancer. What if she's dying? What if she's *dead?* What if I show up and there's a hearse outside?"

"If there's a hearse outside, I'd say it's probably not the best moment to knock on the door." Her friend's dry response forced her to dial the melodrama a bit lower.

Allie pressed the phone against her ear, leaning her head against the leather seat. "What if I'm not supposed to be doing this? What if I'm messing up God's plan?"

Kat laughed. "You can't mess up God's plan. He's a whole lot bigger than that. Look, you're following your heart. And you're doing it for a good reason. God's in that. I don't know what's going to happen, but He does. And He's got you. So stop stressing."

"Okay. Thanks." She blew out a big breath. "Here goes nothing."

"Here goes everything."

Dropping her phone onto the seat, she pulled back onto the road and navigated slowly back into her lane. Thank goodness traffic was light.

Twenty-five minutes later the sign WELCOME TO PENNINGTON. POPULATION 9,649 passed on the road beside her.

Following the directions her phone dictated, she drove through a small but picturesque town center. Quaint shops encircled a town square. Flowers peeked out from hanging baskets, and crisp white frontages set off display windows.

Five minutes later she sat outside 12 Moray Avenue.

What if no one was home? What if there were lots of people there? Odds were slim on a Tuesday morning, but who knew? She hadn't really let herself think beyond finding their address. She'd rehearsed words on the off chance that she would, but they'd all fled, leaving her with a blank mind and a palpitating heart.

C'mon Allie. You didn't come all this way just to sit in your rental car and stare at their house.

Brushing the crumbs of a drive-through breakfast off her shorts, she exited the vehicle and closed the door.

She forced her legs to walk up the cobble-stoned path, and up the stairs to the porch, where she knocked on the cheerful red door.

"Hello?" A slim woman, headscarf around her head, opened the door. Allie would have been able to spot her as Jackson's mother a mile away with her same stunning blue eyes, the feminine version of his face.

"Mrs. Gregory?" Not that she needed to ask. She just needed time.

The woman laughed. "Please, call me Steph. Mrs. Gregory was my mother-in-law."

"I was wondering if you could tell me where to find Jackson." Allie almost banged her head against the doorframe. That was not the speech she had practiced most of the way from Des Moines. Not the opening lines, anyway.

She looked up to see the woman smiling the kind of smile that takes over a person's whole face. "You're Allie."

Allie just stared at her for a second, the ability to form words lost.

Steph laughed. "Oh, honey, that accent is from somewhere far away from here. And I've been praying for you since the first time he said your name."

She what? Allie sagged against the porch, knees taken out by sheer surprise.

"Of course I can tell you where to find him."

Steph looked at her watch. "They're probably just about to break for lunch."

"He's here?"

Steph studied her, smile softening. "Yes, he's here. He's been here ever since he got back from New Zealand."

Allie opened her mouth but no words came. This was not what she had prepared for. Not in a million years. Him being in Pennington. Mere miles away. The possibility of seeing him today. She looked down at her travel-rumpled clothes and had a flashback of her weary face reflected in the rearview mirror. She couldn't see him looking like a hobo and smelling like a pair of two-day-old gym socks.

"Would you like to come in and freshen up before you go see my boy?"

"Yes." Allie blinked back the tears that sprang to her eyes in the face of such unexpected kindness from a woman who'd known who she was before she'd even said her name. "Please."

It was going to break ninety today, Jackson was sure of it. Splashing some water on his face from the hose, he relished the cool liquid dripping down his neck.

Picking up the brush, he continued scrubbing down the new tractor that had just been delivered the week before. His father's new pride and joy.

He'd never seen the man so happy. All the joy of working on the farm he loved, with none of the stress about cash flow. There was nothing Jackson would ever be able to do or say to thank Louis for the life he'd given back his parents. How ironic that in the middle of his mom's illness, he'd never seen the two of them with so much zest for life.

Movement sounded behind him. "Did you find it?" His father had gone on the hunt for a bigger brush.

"Jackson Gregory scrubbing a tractor. Can't say I ever imagined that."

His hand froze. All of him stuck in his awkward half-crouched position.

It couldn't be. Not here. But it was. He would have known that voice anywhere. It was the same one that still saturated his thoughts and showed up in his dreams.

Finally managing to force his legs to move upward, he turned.

Allie stood there, the sun bouncing off her loose hair and shooting it through with copper threads. Blue T-shirt, black shorts, and flip-flops. Behind her he snatched a glimpse of his father retreating to the barn.

He tried to catch a breath. His mouth opened, but nothing came out.

"Nice tractor."

"We just got it. It's a Massey Ferguson MF 8690.

A red one." His last sentence had him flushing the same color.

She laughed. It was the best sound he'd heard since, well, the last time he heard it. Jackson walked toward her, his rain boots sloshing through the puddle surrounding the tractor. "Hi."

Her smile almost turned him into a puddle. "Hi."

"Hi." It was more of a croak than a word. He looked down, saw he was still holding the hose, its stream splashing down around his feet. He gestured at the water spraying across the ground. "Just let me go turn this off."

"Sure."

Jackson retreated back to where the spigot stood, unable to stop himself from checking over his shoulder to make sure she was really there. That she wasn't a mirage conjured up as a result of too many days staring at stalks of corn.

Turning the tap off, he dropped the hose on the ground and walked back to where she was standing. Her hands were in front of her, fingers twisting around themselves.

Allie. In Pennington. Here. His mind was misfiring trying to process it all. He shoved his hands in his pockets. He had no idea what to do with them. No idea what to do with the impulse to wrap his arms around her and bury his face in her hair to see if it smelled like he remembered.

He stopped a few feet in front of Allie and

drank in her green eyes, the smattering of freckles across her pert nose, the way her bottom lip was now tucked under her top teeth. "What are you doing here?" His words came out hard.

She flinched as if she'd been hit with stones. "I'm sorry. I shouldn't have come." She stepped back.

He jolted. "No. No. Sorry. I just . . . I don't think I've been more surprised by anything in my whole life." One of his hands was out of his pocket, reaching for her. He settled for grazing her arm. "Want to sit?" He gestured toward an old picnic table they occasionally used for lunch.

"Sure."

They walked toward the table, feet in perfect rhythm.

She sat down on the bench seat; he sat beside her, unable to maintain distance. The wood creaked and sagged beneath them. Jackson curled his finger around the boards, the roughness grounding him.

His chest felt like it was going to crack open with all the words fighting to burst out. *I'm sorry. I miss you every second of every day. I love you.*

Neither of them spoke for a few seconds, just sat and looked out across the vista of green fields and blue skies. *God, help.* Jackson managed to string the two words together in his mind. He'd had a plan. A crazy far-fetched plan of how he would know if God meant for them to have another chance. It was all in motion. It did not include Allie showing up here before he knew what the answer was.

"I'm not married." Her voice was small, tentative.

"I know." He looked sideways to see her mouth form an O. "Louis told me."

She managed a wry smile. "Is there anything he doesn't know?"

"Apparently not." His heart thundered in his chest. He leaned forward, clasping his hands to stop them from doing what they were determined to do. Hold her hand. Run his fingers through her hair. Cup her chin.

"I have an interview at Oxford on Friday."

"That's great. Congratulations."

She smiled, her face lighting up. "Thanks. I'm excited. Super nervous, but excited."

"So you might be going to England?"

"Maybe." She shrugged. "Hopefully. Who knows? It's just to cover for someone on maternity leave for the next academic year. Nothing permanent." Though she tried to feign nonchalance, he could feel the heady hope emanating off her.

"So what brings you to Pennington, Dr. Shire?" A whisper of wind picked up and blew a strand of hair across Allie's face. It took everything he had not to tuck it behind her ear.

Allie tilted her body so she could look right at him. "I needed to thank you." She pursed her rosy lips.

Jackson forced his eyes away from them. *Look at anything but her lips.* Not that the deep green eyes he could fall into like a cold pond on a summer's day were much better.

Allie ran a finger across the small space of wood separating them. "When I met you I was so tired. Everything with Derek, my job, my family . . . I was just doing whatever it took to survive each day. You reminded me what it was like to really live again—to feel. You reminded me that you fight for what you love. I fell in love with Tolkien again because you forced me to remember why I've loved him so much and for so long. I know we left things badly and there's nothing I can ever say to make up for that. But you changed me. You helped me understand that God doesn't want me to live a life that's defined by my mistakes. And I'm so grateful for that."

At some point during her words their fingers had become intertwined. They both looked at them for a second and then back up at the same instant. Their gazes locked, the electricity arching between them strong enough to power Vegas.

The desire to drop down to one knee, right there, in the dusty farmyard and propose with a blade of grass, a piece of string, anything, was almost overwhelming. Except a stronger force kept him pinned right where he was.

Allie didn't belong here. He was certain about that. Neither did he. He didn't know where he belonged, but she belonged at Oxford. He knew she would get the job with the same certainty he knew they were in for a bumper harvest.

Something flickered in Allie's eyes. "Can I ask a question?"

"Sure."

"Your mom, she already knew who I was."

He smiled. His mom had managed to wrangle bits and pieces of the story out of him over the last month. "She does. She loves you."

"Why?" Another gust of wind. She grabbed her flyaway hair with her right hand and held it off her face.

"You changed me too. You got me back here. You helped me realize there are more important things in life than making money or climbing the corporate ladder."

"Like what?"

"Like faith. Like family." He turned and held her gaze. "Like love."

Her eyes widened. "Jack—"

He put a finger against her lip, allowing it to linger. He bit back a groan, but a ragged sigh escaped instead. "Allie, I am totally crazy about you. I miss you every second of every day. I was so hurt and I came here to lick my wounds and spend time with my family. I needed to recalibrate who I was and who I want to be. I would love nothing more than to sit here right now and say all the words that bubble up every time I'm around you." His thumb roamed across her bottom lip and he leaned back slightly before he gave into the desire to kiss her senseless. "But I can't. It wouldn't be fair. You have this great opportunity at Oxford. I'm a farmhand trying to figure out what God wants him to do with his life. I can't—I won't—say things because they feel right when I can't make them right."

She swallowed, tears pooling in her eyes.

He closed his eyes for a second and tried to gather himself. When he opened them, a couple of tears were trailing down her cheeks. He wiped them away with his thumbs. One left a streak of dirt in its wake. "You are brilliant, and funny, and feisty, and beautiful, and I hope with everything in me that I'm the man for you. But if I am, I know it's not right now. And if I'm not, I need to set you free to go and find him, because you deserve every single moment of joy that he can give you."

"I don't want anyone else. I want you." Her soft words almost undid him. Winding his fingers through hers, he lifted her hand up and pressed a kiss into her skin as he held her gaze.

"I want you too. It j—"

"Stop talking, Jackson." Before he could even process what was happening she'd grabbed his T-shirt between both hands and tugged him down. Allie leaned into him, kissing him like her survival depended on it. He closed his eyes and kissed her back. Poured everything into the kiss that he couldn't say with words. Her hands framed his face as his fingers wove through her hair, down her back, pulling her closer. By the time it ended they were both breathing like they had just sprinted a mile.

Allie let go of his T-shirt, smoothing it across his chest, and slid back along the bench a few inches.

Jackson tried to get his heart rate under control. He curled his hands back under the bench before he could pull her back to him to fill the gaping void she'd just left.

She stood up. "Okay. I'm going to go. Because if I don't leave now, I'm never going to."

If she stayed for one second longer, there was no way he was going to let her.

Allie walked across the yard, toward the fence, heading for a red car beyond it.

He stood up, followed after her, mind scrambling for something to say.

The car beeped and Allie opened the door. She turned, just as he was opening his mouth and spoke first. "Don't say it. Don't you dare say good-bye."

Thirty-four

Allie squared her shoulders at the door to the Gulbenkian lecture hall. *God, please help me.* She'd repeated the same desperate prayer before every single lecture in the last two weeks. She forced her feet to move beyond the threshold and pasted on her lecturer's face. Getting her dream job hadn't magically erased all her fears, but every day things got a little easier.

It was a first-year undergraduate English-literature class: Introduction to Tolkien. She could have taught this in her sleep. Given that it was nine in the morning on a Friday, half her class of mostly eighteen- and nineteen-year-olds probably still were.

Not only could she have taught this class with two arms tied behind her back, but much to her surprise, once she got over the hump of her fear and started talking, she loved it. She'd told Jackson he'd reignited the passion for Tolkien she thought was gone forever, but until she'd started teaching again she hadn't realized how true it was.

Just thinking his name brought the familiar ache of never-to-be-fulfilled yearning. Still. After four months. She longed for the day when it didn't. Even better yet, for the time when she made it a week without the first thought when she opened her eyes in the morning being the hope that today would be the day he'd walk back into her life. So far her best run was four days. Once she'd even made it all the way to lunch before it found her. He was right. They both had to move on. Though there was one thing she did know: she would never ever regret that kiss.

Opening the classroom door, she walked in with her papers tucked tightly against her chest and the USB holding the morning's presentation in her hand.

Love and Tolkien. She planned to skip over the obvious couples in her lecture. Aragorn and Arwen. Celeborn and Galadriel. She would spend most of her time homing in on the true love that weaved its way through the stories. Brotherly love. Sacrificial love. A love where the desire for justice conquered fear. A love for light and life that took on the powers of darkness.

Placing her papers on the desk, she plugged the USB into the university's system and pulled up the slides. Then, closing her eyes for a second, she took a deep breath and turned to face the room.

Almost two hundred pairs of eyes stared back at her. A wave of colors and faces, genders, and hairstyles. Fancy that. Most of them had managed to drag themselves out of bed after all.

Picking up the microphone, she leaned back against the desk and felt her lecturer persona settle over her.

She could do this. She was good at this. "Good morning, everyone. When we left off on Tuesday, we were discussing the important role of symbolism in Tolkien's work. Hopefully, this was continued in your tutorials this week. Today we're going to turn our attention to one of these overarching themes. Love." She heard her voice falter at the four-letter word.

How long was it going to take before she could say the *l*-word without the face of a certain American flashing up in her mind? Or before she was able to reconcile herself to the fact that she was never going to know if that was what they'd had?

Jackson sat awestruck. He'd gotten here early to claim a seat toward the back of the lecture hall, even paid a fee under an assumed name to attend the class, just in case there was someone checking such things. He watched as students started wandering in, wave after wave, until the room was almost full.

Clearly, even undergraduates took things seriously in England. When he'd been in college, you did everything you could to avoid signing up for lectures on a Friday. And if you had to attend one, you only showed up if you absolutely had to.

It was clear after the first five minutes why that wasn't the case here. Allie was amazing. Poised, confident, holding the microphone as she leaned back against the desk and chatted away like she was having a conversation at a dinner party and not speaking to hundreds of people.

He drank her in. She had cut her hair. It now sat in a sleek bob just above her shoulders. She was wearing some kind of dress-and-jacket combo that managed to be both professional and crazy sexy, which was helped by the high heels that gave her an extra four inches. He could sit here and watch her all day.

She kept talking, her words rolling over him. She never referred to any notes. The only time she even looked at the screen was to move on to the next slide. Most of the people around him held pens, but their pages were empty, so captivated were they by her seamless weaving of material from the books with movie references and personal anecdotes about her work with the movies and as a tour guide.

His insides twisted, his hands slick. This had seemed like a terrible idea when it first came to him. The day his acceptance letter had arrived. The moment he realized there was a chance God might have managed to do the impossible and create crossing paths for them. Cambridge and Oxford. Both of them in England. Only a couple of hours apart by train.

It was a rash, crazy idea. He'd shoved it away, thinking there couldn't be a worse thing to do to her, but it kept coming back, the small voice prodding him.

It had grown into an insistent drill sergeant the moment he'd clicked on the Oxford English faculty page to see her picture smiling back at him.

He looked around the room at all the entranced upturned faces. Not a single student was sleeping, or even surreptitiously texting, that he could see.

He couldn't believe he was going to do this. Here. Today. It was insanity.

But then, more miraculous things had happened. Like his mom's cancer treatment being so successful that specialists had used words like *unprecedented* while trying to hide their surprise as all her markers defied the most optimistic of predictions.

Or like Cambridge being the only school, out of twenty-something, to accept his application to their MBA program. His very late application, at that.

He blew a breath out and focused back on Allie. Her smile. The way her hands gestured as she told a story about something that had happened during filming. The way the sound of her voice slid down his spine like maple syrup on pancakes.

Seeing her now made him marvel at how he'd

survived months without her. He was even more determined that it wasn't going to continue for one more day. If she said yes.

This was always going to be a bit risky, given what had happened before. And that was when he'd thought he'd be dealing with a small class of maybe fifty students.

He swallowed, his mouth like sandpaper. It had been forty minutes, which meant she had to be wrapping up soon.

Why couldn't he just lie low? Go and find her in a café or something like a normal guy? Spend days wandering around the English department, if need be, until they ran into each other.

But he'd prayed. And this was what kept coming back. Lord help him—He was the only one who could.

She was finishing up, segueing perfectly to the final bullet point on the slide. She looked up and across the room. "Any questions?" No one else would have noticed the sudden stiffening of her posture or the trepidation that flickered across her face for a split second.

Two hands went up. Two easy questions dealt with in a couple of minutes. "Anyone else?"

Silence. He was frozen.

"Okay, well, first essays are—"

"I have a question." It took a moment for him to realize it was his voice booming out, causing people to look around to see where it came from.

Allie looked in his direction but didn't see him. "Sure. Go ahead." Again, a slight tremor in her voice.

This was either going to be a story they'd be telling their grandchildren or an epic disaster. There was no middle ground.

Dear God, please let me have heard You right.

He got to his feet.

Allie had finally let herself relax, congratulating herself on another lecture down. She'd even enjoyed most of this one—the upturned faces of all the students, most of them actually looking engaged and interested in the material.

Then the guy's voice boomed out, the American accent sucking her back into the past. So at odds with the softer English lilt she'd gotten accustomed to spending most of her days surrounded by.

It had taken two months, but she'd finally stopped turning her head at every American male voice, hoping she would find the impossible face behind it.

She hadn't heard from Jackson since the day she'd shown up in Pennington. She'd thought she might be finally starting to get over foolish, nonsensical hope, but the way her heart lifted for a second, tried to make her believe this one, this American accent belonged to him, told her she'd been kidding herself.

"Sure. Go ahead." Her voice wavered. Had she missed a hand somewhere? It had sounded like the voice came from the back of the room.

A ripple of movement toward the top left of the lecture hall. Someone was standing and seemed to be walking toward her.

"You haven't talked much about Aragorn and Arwen." Allie's breath caught. She knew that voice. She did. "Or even Faramir and Éowyn."

Her eyes searched the upper reaches for him, but the glare of the fluorescent lights temporarily blinded her. Then he appeared out of the haze. Three-quarters of the way up on the left-hand side, standing in the aisle. His gaze focused unwaveringly on her.

Those ocean-blue eyes she'd finally managed to convince herself she was never going to see again. Here. In her lecture.

She found her voice. "You're right, I haven't. Everyone knows about them. I prefer to focus on the other types of love woven through the stories. They're even more important—like Sam's love for Frodo. What would've happened without 'I may not be able to carry the ring, Mr. Frodo, but I can carry you.'?"

Jackson kept walking down the stairs. "But she gave up her immortality for him. Surely that must count for something?"

"Something, yes, but not everything." Her words came out raspy. He'd had a haircut. It made his cheekbones stand out even more. That bone structure belonged to a Renaissance sculpture, not a man.

His gaze was still locked on hers, almost making the hundreds of spectators disappear. Except for the murmurs rippling across the room and the phones being lifted up. She abandoned any pretense they were talking about Tolkien. "What are you doing here?"

He quirked a smile at her. The same one that still caused her heart to stop. "An MBA at Cambridge."

"An MBA?" She repeated the words. *At Cambridge?*

He was nearly to the bottom of the stairs and turning over ground fast. "Turns out being a spectacularly failed entrepreneur does have some benefits, after all. Got me admission to one of the best programs in the world."

"Here? You're *here?* In England?" Her voice boomed around the room. She was still holding the microphone. She put it on the desk behind her with an amplified *thump.*

"I am. The first scholarship recipient of the Louis and Mavis Duff Foundation."

It took her a second to realize what he was saying. "Louis and Mavis got *married?*"

He laughed. "They eloped—two weeks after the tour. Sorry I forgot to mention that."

Good grief. Who would've put money on the

eighty-year-olds taking the gold medal in the whirlwind-romance race?

She pulled herself back to the infinitely more important matter at hand. How long was the MBA program at Cambridge? For the life of her, she couldn't remember. "How long are you here for?"

"At least the next ten months. Maybe more." He hit the bottom step, then started walking across the front.

"Maybe?" She tried to absorb everything. His haircut—she liked it. His insane blue eyes looking at her like she was the only thing on the planet. The fitted red T-shirt and jeans that accentuated his athletic physique. Her breath stalled.

"It depends."

Her hands gripped the edge of the desk behind her. "On what?"

His legs were carving up the remaining distance between them with sure, unwavering strides. "On you."

She couldn't breathe. In a good way. If there was a good way not to be able to breathe.

He stopped in front of her. "The last four months have been the longest months of my entire life. And I cannot spend another day without telling you how I feel."

She had no words.

"Allison Marie Shire. I have loved you since

the day you told me I don't drink real coffee. I went to New Zealand thinking I knew what I was there for but, as always, Tolkien was right."

"About what?" The words just squeaked out.

" 'You certainly usually find something, if you look, but it is not always quite the something you were after.' "

Allie almost fell over as he quoted *The Hobbit* to her.

Jackson reached out and brushed her cheek. The girls in the class let out a collective sigh. "I found something so much better than what I was after. I found you. And I know we haven't even been on a proper date yet, so this may be a little unexpected, but I never want to say good-bye."

I love you too. The words resounded in her head but didn't make it out of her mouth. After months of self-analysis, she'd worked out that she'd fallen for him at the stupid dinner where he'd eaten her torte.

Her vocabulary had abandoned her, so she did her best to tell him with her eyes.

He stood right in front of her. "But this is what God told me to do, and I figure you don't mess with the creator of the universe."

Wait. What? God had told him to do what now? What was he talking about?

He started kneeling and opened his hand to

reveal a small box in his palm. What was he doing? *What* was he doing?

"So, Allison Marie Shire, will you accept this as the one ring to rule them all for the rest of our lives?"

He was on his knee, flicking open a black velvet box. Nestled in there was a sparkling, princess-cut diamond set on a platinum band.

Her pulse hammered in her ears. This was the worst thing in the world he could do. What was he thinking? Of all the places. Here. When he knew everything that had happened. The very same scenario where she had been humiliated and had her heart broken.

Allison. Remember, I take broken dreams and redeem them. I'm the One Who writes a story for you that is better than you could even ask or imagine. The quiet words whispered through her soul and soothed away her fears.

Here. Was perfect.

"Are you sure?" The words whispered out.

His gaze captured hers. Steady and strong. "Never been more sure of anything in my whole life."

"Okay."

"Okay . . . ?"

He didn't know which question she was answering. "Yes, Jackson Gregory, I would like to marry you. Please." His face lit up like Times Square on New Year's Eve as she held out her left hand.

Slowly, carefully, he slipped the ring onto her finger. It fit perfectly. "How did you know?"

"Told you. Creator of the universe." He whispered the words in her ear as she was swept into his arms and off her feet.

She was in the air. Arms around his neck.

He pulled back, tipped his forehead against hers. Just like the day they'd been lost in the bush. "Is it weird we're going to have our second kiss in front of like two hundred people?"

Allie looked over his shoulder at the class, who were now on their feet, cheering and whistling. "Do you want to wait?" She wanted to kiss him so badly she wouldn't have cared less if the university marching band wanted to stage a concert in the hall.

Her answer was found in a split-second throaty laugh before his lips claimed hers and gave her the kind of kiss that rivaled anything any fairy tale had ever woven.

Jackson pulled back, leaving her breathless. "You still prefer the Sam-and-Frodo kind of love?"

Allie shook her head, her ears hurting from the noise rolling across the room. But all she saw were the eyes of the man she would love for the rest of her life.

Acknowledgments

When I started writing, in the beginning of 2006, it was as a young, single twenty-something who had big dreams of putting words on pages that might one day be good enough for other people to read. I dreamt about the day I would be sitting at my laptop, tapping out my own words of thanks. Admittedly, my vision was a lot more glamorous than the reality of sitting in old track pants, surrounded by piles of washing, after an extended sleep negotiation session with a three-year-old.

The idealistic young writer had a different name, a different hair color, a much bigger disposable income, exponentially fewer stretch marks, and a lot more sleep. But the thrill of writing these words is even greater than I imagined it would be. The task of putting on paper my gratitude to the very large tribe who made this dream a reality is even more daunting.

So, without further ado, my inadequate words of thanks to my people:

Jesus, because it's only thanks to Him that the crazy, impossible dream of this girl from New Zealand could ever come true.

My amazing husband, Josh. Surprise! Of course I was always going to dedicate this to you. Sorry (but really not sorry) for all the elaborate subterfuge to convince you I wasn't.

My sister, Melody, my first ever reader, #1 fan, and most brutal critic, who has been cheering me on since I wrote that first (truly awful) chapter.

The rest of my amazing family and family-in-love, for never suggesting that maybe it was time to quit trying and accept that the odds were never going to be in my favor. Especially to my parents—from you I know what it looks like to love God and live a life that takes the road less traveled.

My amazing Sister Chucks: Jaime Jo Wright, Laurie Tomlinson, Halee Matthews, Anne Love, and Sarah Varland, for talking me off more ledges than I can count, riding this crazy writing-life-wife-mom-friend roller coaster together, brainstorming over text when I'm totally lost in plot holes entirely of my own making, the 24/7 living over Facebook messenger, the emergency Double Stuf Oreo deliveries across the globe, enriching my life with your friendship, and making my stories so much better than I ever could on my own.

The dream team. My wonderful agent/fairy godfather, Chip MacGregor, for signing a girl who lived half a world away and having an unswerving belief this would happen. My amazing editor, Beth Adams, for loving Jackson and Allie's story as much as I do, your ability to see exactly what the story needed and stretching me to make it the best I could. I still can't believe I got to do my debut novel with you! The team at Howard Books: Katie Sandell, Ami McConnell, Bruce Gore, and everyone else who has embraced this story. I am beyond honored that I get to be on your team.

Kathleen Kerr, for the perfect encouragement at the time when the dream felt too hard and I was so close to giving it up and taking up something more achievable, like learning to play the piano with my toes. I will never be able to express what having you love my writing so much meant when I felt like this was never going to happen.

Charlene Patterson. Remember that day when you asked me, "Have you ever thought about writing a romance to do with *The Lord of the Rings*?" I thought it was crazy and there was NO WAY I would be able to pull it off or that anyone would want to buy it. I've never been more glad to be proven wrong.

Ann-Maree Beard, Olivia Williams, Fee Conway, Anna Holmes, Nicky Parlane, Elizabeth Norman, Myra Russell, Ally Davey, Steph Mowat, Heidi Benson, Wendy Harper, and my amazing Mosaic Table 3 girls, for feeding my family and watching my little people when I was on deadline, for cheering this book on and telling me how much you already loved it even when you knew nothing about it, but most of all, for being incredible friends I am blessed to do life with every day.

To my two little hobbits, aka the Buddy and the Buzz. There is no book that could ever compete with the joy of being your mum.

Last, but definitely not least, to whoever you are, reading this. The world is full of incredible literary voices whose works deserve your time. Thank you for taking a chance on mine.

Center Point Large Print
600 Brooks Road / PO Box 1
Thorndike, ME 04986-0001 USA

(207) 568-3717

US & Canada:
1 800 929-9108
www.centerpointlargeprint.com